PRAISE FOR GL[illegible]

"Glenn Cooper is no ordinary thriller writer, but one who asks big questions."

— THE SUNDAY TELEGRAPH

"Cooper's intelligent, heart-pounding homage to Raiders of the Lost Ark and The Da Vinci Code will appeal to fans of action, thriller and conspiracy genres."

— BOOKLIST ON *SIGN OF THE CROSS*

"Cooper's name on a book's cover guarantees two things: an elaborate story with plenty of twists and turns and a swift pace that carries the reader through to the end."

— BOOKLIST ON *THE DEBT*

"The debut of a startling new talent... a seamless blend of modern-day thriller and historical mystery"

— JAMES ROLLINS, #1 NEW YORK TIMES BESTSELLING AUTHOR

"Fast-paced, cinematic, and incredibly well-researched. Cooper's ability to weave history into a high-stakes conspiracy is second to none."

— THE BOOKBAG

"Cooper understands the architecture of a mystery better than anyone in the genre."

— CORRIERE DELLA SERA

"Pitch perfect. Cooper knows how to keep the reader turning pages from start to finish."

— STEVE BERRY, NEW YORK TIMES
BESTSELLING AUTHOR

COVENANT OF THE DEAD

GLENN COOPER

Cover design by Spike Gragard.
Author Photo by Giliola Chistè.

ISBN(eBook): 978-1-971648-08-8
ISBN(Paperback): 978-1-971648-09-5

Published by Lascaux Media
Title Production by The Bookwhisperer

CHAPTER ONE

WELLSPRING HOUSE, THE RESIDENCE OF THE SISTERS OF THE LIVING Well, was one of the older dwellings in Roslindale, a melting pot neighborhood in Boston. Its clapboards needed a fresh coat of paint, and its roof was on its last legs, but the 1882 Victorian was otherwise in fairly good shape for its age. The eight nuns who lived there were happy to call it home.

Mealtimes at Wellspring House were carefully choreographed. Sister Gabriela, its venerable leader, posted a monthly rota on the corkboard assigning cooking, shopping, and cleaning chores. Tonight, Sister Lidia's haddock garnered fulsome praise, and after dinner, while others did the washing up, she was the first to retire to the lounge. Soon, she was joined by one of this month's shoppers, Sister Claudine.

"How was hospice?" Claudine asked.

"All in all, quite a lovely day," Lidia said, kicking off her orthopedic shoes and resting swollen, stockinged feet on an ottoman. "One of the girls who volunteers with therapy dogs brought the sweetest labradoodle in. The patients loved him."

"What's a labradoodle?"

"You don't have them in Haiti?" Lidia asked.

"We don't have dogs with fancy names like labradoodles," Claudine laughed. "We have mutts."

"They're brown, fluffy, and adorable."

The other women filtered in and talk turned to the evening's television.

"Isn't that show with the policemen on tonight?" Sister Belinda asked.

"Which show?" Gabriela asked.

"You know, the one with the actor we like—what's his name?" Belinda said.

"Oh, yes, his name's on the tip of my tongue," Sister Dora said.

"Well, I don't know who you mean," Gabriela said.

"It's Thursday, so it must be on," Belinda said.

"No, it's not. It's Wednesday," Claudine said.

The nuns began to laugh, and Sister Gabriela said, "That was too many senior moments to count!"

When they couldn't agree on a show, the TV remained off, and the women split into smaller groups. Lidia and Gabriela worked on a jigsaw puzzle of the Boston skyline. Claudine and her younger cousin, Fabienne, put on sweaters and sat on rocking chairs on the porch, chatting in Creole. Belinda and her best friend, Sister Carol, who worked in the same hospital, stayed in the lounge and played gin rummy. Dora retired, climbing the two flights of stairs to her attic rooms.

Kristin, the youngest resident, was about to join her, when Gabriela pulled her aside and said, "Please, Sister. Less makeup tomorrow, and no lipstick. How many times have we talked about this?"

"I'm sorry. I mean no harm."

"Sister Claudine has started using lipstick. She told me she got it from you."

"It looks nice on her."

"Don't be defiant, Kristin," the old nun said angrily. "Now, go to bed and reflect on your intemperate behavior."

Dora liked to read in bed. Kristin—not yet forty, preferred to indulge her guiltiest pleasure—getting under the covers and scrolling TikToks.

At ten o'clock, Lidia and Gabriela were the only ones left downstairs.

Gabriela gave up trying to find a home for a featureless jigsaw piece and said, "I'll lock up. You go on."

Lidia said, "I'll just lay the table for breakfast."

"No, to bed with you," Gabriela insisted. "I'll do it."

Lidia plodded up the stairs on the way to the attic, and Gabriela tackled the remaining nightly chores, setting the kitchen table, locking up, and finally, retreating to her ground-floor bedroom. Before climbing into bed, she thought she heard something in the backyard. She lifted the blind, but seeing nothing, put it out of her mind.

The three sisters who lived in the attic took turns in the communal bathroom, then knelt at their bedsides for prayers. Sister Lidia lowered herself on knobby knees, clasped her hands, and said, "Into your hands, O Lord, I commend my spirit. Watch over me as I sleep. Heal what is wounded, restore what is dry, and draw me deeper into your peace. We go to the well, even when it is empty. Lord, be my well tonight. Amen."

At three in the morning, the house was quiet except for the nocturnal activities of the squirrels scuttling around in the space between the second-floor ceiling and the attic floor. One rolled an acorn toward the midden near its nest, but the noise was too faint to wake the top-floor dwellers.

Likewise, the prowler's footsteps coming up the narrow flight of attic stairs were too soft to disturb them.

Sister Kristin's room was entered first. A cushion pressed over her head muffled the gunshot. The intruder rummaged, found her rosary beads on the nightstand, and slipped them into a pocket.

Sister Dora was next. Her rosary was under her pillow.

Sister Lidia stirred at the muffled sounds next door. At first, she thought the dark shape entering her room was Kristin, but when she realized it was not, she muttered, "Dear God."

The prowler took two steps forward.

"What are *you* doing here?" Lidia said, as a cushion reeking of gunpowder was roughly forced against her face.

Her rosary beads, smooth as glass from decades of prayer, hung from the bedpost. They, too, were thrust into the intruder's pocket.

CHAPTER TWO

There was nothing unusual about Cal Donovan sitting in the audience of a colleague's lecture. As one of Harvard Divinity School's senior faculty, he would occasionally drop in to observe a new hire or listen to a topic that interested him.

Elisabetta Celestino knew he'd be there. When she took the podium in Emerson Hall's Room 105 and scanned the rows, she found him among the three hundred students enrolled in the course *Women and Power in the Catholic Church: History, Theology, and Controversy*. When their eyes met, she gave the faintest flicker of a smile, too brief for anyone else to notice.

The course was her debut as a newly minted professor. For Cal, wrangling her appointment had been a fire-drill operation; he'd promised her a job before consulting anyone at the university. Classic Cal Donovan—a swashbuckling move aimed at sweeping a woman off her feet without sweating the details.

The conclave was over. Victor Macy, Cardinal of New York, the overwhelming choice of his fellow cardinals, had accepted his election and took the name Pope John XXV as an homage to the previous Portuguese-American pontiff, John XXIV. Sister Elisabetta Celestino, the first woman to serve as Vatican Secretary of State, was emotionally spent. She had endured years of withering attacks from traditionalists outraged over the tenancy of a woman at the helm of the Secretariat. She had navigated countless international crises and negotiations, held the Vatican together during an unprecedented terror attack on the city-state, and lost her brother, Emilio, the head of the Vatican Gendarmerie, when he was killed putting down the attack.

Cal had been in Rome for the conclave. As a Professor of History of Religion, a Vatican expert, and a personal friend of the last two popes—"the pope whisperer" to some—he'd been a CNN special correspondent. When the dust settled on the terror incident, he sprang his offer on her. To his surprise, she accepted. With conditions.

His first call had been to Gil Daniels, the Divinity School's dean. Daniels was a flinty Brit with an academic career centered on the history of the synoptic gospels, territory that overlapped with Cal's expertise. He was older, conservative in temperament, and famously methodical. Cal was the departmental rock star, equally at home in scholarly journals and on bestseller lists, a fiftyish, ruggedly handsome, quick-witted bachelor often photographed in Europe in the company of billionaires and beautiful women. Daniels never admitted to resenting Cal's fame, but the faculty assumed otherwise.

Cal was infuriated by Daniels' muted reaction.

"Well, it's intriguing that Secretary Celestino is interested in coming to Harvard—I'll grant you that. But, as you know, Cal, we're not currently recruiting for a faculty position at HDS."

"Gil, this is a once-in-a-generation opportunity for us," Cal half-shouted. "Elisabetta Celestino is arguably the most influential woman in modern Christianity. She's broken every glass ceiling at the Vatican, but given recent events, she's decided she needs a change. She wants to teach, and I've persuaded her that Harvard would be a great fit. If we fumble this, every major university in Europe and the United States will make a play for her."

"I'm not surprised she wants a change, but Cardinal Macy was probably going to install his own man, anyway."

Cal noted the choice of "man." "Maybe yes, maybe no," he said.

"Send me her CV, and I'll take a look."

"Her CV? Seriously? She's the fucking Secretary of State!"

"That's well and good, but she's a nun. Did she even go to university?"

Cal was tempted to say, Gil, you are the most insufferable snob I've ever known, but he shot back, "She has a Ph.D. in archaeology from Sapienza."

"I did not know that," Gil said. "Tell you what—we'll take this up at the first faculty meeting in the fall."

"Not good enough," Cal insisted. "This won't keep."

"If you insist on instant gratification, the best I can offer is a one-year adjunct position. Minimal budgetary gymnastics required."

"Adjunct won't fly. She'll need benefits. And job security."

"Then send me her CV, and I'll schedule a discussion in October."

Cal hung up, went to the French windows of his Rome hotel suite, and flung them open to expose the evening glow of the ancient Piazza della Minerva. Shadows stretched over the cobblestones and Bernini's statue of an elephant bearing an Egyptian obelisk on its back. The dome of the Pantheon loomed nearby.

He was no slave to procedure. His next call was to Darlene Green, the president of the university, who commiserated over the terror attack and pressed him for insider details. When he reached the reason for his call, Green was incredulous.

"We can get Elisabetta Celestino?" she exclaimed. "*The* Elisabetta Celestino?"

"For the right offer."

"What will it take?"

"Best case, Professor of Practice. Worst, Senior Lecturer. Either way, full tenure-track with all the bells and whistles. I recommend the former."

"Competing offers?"

"Imminent," Cal lied.

"Time frame?"

"ASAP."

"All right, Cal. Leave it with me and come home. We were worried about you."

"Thanks. And one more thing—I went over Gil's head on this."

He heard her sucking air through her teeth. "Of course you did. I await Professor Daniels' call with bated breath. Tell Sister Celestino that Heaven is her territory, but the Earth is mine, and I will move it to get this done."

Even with Green's clout, it still took weeks to get the offer nailed down. Back in Cambridge, Cal shared the news over the phone.

"It's done," he told Elisabetta in Italian. "Professor of Practice at the Harvard Divinity School, a tenured position, starting in September. Excellent salary, full benefits including healthcare, pension plan, you name it. I've already laid claim to a nice office near mine. Everything will be outlined in the email you'll receive shortly. For the first year, your only teaching responsibility will be one undergraduate course and one graduate seminar."

She paused long enough that he felt compelled to fill the air.

"I know it's not easy leaving your family and everything else."

Everything *else* included a surprise offer from the new pope to remain as Secretary of State for at least his first year.

"Thank you, Cal," she said finally. "I know how difficult it is to get something like this done so quickly. I've given this considerable thought."

He didn't love the tone. "Why don't you review the offer letter, and we can talk in a few hours?"

"It's not the offer. We need to talk about my other conditions."

"I know your list is extensive."

She took the comment with the humor intended. "You might want to take notes," she said.

"I'm getting a pen."

"One: I won't move in with you. I want my own apartment."

He agreed instantly and told her he'd send a list of faculty rentals.

"Two: I know how generous you are, but I won't be a kept woman. I'll pay my way."

Cal had inherited a small fortune from his parents, and she knew he wasn't shy about spending it.

"Three: I won't be pressured to give up my vows. I haven't decided."

He hid his disappointment. "Of course."

"Four: My father is getting frail. Emilio's death hit him very hard. If Micaela wasn't able to take care of him, I couldn't leave. But I'll need to return to Rome whenever he needs me."

"You don't have to worry. I'll cover your classes. Is there a five?"

She laughed lightly. "Yes, Cal, there is a five. Your drinking. If we're to have a relationship, I need reassurance."

The drinking. Cal had been at it since his teens, never before the sun was somewhere near the horizon, never missing work, never blacking out—but by every definition, a functional alcoholic. With anyone else, he'd have walked, but this was Eli.

Sitting on his sofa, he eyed his ice-cold vodka, set it down, and said, "Eli, you have my assurance. I will do whatever it takes for you to be happy in America. With me."

~

BEFORE HER INAUGURAL LECTURE, he took her to Harvard Yard to scope out Emerson Hall. She pointed to the carved inscription over the door of the red-brick building.

WHAT IS MAN THAT THOU ART MINDFUL OF HIM

"Psalms 8:4," she said.

"Also, Hebrews 2:6," Cal said.

She playfully smacked his shoulder. "I'll never out-Bible you, Cal."

Inside Room 105, she said, "My goodness, it's a large space."

"They originally assigned you a room that held fifty. I told them they'd misjudged your appeal. They didn't believe me until hundreds signed up."

Cal admired her as she stood at the lectern, arranging her papers. They'd met when she was in her thirties, a decade after she took her vows. Pope Celestine had made the bold decision to appoint a nun as his President of the Pontifical Commission for Sacred Archaeology, making her the highest-ranking woman at the Vatican. He'd been in the Vatican Apostolic Library that day, and deep in discussion with a librarian, he paid no attention to the formless, floor-length black habit coming his way. He happened to look up before she passed, expecting the slack visage of an elderly Vatican nun, and instead saw the most exquisite face he'd ever encountered framed in a black veil—dark eyes blazing, full lips curled into a sly smile. Years later, she claimed no recollection of the encounter.

As she advanced through the Vatican hierarchy, becoming Pope Celestine's papal secretary, then Pope John's secretary of state, Cal saw her frequently. All the while, his longing for this unattainable nun steadily grew until it was unbearable.

And now, she was here.

Eli surveyed the audience and looked to the wall clock, waiting for the minute hand to tick over. He wasn't surprised by her composure. This was someone who had addressed parliaments and congresses and had stood down dictators and tyrants—a room full of undergraduates was hardly daunting. But he was surprised at how unselfconsciously she made the transition to the secular world. She remained undecided about abandoning her holy orders, but she'd stopped wearing the black habit of her order, the Augustinian Sisters Servants of Jesus and Mary. When she arrived in Boston, Cal took her downtown to Saks Fifth Avenue, where she spent an afternoon choosing a wardrobe of neutral palettes. After a chat, her salesperson, a savvy Bostonian with a townie accent, had told her, "I can tell what you're after, honey: European sophistication with American reinvention. You've come to the right place. This handsome fellow, your husband? No? Boyfriend? No? Okay, I'll stop asking."

For the lecture, she chose dark-blue pleated trousers, a blue woolen blazer, and a camel-colored cashmere top, and Cal thought she was breathtaking.

"Everyone, please, let's begin," she said. "My name is Elisabetta Celestino. I am very pleased to be here for the first class I am teaching at Harvard."

Women students rose in applause, and men quickly followed.

Eli shook her head in embarrassment and said, "You probably heard I will be an easy grader. As a reward for your kindness, I will give all of you As. Please, please. Basta, as we say in Italian." When the audience settled, she continued, "During this semester, we will examine the historical, theological, and political roles of women in the Roman Catholic Church—from the early Christian communities to the present day. Drawing from scripture, ecclesial documents, feminist theology, and lived experience, we will explore how women have navigated authority, agency, and exclusion within the Church. Topics will include the early female saints and martyrs, the rise of monastic women, the contested legacy of Mary Magdalene, the roles of religious orders, the modern push for inclusion, and the future of women's leadership, a topic with which I have some experience. We will read groundbreaking works by Elizabeth Johnson, Phyllis Zagano, Gary Mason, and Sara Butler, and I will include some public information from my own Vatican service. There will be a midterm exam and a final paper, but no final exam." She smiled at the scattered cheers and said, "I think it is easy to be popular at Harvard. So, the title of this first lecture is Beginnings. I'd like to start by asking you something that might feel a bit unusual in a place like a university. What does it feel like to be invisible in a sacred space? I don't ask as a theologian. I ask as a woman who sat for years in rooms where voices like mine—female, devout, intellectually formed—were politely excluded or openly ignored.

"The Catholic Church has elevated women as saints, mystics, and models of service. It has, however, refused them voice, authority, or governance—except in the rarest of cases. I was one of those rare cases. And the loneliness of it was profound. In this course, we will study the history of that exclusion, but we will not treat it as inevitable. Nor will we treat it as distant. The women you'll meet—Perpetua, Hildegard, Mary Magdalene, Sor Juana—didn't simply survive systems that constrained them. They wrote theology. They challenged doctrine. They held up the Church from inside its walls while standing permanently outside its power. And that raises the deeper question we will ask again and again: What is power in the Church? And who gets to wield it? By the end of this course, I hope you won't just know more about the past. I hope you'll be ready to imagine something new."

AFTER CLASS, they lunched at the faculty club. Seated at a light-filled corner table, colleagues dropped by—a Nobel laureate in physics, a law school dean, a world-famous Shakespeare scholar, a former Treasury secretary. Eli, unfazed, was buzzing from the morning.

She lapsed into Italian. "I loved the class!" she said. "Could you tell I was nervous?"

"Not at all," Cal said. "You looked like an old hand."

"I have a confession. I've been so busy setting up my place, I only have one lesson prepared."

He laughed. "You've got three whole days until you go again."

Her new apartment overlooked the Charles River, a five-minute bicycle ride to Harvard Square. Cal had made a pitch for her to move into her own suite of rooms in his expansive Lowell Street house, but she was firm. She was still in orders, and cohabitation was out of the question.

"Now I want to go to one of your lectures," she said.

"How about tomorrow afternoon?" he said. "I've got a graduate seminar: *Bones, Scrolls, and Relics—Material Religion in the Ancient World.* And maybe my guest of honor would come over for dinner."

"Your guest of honor would be delighted to accept."

The moment was right for the Tiffany box.

"A memento of the day," he said.

She opened it: a silver cuff engraved *Professor Elisabetta Celestino, First Lecture, Harvard University*, with the date.

"I love it," she said, slipping it on.

When their food arrived, she became serious.

"I saw something troubling on the news," she said. "Three nuns were murdered in Boston last night."

"I heard about it," Cal said. "I don't want you to get a bad impression of Boston. It's very unusual."

"I know their order. I've met their Reverend Mother. I should reach out. Is Roslindale nearby?"

"It's not far. I'll take you."

"Thank you, Cal. And thank you for everything. I'm excited about my new life—I really am."

CHAPTER THREE

DETECTIVE JOSÉ "ZÉ" SANTOS WASN'T SUPPOSED TO BE ON CALL, but when another sergeant detective in the Boston Police Homicide Unit called in sick, his commanding officer bumped him onto the duty roster.

Santos told the lieutenant he'd have hell to pay if he missed his daughter's eighth birthday party the next night.

"Zé, we had thirty homicides in the city last year—less than one per week. Unless you're an unlucky bastard, you'll be home in time for cake."

Now, in the warm drizzle of a gray morning, the unlucky bastard stepped out of the crime scene, peeled off his paper booties, and texted his wife as TV trucks rolled up to the BPD barriers on Birch Street.

> I just caught a bad one. Really bad. You'll see it on the news. Zero chance for tonight. Tell Gabby I'll make it up to her.

He added a crying emoji and realized his eyes were wet.

At forty-three, he was a big man with thick shoulders, pock-marked olive cheeks, and the gut of a lazy athlete who played in a low-level weekend soccer league. His partner lagged, jotting notes for the crime scene investigators. He wiped his eyes when he heard her coming.

Maria Trinh, thirty-two, one of the youngest homicide detectives in the city, was promoted a year earlier after five years on patrol in Dorchester. She was five-six—tall for a Vietnamese woman, with a lean runner's frame and long, black hair in a severe ponytail. She was attractive, though she never thought so of herself.

"Big case," she said, bounding up.

"More like a nightmare," he said. "I hate everything about it."

"Really?"

He didn't hide his irritation at her puppy-like enthusiasm. "The whole world's gonna be up our asses—the department, the commissioner, the DA, the mayor, the governor, plus media you never even heard of."

"Yeah, it's exciting, right?"

"Fuck's sake—you're Catholic, right?"

She pulled on the thin gold chain around her neck, liberating her crucifix.

"You know I am."

"And this doesn't rip your guts out?"

"I'll be sad if we don't find the shooter."

Santos blew out a breath. "You're a tough nut. Fine—make a list of all the nuns, along with a map of their bedrooms, and line them up for interviews, starting with the head nun—Sister Gabriela, right? The neighbor in the yellow house took them in out of the rain. We'll use the mobile command post. I'll get uniforms knocking on doors on Birch and Penfield Streets and have them collect Ring footage and anything else. And I'll notify MSP-H we've got multiple homicides."

"Tell me we're not losing this to the State Police."

"Don't worry, hotshot. It's a courtesy call. It's ours. On high-profile cases, they sometimes try to worm their way in through the Suffolk County DA's Office, but, like you said, it's a big case. BPD's gonna be like a fucking dog with a bone."

WHILE TRINH and Santos waited for Sister Gabriela, Santos asked her why her crucifix was outside her shirt.

"I don't want them to think I'm Buddhist or something. It's better if they know I'm on team Jesus."

A District 5 patrol officer escorted Sister Gabriela to the interview room in the back of the BPD mobile command center parked in front of Wellspring House. It was a narrow space with a fold-down table and four chairs bolted to the floor. The detectives stood, bowed their heads, and shook her arthritic hand.

Gabriela wore the water-blue tunic and grey veil of their order, a wooden crucifix at her neck, a five-decade rosary on her belt, and two small emblems of their mission—an embroidered drop of water on her cuff and a small silver pin of a well over her heart.

"Sister, I'm Sergeant Detective Santos, and this is Detective Trinh. We understand you spoke with the responding officers. We'd like to go over some more details."

Gabriela pursed her lips, accentuating the wrinkles on her nut-brown face.

"I will tell you what I know."

"For background, what order are you?"

"We are the Sisters of the Living Water. It's an order founded in the fourteenth century in Avignon during the Black Death by Mother Ysabel of Arles, a widowed noblewoman who left the safety of her estate to nurse the sick. She envisioned religious women living communally in cities and towns, not isolated cloisters, serving the dying and grieving during pandemics and wars, being "living water" for souls in spiritual drought. Our motto is, *We go to the well, even when it is empty*."

"And in Boston?"

"We've been here since the 1950s working in hospitals, hospices, and homeless shelters."

"Okay," Santos said. "Let's start with last night. Walk us through your evening routine. Anything out of the ordinary?"

"It was a typical evening," she said. "Everyone returned from their work assignments before supper. Sister Lidia, God protect her soul, made an excellent fish dish. After supper, we washed up and went our separate ways."

"The deceased—what did they do?"

"Lidia and I worked on a jigsaw puzzle of the Boston skyline. Dora and Kristin went upstairs to read. Lidia and I were the last to retire. She went up around ten o'clock. I stayed to set the breakfast table, checked the house, and then went to my room."

"Your bedroom is on the first floor—off the living room?" Trinh asked.

Gabriela nodded.

Trinh said, "Did the deceased choose to live in the attic, or were they assigned those bedrooms?"

"For several years, our census was only five. Then, providentially, three new women arrived, and we were allocated funds to renovate the attic for three small bedrooms and a bath. We joked that Sisters Lidia, Dora, and Kristin were the new girls, although Lidia and Dora were actually the oldest. Dear Kristin was a youngster compared to us. Lidia and Dora could handle the stairs, and anyway, they weren't the sort to complain."

"What did you check on?" Santos asked.

"Doors locked, burners off, lights out."

"Any unusual calls on the landline yesterday?"

"I don't believe so. No calls or voicemails."

"Do the sisters all have mobile phones?"

"We do. I made a few calls on my cell phone but received none."

"Can we get everyone's numbers? The deceased women, too?"

"I'll provide a list."

"Anyone strange come to the door in the past week or so?" Trinh asked. "Salesmen? Utility workers?"

"I don't believe so."

"Do you know of anyone who might have a problem with your order or any of the nuns, especially the deceased?"

"Lord, no. Who would want to harm a group of religious women devoted to God and community service?"

Santos said, “We saw you don’t have any alarm or cameras. Why?”

“It’s a safe, family neighborhood.” Her chest shuddered, her first open sign of emotion. “We never thought we needed them.”

“What time did you fall asleep?” Trinh asked.

“About eleven. I did my ablutions—I have an en suite—I said my prayers and read for a short while.”

“And you heard nothing suspicious during the night?”

“Just before I went to sleep, I thought I heard something in the backyard. I looked out the window, but nothing was there.”

“What time was this?” Santos asked.

“About ten thirty.”

“But you didn’t hear anything after this?”

“No.”

Santos leaned in. “Would you say you’re a heavy sleeper or light sleeper?”

“Somewhere in between. I used to wake frequently, but a nurse at the Faulkner Hospital, where I call on cancer patients, recommended I take a small pink Benadryl at bedtime, and it works a treat. So no, I didn’t hear glass break in the back door. If I had, I would have called the police.”

“We’re not surprised you didn’t hear anything,” Santos said. “The intruder taped the glass so pieces wouldn’t hit the floor.”

“You told the officers you didn’t hear the gunshots,” Trinh said.

“I don’t think the women on the second floor did either.”

“Tell us what happened this morning,” Santos said.

“I awoke at six as usual. Sister Carol was already working on breakfast. She and Lidia have meal duties this month. Others began coming down at half past. The van that takes us to our workplaces comes at seven-fifteen. At seven, we all noticed that Kristin, Dora, and Lidia hadn’t had breakfast. I asked Sister Fabienne to check on them. A minute or so later, we heard her running down the stairs screaming. When I went to the hall to use the phone to call 911, I saw that the back door glass was broken. The operator told me to have everyone leave the house immediately. We waited outside for the police.”

"Did anyone besides Sister Fabienne go to the attic?" Santos asked.

"No one. We waited on the lawn, as instructed, for the police and ambulances to arrive. We cried and prayed."

"Is there anything else we should know, Sister?" Santos asked.

"I think I've told you everything. When will we be allowed to return to the house?"

Santos opened his hands. "Several hours, at least. The crime scene technicians are going through everything. These things take time. And Sister, we're going to be looking for latent fingerprints in the house. We'll also need everyone fingerprinted so we can spot any that don't belong."

"Excuse me! Detectives!"

A young priest with receding, sandy hair and a neatly trimmed beard was crossing the wet lawn toward them, his clerical jacket beaded with rain.

"I've been sitting at a neighbor's house with the sisters. The officers said I might have a word with you."

"How can we help you, Father?" Santos asked, slipping on fresh booties to reenter the house.

He introduced himself as Father Timothy Bouchard, pastor of the Sacred Heart Church in Roslindale. In the flattened vowels of his Quebec roots, he said the Wellspring sisters worshipped at his church and that he had been their confessor for the past three years.

"Our condolences," Santos said.

"Thank you. They were lovely, gentle women who will be dearly missed. I know it's early days, but is there anything you can tell me for my parishioners? Word has been spreading, and people are frightened."

"I wish we could tell you something, Father, but it's not just early days—it's early hours. We're still gathering evidence. The higher-ups will likely hold a press conference later today."

"Do you visit the house?" Trinh asked.

"Often."

Santos asked him if he'd be available for an interview, and Bouchard readily agreed.

"Since you've been inside, we'll need your fingerprints," Trinh said.

The priest frowned. "Why?"

"To identify latent prints. Any we can't match could belong to the shooter," Trinh said.

"Of course. Makes sense."

Up in the attic, three CSIs and their supervisor worked the narrow hallway outside the bathroom. The supervisor had known Santos for years. They normally traded friendly barbs, but not today. Her mask hid her mouth, but her eyes said enough.

"Yeah, it's a bad one," he said.

"Mega-bad."

"What's your take?"

"The shooter broke in through the back door and turned the deadbolt. Before coming up, he grabbed one of the sofa cushions from downstairs. Its twin is in the sitting room. Makes me think he had a plan and knew where he was heading. I can't say the kill order, but he went room to room, pillow over the heads to muffle the shot, one round each. Looks like it's a small-caliber."

"Care to guess?" Trinh asked.

"Hello, Maria," the supervisor said. "It's probably going to be a .22. No exit wounds. The ME is going to find the bullets at post."

"No casings?" Santos asked.

"Nope."

"So, a .22 revolver," Santos said.

"That's where I'd put my money."

"Any sign of sexual assault?"

"Nothing obvious."

"Even the young pretty one—what's her name, Sister Kristin?"

"Not that I could see, but the ME's got the final say. If it's any consolation, I doubt they suffered. Pillow. Bang. Done. We found their purses and wallets with cash inside. Unless the residents say otherwise, the house doesn't look rifled. Doesn't look like a robbery to me. Oh, one thing. Either of you Catholic?"

"We both are."

"Aren't nuns supposed to have rosary beads?"

"Yeah."

"We didn't find any."

Santos folded his arms. "I don't get it. I can usually read a murder scene. Passion. Robbery. Revenge. Drugs. A hit. This is none of these. Three nuns executed. What's the motive?"

"Maybe it's someone who got the shit beat out of him in Catholic school," Trinh said.

Santos ignored the comment. "Why them, and not the women on the lower floors?"

"Maybe because it's quieter up here," the supervisor said. "He used a pillow as a silencer. He wanted to get away clean. It's a good bet he's been inside before—knew the back door had glass, knew there was no alarm, knew where to find a heavy pillow, knew the attic had bedrooms."

"So," Trinh asked. "One and done, or the opening act?"

Santos started for the stairs. "All I know is, I'm fucked for missing my girl's birthday party."

CHAPTER FOUR

FIVE DAYS AFTER THEIR DEATHS, THE SLAIN NUNS WERE INTERRED AT Mount Calvary in Roslindale, a private Catholic cemetery barely a mile from Wellspring House.

Eli had sent word to Cardinal Reginald Archer of Boston that she wished to visit Wellspring House to offer her sympathies, and on the first Saturday after the funerals, Cal drove her to Roslindale to meet the survivors.

It was one of those rare September days in Boston when the temperature hovered near ninety. Stepping from his chilled BMW, Cal's sunglasses fogged. He wiped them on his linen shirt and surveyed the blue Victorian on the corner lot, a rambling, three-story house with multiple gables and dormers, gingerbread trim, bay windows, and a wraparound porch.

"It's lovely," Eli said, adjusting her silk blouse and long black skirt. "From a fairy tale. We don't have this in Italy."

"Unfortunately, the fairy tale turned into a horror story," Cal said, pointing toward the attic windows."

Inside, the surviving nuns swarmed her like a celebrity, eager to clasp her hands and thank her for coming.

"Ladies," Sister Gabriela said, "let Sister Elisabetta sit. You're suffocating her."

"I'm fine," Eli said. "It's so good to be with you today. I would have come earlier, but I didn't want to impose. This is Professor Cal Donovan from Harvard Divinity School. He's—"

"Oh, we know who the Professor is," Gabriela said. "He was a great friend of Pope John, whom we knew well when he was our dear Cardinal Da Silva. You are very welcome, Professor."

"My sincere condolences," Cal said.

"Sit, sit," the nun said. "We have coffee and cake."

Cal noticed a young priest standing near the kitchen. Eye contact drew him forward.

"I'm Father Bouchard," he said. "The sisters attend my church, the Sacred Heart."

"Father," Eli said, shaking his hand. "It's nice to meet you."

With a thin smile, he said, "I don't know if I should call you Sister Elisabetta or Ms. Celestino—your civvies, you see."

"Civvies?" she asked.

Cal bristled. "He means your civilian clothes."

"I am still a nun, Father, but you may call me whatever you like."

"You could go with Madame Secretary," Cal said, reminding him of her emeritus status.

Gabriela tutted at the discord and parked them on the sofa. The others took to chairs around the spread of sliced cake, cups, and a steaming carafe.

Cal faded into the background, watching Eli ply her considerable skills.

"I was so very troubled when I heard of your tragedy," she said, accepting a coffee. "And moved by the outpouring of community grief. Your order has a proud history, and I think you are most loved for your work in Boston."

"We do not seek attention," Gabriela said. "We prefer to quietly get on with the Lord's work."

"Have you been able to return to your vocations?" Eli asked.

"Monday," Gabriela said. "We will grieve in our hearts, but we must keep drawing water from the well."

"I had a call with your Reverend Mother Pauline two days ago," Eli said. "She told me she had spoken with you, but wanted me to repeat her offer to support your house in any way she can."

"Thank you,: Gabriela said briskly. "We need her to send us three women to replace our fallen sisters."

"I will pass along your request," Eli said.

"She knows what we need, but perhaps, coming from you, it will have more clout."

"I promise I will write her today. Tell me, how have you been coping?"

Four nuns looked to their leader, but Gabriela said, "Ladies? Anyone wish to respond?"

The youngest, Sister Fabienne, a Haitian in her late fifties, said, "We take comfort knowing these beautiful women are in splendor with our Lord."

The other Haitian, Sister Claudine, who had emigrated to Boston two decades ago with her younger cousin, Fabienne, nodded vigorously. "I cried for three days until my tears ran dry. Such a shocking thing to happen to the most gentle creatures on God's green Earth. Things like this happen in Haiti nowadays, not Boston."

Sister Belinda, a large woman with an open, earnest face, politely raised her hand. "I'm scared," she said. "What if he comes back? It's hard to sleep. I lie awake listening for the smallest sounds."

"We had an alarm installed on Thursday," Gabriela said dismissively.

Sister Belinda was in her seventies, still working despite chronic leukemia. Her wrists and hands were purple from blood tests and infusions.

"I do find the alarm comforting," she said in a thin voice, before breaking into a sob. "But why couldn't it have been me? That's what I keep asking. I'll be gone soon enough. It should have been me, not my lovely friends."

Slowly and regally, Eli knelt before her. Taking her hands, she said, "Dear Sister, it was not your time. Know that the Lord has a plan for you, as he had for our three comrades."

Cal studied the way Eli filled the room with quiet command. He had seen her captivate large audiences in the Vatican's Pope VI Audience Hall and enthrall undergraduates, but he had never witnessed her in such an intimate setting. Her empathy was authentic, not something learned or performative. The women nodded, hanging on her words as she guided them into remembrances of the murdered nuns. Only the young priest seemed apart, his lips in a pout. Cal pegged him as a man used to being the parish's center of attention. When Cal was eighteen, he defied his domineering father, Hiram Donovan, a famous professor at Harvard, by giving the middle finger to college and enlisting in the army. In his brief stint as a soldier before being discharged for punching his sergeant, he had seen how a captain looks in the presence of a general. That's the way Father Bouchard looked—outranked and outclassed.

Outside, Cal's car was hot to the touch. He opened Eli's car door and rushed around to blast the AC.

Over the blower, he said, "You were wonderful."

"How do you mean?"

"Your warmth. Your concern. Your strength. They were enormously grateful."

She smiled, shaking her head. "They were the strong ones. I was only being myself."

"Like I said," he repeated. "Wonderful."

~

Shortly after eight, Detective Santos sauntered into BPD's Homicide Unit, a granite and glass complex in Roxbury Crossing, carrying a large Dunkin' iced coffee, only to find Detective Trinh sitting at his desk.

"What the fuck, Maria? Get off my chair."

"You're late," she said.

"First, you don't get to tell me when I'm late. I get to tell you when you're late. And second, it's five past. That's not late. Old guys like me get an extra five minutes."

"Is that in the book?" she asked, smiling.

"Yeah, it's right there on page fuck you. What gives with you this morning?"

She waved a few warm sheets from the printer.

"This just came in from the Crime Lab on the stuff they sent the FBI." She got up. "Have a seat."

"Thank you," he said, plunking down. "I take it from your shit-eating grin they found something interesting?"

"Listen to this," she said.

Two weeks earlier, the State Police Forensic Services Group had told them they were having trouble identifying the bullets recovered from the post-mortems. Pressed, the lead forensics tech in Maynard said there were atypical findings that required the FBI's expertise.

Trinh read from the printout. "In the absence of cartridge casings, the FBI tested bullets recovered at autopsy and the pillow fabric. Every test showed that the three bullets were fired from a common firearm. All had matching striation patterns."

"No surprise," Santos said. "Go on."

"By size and weight, all three bullets were compatible with a .22 caliber LR rimfire class."

Santos sucked on his straw. "Also, no surprise."

"They used two methods for analyzing the bullets," Trinh read. "SEM-EDX and ICP-MS. You want to know what those are?"

"No," Santos said.

"Well, here's what they showed: the bullets were 97.4 percent lead, 1.7 percent antimony, 0.7 percent tin, and 0.2 percent arsenic, with trace copper and zinc."

"This supposed to amaze me?" Santos said.

"Yes—want to know why?"

"Sure."

"Because these days, bullets are over 98 percent lead with less than 1 percent antimony as the primary hardener. And they don't have tin or arsenic. And they have copper or a polymer plating on the surface, which ours didn't have."

"These days?"

"I mean that, according to the FBI, these bullets were made a hundred years ago. Their tests point specifically to Peters Remington-UMC .22 caliber rimfire bullets, made between 1916 and 1920. The gunpowder residue on the pillow matches."

"So, you're saying that the killer used antique bullets?"

"I'm not saying it," Trinh said. "The FBI is. Want to hear about the gun?"

Santos put his cup down, starting a new water stain.

"Yeah," he said. "Tell me about the fucking gun."

She found the section and read, "The grooves on the bullets showed a right-twist rifling of one to sixteen, which has been common in .22 caliber firearms for a long time." She looked up. "But here's where it gets funky. There are other markings they look for—things called cylinder-gap burnishings and forcing-cone signatures. They have a reference collection of firearms in Quantico for test firings. Only one gun in their collection produced the same pattern, the 1918 Harrington & Richardson *Young America* .22 caliber revolver."

Santos said, "What the actual fuck?"

She dropped the report onto his lap and said, "I'm just the messenger. The FBI says the killer used an antique gun and ammo."

CHAPTER FIVE

Eli was at her apartment, running late and hunting for her keys, when her sister Micaela rang.

"Mic, is everything all right?"

Micaela, a gastroenterologist at the Gemelli Hospital in Rome, was a woman who dyed her hair pink or blue on a whim, favored primary colors, and never missed a chance for irreverence. "Why wouldn't it be?" she said. "Italy is going to hell, Papa's a pain in my ass, and my best friend is gone."

"And who is this best friend of yours?" Eli asked.

"You don't know her. Don't get a big head. You're only my second-best friend."

"How are Arturo and the girls?"

"He's a pain in my ass, too. The girls are fine."

"What's going on with Papa? He never answers my emails."

"He's happy you ditched the Vatican, but he pretends you're only in the next room. He won't admit how much he misses you. And Emilio."

Eli's chest tightened. "We all miss Emilio. Tell Papa I want him to visit. Cal said he'd get the Math Department at Harvard to host him. He can give a seminar on Goldbach."

Carlo Celestino, long-retired from his professorship at the University of Rome, had never stopped working on one of the great, unsolved problems in pure mathematics, Goldbach's conjecture.

"He says he'll visit when he can smoke his pipe on the plane," Micaela said. "As for me, I'll come with the girls on their Christmas school holiday. Arturo says he'll stay in Rome to look after Papa and watch football. You're sure we can stay at Cal's?"

"Yes, for sure. He's got six bedrooms! His house is amazing. I'm going there now. He's having a barbecue for his uni friends."

"How many of these bedrooms have you christened?" Micaela said.

"Oh, God, you'll never change! I'm still a nun."

"What the hell are you waiting for? Live your life for fuck's sake."

~

Cal lived on Lowell Street in a leafy Cambridge neighborhood west of Harvard Square, coveted by faculty for its charming old houses and walkability to campus.

Eli pedaled into his driveway and propped her bike against the house beside his charging BMW. Like many of his Tesla-adverse neighbors, he had recently dumped his Model S. She was a regular visitor to the rambling colonial revival house, though emphatically, she had never spent the night. The hundred-year-old antique brimmed with books, maps, paintings, objet d'art, and antiquities, and she was always discovering new treasures.

"It's like a museum," she'd told him.

"That's a compliment," he'd replied, "coming from someone who was a curator at the Vatican Museum."

An only child of wealthy parents, Cal had inherited a lifestyle that suited his tastes and sensibilities. His father, who hailed from a prominent Boston Catholic family, left him a formidable library and a trove of artifacts collected during a career as a Middle Eastern archaeologist. The serious wealth came from his mother, the daughter of a Jewish Wall Street banker raised on Manhattan's Upper East Side, whose legacy included a collection of important paintings, photographs, sculptures, rugs, and period furniture. Cal happily spent down his inheritance, adding artwork, books, and antiquities acquired on his own travels.

His parents' marriage had been a tug of war between two strong-willed people from starkly different worlds. Compromise kept it together. Even Cal's given name was a negotiated settlement. Donovan was his father's Irish Catholic name—that was immutable. His mother chose his middle name, Abraham, an homage to her father. Calvin, a Protestant given name, was the tie-breaker.

The front door bore a handwritten sign instructing people to come in. Eli called out as she stepped inside, then wandered through the library toward the back. On Cal's desk sat a pile of manuscript pages from his book on the Church's thirteenth-century crusade against the French Cathars. She scanned the shelves, looking for volumes she hadn't noticed before.

She loved libraries as much as Cal. Some of her happiest hours were spent in the Vatican Apostolic Library, working among its million-plus books and manuscripts. Cal held the distinction of being the only non-Vatican employee with a "golden library card," granting him free rein to browse, a gift bestowed on him by Pope Celestine for services to the papacy. Other academics had to request titles and wait in the reading room.

From the kitchen, she spotted Cal in the backyard, stationed at his grill in navy shorts and a white t-shirt, black wavy hair tussled by the breeze. The unseasonable warmth of early October had guests in shorts and sportswear. She'd never been to an American barbecue; catching her reflection in the glass cabinets, she made a face, pulled off her necklace, and unbuttoned the top button of her shirtdress.

It was love at first sight when she saw his backyard. "You have a secret garden!" she exclaimed. Designed by Cal, but executed by his Brazilian gardener, it was modest in size but felt deep and layered. In the lingering warmth, it still bloomed: dahlias in burgundy and burnt orange, fading lavender, the last echinacea, pale-pink Japanese anemones, deep-rose sedum, a few stubborn climbing roses, soft purple asters. Hydrangeas near the deck were flushed antique pink. Terra-cotta pots of rosemary, thyme, and sage flanked the brick grilling patio. A gravel path led to a crabapple tree and teak bench—Cal's favorite spot for a book, and in his recent drinking days, a glass of wine or Grey Goose.

Eli wove into the crowd, greeting familiar Divinity School faculty and grad students. Cal spotted her and waved his tongs, but the chicken was at a critical stage, and he couldn't abandon his post. Ruth Steinberg, the effervescent professor of Hebrew Bible, greeted her. Steinberg, a self-described yente with a long-running mission of finding Cal a good match, bustled over. She'd been over the moon at Eli's arrival in Cambridge. After their first meeting, she burst into Cal's office, grabbed his hands, and said, "Honey, I approve."

"How are you, dear?" Steinberg said. "Look how lovely you look! Is that Max Mara? I thought so."

Gil Daniels ambled over, looking self-conscious in freshly pressed blue jeans and a brand-new polo shirt.

"Enjoying our New England autumn?" he asked in his starchy English accent, bending over her like a heron.

"It's so beautiful here," Eli said. "I am looking forward to the trees when they have all their color."

"It's best north of here," he said. "New Hampshire or Vermont—that's the ticket. I would go later this month."

"Yes, I hope," she said.

Someone pulled Steinberg into another conversation, leaving Eli alone with him.

"How are you finding the undergraduates?" he asked stiffly.

Cal could see Daniels had her cornered, and he signaled her with an exaggerated eyebrow raise. Before she accepted her offer, Cal let her know the president had approved the appointment over Daniels' objections. At the Vatican, she was used to wielding power and was only mildly uncomfortable that the department chair had been bypassed. Daniels was less comfortable, and at their introductory meeting, he'd put on a master class in passive aggression. More recently, he had been trying, awkwardly, to be civil.

"They are wonderful," she said. "So smart and engaged. Thank you for asking."

Cal handed off grill duty and swooped in for the rescue.

"Elisabetta was just praising her undergrads," Daniels said.

"You should sit in on one of her lectures. She's a natural."

Just then, Reginald Archer, the Cardinal of Boston, arrived dressed down in a short-sleeved clerical shirt, pectoral cross tucked into his front pocket, Panama hat shielding his bald pate. The jogging enthusiast sported a fitness watch.

"Eminence," Cal said. "I'm glad you were able to make it."

Eli stepped forward, offering her hand. "Cardinal Archer, it is so good to see you again."

"Madame Secretary. I hardly recognized you in your—outfit."

"And I hardly recognized you in that marvelous hat," she countered with a laugh.

"Tell me," he said, dropping his voice and coming close, "are you still in holy orders?"

"I am. I am in a state of reflection."

"If you ever want to talk about it, my door is wide open."

She smiled politely, and Cal steered him toward the food.

"How'd you like some of my not-so-famous barbecue chicken?"

"I would love some," Archer said. "I'm starving after my morning run."

Eli and Cal flitted among his guests before taking their plates up to the deck, where a colleague signaled to the saved seats under a canvas umbrella.

"Eli, I don't think you've met Professor Grace Olufemi Gregory yet."

She touched Cal's arm and said, "Oh my goodness, Cal. So formal. Eli, I'm Grace, and you'll forgive me for not welcoming you earlier. I missed the start of the semester, finishing a research project in Nigeria."

Cal had told Eli about the professor of indigenous African religions, flagging her as someone he thought she'd like.

"I have your marvelous book on my bedside table," Eli said.

A dapper Black man with a goatee asked, "Which one? I ask because they're all marvelous."

Grace said, "And this is my sycophantic husband, Charles Gregory."

"Correction: adoring husband," he said.

"Hello, Charles," Eli said. "It's a good thing to adore one's partner. Where did you two meet?"

"About three miles north of here," he said. "We were undergrads at this fine college. I was a junior in Currier House, and I heard a Nigerian princess sophomore moved in down the hall. The rest is history."

"A nice story," Eli said. "The book I'm reading is *New Hope: The Nigerian Experience in Houston, Texas.*"

"An oldie, but a goodie," he said.

"I was moved by your descriptions of how the local Baptists welcomed the New Hope Church to their diocese," Eli said. "Your book makes me wonder how Nigerian Catholics have integrated into American society."

Grace slapped her chair arm, jangling wrist, and necklace beads. "That's it! Our first collaboration! We were riveted by the heroic work you did on behalf of the abducted Nigerian schoolgirls. I have some data on your question. You must stop by to discuss."

"And what's *your* first book going to be about?" Charles asked.

"If I ever do write one, it won't be for a while," Eli said. "I'm far too busy learning how to be a professor."

"Well, when you do settle on an idea, I know an excellent ghost writer," Charles said.

"There goes my husband, handing out his calling card on street corners."

"Ah, you're a writer," Eli said. "What do you write?"

"I'm known in publishing circles as a ghostwriter who can make awful politicians seem more sympathetic in their awful political autobiographies. But my day job is writing a metro column for the *Boston Globe*."

"Excuse my ignorance. What is a metro column?"

"I write human interest stories about local folks. Political stuff.

Quirky stuff. Whatever strikes my fancy. The paper doesn't keep me on a leash."

Cal said, "When Charles drops a new column, my world stops until I've devoured it. He's an institution."

"I hear institution, and I think old, gray, and stooped," Charles said.

"Actually," Grace said, lowering her voice a little. "I think you might be interested in tomorrow's column, Eli."

"Oh, yes?"

"I dragged Charles to a séance with a medium I go to from time to time. She reads his column and has been urging him to come."

"Séances?" Cal said. "I didn't know you were into that sort of thing."

"I am into it big time, my friend! It started small when one of my students wrote a paper on how Spiritualist beliefs of nineteenth-century Protestant missionaries piggybacked onto Nigerian Pentecostal and Holiness movements."

"It started small, like a cute little puppy," Charles said, "and now it's like living with a big old elephant."

"I'm not *that* obsessed," his wife said, slapping him on the thigh. "It's more like a small pony. How often do I see Eva? Once every three months?"

"Seems like more," he said. "But okay, a pony it is."

"What's the attraction?" Cal asked. "Academic at this point, or personal?"

"Maybe both," she said. "Charles has been pushing me to write off her fees as work-related, but I'm too straight an arrow for that. I do get pleasure communing with my dead relations."

"So, you're a true believer," Cal said.

"I'm an enthusiast. True believer might be too strong. What's your opinion about Spiritualism?"

"You know me. I like to keep an open mind about all sorts of religious beliefs."

"And you, Eli?" she asked.

"There is no tradition of speaking with the dead in Catholicism. We consider it heretical. The Catechism of the Church condemns all forms of divination, including the conjuring of spirits, as incompatible with trust in God. But that doesn't mean I'm not curious. Is your article about the séance?"

"It is."

"And why do you think it would interest me?"

"The nuns who were murdered in Roslindale," Grace said. "I'm sure you heard about them."

"Eli has been involved with the aftermath," Cal said.

"I visited with the survivors," she said. "What do the nuns have to do with a séance?"

"Here's the surprising thing," Grace said. "During the séance, I was speaking with my dead nne, my grandmother. Actually, you don't speak directly to the dead. We direct our questions to Eva, the medium, who passes them to Kay, her spirit guide in the afterworld. Kay finds the departed soul—don't ask me how—and seeks the answers which are delivered via Eva. Well, my nne was offering some advice on a family problem, when Eva stopped talking all of a sudden and said, 'Kay just asked if we want to know who killed the nuns in Boston.'"

"I hadn't said a single word up to that point," Charles said, "but I piped up and said, 'I do.' I mean, I'm always interested in a good story, right?"

"What did Eva tell you?" Eli asked.

"She said the killer was a priest with a red nose who shot them with an old gun," Charles said. "Needless to say, I immediately asked follow-up questions, whereupon Eva snapped out of her trance or whatever you want to call it, and declared that she had lost contact with her spirit guide."

"A priest," Eli said. "With a red nose."

Charles pantomimed downing a shot of booze and said, "In Boston, that doesn't exactly narrow it down, does it?" Then, catching sight of Eli's disapproving face, he added, "Sorry, was that in bad taste?"

Cal put his arm around Charles' shoulder and said, "Yes, it was, but we still love you."

"You wrote about this in your column?" Eli asked.

"Absolutely!" he exclaimed. "How could I not? The column wrote itself."

"You're not concerned that it might cause a witch hunt among the clergy?"

"See, Charles?" Grace said. "Isn't that exactly what I said?"

Charles shook his head and said, "Give me your email, Eli, and I'll send you the column. It's written in a humorous vein, as any piece deserves about a bunch of over-educated Bostonians dropping two hundred dollars a head to sit in a stuffy Brighton parlor and commune with the dead."

"I must tell you this," Grace said wickedly. "My nne never met Charles, but from the grave, she told me I could have done better."

CHAPTER SIX

After the barbecue, Eli stayed into the evening helping Cal clean up. There were leftovers galore, and he persuaded her to stay for dinner. While he reheated side dishes, she read Charles Gregory's emailed column aloud at the kitchen table.

"He has a nice touch," she said, switching to Italian. "Humorous but not cruel to the medium or the people who paid."

"A group that included his wife," Cal said.

"Yes, I suppose he had to be careful. This will be published tomorrow?"

"That's my understanding."

She frowned and said, "This claim about a priest worries me. It will cause trouble, don't you think?"

"I doubt anyone's going to take a séance seriously."

"I hope you're right, but I'm not so sure. The internet spreads rumors fast. I would hate to see an innocent priest suffer."

"It might be a good time for priests with red noses to buy makeup."

She wasn't amused, and he reached into the fridge to top off her wine.

"I'm fine, thanks," she said, covering the glass.

At the kitchen table, he poured himself another club soda.

"Thank you, Cal."

"For what?"

"For not drinking."

"You noticed."

"Yes. I like the non-drinking Cal."

"Cheers," he said, lifting his glass. "And I like the drinking, Eli."

That got the desired laugh, and he plated their food.

Over dinner, she said, "When I get home, I want to do some research on Spiritismo in Italy. It could be an interesting topic for a paper. Publish or perish—yes?"

"I don't think you need to worry about that for a while, but yes. Take my laptop while I do the dishes."

It was a transparent ploy to prolong her stay. Perhaps, the hour would grow late, and she would grow too weary to cycle back to her place. Maybe she would ask for a bed for the night. He knew that she knew. He wasn't hiding it.

She surprised him by saying, "Good. I'll use your computer."

THEY SAT in leather chairs before the cold fireplace that smelled of last winter's wood. She pulled up articles in Italian; he marked up his Catharism manuscript, stealing glances. The domesticity—quiet work together in a shared room—was a long-held fantasy.

She eventually caught one of his glances, smiled back, and sidestepped intimacy by summarizing what she'd learned.

"It's interesting," she said. "Spiritismo arrived in Italy in the late 1800s, inspired by the American and British movements. This coincided with the unification of Italy, which created a cultural climate open to new ideas. But, unlike the American and English movements, Italian Spiritismo incorporated certain elements of Catholic mysticism."

"I'm sure the Vatican was delighted," Cal said.

"The Church condemned it as dangerous and heretical, but

with the rise of Fascism and World War Two, interest in the movement waned in Italy, as in the rest of the world."

"No mediums left in Italy?" he asked.

"Who knows? Maybe some," she said, lowering the screen. "I think I *will* write a paper. Next time I go to Rome, I'll see if they let me into the Archives."

"I'm sure Pope John will oblige," he said. Then, winking, he added, "If not, just tell them you know me."

"Yes, that's the ticket," she said lightly.

"I suppose you'll be looking for letters between the Curia and the diocese during Leo's papacy on how to deal with the crazy heretics."

"Exactly. My first Harvard paper. Wouldn't that be nice?"

"It would."

The library was suddenly so silent that the ticking of one of Hiram Donovan's old pendulum clocks was the loudest sound in the room. At that moment, Cal teetered on the edge of asking if she would spend the night; he wasn't sure the words would come out.

She seemed to sense what was coming and stood, saying, "I had a wonderful day, Cal. I think I'd better be going. I have some work to do on my next lecture."

"Tomorrow is Sunday," he said.

"It needs a lot of work. Perhaps I'll see you at Mass?"

He'd introduced her to his occasional church, St. Paul's, and although he wasn't planning on going, he changed his mind on the spot.

"I'll be there," he said.

She found her backpack in the hall and said, "I was thinking—"

"Yes?" he said, hopeful.

"If I'm going to write a paper, I should go to a séance. And I want to meet the woman who's making these accusations about a priest. Would you come with me?"

"I can be bought with a kiss," he said.

She obliged, lingering in his arms.

"Then, it seems we have a deal," she said.

AFTER HER MONDAY LECTURE, Eli sat on the steps of Widener Library watching students crisscross the sunny yard. A stiff wind that night had shaken the trees, and dry maple, oak, and London plane leaves crunched underfoot. She redialed the number she'd been trying.

This time, a woman answered.

"This is Mrs. Nevins. How may I help you?"

The voice was desiccated, elderly, tired.

"I was hoping to make an appointment for one of your séances."

The listing had been easy to find: *Mrs. Eva Nevins, Spiritualist Medium, Academy Hill Road, Brighton, Mass.* Earlier calls had rung out with no voicemail.

"Oh, my," the woman said. "You read Mr. Gregory's article?"

"Yes, I—"

"I've had so many calls, I'm at a loss. I don't conduct all that many sittings nowadays. I'm getting on, you see. Before this brouhaha, I mainly took longstanding clients, and now, I'm booked for the foreseeable future. The best I can do is to take your details and ring you if there's a cancellation."

Eli puckered in disappointment, but passed along her name and number.

"The Elisabetta Celestino? Sister Elisabetta Celestino?"

"Yes. That's me."

"My heavens," the woman said. "Something good from Mr. Gregory's somewhat disrespectful column. I've always wanted to meet you, Sister. You're such an inspiration. Could you hold the line for a moment?"

A minute later, she returned. Could Eli come Wednesday evening?

"May I bring a friend of mine, a colleague from the Harvard?"

"Yes. It's often best to come with a friend or relative for support if one were to receive distressing news."

WEDNESDAY WAS the first truly chilly night of October. Eli was bundled in a heavy cardigan over a blouse and pencil skirt; Cal pulled on the scuffed-up Bomber jacket he had bought in college at a Central Square army-navy store. They reached Eva Nevin's Brighton Center street less than an hour after sunset, but cloud cover made it full dark. The neighborhood had largely defied gentrification. Many of its houses, dating to the mid-to-late nineteenth century, owned by the same solidly working and middle-class stock as their predecessors. A short row of cars was parked in front of one of them, and that proved to be the place, a weathered circa-1880 Queen Ann Victorian, two and a half story stories, wooden, with a front-facing gable and modest decorative trim. There was a broad covered porch with a long mobility ramp extending from the front door to the sidewalk. The house was unlit except for a porch dome light, a yellow blush emanating from the oval door pane, and a front room glowing orange behind lace curtains.

"It's not lacking in atmosphere," Cal deadpanned.

"I was expecting something like this," Eli said. "I'm not disappointed."

Eva Nevins answered the doorbell seated in a wheelchair she had required since the childhood car accident that claimed her father. She was a sturdy woman, perhaps a few years south of eighty, in a long dark dress with a ruffled front. Pale makeup frosted full cheeks, and her grey hair was piled high in a bun. Hidden beneath the creases of her face, one could imagine a youthful beauty.

She fixed on Eli. "Sister, it is a great pleasure to welcome you to my house."

Her face brightened for the first and only time that night. Communing with the dead, it seemed, was serious business.

Cal introduced himself. "Cal Donovan, a friend of Elisabetta's." He slipped her an envelope with four hundred dollars that she tucked, wordlessly, between her thigh and the side of the wheelchair.

"Is this your first sitting?" Eva said.

Cal nodded. "Yes, our first séance."

Eva seemed to dislike the word, but let it pass.

She turned her chair and said, "My other guests have arrived. Would you follow me?"

They went into the front parlor, a room caught in amber. The gas sconces and chandelier had been electrified a century ago; otherwise, little had changed. The room was square and dim. Honey-colored glass fixtures radiated a moody orange hue on crown plaster moldings crazed with spiderweb cracks. Wallpaper, once deep red, had dulled to a tobacco-rust, patterned with Victorian vines and faint gilt. On a cracked mantel shelf, sat a porcelain dog, a small brass clock that showed the wrong time, and a photograph of an old woman with sharp eyes in mourning black. Above the mantel was an old framed photograph of an imperious man in an Edwardian suit with a walrus moustache.

"A relative?" Cal asked.

"Heavens, no," Eva said. "Arthur Conan Doyle. He attended one of my grandmother's sessions in this very room."

"Really?" Cal said, impressed.

"Who is he?" Eli whispered in Italian.

"Sherlock Holmes," he whispered back.

Mismatched chairs with threadbare velvet seats ringed a round mahogany table polished to a mirror finish. Beneath it was a worn Persian rug, drained of color.

"Laurence, could you pull the curtains?" Eva said.

There were four other guests in the parlor, all in business or formal attire. Cal felt underdressed. A middle-aged man in a brown suit obliged and drew the heavy curtains, giving the room a confessional hush.

The air smelled faintly of beeswax, potpourri, and must. Cal saw Eli taking it all in with a wry smile.

"Friends," Eva said. "I would like you to meet two new guests at the table, Sister Elisabetta Celestino, who has recently been a high-ranking official at the Vatican."

Another man in a tan suit, shoulder to shoulder with Laurence, said, "Bit more than that, Eva. She was Secretary of State."

Eva didn't seem to appreciate the clarification. "Like I said, Martin, a high-ranking official. And accompanying her is Professor Calvin Donovan, also of Harvard."

A frail, elderly man leaning heavily on a cane said, "You're the one they call the pope whisperer, aren't you?"

The man's white-haired wife, elegant in a prim Pierre Cardin suit, tutted and said, "Ronald, be more respectful."

"It's fine," Cal said. "I'm aware of the sobriquet. However, I rarely whisper."

Introductions were made. Martin and Laurence were a married couple who owned an apartment rental agency catering to college students. This was their sixth sitting at Eva's table. Ronald and Melissa Nussbaum, nearing their sixty-fifth wedding anniversary, had lost count of the times they had come. Ronald was a retired lawyer at a white-shoe firm, as he put it. Melissa had been a teacher.

Martin played agent provocateur. He asked if everyone had read the *Globe* article, and lamented he wasn't there as he would have loved to see how Charles Gregory painted him. Then, in a biting tone, he asked Eli, "Is this like a new thing? I wasn't aware Catholics were into Spiritualism. Is that why you're out of uniform?"

Eli parried smoothly. "Exactly," she said. "I'm incognito tonight. Please don't—what's the phrase?—blow my cover."

Eva cleared her throat and rolled to the table. "All right, friends. Let's begin. Take any seat. Hopefully, Kay will bless us with her presence tonight. Will someone dim the lights?"

Cal sat between Eli and Eva; the couples paired up opposite. He could tell from Eli's bemused expression that she didn't know what to expect either. There was nothing on the table—no crystal ball, candles, and there was no mood music, or ethereal soundtrack. He didn't read the elderly woman in the wheelchair as a con, but one never knew. He was happy to be anywhere with Eli, even this musty old parlor, and he let the evening carry him.

"Please take the hands of those on either side of you," Eva said.

Cal took Eli's warm, smooth fingers in his right hand, and Eva's cool, gnarled ones in his left.

"We can proceed," Eva said.

"Sorry," Cal said. "Eyes open or shut?"

"Whichever is comfortable."

Cal watched everyone closing their eyes. He kept his open.

Cal expected Eva would affect a different mannerism when summoning the dead, but she spoke as usual.

"We gather tonight to honor those who departed before us. We seek the comfort and guidance of those we loved and cherished. I seek my spirit guide, Kay. Kay, make your presence known. Everyone, grasp each other's hands tighter and concentrate all your mental energies on summoning Kay."

Eli's grasp was gentle and steady. Eva pinched his pinky with surprising strength. Cal concentrated all his energy on watching the others, not on summoning. Eli's expression hovered near sardonic; the rest furrowed their brows with effort. He waited for theatrics—hidden speakers, vibrating table legs—but nothing came. After thirty seconds, a gentle smile bloomed on Eva's face.

"Kay! Thank you for coming. How are you faring?"

In her barely unaltered voice, she spoke as Kay.

"I am well enough."

"We have four guests tonight who are known to you—Ronald and Melissa and Laurence, and Martin. And two new guests, Elisabetta and Cal."

"All are welcome," Kay said.

"Melissa, would you like to speak to someone?"

"Good evening, Kay. I would like to speak with my sister, Martha."

"I will see if I can find Martha," Kay said.

A long pause. When Cal twisted his wrist enough to check his watch, Eva's hand resisted.

"Martha is here," Kay said at last.

"How is she?" Melissa said.

"She is well enough," Kay said.

Cal suppressed a laugh. Well enough might be as good as it got in the afterlife.

"Please tell her that her granddaughter Emily is enjoying her first semester at Brown."

"Martha is pleased."

"Oh, she'll want to hear this," Melissa said excitedly. "Tell her that her ex-son-in-law's new wife—who's half his age—is pregnant."

"Martha says she has no interest whatsoever in that stinker, Bob Cunningham. She is concerned about Emily's reaction."

Melissa belly-laughed. "That's what she always called him. The stinker. Tell her that Emily's too busy with college life to think about her step-monster's demon spawn."

"Martha still loves your sense of humor."

Cal was unimpressed. *Stinker*, likely came up in an earlier sitting.

The sisters chatted on. Eli yawned, opened her eyes, and when he winked at her, she squeezed his hand and closed them again.

When Melissa bade Martha a tearful goodbye, Eva asked, "Martin? Laurence? Who would you like Kay to summon?"

Laurence spoke, venom in his voice. "I'd like to speak to my father. Ask Kay to find the old bastard."

"Now, now," Eva said. "Kay, Laurence would like you to find his father, Ernest."

"I will look for him," Kay said.

Another pause.

"Ernest is with me."

"Hey, Dad, how's it hanging?" Laurence said.

"Your father is not amused," Kay said.

Cal would later learn that Ernest had killed himself at the end of a rope.

Over the next several minutes, it emerged that Laurence's father had been some sort of broker or financial advisor, and his son wanted investment advice from beyond. The answers seemed authoritative—company P/Es, earnings per share, and Cal wondered how Eva kept up. By the end, Laurence's anger had cooled.

"Ok, Dad," he said. "I do miss you—now and then."

"Your father misses you, too," Kay said.

Martin passed his turn, and Eva asked if Elisabetta or Cal wished to speak with someone. Cal had been thinking about whether he'd try his hand. Maybe he'd ask his father if he regretted his affairs or being so damned aloof during his childhood. He already knew the answer. *I lived as I wished to, just as you do. I regret nothing.* Or, he could ask his mother whether she approved of Eli. But he knew that answer, too. *She's a goddamn nun, for pity's sake. You couldn't find a nice Jewish girl?*

"I'm good, thanks," he said.

"What about you, Sister Elisabetta?" Eva asked.

Eva's hand became moist. A flush climbed her neck.

"I would like to ask about this priest you say killed the nuns. Why do you say such a thing? Many people in the community are upset by this."

Another long pause.

"Kay says she doesn't want to talk about him anymore. You can ask another question if you like."

"Why doesn't she want to talk about him?"

"Kay is upset. You should move on, Sister."

"All right. I would like to speak to my brother, Emilio Celestino."

Cal worried where this was going to lead; he squeezed her hand.

"When did Emilio pass?"

"Five months ago."

"A newcomer," Eva said. "Think hard on Emilio, Elisabetta. Kay will see if she can find him. Kay, our guest, wishes to contact her brother, Emilio Celestino, who has only just arrived."

"I will try," Kay said.

Cal could tell the wait was punishing. Eli pressed her lips together. Her breathing went shallow. When Kay spoke, she softly cried.

"I have him," Kay said. "A young, vigorous man. Such a shame. What does Elisabetta ask?"

"How is he?" Eli whispered. "Emilio, how are you?"

"He says he is well enough."

Cal sneered inwardly. Of course.

"He asks about Papa," Kay said. "He wants to know how he is."

Cal was amazed that a worldly woman like Eli would participate in whatever this was.

"Papa misses you very much."

"He says he misses Papa, too. He wants to know if he's smoking his pipe too much."

Cal heard her gasp. "More than ever," she said.

"He asks if he's still working on his Goldbach conjecture."

Eli swallowed and whispered, "Yes."

"Your brother laughed and he says that maybe he will find Christian Goldbach here and get help for Papa. And he misses you and Mic. He thinks of you all the time."

Cal's face burned with anger. Eva had done her homework. Eli had spoken about her family in published interviews. He wanted to lash out at her brazen manipulation of a grieving woman, but he bottled it up.

"Can he see what we are doing?" Eli asked.

"He cannot," Kay said. "The dead are cut off from the living."

"Does he know people call him a hero?" Eli asked.

"He says he was no hero, but he is proud he did his job."

Cal flashed to France. The cardinals held hostage, the assault on the chateau, Emilio crumpling from a bullet wound, Cal's hand against his gushing thigh, Emilio saying, "Tell Eli—" before he faded away, and Cardinal Manzetti rushing over for last rites.

"He has a question for you," Kay said.

"What does he want to know?" Eli asked through tears.

"He wants to know if you received his dying message?"

"I only know what you started to tell Cal."

"He says he told Manzetti the rest."

"What was it?" Eli asked.

"It was: Tell Eli to go to America with Cal and be happy with him."

"That's what I did," she said through choking tears.

"He says that makes him very happy."

It was too much for her. She pushed back and fled the room.

As Cal rose to follow, Eva said, "The chain is broken. Kay is gone. The sitting has ended."

CHAPTER SEVEN

Cal's electric BMW hummed along Soldiers Field Road. Eli sat rigid, hands clasped. She hadn't spoken since the parlor. Cal was boiling, ready to unload about the despicable old woman who'd played her, but the hurt on Eli's face made him hold it.

On the Eliot Bridge, crossing the black river, she said, "It was a mistake. I shouldn't have gone."

"You couldn't know she'd manipulate you."

"It was stupid to toy with Emilio's memory."

"It's still raw," he said.

An ambulance flashed past toward Mount Auburn Hospital.

"How did she know these things?" she blurted. "About my father."

"You've given a lot of interviews," Cal said. "Journalists always press you for personal details."

"I never talked about him."

"Carlo's work is public. He's got a Wikipedia page. And I'm sure there are pictures of him with a pipe."

"Maybe," she said, retrieving a tissue. "But no one knows what Emilio told you."

"Only you."

"Say it again."

"Eli—"

"Please."

"I only heard, 'Tell Eli—'"

"What did he want to tell me? And how did she know about Manzetti? Of all the cardinals, she picks Manzetti."

"I don't know, Eli. There were a lot of people there. The cardinals. The police. Journalists interviewed everyone afterwards. Someone could have seen him giving Emilio last rites."

"Did you talk to Manzetti? Did he tell you if Emilio said anything?"

Cal turned onto Memorial Drive. He assumed Eli wanted to go home. "After the rescue, I didn't see him. You never talked to him?"

"He returned to Turin the day after the conclave. I heard he wasn't well. He didn't come for the inauguration. I left a voicemail thanking him for attending to Emilio, but he never replied. If my brother gave him a message, wouldn't he tell me?"

"He was gravely wounded. I doubt he said anything."

They drove in silence, and Cal pulled into her driveway.

"If you don't want to be alone—"

Hand on the door, she shook her head. "I'm tired."

"We should expose her," Cal said. "Gregory made it sound cute. It isn't. She exploits grief."

She managed a thin smile. "I'm going to try to put her out of my mind."

~

Detective Santos was at his desk when his commanding officer came by and said, "Hey, Zé. I need you."

Santos put his hand over his phone and said, "Give me thirty seconds."

"Now."

Santos abruptly ended his conversation and followed his boss to his office.

The lieutenant, a stocky ex-Marine who never outgrew crew cuts, said, "Close the door."

"What gives?"

"I've got the Commissioner's office on hold. He wants the lead on Wellspring."

Ten minutes later, Santos returned to his desk, sat down, and rubbed his tired eyes. When he looked up, Trinh was standing over him.

"What's going on?" she asked. "You didn't get fired, did you?"

"Fuck you. I didn't get fired."

"Oh, shit. Don't tell me the State Police are taking over."

"Not yet."

"Then, what?"

Santos moved papers until he found his car keys.

"Get your jacket."

"Where're we going?"

"Brighton."

She froze, then groaned. "Oh, hell no."

~

DRIVING through Brighton on Chestnut Hill Avenue, Santos said, "You know this area?"

"We looked at an apartment when I was at Northeastern, but it was too far," Trinh said. "It's got some nice spots."

He turned onto Academy Hill Road, he said. "This is one of them. These old places don't come cheap. What's the number of that one?—yeah, that's hers."

Trinh sighed. "This is stupid. I can't believe the Commissioner is making us interview a crazy old lady."

"How do you know she's crazy?"

"'Cause I read the article—she'll want to talk to your dead grandma, Zé. Bunch of fools paying money, holding hands, getting their asses conned."

"Then maybe she's crazy like a fox."

"Still, this is high-grade bullshit."

"The Commissioner says the pressure's coming at him from all directions. The article lit up the socials. Hell—you've screened calls on the tip line. People are dropping dimes on every priest with a runny nose. Reporters are up his ass. Mayor's up his ass. I'm glad it's high-grade bullshit, because it rolled down the hill onto us."

"What are we supposed to do?"

Santos switched the ignition off. "Take her statement. Send it up the line. He wants to be able to tell the press that appropriate inquiries were made."

Trinh fished for her phone. "Waste of time."

"We wouldn't be here if we had good leads," he said. "All we've got is eight seconds from a Ring camera of someone dressed in black walking down Birch Street around the time of the murders."

Trinh scrolled through her emails. "I'm speaking to a gun dealer from Ohio this afternoon who did an online sale of a Harrington & Richardson *Young America* to a Massachusetts buyer eight months ago. He's going to give me the details of the transaction."

"Ammo?"

"Just the gun. I'm working on ammo sellers, too."

Santos popped his seatbelt off. "Let's go speak to the dead."

They walked up the mobility ramp, and being detectives, weren't surprised when Eva Nevins came to the front door in a wheelchair. Santos used his speaking-to-an-old-person voice and said, "Hello, dear. Are you Eva Nevins?"

"Yes."

He showed his credentials. "I'm Sergeant Detective Santos, and this is Detective Trinh. We were hoping you could answer some questions."

Eva craned her neck to the tall Dominican. "About what—not Mr. Gregory's article?"

"Yes, ma'am. The article."

Her sitting room, furnished with period furniture and dark paintings, was across the hall from the séance parlor.

"Would you open the curtains?" Eva said. "I keep them drawn because the sunlight fades the fabrics."

Trinh parted the drapes and took out her pad. Santos liked to do the talking. She was usually relegated to notetaker.

"Can I get you water?" Eva asked.

"Thank you, ma'am, we're fine," he said. "We won't take a lot of your time. Is it just you here?"

"I live alone."

"You don't need help getting around the house?"

"Everything I need is on the ground floor," she said. "My bedroom, the kitchen, bath, these reception rooms. I have a chair lift if I need to go upstairs."

"Still, it's a big house to manage."

She made a muscle underneath her cardigan. "I may not look it, but I'm strong. I've always been self-sufficient. After my accident, my mother didn't coddle me. Market Basket delivers groceries. I use Amazon. I've learned how to use all the apps!"

"Good for you. You said an accident?"

"Over sixty years ago. It was a car crash. My father died, and I was paralyzed."

"How long have you lived here?"

"Since I was born. My grandparents had it when it was brand new. Imagine that."

"That's amazing," he said, flatly. "So, your séances."

"I don't use that term. I have sittings where I help clients exchange messages with loved ones."

Trinh couldn't help herself. "Dead ones."

Santos shot her a look.

"Yes, the departed," Eva said with an unconvincing smile.

"Where do you hold these sittings?" Santos asked.

"Across the hall. You may look, if you like."

"Maybe on the way out," he said. "We're not up on how this works. The article said everyone holds hands, and you speak to someone named Kay?"

"My spirit guide."

"Kay is—dead?"

"She is."

"Long dead?"

"She passed quite some time ago."

"And how did you meet her, if that's the right way to put it?"

Eva looked to the ceiling dreamingly. "I've had the gift since I was young. Kay came to *me.* I didn't seek her out. I believe other mediums have had similar experiences. I can't say why she chose me, but we became bookends—one alive, one not."

"I see," Santos said, although his face said that he didn't see at all. "So, you ask her things?"

"My clients pose questions for their mothers, fathers, siblings, and friends. Kay can sometimes—not always—locate the departed souls. Do you remember the old children's game of telephone, where messages are passed down a chain? The client poses the question to me, I pass it to Kay, Kay passes it to the departed. Then the chain is reversed until the client receives the reply."

Santos noticed Trinh's smirk. He stared her down until she lost it.

"When we played telephone as kids," he said, "the messages always got garbled."

"Oh, dear. Perhaps that wasn't the right way to explain the process. Our messages never get garbled. Everything is clear."

"Okay, I got you. *I'm* not clear on who asked about the murders in Roslindale."

Eva tapped her fingers on the wheelchair's arm. "Well, that's the remarkable thing. No one did. Kay came up with it out of the blue. It was a great surprise. I can't recall something like this happening before. Mr. Gregory captured it perfectly in his column. He wrote, 'Mrs. Nevins suddenly looked astonished.' I was astonished."

"What exactly did she say?"

"She said, 'Eva, I must tell you something. A priest with a red nose killed the three nuns with an old gun.'"

"That was it? You didn't ask any follow-up questions? Like, who's the priest? Why'd he do it? Where's the gun?"

"Kay delivered this message toward the end of our session. Everyone around the table had taken their turn. After I repeated what Kay said, Mr. Gregory got excited and stopped holding hands to jot down notes. With that, Kay was gone, and the sitting ended."

Trinh was making her own notes. She looked up and said, "Did you know about the murders already?"

"Oh, yes. I watch Channel 7 every evening."

"So maybe this came from you, not Kay?" she said, putting *Kay* into air quotes.

Santos sputtered, "I'm sorry—" but Eva insisted on replying.

"No, dear," she said patiently. "This came from Kay. I only knew what the news reported about the killings."

Santos reasserted himself. "Mrs. Nevins, here's what I want to know—you've conducted sessions since the one with Mr. Gregory, right?"

"I have."

"How many, would you say?"

"I can tell you exactly." She pulled a small leather notebook from a side flap of her chair. "I've had three sessions since."

"Did this Kay ever bring up the murders again?"

"She did not."

"How come you didn't ask her—I mean, it's kind of important, don't you think?"

"I didn't think to ask, but at my last session, one of my guests did."

"Who?"

"It was a nun—an Italian nun who teaches at Harvard. Her name is Elisabetta Celestino. She was a very important Vatican official."

Trinh interrupted to have her spell the nun's name.

Santos stepped back in. "What did she ask?"

"She asked about the priest—she wanted to know more. She said a lot of people were upset about Kay's accusation."

"And?"

"Kay said she didn't want to say more about it. She was insistent. I urged Sister Elisabetta to ask different questions. She agreed and had a heartfelt conversation with her recently departed brother."

"So, Kay was tight-lipped," Trinh said, "if spirits have lips."

Once again, Santos started to apologize for his partner, but Eva smiled and raised her hand.

"It's okay. I'm not offended. I'm used to skeptics. If you believe in my abilities, that's fine. If you're a non-believer, that's fine, too. When the race is run, everyone will find out for themselves."

"I want to go back to the priest with a red nose," Santos said. "That was all she said? No other identifiers. Old? Young? Big nose? Small nose?"

"No, just a priest with a red nose. Those exact words."

"The same with the gun? Pistol? Revolver? Silver? Black? Big? Little?"

"Just old," she said.

"Do you own a gun?" Trinh asked.

"I don't."

"Did you ever?"

"I never did."

Trinh pressed her. "You didn't inherit an old gun—maybe a family heirloom?"

"My parents didn't own a gun."

"You sure?"

Before she could answer again, Santos pushed himself from his chair. "I think we're done. Thank you, Mrs. Nevins. Here's my card. If you get any more messages about the killings from the dead—or the living—please give me a call."

Trinh and Santos bickered on the way back to Roxbury Crossing. He told her she was unprofessional and insubordinate. She countered that he was too respectful of Eva Nevins' bullshit. He pulled rank to end the conversation, but she was uncowed.

"I'm sorry, but sending us to interview this crackpot was inappropriate and a giant waste of time. I know it. You know it."

"There's a chain of command. I follow it. I'm beginning to wonder how you made detective with your bad attitude."

"I made it *because* of my bad attitude." She fumed for a while and said, "Did you ever think that *she* could be the killer?"

Santos backed into his parking space at the station.

"She's paralyzed, if you didn't notice. The murders were in the attic."

"Maybe she's faking it."

"Come on, Mary."

"I want to subpoena her medical records."

"Jesus. You're out of your mind."

~

Cardinal Guido Manzetti had barely qualified as an elector at the last conclave, as he was only five months shy of the cutoff of eighty when the conclave convened. Per Vatican protocol, on his seventy-fifth birthday, he submitted the standard letter to the pontiff. *Most Holy Father, in accord with canon law, I submit my resignation from the office of Cardinal Archbishop of Turin upon reaching the age of seventy-five.*

The letter had arrived on Elisabetta Celestino's desk at the Secretariat of State, and after consultation with the pope, the decision was taken to have him continue in office. Although Manzetti's health wasn't the best, he was popular, his diocese was well-run and scandal-free, and he didn't want to retire. And he was a great ally, completely aligned with the pontiff's social agenda. So, Manzetti received an equally concise reply from the Holy Father. *I have received your letter of resignation. I ask that you continue in your role for the present, until other arrangements are made.*

Other arrangements were never made.

Worsening emphysema made Manzetti's next five years increasingly challenging, and the trauma of the terror attack on the last conclave left him an invalid. The new pope was in the process of elevating a bishop to replace him as cardinal.

Manzetti was propped in bed at his residence at the Palazzo Arcivescovile in Turin, looking over papers, oxygen hissing into his nostrils, when his secretary entered.

"Eminence, I have Sister Elisabetta Celestino calling you from America. Would you like to take it?"

Manzetti motioned for the phone and removed the oxygen prongs.

"Madame Secretary," he wheezed. "How good to hear from you."

"Your Eminence. I hope this finds you well."

"I've been better. My breathing, you know. And to be honest, I'm forgetting things—at least that's what the people around me say. What can I expect? I'm getting old and feeling old. Anyway, I'm in God's hands. I heard you left Rome. I'm sorry I couldn't return to the Vatican to say farewell."

"Once I made my decision, I had to move swiftly to be in place for my teaching responsibilities."

"Harvard, yes? How is it?"

Eli was standing at her living room window, watching Harvard's rowing team sculling on the Charles, a broad, slate-gray river trimmed with boathouses and brick façades. How different it was from the coiling and restless Tiber, churning green under ancient bridges.

"It's quite a change, but change can be good."

"I'm getting ready for the biggest change of all—being at the Lord's side."

"Nonsense," she said. "You have a long way to go before that."

He laughed, then coughed. "Are you still in holy orders? I heard things, but I don't know what to believe."

"I am. For now.

"For now," he repeated ruefully. "It would be a shame if you abandoned your vows. You're an inspiration to religious women."

"It's a difficult decision, Eminence."

"Pray on it. Pray on it hard."

"I will."

"How can I help you?"

She pulled a breath, then let it out. "We never talked after the rescue. I left you a voicemail thanking you for what you did for my brother."

"I appreciated it. I should have called you, but—"

"No, it's okay. I wanted to ask you something about that day."

"Yes?"

"When you came upon him dying, what rites did you give?"

"Such a painful memory—that I remember like it was a minute ago. He was a fine man. Professor Donovan was the first one to reach him after he was shot. When he withdrew, I was the nearest priest. Time was of the essence. All I could do was render conditional absolution—he couldn't respond, you see—and then, the apostolic pardon. That was it."

"He wasn't conscious? He didn't say anything?"

Manzetti went quiet. He adjusted himself on his stack of pillows. Finally, he said, "I must tell you the truth. My conscience—it's been bothering me."

"The truth?"

"I gave him absolution. I was waving at the French policemen to come over. It was a chaotic scene. Then, I saw his eyes flutter open and his lips move."

Eli gasped. "He said something?"

"I had to put my ear to his mouth."

"What did he say?"

"I'll tell you, but I want to explain why I avoided your call before. It's because I have so much respect for you. I saw how the Vatican wolf pack tried to rip you apart. For what? For being a strong woman atop the male Curia. I didn't want them to win. I wanted you to remain a nun. I wanted you to remain in the Vatican. I didn't tell a soul what he said—I'm certain of that, even though my memory is like a colander. Now, I'm ashamed of my selfishness, and I beg for your forgiveness."

Her hand clamped so hard on her phone, it ached. "What did my brother say?"

"Tell Eli to go to America with Cal. Tell her to be happy."

CHAPTER EIGHT

Santos was working through the multiple voicemails on his office line when he came to one that stopped him in his tracks.

"Oh, hello, this is Father Timothy Bouchard. I hope I'm calling the right extension. I'm the pastor of the Sacred Heart Church in Roslindale, and a frequent visitor to Wellspring House. I've been wrestling with something, and I think I need to speak to the police. Please call me."

Santos finished the last glug of office coffee, tossed the cup, then shouted across a desk to Trinh.

"Hey, do we know anything about a priest named Bouchard from Roslindale?"

"Never heard of him. Why?"

The detective whose desk was between them complained. "Fuck's sake, Zé, I'm on the phone here."

Trinh sidled over to Santos's workstation.

"He says he knows our nuns and wants to talk to us about something. Didn't say what."

"You going to call him?"

"Absolutely. What happened with the Ohio gun dealer?"

"Dead end. He shipped a working model of the Harrington &

Richardson *Young America* to a buyer in Dedham, who resold it to someone in Florida a few months ago. I'm talking to a new guy who runs a subreddit on antique firearms. He says he knows people in New England who own *Young Americas*. He's agreed to reach out to them to see if anyone knows anything, but he's not going to give me names—big Second Amendment dude who thinks the government's going to confiscate the guns."

Santos grunted. "The only one I want to confiscate is the murder weapon."

~

CAL'S MOBILE vibrated during an office meeting with a first-year grad student who was pitching a thesis idea. He ignored it twice, but when it went off a third time in quick succession, he flipped it over and saw it was Eli calling.

"I'm sorry, I've got to take this."

"Should I leave?"

"No, stay." He answered the call in Italian. "Ciao, Eli. Is everything all right?"

"I talked to Manzetti."

He could tell that something was seriously off.

"I'm coming over."

He'd walked to work that morning, so he got an Uber to her apartment. At the door, she was pale and tremulous, with the drawn countenance of someone who'd cried herself out. His instinct was to offer a hug, which she accepted, melting into his arms.

"Let's sit," he said.

Her furniture was rented; the sectional was hard, not the best. They faced each other on the diagonal.

"What did Manzetti say?"

"He gave Emilio absolution. He opened his eyes. He spoke." Her eyes burned. "The same words."

"As what?"

"What Kay said, or Eva said. It started with the two words he said to you—Tell Eli. He said to Manzetti, Tell Eli to come to America with Cal and be happy."

Cal went to the window. A cold front was bringing rain and wind from the ocean, and the river was running wild. Across from it, the buildings of the Business School were shrouded in fog.

"Why didn't Manzetti tell you this before?"

"The dear old fool wanted me to stay at the Vatican and keep fighting the good fight. He didn't want the bastards to win. He says he's ashamed of his selfishness."

"Who else did Manzetti tell this to?"

"He swears no one."

"Then, how did—?"

"How did Eva know?" she said. "How in God's name did she know?"

~

Father Bouchard sat uncomfortably on an aluminum chair in one of the interview rooms at BPD's District 5 headquarters in West Roxbury, which the homicide detectives had borrowed for the interview. He took a pen from inside his black suit jacket and clicked it nervously.

Santos and Trinh didn't keep him waiting long. They passed him business cards and faced off. Their presence seemed to unnerve him more, and he began shaking his head in some sort of internal debate. Trinh had taken to wearing her crucifix outside her shirt, and the priest's eyes were drawn to the shiny gold.

"You okay, Father?" Santos said. "You need a water?"

"No, thank you. I'm fine. It's just—"

"Look, Father," Santos said, "I don't need to tell you that sometimes it helps to unburden yourself. Whatever you have for us, we'll treat it with discretion."

Bouchard put his hand through his hair. "It's the article in the *Globe*."

"The priest with a red nose," Trinh said.

"Yes, that. My parishioners are talking about it. Some are making accusations."

"Against who?" Santos asked.

"Father Malloy, my associate pastor."

"Why would your parishioners be talking about him?"

"He has a skin condition. It's called rosacea. It leaves a person with red, thickened skin."

"You're saying he's got a red nose?" Trinh said.

"He does."

"You think he killed the nuns?" Trinh asked impetuously.

The priest stiffened. "When you put it that way—gosh. I've struggled with this, especially because the killer's description came from a séance! Séances are contrary to Church doctrine. Perhaps it wasn't the best idea to come, but my parishioners are buzzing like an angry hive. Honestly, I didn't know what to do."

"Let's take a step back," Santos said. "Is there anything else about Father Malloy that's concerned you?"

"Well, he knows the sisters at Wellspring House. Sometimes, when I'm not available, he goes there to take the sisters' confessions."

"So, he knows the house," Trinh said.

"He's been there several times."

Santos laid his hands on the table. "Father, these are interesting facts, but tell us what *concerns* you."

"Here's my concern," the priest said, his Québécois accent thickening under pressure. "Father Malloy is a bit of an odd duck. He's had something of a checkered career. He's pushing sixty, and he's never had his own parish. He came to Sacred Heart from a spell at a residential treatment facility, followed by an extended aftercare plan."

"What kind of treatment facility?" Santos said.

"He had a drinking problem. By all accounts, he's been abstinent for two years."

"That makes him an odd duck?" Trinh asked.

"Not by itself, no. He's—on the awkward side. Ray isn't what you'd call a people person, which makes pastoral care an unusual calling. Nevertheless, he's dedicated his life to service, and he tries hard. Unfortunately, when he tries too hard, he makes some parishioners uncomfortable."

"Like how?" Santos said.

"I can't give you specific examples off the top of my head. It can be the odd stare, an awkward turn of phrase, or inappropriate comment. It's enough that some won't go to him for confession."

"He's aware of this?"

"He is, and it frustrates him. We've talked about it many times. I've counseled him on trying to relax when he's one-on-one, but it's easier said than done. Also, he's told me he's embarrassed by his skin condition—he thinks people won't believe he's on the wagon. He's seen a doctor, but the creams don't do much."

"What do the nuns say about him?" Trinh asked.

"Sister Gabriela tells me they prefer to deal with me, but she's a respectful woman. She's never raised specific concerns."

Trinh, as always, was blunt. "Does he creep people out? Any known sexual misconduct?"

"No! Nothing like that—at least that I'm aware of."

"Where does he live?" Santos asked.

"He has a house in Dorchester. It's close enough to the parish that he didn't need to relocate."

"What about guns? Does he own a gun?" Trinh asked.

"Not that I know of."

"Anything else we should know about?" Santos asked.

"No, that's it. I'm sure he's not responsible, but I couldn't in good conscience keep silent. What will you do with this?"

Santos shrugged his bulky shoulders. "I guess we're going to have to talk to him, Father—but don't worry—we'll leave your name out of it."

~

THAT EVENING, Cal and Eli caught a bite out, hit a few bookstores, and got to work in his home library. It was cool enough to light the first fire of the season, and as flames leapt and wood hissed and popped, they spread out their new purchases and manned their laptops.

Eli had set the wheels in motion as soon as they sat for dinner.

"I've thought about it all day. I can't ignore it. I can't dismiss it. I need to understand Spiritismo."

Cal unfolded his napkin and said, "I'll explore it with you, if you like."

Her eyes lit up. "Would you? What about your book?"

"It can wait. I'd rather work with you than my editor."

As the night progressed, Cal added logs to the fire, and they read to each other, jotted notes, laughed a little, and cried a little whenever Emilio's name was invoked. He opened a good bottle of red from his cellar, and when she took pity on him for drinking soda water, she told him it was okay to have some. He declined and was rewarded with a peck on his cheek.

At midnight, they took stock.

"So, what have we learned?" Eli asked.

Cal looked at his notes and said, "We can credit the Fox sisters from New York for putting Spiritualism on the map in 1848. Their national tour, demonstrating the ethereal rappings they'd heard in their Hydesville séance parlor, popularized the hallmarks of the movement: table-tipping, automatic writing, and trance speaking."

Eli sniffed, "Teenage girls who confessed years later they were making the noises themselves—what a way to start a movement!"

"Yes, but look at the breeding ground," Cal said. "The movement's promise that clergy weren't required to commune with Heaven fit the zeitgeist of the time," Cal said. "The Civil War and waves of epidemics created a vast audience of grieving relatives, desperate for closure. Millions of them went to séances and camp meetings. From America, it spread like wildfire across the Atlantic."

From the start, Spiritualism drew both scientists and conjurers. The Society for Psychical Research sprang up to investigate notable mediums. Daniel Dunglas Home, famed for levitations and handling hot coals, impressed elite observers and was never definitively caught cheating. Leonora Piper, who was studied by the Harvard luminary William James, produced striking personal details during her séances that convinced many of her sitters. Eusapia Palladino baffled and infuriated investigators in equal measure, sometimes producing phenomena under controlled observation, sometimes plainly cheating. In the early twentieth century, the séances of Boston's Mina Margery Crandon were relentlessly challenged by the world's most famous magician and Spiritualism skeptic, Harry Houdini. In Britain, Florence Cook's spirit guide, Katie King, persuaded the noted scientist William Crookes with her materializations, but later a woman named Eliza White came forward claiming to have masqueraded as Katie. Ectoplasm mediums such as France's Marthe Béraud were repeatedly exposed. The American spirit photographer, William Mumler, was tried for fraud (and acquitted), and the Scottish medium, Helen Duncan, was famously prosecuted in 1944 under the Witchcraft Act (and convicted).

"And in Britain, we get the surprising voice of Sir Arthur Conan Doyle," Eli said. "At least, it surprised me. Growing up, we watched Sherlock Holmes movies and loved them. I didn't even know the author was a physician, let alone the most influential promoter of Spiritualism."

A series of personal bereavements during World War I, particularly the death of his son, and the influenza pandemic deepened Doyle's conviction. In his books on Spiritualism, he argued that evidence from respectable witnesses convincingly proved the survival of the soul after death. His friendship with Houdini collapsed over the issue—Doyle saw genuine spirit agency where Houdini saw stagecraft—but his prestige kept Spiritualism in the headlines and lent it a certain cache among educated readers.

On the Continent, France produced a related but distinct current. Spiritism, codified by Allan Kardec, framed spirit communications as a moral and quasi-scientific doctrine of soul progress, setting patterns that spread across Europe and, later, explosively to Brazil. Germany and Austria formed their own research cultures, often through medical practitioners. Physician Albert von Schrenck-Notzing investigated physical mediums and documented the French medium, Marthe Béraud, whose dramatic ectoplasm displays alternated between baffling and debunked. German scientists established laboratory-style controls in séance rooms—cameras, seals, dynamometers.

"Of course, the story in Italy interests me the most," Eli said. "Spiritismo seems like a theater where science and séance collided. The star of the show is this Neapolitan medium Eusapia Palladino. If I write a paper, she needs to be the focus. The Vatican must have been greatly concerned about her influence."

Palladino, born into a peasant family and orphaned as a child, claimed to possess extraordinary powers, including the ability to levitate tables and communicate with the dead through her spirit guide, John King. She toured Europe, where her sittings drew famous criminologists, physiologists, and psychical researchers. Some reported striking phenomena under seemingly controlled conditions, whereas others revealed unmistakable trickery. That very tension kept Italy at the center of debate and popularized Spiritismo for a generation.

Cal tossed his pen aside. "So, we get to the mid-twentieth century, and the movement fizzles as more sophisticated research methods expose one fraud after another. People lose faith in it, mediums vanish, and here we are today with only a few of them left servicing a small number of people willing to pay for messages from beyond."

"Eva Nevins is one of the survivors," Eli said. "What are we to make of it, Cal? It's tempting to say that all of them, starting with the Fox sisters, were frauds. Is Eva a fraud, too?"

"I mean, probably, but we need to understand how she knew what Emilio told Manzetti.

"Manzetti mentioned his failing memory twice in our conversation," she said. "Maybe he forgot who he told. What's a possible connection between Manzetti and Eva?"

The penny dropped. "Archer," he said. "Cardinal Archer was there when Emilio was shot. Maybe Manzetti told him on the way back to the Vatican."

"And Archer told Eva?"

"It's not likely," he said, "but we need to run it to the ground. You or me?"

"I'll talk to Archer," she said.

"I'll talk to Charles Gregory to see if he did a background check on Eva," he said.

She groaned at the time. "I've got a class tomorrow. I've got to go."

"I'll get my keys."

Outside, the smoke from his fireplace trickled from his chimney, perfuming the night air. He started the car and cranked the heater.

Eli clicked her seatbelt and said, "We know more than a few hours ago, but we know nothing."

FATHER RAY MALLOY lived in the house he inherited from his mother in Dorchester's Franklin Field North neighborhood. It was a pleasant part of the city bordering the park and the zoo, but the McLellan Street house was sorely neglected.

Santos slammed his car door and said, "Jesus, it's a wreck. Are we sure this is right?"

Trinh checked her notes. "It's the right address. It looks condemned."

"Watch yourself on the stairs," Santos said.

The rotting stairs weren't the worst of it. The house hadn't seen much work in the past hundred years. The yellow shingles were on their last legs, but they were mint compared to the sagging porch and rotten sills and window frames. Santos gestured at the brown, dead yard.

"My kind of lawn. No mowing necessary."

The man who came to the door looked like the sort to live in such a house, for he too was a wreck. He wasn't dressed as a priest. He wore baggy denims held up by a battered leather belt buckled into one of the extra holes he'd punched. His stained, dark blue shirt was half-tucked in, leaving one shirttail flapping. Several days of stubble carpeted a pale face that was fleshier than his emaciated body. Heavy lids fluttered over large, watery eyes, and at the sight of visitors, he instinctively tried to hand-comb some hair over a swath of baldness. The maneuver accomplished little more than robbing Peter to pay Paul. There was no hiding his bulbous, dusky-red nose.

"Father Malloy?" Santos said. "Ray Malloy?"

"Yes?"

Wallets flashed.

"I'm Sergeant Detective Santos, and this is Detective Trinh with the Boston Police Department. We were hoping to ask you a few questions. Think we could come in?"

The priest took a half-step back. "About what?"

"We're investigating the murders of the nuns at the Wellspring House."

"Oh! Why would you want to speak with me?"

"It's routine. We're talking to anyone who knew them. We understand that you had interactions from time to time."

"Yes, such a tragedy. They were parishioners. I occasionally subbed for Father Bouchard and took their confessions. I wouldn't say I knew them well."

Santos waited a few beats for an invitation, and when it didn't come, he made a joke about not wanting to fall through the porch.

"Yes, very well," Malloy said. "It's a bit messy. I wasn't expecting company."

Santos bent for a copy of the *Boston Globe* in a blue plastic sleeve. "Your paper."

The sitting room was strewn with weeks' worth of old newspapers, which the priest had started gathering.

"Don't mind us," Trinh said as he continued clearing furniture.

"It's the one room I don't let the cleaner into," he said. "It's not that I don't trust her, but I've got valuable breakables—well, valuable to me."

With lamps on and louvers open, the detectives got a sight of a room straight from a roadside antique store. There were curio cabinets filled with glassware, goblets, vases, and cups; bookcases packed with pewterware; tables strewn with decorative ashtrays; and a mantel lined with candlesticks.

Malloy preempted any comments. "My mother was a great collector of early American pressed glass, milk glass, and ruby-stained and goofus glass—these ones with flakes of red and gold paint. She'd buy them for twenty-five, fifty cents a pop in her time. They're only worth tens of dollars today, but the trick is collecting complete sets. That greatly helps the price. Since she passed, I've kept an eye out for missing pieces, but my greatest interest is in pewter—not early colonial pewter—heavens, that's astronomical—but nice reproduction pieces and mid-century Scandinavian ware that are affordable to someone with a small inheritance and a clerical stipend."

Santos blinked, unsure how to respond to the unsolicited tutorial. It all looked like junk to him. The priest sank into a sagging cushion and asked how he could assist.

"So, you knew the nuns," Santos said.

"As I said. In my role as associate pastor at Sacred Heart."

"We understand you're a regular visitor to their house."

"Regular? No. I'd say irregular. Father Bouchard—you've spoken with him?"

Trinh said they had.

"Father Bouchard is their principal spiritual advisor. He brushed a leaky nostril with a knuckle, drawing his attention to his red nose. "Is this about that silly article in the *Globe*?"

Santos looked sheepish. "I'd be lying if I told you it wasn't the case, Father. We don't have any suspects, and people are on edge. There's a lot of rumors and unfounded speculation. We agree. The article's a distraction, but we're obligated to make contact."

Malloy's face contorted. "I understand. I do. People have stared at me for years. I pray for a cure—I have an upcoming appointment to see a new specialist. Ever since the article, I've had people whispering behind my back. It's terrible."

"Then help us put the rumors to bed."

"What can I do?"

"You can start by answering a few questions. Where were you on the night of the murders?"

"I was here. I rarely go out unless it's to attend to a parishioner in crisis."

"Can anyone vouch for you?" Trinh asked.

"I was alone, so no."

"Did you speak to anyone on the phone that night?"

"I don't think so."

"When was the last time you saw the murdered women?" Trinh asked.

"They attended Mass the Sunday before the tragedy. That would have been it."

"Do you remember the last time you were inside the house?"

"Not without looking at my day planner. It has to be several months. Before summer."

"Were you particularly close to any of the murdered women? Closer than with the others?" Trinh asked.

"I wouldn't say so. I believe all of them simply saw me as their associate pastor."

"Have you ever been in the attic?" she asked. "The bedrooms?"

"I've never been anywhere but the ground floor."

Santos suddenly said, "Do you own a gun?"

"I do not," the priest retorted sharply. "I've never even held one."

"You're a collector. You come across antique pistols?"

"I've seen them in shops, but they aren't the slightest interest."

Santos lightly slapped the arm of his chair. "You know, Father, the fastest way to put this to bed is to let us have a look around your house. Would that be something you'd consent to?"

The priest's spine straightened. "You mean now?"

Santos nodded and said, "We whip around, and if we don't find anything helpful to our investigation, we'll be able to tell our bosses we checked the box, and that will be it."

Malloy puffed his cheeks in frustration. "A box created during a séance?"

"I don't disagree with you," Santos said, rising. "It's an unusual development in a difficult case. What do you say?"

The priest had sunk so deeply into his sagging sofa that he had to fight to get up.

"When you say search, what do you mean?"

"We go through things. Look in drawers, closets—"

"I have breakables!"

Trinh reassured him they'd be careful.

The priest closed his eyes and rubbed his face. "I'm not sure what to do. I've never been involved in something like this. Do I need to speak to a lawyer?"

Santos flashed a reassuring smile. "You're not a suspect, Father. You're not a person of interest. You're someone who's assisting our investigation. It would help us check that box and move on. But it's completely up to you. And at any time, if you're not comfortable, you can withdraw your consent, and we'll take off."

"What would I do when you're searching?"

Santos reached for the sleeved newspaper. "You can hang out here and read this. By the time you get to yesterday's miserable Sox game, we'll probably be wrapping up. What do you say?"

Malloy whispered, "Go ahead. Please excuse the mess."

After Santos collected a signature on the one-page form, the detectives re-grouped in the hall and wandered into a tomb-dark kitchen with dirty dishes piled in the sink and a cold pot of congealed soup on a burner.

"Let's move fast before he gets squirrely and pulls consent," Santos said. "This place creeps me out. I don't want to have to come back."

"Look at that," Trinh said, pointing at a half-full bottle of cheap vodka on the counter. "Looks like he reset his AA clock."

They donned gloves and divvied up the job. Trinh would take the upper floor and attic, and Santos would do the lower level and detached garage.

"I'll do the living room last," he said. "He's going to freak out watching me poke through his junk."

Santos began opening the kitchen cabinets, and Trinh went up the stairs for a quick survey of the layout—three bedrooms and a bath. A rope hung from the hall ceiling. When she pulled it, a set of folding stairs squealed on their hinges. Climbing up, she saw it was more of a crawl space than an attic. It wasn't as bad as she feared. There were a few cardboard boxes and small pieces of furniture sitting on a bare wooden floor littered with carcasses of flies and wasps. As she was already up the ladder, she decided to start the search there. The boxes were filled with women's clothes and handbags, belonging, no doubt, to the priest's mother. She shone a flashlight into the nooks and crannies of the unfinished area, and satisfied, climbed down, and raised the stairs.

Father Malloy's bedroom was untidy. The bed was unmade, and there were piles of clothes on the floor. She sniffed at the bedside glasses. The large tumbler contained water, and the small one was alcohol. She rummaged through his dresser drawers and bedside tables, and then moved to the closet. Clerical clothes hung neatly on hangers, one set in dry cleaner's plastic—the only articles that seemed to be treated with care. She grunted at the large number of double-sized shoeboxes stacked on the floor, and let out a curse when she found that the first few she checked were packed with papers—bank statements and the like. There was nothing to do but get down on hands and knees and sort through them. She made quick work of it by grabbing a handful of papers with one hand, probing the box with the other, glancing at a few documents, and moving on to the next.

One box seemed heavier than the others, so she pulled it onto the rug, crouched on her haunches, and opened it. There were legal papers, yellowed with age, that resembled deeds or property documents.

She lifted out a handful and almost fell backwards onto her butt.

"Fuck me."

She kept whispering *fuck me* like a bad mantra as she ran down the stairs. She found her partner's legs protruding from the hall closet.

"You've got to come upstairs."

The two of them stood over the open box until Santos lowered himself to his knees.

"You pick it up?"

"I didn't touch it."

He took a picture on his phone, then said, "Damn."

It was small—pocket-sized. The nickel-plated barrel, cylinder, and body gleamed like the day it left the factory over a hundred years ago. The grip, made of hard black rubber, was pristine. The lettering stamped onto the octagon barrel was large enough that Santos didn't need his glasses.

H&R ARMS COMPANY, WORCESTER, MASS, U.S.A. 22 RIM FIRE

But he had to fish for his glasses to read the curlicue inscription etched into the chrome body.

To Piggy

"Is it loaded?" Trinh asked.

He carefully picked it up with gloved hands, found the cylinder release, and sniffed at the seven chambers.

"It's loaded." He clicked the cylinder in place, put the pistol back into the shoebox, and closed the lid. "Four live rounds—"

"What?" she said impatiently.

"Three spent."

CHAPTER NINE

Eli was in a meeting at the Divinity School with a student journalist from the *Harvard Crimson* when she saw that Cardinal Archer was calling her mobile. She silenced the ringer and carried on with the interview. At its conclusion, she complimented the woman, telling her she was tougher and more thorough than most professional journalists. As the student floated away on a high, Eli closed her door and reached for her phone.

Archer apologized for not returning her call earlier, explaining he was at a conference in Chicago.

"I read about it," she said. "It sounded—eventful."

He snorted at the euphemism. During his keynote address, a group of activists invaded the stage, unfurling a banner calling for the ordination of women, and had to be removed by the police.

"As if that wasn't enough," he said, "Father Malloy was arrested the next day. It's been wall-to-wall crisis meetings."

"Is the Vatican involved with Malloy?"

"Oh, yes. The Press Office has been sending me love letters."

"I'm not surprised," she said. "It's become an international story. Actually, Eminence, I called you on a personal matter."

"How can I be of assistance?"

"It's about my brother. I don't know if you are aware, but Cardinal Manzetti gave Emilio absolution as he lay dying."

"It was chaos," Archer said. "So much shooting and bloodshed. I didn't see Manzetti with him, but I heard about it afterward. I'm glad he had the presence to be a minister."

Talking about Emilio's last moments was still raw, like picking at an open wound. She wiped her cheek and pressed on. "As am I. I only recently learned that Emilio had some final words intended for me. I'm wondering, Eminence, did Manzetti tell you what he said?"

The cardinal was quick to respond. "No, never. I know nothing of this. Why do you think I might?"

"It's because I met someone in Boston—someone with no connection to the Vatican—who knew exactly what he said to Manzetti. You were there when he died. You and Manzetti are colleagues. You returned to Boston. As tenuous a connection as this is, I feel compelled to ask."

"Did Manzetti say he told me?"

"He says he told no one. Nevertheless, someone in Boston knew, so I'm checking."

"It wasn't me, I assure you. How did you find Guido?"

"He seemed fine, but he claimed his memory is like a colander these days."

"It's open knowledge that his mental acuity is declining. The Holy Father had him stand down from front-facing responsibilities. Perhaps he doesn't remember whom he told."

"The mystery remains unsolved," she sighed. "I'm sorry to have bothered you."

"It's never a bother. Actually, I was going to call you about Father Malloy. I could use your help."

"I'm at your service."

"As you know, the police say they found a firearm of interest at his house. Nevertheless, he vigorously professes his innocence. Frankly, we were surprised he was able to come up with the substantial bail—apparently, he pledged his house and bank accounts as security."

"I saw that he's been confined at home with an ankle monitor," she said.

"Where he remains isolated, and by all indications, in a terrible state. As head of his diocese, I have a responsibility to attend to his spiritual well-being. Unfortunately, Father Bouchard—whom you've met—cannot fulfill the role, as he might be called to testify in judicial proceedings. Likewise, there isn't a priest in the diocese who doesn't know him or the victims, and I don't want to get any of them in a legal tangle."

Just then, Cal looked through the glass panel at the side of her door. She held up a finger.

"You'd like me to see him."

"Indeed, yes," the Cardinal said. "You're familiar with the case, and I know you've dealt with far thornier issues in your time."

"Let me ask you, Eminence. Do you think he's guilty?"

She heard a nervous laugh. "I ask myself, how could a priest—one of their pastors—kill these nuns? Yet, as I understand it, there are damning facts: The weapon found hidden in his house, his lack of an alibi for the night of the murders, his history of alcoholism. Father Bouchard tells me he's smelled alcohol on his breath despite his claims to abstinence. Bouchard let the incidents pass—too leniently in my estimation. Maybe he was drunk that night and acted in a diminished capacity. All I know is that this affair is putting our diocese on the map in a very unfortunate way. I pray for a swift resolution so we can heal the wounds as quickly as possible. A long, drawn-out legal process with a televised trial would have the opposite result."

She understood where this was going and shook her head at the Machiavellian cunning.

"Canon law's sacramental seal does not protect communications between a priest and a nun. You'd like me to get him to bare his soul and confess, thereby achieving the rapid resolution you seek."

She detected a breath of relief. "As usual, you see things clearly, Madame Secretary."

Archer was not among her favorite prelates, but she lived in

Boston now, and he was her cardinal. "How could I ever refuse you?" she said coyly.

She took down the priest's particulars and signaled Cal her availability.

"Lunch?" he asked through the open door.

"Gladly. Question. Where is Dorchester?"

~

WHEN CAL ARRIVED at her apartment on a cool, rainy night, Eli told him he was more reliable than an Uber driver.

"Five stars?" he asked.

"Definitely," she said. "And you have a nice smile."

On the way to Dorchester, he let her know that he and Charles Gregory had met for a coffee in Harvard Square.

"Charles has been in the spotlight since the arrest," Cal said. "He's no longer the Metro columnist. He's the reporter who outed a triple murderer. Every TV station in Boston and beyond wants him on the air."

"How's he handling that?"

"He's a very private person. He likes to say he's a shoe-leather journalist who puts the work in, goes home, and doesn't care to dissect his columns publicly once they're published. He's ducking media requests. He says he's happy if they've caught the real killer, but on a personal level, he kind of wishes he never wrote the damned thing."

"Did he have anything to say about Eva Nevins?"

"Some. Not a lot. When I asked him over the phone if he'd done any background checks before he wrote the article, he laughed and said, 'What am I? The FBI?' He said he makes it clear to his readers that he only reports what he sees and hears—and sometimes smells when he's doing an article about missing trash pickups—but he doesn't do heavily researched pieces. But after our séance, he started doing some checking, and he went into overdrive after the arrest."

"What did he find?"

"This is from memory, so—"

"You have an excellent memory."

"Thank you. She was born in 1955 at the Boston Lying-In Hospital and grew up in the house we visited in Brighton, the only child of Edwin, a salesman, and Winnie, a stay-at-home mother. In 1963, when she was fourteen, she was riding with her father in his car when he ran a red light on Commonwealth Avenue in Brighton, and was hit broadside by a city utility truck. He was killed outright, and she was severely injured. The police report said he reeked of booze. She was taken to Saint Elizabeth's Hospital in Brighton with a broken back. They saved her life, but she was paralyzed from the waist down. Eva graduated from high school, then went to Katherine Gibbs, a big secretarial school in those days. She got a job as a typist at the John Hancock Insurance Company and worked there until her early thirties, when she left the company and applied for a license to be a medium."

"You need a license for that?"

"According to Charles. It's called a fortune-teller's license."

"Even now, this is done?"

"Apparently, she has to renew it every year. Charles said she's in good standing with the Boston Licensing Board."

"This seems quite archaic for a modern city like Boston. I don't think there's such a license in Italy. It must be a strange procedure."

1982

THE SMALL CHAMBER in Boston City Hall smelled of coffee and carbon paper. Three Board members sat behind a long oak table. There were only a few people in the audience, half of them dozing.

The clerk called the docket for May 16, 1982, and said, "Application of Eva Nevins, 125 Academy Hill Road, Brighton, for a license to tell fortunes for hire, pursuant to Chapter 140 of the General Laws."

The chairman looked at his paperwork and said, "Good morning, Ms. Nevins. Please step forward."

A young woman wheeled Eva toward the front of the room.

"I'm sorry," he said, looking up. "Do you need any assistance?"

"I'm fine, thank you. I have a helper."

Eva was thin and pretty, dressed demurely in her secretarial ensemble of skirt, blouse, and sweater. Perms and curls were the rage, but she wore her hair in a short pixie cut.

"Now, you've lived at that address how long?"

"All my life. My family's been in the same house since the 1890s."

"And this is the first time you've applied for a fortune-telling license?"

"Yes. I've entertained friends and neighbors for years, but I want to be aboveboard now, do things properly, and begin charging for my services."

It was a gentle lie. She'd been accepting payments to supplement her income since her mother died four years earlier.

"So, I take it you'll be holding the séances in your home?"

"I don't call them séances," she said, thrusting her small chin forward. "They are sittings where I help people communicate with the departed."

"Fine, but we call them séances per the licensing ordinance. I asked if the residential address is the same as the business address."

"It is. I'll be holding my meetings in the front parlor. I've enclosed the floor plan, as requested."

"And you understand the license allows only what's specified—fortune-telling, readings, séances—for a fee. Nothing else."

"I understand."

"Have you installed exit signs?"

"I have."

"Procured a fire extinguisher?"

"Yes, sir."

The chairman asked his board members if they had any questions, but there were none.

"I think that's all we need from you, Ms. Nevins."

Eva looked surprised. "You don't need to hear about how I discovered my gift when I was a young girl? Nothing about my spirit guide? I want to assure the board that my methods are above board, and my results are valid."

A couple of board members smirked, but the chairman kept a straight face.

"That won't be necessary. We don't go into that. If the board receives complaints from the public about a licensee, we might require a hearing on the matter of consumer fraud, but if you do right by your customers, you should be fine."

"Can I charge what I like?" she asked.

"You can charge whatever people are willing to pay. Fee regulation is not within this board's jurisdiction. Are there any comments from the public on this application?"

A woman representing a citizens' group in Brighton rose to say that parking on Academy Hill Road was tight and asked the applicant to keep her gatherings small.

"Most sittings are six or seven people, no more," Eva said. "I don't plan to make it a circus."

"Very well," the chairman said. "The license, if granted, runs one year. You'll need to renew annually before May 1st. Any violations or complaints, and you'll be back here in person. Do you understand?"

"Yes, sir."

"I don't see any red flags. You'll receive a written communication from us soon," he said, bringing the gavel down.

Eva wheeled around, smiling broadly. Her young companion came forward to grab the chair's handles.

Eva gushed to her, "We're in business!"

Charles Gregory found nothing unsavory in Eva's past. Her online reviews consistently received four or five stars, with customers praising her for the sensitivity and uncanny accuracy of her mediumship. No one accused her of fraud or subterfuge. *Her spirit guide knew that my Leonard loved licorice*, said one. *My mother told me her pearl necklace was fake. I took it to a jeweler, and she was right.* He also paid a few dollars for an online background check, and it came back squeaky clean with no civil or criminal blots.

"So, we're left with a woman with a spotless record who's been doing this for most of her life," Cal said.

"And no closer to understanding how she knew what Emilio told Manzetti or that Father Malloy might be a murderer," Eli said.

The car whirred quietly through Jamaica Plain. Cal mentioned something about taking her to the Arnold Arboretum one day, but she was deep in thought and didn't respond.

"There's always the possibility—" he began.

"Oh, God," she said. "You're not going to suggest she actually communicates with the dead."

He laughed. "From one Catholic to another, Christianity is built on the bedrock of miracles and fantastic occurrences."

"Surely you're not equating Christ's miracles and his resurrection with Eva Nevins' séances," she huffed.

"All I'm saying is that not everything is knowable and explainable. If one believes in Heaven and Hell and eternal life, then maybe—just maybe, some mortal souls might possess the ability to communicate with them."

"I'm sorry, but it's hard for me to be as open-minded as you. I believe she engages in fraud. We just don't know how she does it."

"Said Harry Houdini to Arthur Conan Doyle," he said.

The joke lightened her mood, and she said, "Me, Houdini? I can't do a single magic trick."

"And I can't write a detective story."

Content to change the subject, she asked if he'd finalized his itinerary for his Rome trip.

"Pretty much. A few side meetings still up in the air."

"Mic told me you're seeing them on Thursday."

"We're going to have dinner at Tonnarello."

"You're making me homesick."

He brushed her hand. "Sorry, it can't be helped."

"Give them the hugs they need. Which day will you go to the Archives?"

"Friday. I need my fix."

Cal hadn't been sure that his "golden library card" was going to be honored during the new papacy, so he checked with Pope John XXV's private secretary to make sure the new pope was happy to continue the privilege of unlimited browsing. The two-word message from the American pontiff, who, in his youth, was a college basketball star, was "Hell, yes".

"Is one day going to be enough?" she asked.

"Probably not, but it's better than nothing. If I find interesting leads, Maurizio can keep looking."

"He adores you," she said.

Maurizio Orlando, the Vatican Archive's Vice Prefect, had become a trusted friend over the years, always willing to help Cal with research.

"He likes me," Cal said. "He *loves* you. When he hears it's your project, he'll drop everything."

She thrust her lower lip into a pout. "I really want you to be a co-author."

"Nope. If it comes together as something publishable, it's all yours. Toss me an acknowledgement as a research assistant if you want. Have you thought more about search parameters?"

"I think the focus should be on the correspondence of the three popes who spanned the peak Spiritismo years. The Vatican's formal position on the movement is well known, but there may be illuminating letters between the Holy See and the diocese in those countries where the movement was strongest."

The GPS announced they were about to reach their destination.

"Give me a list of the cardinals you want me to look at. This is his street. You ready for this?"

"Barely. I don't know if we'll be looking at the face of a monster or a victim. Are you coming in?"

Cal put the car into park. "I'm not leaving you alone with him."

Standing on the sloping porch, Cal said, "The place could use a little work."

Father Malloy appeared in clerical garb, freshly shaven, his hair combed. When they shook hands, his trembled. In the days since his release on bail, he had been dealing with the aftermath of the search warrant. The police were looking for the missing rosaries, ammunition, and clothing with gunpowder residue, and they had tossed the contents of every drawer and cupboard, and rifled the cabinets and bookshelves. Malloy dealt with it stoically until he found they had broken the handle of one of his mother's favorite porcelain teacups. That small transgression triggered a full-blown meltdown, causing him to collapse, sobbing on the kitchen floor.

"Please come in, Sister," he said. "I've been looking forward to meeting you."

"This is my friend and colleague, Calvin Donovan. He was good enough to drive me. Do you mind…"

"Oh, yes! Professor Donovan. You're nearly as famous as the Madam Secretary. Please come in, too."

He took them into his living room, which he had returned to its pre-ransacked state. Eli delighted him with the comment that it was like walking into a museum.

"I inherited the collecting bug from my mother," he said. "It's only bric-a-brac, but it's my passion. Please, can I get you something to drink?"

"We're fine," Eli said.

"Really? Nothing? I read you're a vodka man, Professor. I have a bottle—not a top-shelf brand, but—" His voice trailed off, and he lifted a trouser leg to show an ankle bracelet. "I'm not allowed. They call this a SCRAM monitor. It detects alcohol. If it transmits a positive reading, they can revoke my bail." He continued the show-and-tell by lifting the other trouser leg. "This one goes off if I leave my house. How did I wind up like this?"

Cal didn't think the agonized question required an answer.

"Thanks, I'm good."

The priest sat opposite them and crossed his legs tightly, exposing both monitors.

"As you know, Cardinal Archer asked me to visit with you to provide a measure of pastoral support," Eli said.

"Yes, yes, I completely understand. I'm radioactive. No one within my diocese wants anything to do with me. Why would they? And I appreciate your willingness to see me. But, Sister, please believe me. I am innocent of this heinous crime."

Cal sat back and watched her handle the moment. She told him she wasn't there to be his judge, but that the Lord is there for all men, in the best of times and the worst.

"I'm not a priest, and this isn't a confessional," she said. "Cardinal Archer is a friend. I've been to Wellspring House. He knows I care deeply about everyone touched by the tragedy."

Malloy wanted to talk about his legal situation, not his spiritual one.

"Yes, but it's important for the Cardinal to know—for everyone in the diocese and beyond to know—that I had no involvement in this. I am not a perfect man. The Lord knows I'm a sinner, and I beg for His grace and redemption every day of my imperfect life. Not only am I a flawed man, I am a flawed priest. I don't put parishioners at ease—I'm aware of this. I can be awkward. I don't have the gift of the gab. I've never been entrusted with my own parish. I don't fault my superiors for this. But I've been a faithful servant of God, and I've never harmed a living soul."

She asked about his dealings with the sisters at Wellspring. He replied that he thought they were professional and always appropriate. He respected them personally and for their vocations. He knew they preferred Father Bouchard, but they never showed him anything but courtesy. And the three murdered women? Was there any bad blood with any of them? On the contrary, he responded. If anything, he felt closer to the older nuns. Lidia, especially, reminded him of his deceased mother, whom he lauded in a lengthy monologue, revealing she had been the one who encouraged the shy young man to become a priest. Afterwards, he circled back to his defense.

"I can't explain how a gun wound up in my house. I've never even held one. I was home the night of the murders. I rarely go out. I wish I were more sociable, but I am who I am. If I'd been visiting with someone that night—playing poker with the boys, or whatever the boys do—I wouldn't be in the impossible position of having to prove the negative that I was home and asleep in my bed. I beg you—please tell Cardinal Archer I am innocent."

After half an hour, there was no more to be said, and no confession obtained. Cal remained silent until they were at the front door, and the priest asked him how close he was to the new pope.

"I know him quite well, though not as well as his predecessor."

"I've read about your close bond with Cardinal Da Silva. I was overjoyed when he was elected, although losing him was bittersweet. He was the leader Boston needed."

"Rodrigo was irreplaceable," Cal said, "but Cardinal Macy was terrific in New York, and I'm sure he'll be a terrific pope."

Father Malloy let out a shuddering breath and said, "I hope and pray I can attend one of his general audiences in the future. My fate is in God's hands."

Cal and Eli said nothing to one another until they were buckled in their seats.

"What do you think?" he said.

"He's a pathetic soul, isn't he?" she said.

"Pathetic in an innocent or guilty way?"

She considered the question before saying, "I cannot picture this man sneaking into Wellspring House in the middle of the night and executing three women in their sleep. Do you feel differently?"

"I don't know. Gun—check. Red nose—check."

"That infernal séance!" she cried.

"I understand, but he also knew the victims and doesn't have an alibi. If you ask me, Cardinal Archer's going to be disappointed he didn't confess."

"I know he wants the diocese to put the sordid affair behind it quickly," she said, "but not at the expense of a rush to judgment."

She checked the dashboard clock and wondered if it was too late to call the cardinal.

"Sure. Give him the bad news. Put it on Bluetooth."

Archer answered the phone somewhere noisy with background voices and clattering cutlery. He listened to Eli's debriefing without interruption.

When done, he asked, "You say he had no explanation for the gun in his bedroom."

"He says he's mystified."

"What's your woman's intuition on his story?"

Cal gave the car speaker the finger, and Eli swatted his hand playfully.

"I went to provide pastoral support. I didn't go as your investigator, Eminence. However, despite the incriminating evidence, I don't believe he's a murderer."

"Well, I beg to differ," he sniffed. "I've put him on administrative leave with a subsistence stipend, and will be opening a canonical investigation into his suitability to remain a priest." She heard a waiter announcing desserts. "Ah! I have to go," Archer said. "It's a pity we don't see eye-to-eye on Father Malloy, Madame Secretary, but I greatly appreciate your assistance."

CHAPTER TEN

It was only the second time in his career that Santos had been summoned to a meeting with the Suffolk County District Attorney. The first time was also for a high-profile case—the murder of a city councilor's wife. Santos was all nerves, but his partner was loose, even though it was her maiden visit to One Bulfinch Place. As they waited in a nondescript conference room in the Homicide Unit, he got annoyed at her yawns and insouciant posture.

"How the hell are you so goddamn chill?"

Trinh puffed her cheeks and blew air. "Why stress? It's not like we did something bad, right?"

"Maybe they think we fucked something up."

"We caught the killer. Remember?"

The room got crowded fast—first with the prosecuting lawyers from the Homicide Unit and their investigators, and finally, the DA.

Marilyn Meeks slapped a briefing book on the table and began unceremoniously. "Detective Santos, do you have any idea how many calls I've gotten from the governor's office and legislators to give this case to the State Police?"

Despite vigorous head movements, her platinum hair didn't budge.

In a moment of madness, Santos regurgitated the last thing his partner said, "Before or after we caught the guy?"

He was rewarded with a withering stare. "This office has its eye on the prize. You made an arrest, Detective. Bravo. The prize isn't an arrest. It's a conviction. What have you done since the arrest to help us build a winning case?"

"We haven't stopped working," he said defensively. He counted their accomplishments by sticking out fingers, starting with his thick thumb. "We've gotten confirmation from the FBI that the gun we seized at the priest's house was the murder weapon. We got a new doorbell video from an across-the-street neighbor who'd been in China. It has another view of the person dressed in black going down the driveway toward the rear door of Wellspring House. It's compatible with Malloy's height. We found out that he turned his cellphone off the night of the murder to mask his whereabouts, we believe."

"That's it?" the DA asked.

"So far."

"Did you hear who Father Malloy has hired to defend him?"

Santos shook his head.

"Barry Weintraub. You've heard of him, right?"

Everyone in town knew who Weintraub was. He was a motor-mouth, sharp-dressing criminal defense lawyer who liked high-profile cases and winning.

"He can afford Weintraub?" Santos said.

One of the senior prosecutors, the only one with a bowtie, said, "Barry's trading fees for camera time. Every hearing's going to be televised and clipped for the nightly news, and if it gets to trial, it'll be boom days for YouTube lawyers. For Barry, the exposure is gold."

The DA said, "All right, Jack, why don't you tell the detectives where the holes are in the Swiss cheese. Jack Harrigan's going to be first chair for the prosecution."

Harrigan, the one with the bowtie, was lanky to the point of bony. He was marginally less abrasive than his boss by dint of sugaring his barbs with smiles.

"I've looked at Father Malloy's interrogation video a few times, and there's nothing that's helpful to the prosecution, but plenty for the defense. The jury's going to find his denials credible. He comes across as sincere and genuinely confused about the gun being in his house. He might have opportunity against him—he knew the victims, he's been to their house—but where's the motive? There's no history of bad blood with the victims. This wasn't a sex crime. You didn't find a stash of nun porn or whatever on his devices. The videos on Birch Street? You can't make out the perp's face. It's not a giant or a dwarf—can you still say dwarf?—but most adults aren't excluded. The gun. It's an antique, and we know the guy's crazy about antiques, but he had to get it from somewhere. Have you canvassed all the physical and online stores he buys from?"

Trinh hadn't said a peep yet, but she decided to weigh in. "An antique store couldn't sell it. It's post-1899, so it's legally a modern firearm in Massachusetts. You need an FFL to sell a modern gun."

"Thank you for educating me, Detective," Harrigan said. "Here's a list of fifteen antique dealers in the state who have federal firearm licenses. Do you know if Malloy buys from any of them?"

He slid the piece of paper across the table. Trinh glanced at it and mumbled that they'd look into it.

Harrigan had another report ready. "You mentioned his phone going dark the night of the murders. Our investigators got a Carpenter warrant for a more expansive CSLI. It seems that Malloy turns his cell phone off every night. He's done it for ages."

Santos swallowed. "That's very interesting. Noted."

"Let's talk about the gun. You ever worked a shooting case where the gun and ammo were a hundred years old?"

"First time for everything," Santos said.

"Very good response. Make it at trial, and Weintraub will mop the floor with you. Not only is the gun rare as hell, it's got *Piggy* engraved on it. That makes it a one-of-one. Some dealer out there is going to see it and say, I sold that puppy. Have you gone wide with the photo? Trace the sale to Ray Malloy and it's game, set, and match."

It wasn't hot in the room, but Santos was sweating. "We can do that," he said

"Let me continue," Harrigan said. "The victim had their rosaries stolen. Where are they? If the priest took them as some kind of trophy, why didn't you find them at his house? And why didn't you find any gunpowder residue on any of his clothes? The FBI reports say that the revolver's large cylinder gap would have spat out considerable residue toward the shooter."

"He could have thrown out the clothes he was wearing and the beads," Santos said.

"Yep. Could have," the prosecutor said. "Could have doesn't help us win the case. Want me to go on? The defense is going to say he was framed and that the gun was planted. And they're not going to have to identify that hypothetical person. They're only going to have to raise reasonable doubt in the minds of one or more jurors. Take Father Bouchard. He's the one who put you onto Malloy. How do we know he's not the perp?"

"Bouchard?"

"Sure. Why not? One of the victims was a very attractive young woman. How do we know he didn't have a thing for her? Maybe he snuck up there and shot her when she refused his advances. Maybe he killed the other two because they heard the shot."

"That's pure speculation."

"Yes, it is, and that's what Barry Weintraub does for a living. Tell me, where was Father Bouchard that night?"

Santos stared blankly at Harrigan. "We'll go ask him."

"Good idea," Meeks said, throwing her head back.

"And what about the fortune teller or the medium—whatever the hell she is?" Harrigan asked. "She's the one who got the ball rolling with the red-nosed priest story. Barry Weintraub will call her as a witness and turn the trial into a circus or worse. Maybe he'll throw shade her direction."

"She's kind of kooky, but she's not our shooter."

"How do you know?"

"For one thing, she's paralyzed."

"Are you sure she's not faking it?"

Trinh smiled wickedly. She'd asked the same question.

Santos fibbed and said they were trying to get her medical

records. He signaled his partner with an eye raise to make sure she didn't rat him out.

"Could she have hired someone to do the killings?"

"Why would she do that?" Santos blurted.

"Aren't you the least interested in ruling it out?" Harrigan said sarcastically. "Barry Weintraub is sure going to bark up that tree. I can see him now hamming it up in front of a jury—My client had nothing to gain by killing these women, but this woman in Brighton who calls herself a medium falsely implicates him and makes a killing fleecing a boatload of new customers."

"We'll interview her again," Santos said, looking down at his hands.

The DA shut her briefing book and said, "Grand jury's next week. Barry can't stop the bill, but he'll start the show. The Mayor wants BPD to keep it, but I'll move it to MSP in a heartbeat if you're not cutting the mustard. Use Jack's team. If you don't, your next trip to Bulfinch is your last."

Following the mass exodus of prosecutors, Trinh and Santos were left alone in the room.

"Fuck me," Trinh said, shaking her head in disbelief. "What if we hadn't caught the guy?"

"I told you not to be so chill," Santos said.

"NICE CHURCH," Trinh said.

The Sacred Heart Church was a Gothic Revival gem nestled in a corner lot within a crowded neighborhood of single-family homes. For over a hundred years, it had been the beating heart of Roslindale's Catholic community. Originally, it served Irish-Americans, but their lot were dwindling, replaced by Dominicans and Haitians. These days, Mass was offered in English and Spanish, with a monthly one in Creole.

Santos liked to show up unannounced to get an interviewee's unprepared versions of events. They checked to make sure they weren't going to bump into a scheduled service, and arrived at a mostly empty parking lot.

"Let's try the office over there—or maybe it's the rectory."

The attached wood-framed building was both a parish office and the pastor's residence, and a woman they encountered summoned Father Bouchard. The priest didn't seem particularly surprised to see them and took them to an office decorated with crayon and finger-painted pictures from the preschool program.

Bouchard took his place in an oversized desk chair that made him look like a youngster, and tented his fingers over his lips, waiting for them to explain their presence.

"Thanks to your tip, we were able to make an arrest," Santos said. "We're here to button up a few things."

"Our community is in shock," Bouchard said. "I'll help in any way I can to bring a measure of closure."

"Thank you. Just a few questions."

"Will my role in Father Malloy's arrest become public knowledge?"

"I really can't say."

"Will I be asked to testify in court?"

"Again—no idea. It'll be up to the lawyers on both sides."

"I hope it doesn't come to that. It wouldn't be pleasant."

"Nothing about murders is pleasant," Trinh said.

"Hmm. Ask away."

Santos had told his partner she could do the questioning, and she eagerly jumped in with both feet. "How often do you go to Father Malloy's house?"

The priest smiled. "His house? Only once. It was three years ago during that big February blizzard. He couldn't get to Roslindale, and we had a check that urgently needed to be sent out, requiring two signatures. I braved the elements and drove there."

"Did you go inside?"

"I did. He made me a coffee. It was quite the place. If there's a line separating collectors and a pack-rats, I didn't see it." He closed his eyes in thought, then volunteered more. "He was a mess that day. It was before noon, and he'd obviously been drinking. I know the smell of alcohol and mouthwash—my father was an alcoholic. His hand shook when he signed the check."

"Did he show you around?"

"I only went to the front room—the one with his glassware collection, and the kitchen."

"You didn't go upstairs?"

"I didn't, no."

"You didn't see a gun there, did you?"

"A gun? No! I'd remember that."

"Did he ever talk to you about owning a gun or looking to buy one?"

"Never."

Trinh glanced at her partner before making the transition to her next line of questioning.

"We've gotten a lot of questions internally about why you called us about Father Malloy. Can we go into that?"

Bouchard frowned deeply. "I think I explained to you how conflicted I was. On one hand, there's this crazy *Globe* article about séances and priests with red noses, which I found ridiculous, and on the other, there's been a horrific murder in my parish. Do I make a fool of myself by coming forward and subjecting a colleague to police scrutiny, or do I risk withholding critical information? I chose to come forward."

"How did you feel after we made an arrest?"

"I was happy my decision to call you was vindicated, but I was deeply shocked and saddened that my associate pastor might have been the monster who killed these dear women."

"Was there any bad blood between you and Father Malloy?"

"Bad blood? I wouldn't say so. We had stylistic differences, and as his superior, I tried to counsel him on how he might connect more effectively with our parishioners, but I thought he was a decent fellow. He disappointed me sometimes, but never angered me."

"You weren't friends."

"We were not friends."

"You never talked about personal things?"

"Ray is a very private man, and I suppose I am too. We stuck to parish business."

Trinh shifted gears again, her voice becoming scratchy. "I think you told us that you went to Wellspring House fairly often."

"Yes?" he said warily.

"You ever go up to the bedrooms? The attic?"

He cleared his throat and asked to think about it. "I toured the attic with Sister Gabriela after the space was converted to bedrooms."

"When was that?"

"I'd say four years ago. It must have been summertime because the window boxes hadn't gone in yet, and it was very hot."

"Before the three new nuns arrived?"

"Shortly before, yes."

"Did Father Malloy come on this tour?"

"No."

"Once the nuns moved in, did you ever go to their bedrooms again?"

"Goodness, no! Why would I?" When the detective didn't answer, Bouchard vented to Santos. "I feel like you're trying to turn the spotlight. Is there any doubt it was Ray?"

"We're just covering all bases—doing our job," Santos said.

"Is there anything else? I have a counseling session in a few minutes."

"Are you on social media, Father?" Trinh asked.

"I am."

"TikTok?"

"All of them, why?"

"Are you active on them?"

"Only the church's official Facebook page."

"What do you do with the other accounts? Follow any parishioners?"

"I'm also the youth minister. If I think one of our kids is having difficulties, it's a way to see what's going on with them in their version of the real world."

"Sister Kristin was heavily into TikTok. Did you follow her?"

He screwed his mouth while holding his breath. On the exhale, he said, "I don't remember."

"Could you check?"

"My phone's upstairs. Can I get back to you?"

"We can wait."

"I'll email you later. I've got your cards. I really need to get ready for my session."

"Sure thing," Trinh said. "One more thing. Do you have any sock-puppet accounts?"

"I don't know what they are."

"Fake online identities so you can follow, maybe talk to people anonymously."

He raised his voice. "I do not."

Santos stood, forcing his partner to follow suit. "Any chance you'd consent to having us look at your phone to see if there've been any private messages exchanged between you and the victims?" he said.

"Really? You're really asking for my phone? Look, Detectives, I'm actually getting uncomfortable. I might need to seek advice from diocese lawyers."

"We understand, Father. Just one more question. Where were you the night of the murders?"

Bouchard thrust his finger toward the ceiling. "I was upstairs, in bed."

"Can anyone vouch for that?"

The priest sprang from his giant desk chair and said, "I think we're done."

ON THE DRIVE TO BRIGHTON, Santos and Trinh mulled over the priest's responses.

"He's acting like he's hiding something," Trinh said.

"It's not the murders," Santos said. "We've got the murderer."

"I've got a feeling he's been a naughty boy and doesn't want us to see what's on his phone," she said.

"You think he was messaging Sister Kristin?"

"Maybe."

"If he doesn't want to let us search it, there's no fucking way a judge is going to give us a warrant. Where are we with Kristin's phone?"

The detectives had found nothing of interest on Dora and Lidia's non-password-protected phones. They couldn't get into Kristin's.

"I heard back from Apple with their usual response that they refuse to break a locked device for law enforcement. I've got a subpoena in for her iCloud account. I'm just waiting for the chief to authorize a requisition to send the phone to Cellebrite to try to crack it."

"Waste of money. Never works."

"That's what the chief said, but I think he's going to approve it."

"Meanwhile, back to Brighton to make the case Weintraub-proof," Santos grumbled.

Trinh grinned. "Aren't you glad I didn't rub it in about getting her medical records?"

"You're rubbing it in now. Where are we with that?"

"Medical records are tough. They're HIPAA-protected."

"I know that."

"I did the paperwork. It'll take a while."

"We could stick a pin in her leg and see if she feels it."

She giggled at that. "Sounds like something I'd say."

Eva Nevins was in the kitchen when the detectives showed up at her door. She invited them in, and seeing the napkin on her lap, Santos apologized for interrupting a meal.

"It's only soup and a sandwich," she said, wheeling down the hall. "Can I make you one?"

"We're fine, thank you. We can talk while you're finishing your lunch."

They followed her to the kitchen table, where she poured a bag of potato chips into a bowl and encouraged them to help themselves. Trinh nudged him to notice the second plate and silverware setting on the table.

His mouth was full of chips, when a young woman with highly distinctive looks walked in. He swallowed and apologized again for interrupting their lunch.

The woman, dressed in black, was short and a little stocky, with bloodless-white skin, midnight-dark hair cut short and geometrically, black lipstick and nail polish. And she had enough facial piercings to set off an airport scanner.

"That's all right," Eva said. "This is my friend, Felicia. She's learning how to do what I do. Felicia, you don't mind if I speak with the detectives investigating the murdered nuns?"

"It's your house, Eva. You can talk to anyone you like. Should I sit somewhere else?"

"You can stay, if you like," Santos said.

"Yes, stay," Eva said. "Have your sandwich."

Santos began, "We wanted to circle back and ask a few more questions following our arrest of Father Malloy."

"I'm happy we were able to help catch him."

"Did you tell Kay?" Trinh asked wickedly.

Felicia looked over her turkey sandwich, her eyes narrowed.

"One of my clients asked her if she was pleased," Eva said.

"Was she?"

"She was unaware, of course. The departed don't have the evening news. When informed, she expressed satisfaction that justice was done."

"Here's something I don't get about the whole Kay thing," Trinh said. "If dead people don't know what's happening on planet alive, how'd she know about the priest with a red nose?"

Santos reached for more chips and let his partner do her thing.

"That's a good question. I imagine she spoke to the dead nuns."

Trinh blinked hard and widened her eyes theatrically. "Well, that's interesting! Could we talk to them? It'd be useful to ask them about their murderer."

"We could try," Eva said helpfully. "When I've finished my lunch, we could go to my parlor."

"Jeez, I don't know—" Santos began, but Trinh cut him off and said with a sparkle that they'd love to have a go.

"Very well," Eva said.

"Can I ask about your childhood injury?" Trinh said.

"Of course."

"You're completely paralyzed below your waist?"

"I am. I've lived with it for so long, I don't even think about using my legs anymore."

"You said you don't have much help around the house. How do you do it?"

"It's no mystery. I have strong arms and shoulders. I have my chair lift for the stairs. My bed is low. I can slide onto it from my upstairs wheelchair. I have handrails in the bathroom. For a small extra something, the deliverymen take my shopping to the kitchen. You'd be surprised what you can do out of necessity."

"Could we talk to your doctor about your condition? Just to verify a few things?"

"Really?"

"Yeah, really?"

Felicia had been squirming with anger and it bubbled over. "For fuck's sake, lady. Her legs are dead. Are you fucking kidding me?"

"Now, now, Felicia, it's all right. I'm sure the detective has a good reason to ask. It's Dr. Aitken at Mass General. I'll ring his office and give permission."

Trinh tapped the table and smiled at her partner. "That would be very helpful. Did you ever meet Father Ray Malloy?"

"I don't think so. I'm a Methodist."

"Do you harbor any dislike for priests in general or Father Malloy in particular?"

Eva had the last bite of her sandwich, finished chewing, and wiped her mouth. "As I said, I don't know Father Malloy. I'm not acquainted with any priests, but I certainly don't have ill will for them, or any Catholics."

"With all the publicity you've had, how's your business?"

She threw her hands in the air and exclaimed, "It's too busy! I've never had this many calls. Felicia will vouch for that. She has the gift, you know. She started as a client and has become my protégé, haven't you, dear?"

"That, I have."

"I hate turning people away, but there are only so many I can accommodate. I'm not young anymore. It's too much."

"The money must be good," Trinh said.

"I don't need the extra money. My necessities are covered. I've nothing to spend it on. I rarely buy new things, and my shoes never wear out!"

Santos didn't show any surprise when Trinh turned her attention to Eva's young friend.

"I didn't catch your last name, Felicia."

"I didn't say it."

"Would you mind? For my report."

"King."

"Do you work, Ms. King?"

"I'm a massage therapist."

"You don't have your ID on you, do you?"

Felicia smiled stiffly and pulled a purse from her bag slung over her chair.

As Trinh jotted down her particulars, Eva said, "So, are you ready for the parlor?"

Trinh almost had to drag Santos down the hall. She whispered to him that it would be a hoot.

Eva had Felicia pull the parlor curtains, turn on the small lamps on the side table, and close the door. Santos took the chair facing the mantel and went eyeball to eyeball with the framed photo of Arthur Conan Doyle, and Trinh sat on Eva's other side. Felicia didn't join the little circle. She took a side chair and quietly observed.

"We'll hold hands," Eva said. That's right. Reach for her hand, Detective."

Santos scowled and obliged.

"We can begin, if you're ready. Close your eyes, or keep them open. It doesn't matter."

"I was born ready," Trinh said mischievously.

Eva closed her eyes and said, "We gather tonight to honor those who departed before us. We seek the comfort and guidance of those we loved and cherished. I seek my spirit guide, Kay. Kay, make your presence known. Please grasp hands tighter and concentrate all your mental energies on summoning Kay."

Trinh and Santos each kept their eyes open and saw Felicia staring hard at them.

"Thank you for coming, Kay!" Eva suddenly said. "How are you faring?"

In her Kay voice, she said, "I am well enough."

Trinh let out a small snort.

"Kay, my guests wish to speak with the nuns recently murdered in Boston. Their names? Detectives, please tell me their names."

"Lidia, Kristin, and Dora," Trinh said.

"Kay, their names are Sisters Lidia, Kristin, and Dora. Are they there?"

The room fell silent for several minutes until Kay spoke. "I cannot find them."

"Why am I not surprised?" Trinh said.

"I think we need to get back to work," Santos said.

"Wait," Eva said. "Is there anyone else you would like to speak to?"

In a snarky voice, Trinh said, "I wouldn't mind saying hi to my father."

"What is his name?"

"Bao. Bao Trinh."

"Concentrate on your father," Eva said.

"Will do."

"Squeeze hands tighter—both of you."

Again, the room fell silent until Kay said, "Bao is here. What would you like to ask him?"

Trinh angrily shook her head and spat out, "Okay, why don't you ask him why he stepped in front of a train?"

"He says he was in despair."

"Sure. Good generic answer," Trinh said. In a mocking tone, she added, "How about this, *Kay*, why don't you ask him what he gave me for my tenth birthday?"

The answer came quickly. "He says he gave you a gold crucifix."

Trinh realized her crucifix was shining against her black shirt like a tiny mirror. "Lucky guess, Kay. Ask him what's engraved on it."

After a long pause, Kay said, "Oh, my, it's very sweet. It says, To my little angel."

Trinh stood up, shouted, "Fuck this! I am so out of here," and bolted from the room.

The whole house shook when Trinh slammed the front door.

Santos slowly rose, shaking his head. "I'm sorry, Mrs. Nevins. I don't know what got into her. That was unprofessional."

"It's quite all right. I've seen far stronger reactions."

"You've been generous with your time. I think we're all set." He turned, face-to-face again with the mantel photo. "Can I ask you who this is? Your father? Grandfather?"

"You have more kinship with him than me. He's the father of all detectives, Sir Arthur Conan Doyle, the author of Sherlock Holmes. He attended a Spiritualist gathering conducted by my grandmother in this room."

"Isn't that something? I can see myself out."

Eva remained at the table and said, "Well, Felicia, what did you think?"

"I think she was an asshole. Maybe that's why her father walked in front of a train."

Santos found Trinh crying inside his car.

"What the fuck, Maria? What the hell was that about?"

She pulled the gold chain over her head and handed him the crucifix.

"Read the back."

He squinted at the metal and said he couldn't see it without his glasses. When he started fumbling for them in his console, she grabbed it back and said, "It says, To my little angel, Love Bo. There's no way she could have seen it."

"What's Bo?"

"It's Vietnamese for daddy."

CHAPTER ELEVEN

1922, The North Atlantic

THE BOY WHO GREW UP IN SQUALOR IN AN EDINBURGH TENEMENT AS the son of a mentally disturbed, alcoholic father could never have conceived of the glittering life he would live. But thanks to a wealthy uncle who swooped in like a benefactor from a Dickens novel, the boy received a top-notch primary education in England and the Continent before returning to Edinburgh to study medicine. Without that helping hand, the world might never have been blessed with Sherlock Holmes.

Now, in the twilight of his life, Arthur Conan Doyle wrapped his hands around the brass railings of the White Star liner, RMS Baltic, and watched the sun slowly dip below black waters at the horizon.

"Sir Arthur! There you are."

Mr. Preston, a young Cambridge graduate who took a bullet to his hip in the war, limped to his side.

"Ah, Preston," Doyle said, sweeping his arm toward the west, "have you ever seen a finer sunset?"

"It is magnificent, Sir. The family awaits you in the saloon. As it's our last night, the Captain has us at his table again."

"Splendid," Doyle said. "Give me a few minutes longer and I'll be along. I want to see the great flaming orb fully quenched."

Along the way to the first-class dining room, he was pleasantly accosted by an American woman in an excited state.

"Sir Arthur," she gushed. "Finally."

"Finally, what, madam?"

"Finally, there you are on your own. Every time I've seen you, you're surrounded by admirers. And it's just in time!"

He was an imposing figure, tall and bulky, with a massive, drooping gray mustache. He glared at her. "In time for what?"

"We dock tomorrow in New York! She reached into her purse and produced a book. My son, Jack, would be so thrilled to have your signature on his favorite novel."

He glanced at the all-too familiar cover of *The Hound of the Baskervilles*, and grunted, "Holmes is behind me, Madam."

"Is he? What is in front of you, if I might ask?"

"Something infinitely more important involving the destiny of all men. Now, if you'll excuse me, my family is waiting."

She prattled on about how she rushed to buy the book when she heard they'd be on the same crossing, and how disappointed her son would be if she failed in her mission. And in a final plea, she pressed her palms together in prayer. With that, the book slipped to the deck.

Doyle picked it up and reached into his jacket for a pen. "Jack, you say. How old is young Jack?"

"He's thirty-two. It was his favorite childhood book!"

He hastily signed the title page, *To grown-up Jack, A. Conan Doyle.*

Doyle's traveling party was seven strong, comprised of Doyle and his wife, Jean, three of his children, Mr. Preston, and Miss Stable, the daughter of an old friend who had come to look after the children. Doyle embarked on this journey only a year after a grueling tour of Australia. He had been reluctant to undertake another taxing tour until he received spiritual guidance during a séance that an American tour would be a roaring success. The assurance came from a trusted friend who perished in the war. "You have no idea what great and glorious work you are going to do. You will leave your mark forever upon America. We will be with you, giving you inspiration and power and health."

At dinner, Doyle sat between the captain of the vessel and a prominent American financier who played the cheerful skeptic.

"We Jews are a little vague on the afterlife question. Orthodox Jews think there's a physical place called Olam-Ha-Ba, the World to Come, but we Reform Jews don't go that far. Sure, the soul might be immortal, but who knows what that even means? We sure as hell don't go in for mediums and séances."

"Allow me to invite you to one," Doyle said. "You might conclude otherwise."

"Put it this way, Doyle—when Harry Houdini changes his mind, I'll change mine."

"You might not have long to wait. Mr. Houdini and I are scheduled to meet in Atlantic City in two months for a séance with my wife and I."

"If Harry buys into it, I'll eat my hat," the financier said, "which would be unpleasant because my hat was very expensive and I don't think I'll like the taste."

Doyle and Houdini, surely the most prominent Spiritualism doubter, met for the first time in 1920 during Doyle's last visit to New York City. Houdini sought him out after a lecture. The magician, who knew a thing or two about pulling the wool over audiences, had a flair for exposing fraudulent mediums. Yet, following their get-together, the two men became highly amiable foes.

The captain rescued Doyle from having to defend himself. "Tell me, Sir Arthur, are you planning to take in a baseball game during your visit?"

"I would relish it. Perhaps my people can arrange for us to see a game at the Polo Grounds. It would be memorable watching Mr. Ruth hit one of his towering home runs."

"You were a sportsman in your day, were you not?"

"Indeed, I was. I've dabbled aplenty. I was goalkeeper at Portsmouth, bowled at Marylebone Cricket Club, did some amateur boxing, captained a golf club in Sussex, and was quite a fair marksman. That was my younger self. It's all behind me."

After dinner, Doyle and his party retired to the first-class social hall for his promised shipboard lecture, a low-key warm-up for the tour that lay ahead. A majority of the four hundred first-class passengers gathered in the high-ceilinged room paneled in polished oak with gilt trim that more resembled an elegant country-house drawing room than a ship's interior. The hall, illuminated by electric chandeliers and wall sconces, was filled with upholstered armchairs and settees, arranged in conversational groupings facing a raised platform. At the back of the stage stood a projection screen.

The ship's captain leapt onto the stage and said, "Our speaker tonight needs no introduction unless you have been in a deep slumber for several decades. In the event a Rip Van Winkle is present, I will give a brief one. Sir Arthur Conan Doyle is an eminent physician, keen sportsman, as we have been discussing over dinner, and one of the most beloved writers of our time. He has authored four novels and numerous stories about the world's favorite detective, Sherlock Holmes, as well as dozens of other novels, plays, essays, and historical works. Recently, he has become a passionate advocate for the cause of Spiritualism, and it is for this reason that he is embarking on a lecture tour of America to educate the public. Sir Arthur has graciously agreed to give us an exclusive preview of the message he is to bring to our American cousins."

From her seat at the front, Jean Conan Doyle, a sturdy, matronly woman, patted her husband on the hand and watched him slowly climb the platform to great applause.

He laid one hand on a grand piano, the other on his heart, and began, "Ladies and Gentlemen, I stand before you tonight to speak about far the most important thing in the world, since it involves the fate of every man and woman in attendance tonight. And no, it is not the resurrection of Professor Moriarty!"

The hall erupted in laughter.

"I believe there is one proposition upon which everyone would agree, and that is, whether our claim to have pierced the barrier of death is one of the greatest delusions ever offered the human race, or else, the greatest achievement ever done. I ask you to form yourselves into a jury so that you may render a verdict in the case I will now state."

For the next hour, he laid out his evidence for physical manifestations from the afterworld and how foolish it was for people to deny them in the face of the deliberate conclusions of the esteemed men who had thoroughly examined the matter. He quoted his friend, Professor Hyslop, who had recently asserted that a man who denies these things is either ignorant or a moral coward. He projected lantern slides of ectoplasm, a mysterious, thick, vapory, slightly luminous substance that exuded from some mediums in the throes of communicating with the other side, and spirit photos of winged garden fairies.

Doyle scanned the audience. He noticed a young man of university age taking notes and smirking. An elderly couple locked arms, gasping at the fairies. A Baltic officer standing against a pillar ambiguously blew his nose.

He outlined his own search for truth, which began, he said, with an utter lack of belief in any life beyond this one. It was only after a long course of reading, innumerable sessions with notable spiritual mediums, and his own psychic experiments that his views began to shift.

"I am supposed to know something about detective work," he told the crowd, "and I am not easily imposed upon. I always want proof. I struggled against the facts until my final forced acceptance of the phenomena. Tonight, I will show you how the messages from beyond vary very little, whatever the means by which they were obtained, or whatever the land of their origin. I will demonstrate that they constitute an organized philosophy and explanation of life and fate quite different from any held by the world before, but simple, reasonable, and credible, when once we have cleared our minds of prepossessions and prejudices. I will explain how they bear every sign of being a new revelation from God to man, sent to the human race at the hour of its need."

He described the transition from this world into the next as heralding a glorious reunion of loved ones and the realization of everything that is beautiful.

"When we die, our physical body dies, but our etheric body continues to live," he claimed. "There is no change in our intellectual standing. If we were brainy here, we would be brainy there. If we are fools on this side, we will be fools on that side."

The audience stirred and whispered, a mix of wide-eyed believers and squinting skeptics. However, when Doyle got personal, the salon became so quiet that whenever he paused for a breath, the sound of the liner cutting through the waves came through.

"Arthur Alleyne Kingsley Conan Doyle. Born 15 November 1892, died 28 October 1918," he said. "Kingsley was as fine a young man as the world has ever known."

He looked his wife in the eye and watched her draw a handkerchief.

"Wounded in France, he survived the war, only to be cruelly taken from us by the cursed Spanish influenza soon after he resumed his medical studies. Yet, with the help of mediums, we have been able to pierce the eternal veil and once again communicate with our dear boy. I will give you examples. Ten months after his death, my wife and I attended a sitting with a well-regarded medium in Portsmouth. The medium, Mr. Fletcher, was, for a time, groaning and muttering, but suddenly, we heard from his throat a voice that we immediately recognized. I said, Is that you, boy? And a reply came in a tone all Kingsley's own, 'Father!' and then after a pause, 'Forgive me!' I took that to mean forgive his earlier doubts about psychic activities. Then, I felt a strong hand pressing down on my shoulder, followed by a kiss on my forehead. And do you know what our boy said next? He said, 'I am so happy.'"

Doyle paused to let emotions ripple through the salon.

When the audience settled, he said, "Recently, I snapped a muscle in my calf. I consulted an eminent surgeon, Mr. Wallace, who told me that the fibers were torn and that it would be a long job. I answered that I had to lecture the next evening, and would do so, if need be, on one leg, like a stork. He did not seem hopeful. That evening, we had a sitting in my home. Kingsley came at once and said via the medium, 'I will help you, daddy.' The next moment, I felt a strong hand upon the very seat of my injury—the medium had no idea where it was—and for some minutes the whole circle could hear the *swish, swish* of the steady massage. The result was that I had the pleasure of lecturing the next day on two good legs, and of seeing the surprised and smiling face of Mr. Wallace among my audience, who afterwards told me it was a miracle. So it was, but a miracle is only the interposition of some higher natural law."

The anecdotes continued. A Welsh medium, Doyle said, connected with his mother, producing a sample of her distinctive handwriting, and produced details about her earthly correspondence that would be impossible for any medium to know. Doyle's dead brother had given him the correct name of a doctor in Copenhagen whom he wished his widow to consult. He had participated in numerous sittings where others had received accurate messages from loved ones that no fraudster could have had prior knowledge of.

"These are but a few cases drawn from my experience," he said, his voice rising to a thunderclap. "How long will the world wait before it realizes these things? Will these outer forces wait indefinitely for recognition? Or will they find their own way, breaking through? The future will show. Meanwhile, an ever-increasing number of us have come to be thankful for the greatest gift that life can bring. No religious system on earth could survive the destructive criticism which has shaken the psychic revelation founded upon the rock of actual personal observation. Those who have not observed it are like astronomers without telescopes. They must accept the conclusions of those who have the necessary knowledge and instruments. Ladies and Gentlemen, I feel the hand of destiny upon me. We do not embark on a mere lecture tour. No, I say! It is a mission! What greater message can we bring to mankind than that death is not the end?"

AT THE RMS BALTIC's port of call at the White Star Line terminal on the Chelsea Piers, in Manhattan, Doyle's party was greeted by his American manager, Lee Keedick, and the esteemed private detective, William J. Burns, who would attend to their security. They were whisked through Customs Hall and were immediately surrounded by a pack of over-eager journalists and photographers lying in wait.

"Oh, Lord!" Doyle's wife exclaimed. "The wolves are circling."

"It is to be expected, dear," Doyle said. "Allow me to toss them a few morsels of meat. I won't be long."

Doyle adjusted his jacket and waistcoat for the photos and stood before an erupting gaggle of people.

"Sir Arthur! What is the purpose of your visit?"

"The Protestant and Catholic Churches have condemned Spiritualism. What's your comment?"

"What do you say to the allegations that psychic mediums are frauds?"

"Gentlemen, gentlemen," Doyle said, holding an arm above his head, seeking quiet.

When the hubbub failed to abate, the detective shouted, "Fellows, you settle down right away and let the man speak, or you're going to get nothing."

The admonition was effective, and Doyle said, "Thank you, Mr. Burns. Permit me to make a brief remark or two. I'm delighted to return to America to begin a tour that will take me to two dozen cities here and in Canada. Making every allowance for fraud, which has been greatly exaggerated, the psychic movement is not antagonistic to religion. On the contrary, it is destined to revivify religion, which has long been decaying and becoming a mere formality. This new knowledge enables one, for the first time, to understand the actions and views of the early Christians and of their great Leader.

"There remains a great residuum of proved fact which makes this psychic movement the most serious attempt ever made to place religion upon a basis of definite proof. The true aim of communication with spirits is consolation, knowledge of spiritual matters, including conditions of life after death, and above all self self-improvement. Thank you. That is all for now. The children have had a long journey, and we must get them to their beds."

The weary and bedraggled party proceeded in two taxicabs

through the city's canyons, arriving at the Ambassador Hotel, where the general manager attended to their needs.

In their suite, Doyle exhaled deeply and told his wife, "Here we are, happy and safe. Our American adventure begins."

AFTER A DAY of sightseeing for the pleasure of all, but especially the children, Doyle held the first of his lectures, playing to a packed house at Carnegie Hall. Armed with lantern slides and a booming voice, he beguiled the assembly for two hours, stopping only for sips of water. At its conclusion, hot and exhausted, he retired to the dressing room where the ordeal continued. Management had given a flock of reporters, well-wishers, and autograph seekers unfettered access, and it wasn't until late at night that he was able to escape into a cab.

The glowing reviews in the morning papers dispelled any lingering questions about his New York reception. *The Tribune* began its account:

With utmost earnestness, Sir Arthur Conan Doyle impressed upon a large audience his belief in spirit communication at Carnegie Hall last night. Scores of women in mourning were present, and tears were brought to the eyes of many when Sir Arthur told of his personal communication with his son.

Said *The Times*:

It was a quiet and solemn audience during part of the time that Sir Arthur delivered his lecture. Nearly every seat was taken ten minutes before he began, and lines were standing at the box office windows buying standing-room. The audience, which numbered 3,500 people, evidently saw a manifestation of the coming of a newer and finer religion that would clear out most of the weeds in the old religions and show the human race what God has written down in His eternal law.

Doyle had a day of rest, followed by a somewhat lackluster

reception at his lecture in Brooklyn. Undeterred, the following morning, the family had a shopping spree on Fifth Avenue, followed by the baseball game that Doyle had requested —an afternoon clash between the New York Giants and the Brooklyn Robins.

There would be seven more lectures and a string of psychic sittings with local mediums of repute before Doyle bid farewell to the city and boarded the train to Boston. His manager, Keedick, saw him off.

"I'll see you in a few days, Sir Arthur. I'm sorry I can't accompany you, but my man, Widdecombe will meet you in Boston. As you've been there before, you'll know the city has a reputation for conservatism and hide-bound tradition. Protestant Brahmins and Irish Catholics rule the roost. Their ministers and priests say jump, and the people say, How high? You're going to run into some strong non-believers. Don't expect the same reception as in New York. It's a tough town."

CHAPTER TWELVE

Eli was heading to the Divinity School as Cal was leaving. They bumped into each other on Francis Street in the crisp morning air. It was a struggle, but he resisted the urge to give her a public embrace. Enough tongues were wagging about them already.

"I'm glad I caught you," he said.

"Me too. What time is your flight?"

"A few hours."

She pointed to his bulging shoulder bag and said, "Looks like you'll be busy."

"In the old days, I'd only get about four hours of work in. Thanks to you, I should get eight.

"Oh, yes? What have I done?"

"Kept me sober, Madam Secretary."

"You've done that, not me, Professor Donovan."

"We'll call it teamwork, then."

She laughed. "A very American thing to say."

"If you haven't noticed—" he said. "I'll WhatsApp you when I get to the hotel. I'll have a little rest before meeting your family."

Her sigh said it all. She was thinking about Emilio.

"I know," he said. "It's going to be tough not seeing him there."

She choked back tears, and on parting, brushed his cheek with her hand. With that small gesture, he'd never felt more in love.

ELI HAD ALWAYS PLANNED on including a lecture on violence against religious women, but spurred on by the Wellspring killings, she decided to give it sooner, rather than later.

At the top of the hour, she stepped to the lectern.

"Good afternoon. Today, we open a difficult but necessary chapter in our course. Our focus today is the history of nunicide—the intentional killing of religious women. The term is not a canonical category. I'm using it descriptively to gather under one lens episodes in which consecrated women were slain because they were women, because they were religious, or because they were accessible and unprotected. Studying nunicide is not voyeurism. It is a way to ask: What do these killings say about gender, power, and the social meaning of the Church? And what do institutional responses—legal, ecclesial, cultural—reveal about who is protected, who is believed, and which lives are grieved as public losses? Of course, we are mindful of the killings that took place in Boston only last month. At this point, it is too early to say how they fit into the historical framework we will be discussing during the next hour.

"We will move across time and place, because the motives and contexts change. In revolutionary France, anti-clerical ideology viewed nuns as symbols of the Ancien Régime. The Carmelite Martyrs of Compiègne, guillotined in 1794 for refusing to renounce their vows, show how cloistered women became symbolic enemies of the state. In 1930s Spain, radical militias killed hundreds of sisters as part of a campaign to purge the Catholic presence. Violence against nuns functioned as political theater, desecration, and terror.

"War scrambles motives further. Under Nazi occupation, some nuns were executed for resistance or for sheltering the persecuted. In the Soviet advance of 1945, mass sexual violence swept through convents in Silesia and elsewhere, with sisters killed while resisting rape. Here, gender is foregrounded. Vows of chastity became a provocation to soldiers bent on humiliation as domination.

"In the late twentieth and twenty-first centuries, we see ideological targeting persisting in smaller incidents and in mission territories, where nuns have been killed because their presence signals the Church's or social advocacy."

A student seated up front wearing a Celtics hoodie, stared at Eli and nodded emphatically.

Her TA dimmed the lights, and Eli went on to give a series of case studies of murders of sisters from the Middle Ages to the present. Some of the examples, particularly contemporary ones with photos of the victims in life and death, hit hard with some. A kid sobbed at a photo of a young nun her age, smiling into the camera in one shot, and crumpled in a ditch in another. Eli stopped to acknowledge the distress, saying that it was a difficult topic, but one that needed to be studied with heavy hearts but clear eyes.

"Across these cases, the death of a nun is never treated as a private tragedy. It is a communal, international shock because nuns stand for care, constancy, and a life freely given. That cultural standing also shapes institutional behavior: at times, the Church has canonized or beatified victims, reframing atrocity as witness; at other times, particularly in abuse-adjacent cases, it has been accused of obscuring facts to guard reputation. Civil systems, too, have evolved from cold cases neglected for decades to prosecutions that finally hold once-untouchable suspects accountable.

"The deaths of the three nuns in Boston belong to a long, painful archive. A suspect has been arrested. He has not gone to trial, so we cannot assign guilt to him. We have no indication of motive.

"Motive matters, but so does meaning beyond motive. Revolutionary guillotines, Red Army assaults, thrill killings in a Lombard alley, cold-case conspiracies, and burglaries becoming lethal differ radically. Yet each struck a nerve because the victims embodied mercy and stability. That is why public response—from French streets falling silent as Carmelites sang, to Mississippi towns holding candlelight vigils—has often been liturgical in tone. Society senses that an attack on vowed women is an attack on a shared moral reserve.

"Gender is not incidental. Even where anti-clericalism or opportunism dominate, misogyny and sexualized domination recur: rape as a weapon of war, elderly sisters targeted because they are presumed defenseless, purity chosen for defilement. Reading these cases as part of the larger story of violence against women clarifies our obligations to strengthen environmental safety for sisters in clinics, schools, and missions, to fund trauma-informed support, and to insist that law enforcement treat crimes against religious women with the same urgency and sophistication shown when victims are culturally powerful.

"Let me close by pulling threads together and pointing toward action. The archive of nunicide is small in number but immense in meaning. It maps the fault lines where women, sacred authority, and social power meet.

"The three Wellspring sisters belong to this wider communion of witness. If their deaths become only a news cycle, we will have failed them. If, instead, their memory helps secure other sisters, purifies institutional practice, and deepens our collective refusal of violence, then their last act will be to teach.

"For your next section meeting, I invite you to bring one case from today's lecture, or another case you discover through your readings, and trace who had power at each step—perpetrator, police, press, parish, and public. Ask where power protected the vulnerable and where it failed. The history of nunicide is not only about death. It is about whether the Church and the societies around it can convert grief into truth, protection, and hope."

When she was done, the kid in the Celtics hoodie came up to her with tears in her eyes and said, "My aunt's a nun in Colombia. I worry about her. Thank you."

Eli could only nod and take her hand.

When Cal arrived at Tonnarello in the Trastevere neighborhood of Rome, Micaela Celestino was already seated. The restaurant was near the large apartment where the mathematician and his wife, a historian who died tragically young of cancer, raised their three children. It was a family restaurant with a rustic menu, and the Celestinos, who began coming decades ago, were treated like family. When Elisabetta became a high-ranking official at the Vatican, bishops and cardinals dined with her regularly, and one of them, Cardinal Da Silva, became a pope. Needless to say, the owners would do anything to accommodate the Celestinos, and since Emilio's death, they sent dinner to Carlo every night.

The owner knew that Cal would be joining them and greeted him warmly, pulling him out of the line of tourists.

"Professor! So wonderful to see you again. Come, this way."

Micaela jumped up, her outfit blazing the bright colors she adored, and gave him an everlasting hug.

"When I see you, everything seems normal," she whispered in Italian.

The waiter appeared with a glass of clear liquid.

"Your usual, Professor."

Cal thanked him, but told him he wasn't drinking tonight. "Just a Pellegrino, please."

Micaela looked shocked. "Either you're not well or Eli's gotten to you."

"The latter," he said with a smile. "Where's Carlo?"

She waved toward the back. "In the toilet."

"How's he doing?"

"Truthfully, not well. He rarely goes out. Even tonight, it was a struggle getting him out the door. He brightens a little when I bring the girls over, but mostly, he just sits in the dark and smokes his pipe." The expression she used was *essere a pezzi*—he was in pieces.

When Carlo emerged, Cal thought that for the first time, he looked his age. Although he was a brilliant mathematician, he grew up in a family of poorly educated farmers, and he always had the rugged appearance of his ancestors, rather than that of his pale university colleagues. Now, the octogenarian stooped and shuffled toward the table. Cal got up to greet him, receiving a weak handshake.

"Thank you, thank you," he said, which Cal took to mean gratitude for everything he had done for Eli.

Carlo long lamented Eli's decision to ditch her academic career to follow her heart into the nunhood. Even when she attained the loftiest Curial positions achieved by a woman, he derided the Vatican, calling it a nest of vipers, sexists, and charlatans, and urged her to do something better with her life. He and Micaela were sad to see her go—after Emilio, it almost felt like a double loss—but they were relieved she decided to leave the Vatican.

They didn't need the menu. The owner knew Carlo's favorite dishes, and over antipasti, Carlo asked, "So, how's my girl doing?"

"As expected, she's amazing," Cal said. "Her first lectures were a triumph. Students rave about her. She's getting along famously with faculty members. It's a wonderful start."

"I'm not at all surprised," he said. "Students used to love my wife, too."

"What about your students, Papa? What did they say about you?"

"What do you think?" he barked.

"That you were an ass?"

"Exactly."

"How's Goldbach going?" Cal asked.

The old man cursed and looked like he would have spat if outside. "I'm done with it. Defeated. Some idiot coder with pimples who doesn't know any math will probably solve it soon with an AI program. When it's done, the goddamn AI will throw in an elegy for the last human mathematician. Humanity is going to become irrelevant, and I say, good. We're a failed species."

"Oh, my God, Papa!" Micaela exclaimed. "Either you go on antidepressants or I'll have to."

Cal quickly changed the subject and asked Micaela about her work at the Gemelli Hospital, where she ran the gastroenterology clinic.

"Too many patients and not enough time. I know I always say

this, but it's gotten worse. It's like I have an assembly line of anuses to scope."

"Charming as always," her father said.

"Where do you think I got it, Papa?"

"How're Arturo and the kids?" Cal asked.

"The hospital overworks him, too, but at school, the kids are under-worked, so it all balances out. The only real tragedy is that Roma's doing awful this season, so Arturo's been impossible to live with. So, Cal, why are you in Rome?"

"I'm giving the keynote address at a conference at the Pontifical Gregorian University called, *From Papal States to Soft Power: The Holy See's Diplomacy and the Making of Modern Europe, 1870–1965.*"

Micaela moaned. "It makes what I do sound interesting."

Cal laughed, "You stick to your assembly line, I'll stick to mine. But I'll be doing something more interesting on my day off. Did Eli tell you about our adventure with séances?"

Micaela nodded, but Carlo was in the dark, so Cal filled him in.

"I don't like nuns, but I don't approve of killing them," Carlo said, tucking into his bowl of straccetti.

"We're happy to hear that," Micaela sniffed. "I've always wanted to do a séance. Eli told me what happened to her."

"What happened?" Carlo demanded.

"I shouldn't say. You'll get upset."

"I'm already upset."

"Against my better judgment, I'll tell you."

The old man listened impassively to the story about Emilio's last words and Manzetti's after-the-fact account, poured himself another glass of wine, and said, "It's a magic trick for the gullible. You watch—this medium will want to sell you more lies. Manzetti, the old fool, is probably in it with her getting half the cut."

"Well, at least you didn't get upset," Micaela said.

"Whatever you think of the experience," Cal said, "it got Eli interested in writing a paper on the Vatican's reactions to Spiritualism during its peak era. I figured I'd spend a day at the Archives seeing what I could dig up."

At the end of the evening, Micaela and Cal walked Carlo home, then shared a taxi.

"So?" she asked, shaking her bright-red hair.

"That's a small word and a big one at the same time."

"You know what I'm asking."

Cal laughed. "I don't know, Mic."

"When is she going to stop all this silliness and move in with you?"

"It's up to her. As far as I'm concerned, she can take all the time she needs. When she's ready—if she's ever ready—I'll be waiting for her."

She took out her phone and snapped a selfie with him.

"What's that for?"

"When you become a saint, I want to be able to say I knew you."

~

Eli was at his house when Cal called to talk about his dinner. He'd offered her the use of his library and a guest bedroom while he was away, and she took him up on it. While they chatted, he could hear a log fire crackling away. When he finally begged off, dog-tired, she resumed her reading.

Doorbell chimes startled her, and she cautiously went to the hall to open the door a crack.

An attractive woman near Eli's age, decked out in designer clothes and a rain-spattered overcoat, said, slurring her words, "Oh! I'm sorry. Is Cal home? I saw his car."

"No, he's in Rome."

"Rome. Typical." She squinted at Eli and added, "Hey, I know who you are. You're her. Where's your habit?"

Unsure of what she was dealing with, Eli said, "May I know who you are?"

"Me? I'm Jessica. Jessica Nelson."

Eli knew the name. It had surfaced during a lunch with Ruth Steinberg, the Hebrew Bible professor. Steinberg had been lightly dishing on Cal's checkered past with women, mentioning Jessica as a cut above, but someone he simply wasn't in love with.

"Cal's mother passed away a few years back," Steinberg had said, "and I had to step into the Jewish mother role. I don't give him advice on his professional life—he doesn't need it. I tell him what I think about his personal life, whether he likes it or not. He has a history of going for the wrong type. Thank God, he found you."

"Ah, you approve of me?"

"Honey, you check every box God ever made."

The rain and wind were picking up. Jessica's car was parked at an awkward angle, half in and half out of the driveway. She was rocking back and forth in the porch light, as if she were at sea. Her breath was flammable.

"Would you like to come in for a coffee?" Eli asked.

"A coffee? Yes, I would."

"Please, this way."

"I know the way, Sister," Jessica said, emphasizing *Sister*. "I used to live here."

Jessica had been in the picture far longer than Cal's previous partners, and his friends had placed bets on whether she might be the one. On paper, they were a formidable match. She was a Ph.D. geneticist, the CEO of a major biotech company, and the youngest woman to lead a Fortune 500 healthcare firm. Cal had been one of the youngest faculty members at Harvard to be named to a full professorship.

They were both good athletes. She had been a competitive golfer who still played regularly at a tony country club. Cal had boxed in the army, and he continued to train and fight at a Harvard club. Both were practicing Catholics—she born and bred, he a latecomer by choice. Both were financially well-off—she from stock options, he from inheritance. And they could hold their liquor, or in her case, wine. While they dated, she kept a selection of rare vodkas for him in the legendary wine room of her Boston penthouse.

Their relationship worked best when travel schedules kept them apart for extended stretches. Things finally unraveled during a long period of cohabitation, when both were planted in Massachusetts, and domesticity crept in—to use Cal's words—like a choking vine. He came to realize that their perfect match was only perfect on paper, and that he wasn't in love. The perfect woman was in Rome, an Italian nun. After a trivial argument fueled by vodka and wine escalated into a major dust-up with words that couldn't be retracted, she angrily packed the things she kept at his house and left for good in the middle of the night. Cal moved on; she never did.

Jessica watched gloomily as Eli opened cupboards and ground the beans.

"Looks like you know your way around the place."

"Not really," Eli said. "I know where he keeps the coffee."

Jessica darkly smiled when she saw Eli reaching for Cal's favorite set of mugs.

"I read you took a job at Harvard. Must be quite the change."

"It's very different, yes. But, change can be good, don't you think?"

"Theoretically," Jessica said.

"You must be an expert in change. You were a scientist who became an entrepreneur, no?"

"Oh, you know who I am!"

"Maybe we both know a little about each other."

"Ha! Two members of the Cal Donovan fan club—well, I'm an ex member, or member emeritus, maybe. You live here now?"

"No, no. I have an apartment. Cal is letting me use his library while he's gone. It's conducive to work. My place is quite sterile. How do you take your coffee?"

"Just some milk. Did you notice he alphabetizes his books within each section?"

"I did notice, yes."

Jessica watched her prepare the drink, thanked her, and took a sip.

"Cal used to tell me that before you came along, most of the nuns at the Vatican were there to make coffee and Xeroxes."

"It's true, I'm afraid. Things are better now—not good, but better."

"You're a trailblazer. I know—I'm a Catholic. I admire you."

"Thank you."

Jessica drank more coffee and said, "I was in Cambridge for a dinner. I wasn't planning on taking Lowell Street. I just did. I saw his car. It was a mistake—obviously. I don't know what I thought was going to happen."

"I understand," Eli said. "You don't have to explain."

Jessica looked her full on. "You're very beautiful."

"I don't think of myself that way, but I appreciate your words."

"Are you still a nun?"

"I remain in my vows."

"So, you and Cal? Oh, God, you don't have to answer. It's none of my business."

"I'm in a period of self-examination. I'm not sure what I'll do."

The coffee was cool enough for Jessica to drink in a few gulps, medicinally.

"When I was with him," she said dreamily, "I always knew there was someone in Rome he lusted after. Then, someone told me it was a nun, and I thought that was peak Cal. A perfect scenario for a guy petrified of commitment. He'd spend the rest of his life like a dog chasing a car. And here you are. Looks like he caught the car. Question is: what's he going to do with it now?"

Eli deflected. "Are you still in love with him?"

Jessica got up and reached for her coat. "I tell people I hate him." She did up a few buttons, thanked her for the coffee, and took a few unsteady steps toward the door. "But, yeah, I'll love that fucker till the day I die."

Eli saw her fumbling for her keys and said, "The weather's bad. Let me get an Uber for you. You can return for your car in the morning. We can talk some more."

CHAPTER THIRTEEN

Eli was in her Divinity School office when one of her teaching assistants stopped by to see if she needed anything for the next class.

"Thank you, Miriam. I'm not going to use slides on Thursday."

"That's fine. I held my section this morning."

"Oh, yes? How did it go?"

"We had a very good discussion. Their examples of nunicide spanned four centuries."

"All from my lecture?"

"All but two."

"What were the new ones?"

"There was a Spanish incident from 1835 during the anti-clerical riots in Barcelona. Twelve women in a teaching convent were burned alive in the Raval quarter by a mob who accused them of harboring Carlist spies."

"I never heard about this," Eli said, reaching for the student's paper. "Who wrote it?"

"A junior—a history major. His articles were in Spanish."

"Good for him. I'll include it the next time I give the talk."

"The other one happened locally in 1944," Miriam said. "The student is from Boston—she's a computer science major."

"Computer science! Why is she taking the class?"

"She's religious, a Catholic—and she's one of your fangirls."

"I have fangirls?"

The TA broke out laughing. "Clearly, you have no idea."

"Clearly, not," Eli said. "What was her incident?"

Miriam passed the student's paper along. "She was talking to her family about the assignment. Her grandmother told her about a killing she remembered when she was a girl. There was a shooting—"

Eli's office phone rang. One of the department secretaries asked if she wanted to accept a call from Sister Lisetta Houseman, the President of The Leadership Conference of Women Religious.

"Miriam, I've got to take this. Can you leave the papers with me?"

Eli picked up the flashing line and was greeted by an energetic voice.

"Oh, Madame Secretary," the woman gushed. "Thank you so much for speaking with me! I know how busy you must be. I'm unsure if you're aware of us, but—"

"I'm familiar with your organization," Eli said. "You do marvelous work."

The LCWR was a progressive association of Catholic nuns and sisters, representing the majority of the thirty-five thousand women religious in the United States. In the past, it had attracted the ire of the Vatican over social stances perceived to be contrary to doctrine.

"I am so pleased to hear this," Sister Lisetta said. "As you know, our relations with the Vatican have been challenging at times."

Under Pope Benedict, the LCWR was mandated to revise its statutes, undergo oversight of programs and publications, and vet conference speakers under the watchful eye of a Vatican archbishop. Relations thawed and the mandate was lifted under the liberal pontificate of Pope John XXIV. Behind the scenes, Eli had played a role in the decision.

"Yes, that is true," Eli said diplomatically.

"The reason for my call is this: our organization is having its annual convention in Boston first week of December. I know it's short notice, but given your relocation to Harvard, we would be absolutely delighted if you could give a talk to our members."

Eli was no stranger to public-speaking requests. As Secretary of State she routinely fielded them and had to pick and choose carefully, balancing geopolitical, Curial, and time-management issues. Free of Vatican constraints, the only considerations that mattered were her level of interest and availability. She admired the organization, so she inquired about dates. One of the proposed time slots was on a non-teaching day.

"What topic were you looking for?" she asked.

"Anything you'd care to talk about," the president gushed. "I think our members would love to hear about your personal journey. It's remarkably inspirational."

Eli asked to see the details, promised an answer in a few days, and turned her attention to the assignments. She scanned the paper on the 1944 murders in Boston and saw the student had closely followed her prompt. Following a paragraph about her grandmother's recollection and a PDF of an article from the *Boston Globe* archive, there were sections on the power dynamics from the perspectives of the perpetrator, police, press, parish, and public. The perpetrator section was the shortest: Unknown. The crime was unsolved.

The front-page newspaper article included a picture of a police car in front of a clapboard house on a tree-lined street.

THREE NUNS SLAIN IN BRIGHTON CONVENT: CITY SHOCKED

No sign of robbery—Neighbors heard "pops" after midnight—Archdiocese calls for day of prayer

BOSTON, June 15— Three nuns of the Sisters of the Sisters of the Immaculate Shepherd order were found shot to death at dawn today in their residence at St. Joseph's Convent of the Sacred Heart, Chestnut Hill Avenue, Brighton—a quiet street within sight of St. John's Seminary. Police termed the crime "deliberate and cold-blooded." No arrests have been made.

The bodies were discovered shortly after 5:30 A.M. when the superior, Mother Ignatia Marie, making her rounds with the rising bell, found Sister Mary Perpetua, 23, Sister Hilaria Imelda, 29, and Sister Angelica Catherine, 34, lifeless in their narrow cells on the top floor of the three-story brick house. Ambulance men and the Medical Examiner were summoned; all were beyond help.

Four Sisters survived: Mother Ignatia, Sister Aloysia, and Sister Columba, who were sleeping on the second floor, and Sister Magdalen, an elderly invalid in the small infirmary on the ground level.

Detectives said early examination showed no ransacking and no theft. The convent's modest safe, used for school receipts, was untouched; drawers and trunks remained closed; wristwatches lay on bedside tables.

"There is no evidence of a struggle," a ranking officer stated. "The Sisters appear to have been shot as they slept or as they rose." Entry is believed to have been gained through a side delivery door leading to the kitchen. The front and chapel doors were found secured. The kitchen key, typically kept on a peg near the scullery, was missing. A rear pantry screen bore a fresh slice in the mesh; faint impressions in damp earth beneath the sill are being examined.

Neighbors reported hearing several 'pops' shortly after one o'clock. Patrick J. O'Rourke, a streetcar motorman, said he was returning from a late tour and "heard three, maybe four, quick snaps." Mrs. Rose Carbone, who keeps a boarding house on the corner, told police she observed a "slender person in a raincoat" near the convent gate at about that hour. "It was misting. I thought nothing of it," she said.

From the Chancery, the Archdiocese announced that a Solemn Requiem Mass will be offered and asked the faithful of Greater Boston to keep a day of prayer. A spokesman said the Archbishop was "deeply grieved by the untimely and shocking deaths of devoted women who gave their lives to God and to the children of this city."

Classes at St. Joseph's School for Girls (Grades 1–8) were suspended. Parents and alumnae gathered quietly outside the iron fence; by noon, the steps were heaped with peonies and small American flags. Priests from nearby parishes comforted the surviving Sisters and recited the Office of the Dead in the convent chapel.

War-time service lent special sorrow. The slain Sisters organized Red Cross sewing circles and bond drives, and counseled wives and widows of men overseas. "Everyone knew their quiet ways," said Mrs. Catherine Doyle, mother of three in the service.

Police said every resource of the department is engaged. Identification Bureau men photographed the rooms, and ledger books and visitor logs were removed for study. Officers canvassed shops on Commonwealth Avenue and Beacon Street and questioned taxi drivers near the Reservoir. Citizens out late last night—war workers, drivers, returning servicemen—are urged to report any loiterers or unfamiliar motorcars seen in the vicinity.

At press time, no motive had been established, and the weapon had not been found.

In a brief statement, a senior officer said, "This grievous deed strikes the city's heart. We ask the public's help and its patience. Whoever committed this crime will be found."

Funeral arrangements will be announced by the Archdiocese. Persons with information are requested to telephone the Brighton station, No. 14, or the Homicide Unit at Headquarters.

~

Eli had to run to a faculty working group on admissions requirements for international applicants, but for the rest of the day, she kept returning to the *Globe* article. She was anxious to share it with Cal, but didn't want to distract him from his speaking engagement, so she waited until he'd likely returned to his hotel before sending him a scan with the annotation: *3 nuns were shot in Boston—in 1944! Call me when you're free.*

She was walking through the door of her apartment when he rang.

"Holy shit!" he said, forgetting his vow not to swear around her.

"Holy shit, indeed," she replied. "The similarities—"

"I mean, it's crazy," he said, jumping her sentence. "It's only a few miles from Wellspring House. Do you know if they caught the killer?"

"I checked as well as I could. I didn't see anything, but I'm not sure."

"So, what do you think?"

"It's surely a coincidence," she said, "but it's eerie. I'll leave it at that. Are you finished for the day?"

"I'm back in my room."

"How was your talk?"

"They laughed. They cried."

"Oh, my God! You're terribly impressed with yourself."

"You noticed?"

He heard her taking an airy breath. "So, I should tell you about something that happened last night. I was at your house. You had a visitor. Jessica."

Cal sat on his bed and closed his eyes, literally counting to five to corral his anger.

"I'm sorry."

"Why should you apologize?"

"Because you had to deal with her. What did she want?"

Eli lightly laughed. "She wanted you."

"Christ," he sputtered. "I haven't seen her or talked to her for ages. Why now?"

"I think wine had something to do with it. She had a dinner in Cambridge. I gave her coffee and got her an Uber. She came back for her car this morning but didn't ring the bell."

"You're a saint."

"I am most definitely not. I did have something of a revelation about you."

"That sounds ominous."

"I've concluded that you have an effect on women."

He flopped onto his pillow and said, "Oh, yes? Do I have the desired effect on you?"

He heard that magical laugh again. "That remains to be seen."

Detective Santos hung up his desk phone and popped up like a jack-in-the-box.

"Maria, get your coat."

Trinh, who was also on the phone, gave him a what's-up look.

"Now!"

When they pulled up in front of the rickety house in Dorchester, the street was clogged with patrol cars. They paused on the sagging porch just long enough to don paper booties.

"Where is he?" Santos asked an officer in the front hall.

"His bedroom. It's—"

"I know where it is."

Father Malloy was lying on his back on his made bed, his eyes closed, dressed in an undershirt and sweatpants. Right and left ankle monitors peeked out from under elastic cuffs. If not for the streak of vomit running from mouth to neck, he might have been mistaken for sleeping.

"Fuck me," Trinh said.

Santos grunted something and put on a pair of gloves to handle the empty prescription bottle on his nightstand.

"Zolpidem," he said. "What's it for, do you know?"

"My mother takes it," Trinh says. "It's Ambien. For insomnia."

"He should've saved me one," Santos said, "'cause I ain't sleeping tonight."

She put on gloves and took the bottle from him.

"He filled it two weeks ago—sixty tablets, ten milligrams each. If he took all of the rest of them, that's forty-six tablets. Is that enough to kill you?"

Santos stooped to pick up the empty vodka bottle on its side by the bed.

"This could've helped the effort. Let's see what the ME says. The SCRAM monitor should have registered the vodka. Check with probation to see what time got recorded."

"Will do," Trinh said. "I never heard of a priest offing himself. Thought it was a sin."

"He already checked that box with murder," Santos said, "but let's not jump the gun. It could have been accidental. Who was the responding officer?"

A young policewoman stepped into the bedroom from the hall. "I was."

"Who called it in?"

"His cleaner. It's her usual day. He didn't answer the door, so she let herself in. I kept her here in case you wanted to talk to her. She's in the kitchen."

The cleaner was heavy-set with a gray bob, hound-dog jowls, and orthopedic stockings.

"Ma'am, my name is Detective Santos, and this is Detective Trinh. What time did you arrive here this morning?"

"Eight-thirty."

"How often do you clean for him?"

"Every two weeks."

"So, the last time you saw him was two weeks ago?"

"Yes."

"How did he seem to you, then?"

"He didn't say anything to me. He almost never did."

"He never talked about the nuns who were killed?"

She shook her head. "He didn't have milk. He wasn't allowed to go out, so I got him a half-gallon. He paid me for it."

"How long had you cleaned for him?" Trinh asked.

"Two years. There was another girl before who quit. They had me do it."

Santos and Trinh shrugged at each other, and Santos said, "Thanks for sticking around. The officer took your details. If we have any more questions, we'll be in touch."

"It's sad," the woman said, groaning as she pushed herself to her feet.

Santos and Trinh lingered on the sidewalk, clearing their nostrils in the fresh air. The priest's house smelled of death and vomit.

"She wasn't the sharpest knife in the drawer," Santos said. "You want to write this up and close it down?"

"Yeah, I'll do it."

"Do we have any loose ends?"

"I told you I talked to Eva's doctor at Mass General who confirmed her paralysis, right?"

He nodded. "She's hundred-percent, not our shooter. What about Felicia King?"

Both of them had suspicions about Eva's protégé, the woman in black with a face full of silverware and a sandpaper attitude.

"I was going to tell you. I interviewed the manager of her massage studio over the weekend. She was with Felicia and a bunch of people at Elements, the rave club in Cambridge on the night of the murders. The club closed at 2 a.m. Afterwards, they all had a few more drinks at someone's apartment in Sommerville. So, creepy-ass Felicia's not the shooter either."

"You happy if we close the case and declare Ray Malloy the killer?"

"Happy?" she said, zipping her windbreaker against the sudden gusts. "I don't know about that, but I guess he's the twisted fuck that did it."

CHAPTER FOURTEEN

1922, Boston, Massachusetts

Arthur Conan Doyle arrived in Boston's South Station following a pleasant train journey through the New England countryside. He had judged his lectures, interviews, and Spiritualist sittings in New York to be unqualified successes and looked forward to getting his message across to the city he regarded as being the center of American literary culture. He left his family and aides in the comfortable quarters of New York's Ambassador Hotel, where he would unite with them on his way to Washington in several days. At the station, he met his manager Keedick's deputy, Captain Wallace Widdecombe, a formidable ex-soldier tasked with smoothing the way in Boston for Doyle and his private detective, William Burns.

"Good to meet you, Sir Arthur. Just to warn you, there's a bunch of folks waiting for you out there. Quite the reception committee."

"Sounds ominous," Doyle said.

"I'll see to your bags. You and Mr. Burns should head straight for the car out front. I wouldn't stop to chew the fat, if you know what I mean."

Widdecombe wrangled the luggage, money in one hand, a cigarette in the other, and dispatched the porters to the waiting limousine. Clearing the platform, Doyle saw that the arrivals hall was mobbed.

As soon as he entered the hall, Doyle was blinded by brilliant magnesium flashes of photographic lamps. Reporters hurled questions, but there was something else in the air. It was the clamor of men and women, hurling insults and shouting at him to go back to England.

"Come on, Doyle, stick by me," Burns said.

The loudest voice came from a man holding a placard that Doyle read through the haze of magnesium smoke.

We Condemn Necromancers: Deuteronomy 18:10-12

The man howled out the Biblical verse, "Let no one be found among you who practices divination or sorcery, interprets omens, engages in witchcraft, or casts spells, or who is a medium or spiritist or who consults the dead. Anyone who does these things is detestable to the Lord!"

At that, the fellow charged, brandishing the placard's pole like a lance.

The sharp-eyed detective spied Doyle reaching into his coat and yelled, "Doyle, don't!"

Burns stepped forward, parried the length of wood with one arm, and flattened the protester with a well-placed punch to his temple.

"Let's move!" he shouted, pulling Doyle to the limo.

On the way to the hotel, Burns said, "What were you reaching for?"

Doyle wiped the sweat from his brow and showed him.

"Good God, man! Put that away. There are laws here."

Doyle nodded and said to Widdecombe, "Mr. Keedick was spot on the money. He said that Boston was a tough town, and indeed it is." Still breathing heavily, he gestured out the window. "It has been twenty-eight years since I was in Boston. I can hardly recognize the place! Where are the dear old crooked streets of faded brick? Replaced it seems by these broad and spacious avenues. I do hope the Parkmans, Emersons, Lowells, the Longfellows—all the wonderful circle which put New England above old England in culture—have not departed to the Middle West or some such place."

Burns was more interested in practical matters and asked Widdecombe if he was aware of more protests brewing.

"We were unscathed in New York," Burns said, "but Boston is clearly a different kettle of fish."

"I will keep an ear to the ground," Widdecombe said.

Pulling up to the Copley Plaza Hotel, Doyle remarked that at least this area seemed unchanged. The grand hotel was situated on a busy triangular traffic space with Huntington Avenue cutting diagonally across the square, Trinity Church on the south, the Boston Public Library's McKim Building on the north, and Old South Church on the northwest.

Doyle was whisked through a dignitary's registration in the hotel's Empire reception hall, its gilded, coffered ceiling brightly lit by crystal chandeliers. A few of the guests taking afternoon refreshments in clusters of armchairs and settees recognized the famous author and murmured discreetly.

"No press here," Burns said. "Good work, Widdecombe."

"I registered him under an assumed name. Dr. Watson."

"Very droll," Burns said approvingly.

Doyle settled into his ornate suite, spending the remainder of the day on correspondence. That evening, he dined with Frederick Wiggin and Frederick Nicholson, both reverends of Boston Spiritualist churches. Doyle, who had rejected his Catholic faith, was an enthusiastic member of the Church of Spiritualism, a denomination that borrowed Christian language and hymns, but was organized around the premise that we never die, and that communicating with the Spirit World is a fact. The two Fredericks were delighted to have the great Conan Doyle in their midst, and Nicholson, an Englishman by birth, helpfully called himself Fred to avoid entanglements. At meal's end, they invited Doyle to attend their Sunday services the next day, and Doyle enthusiastically accepted.

After an exhilarating Sunday of churchgoing and sightseeing around Back Bay, the Public Gardens, and the golden-domed State House, Doyle retired to his suite to pen a letter to his wife.

"I plunged instantly into spiritual exploration," he wrote. "Today, I attended Sunday services at two churches, and was forced to address the congregation each time, so that my much-needed day of rest did not come up to expectation. But I was repaid by what I saw, and by the fine, sane, well-groomed, and well-balanced Spiritualist audiences who listened kindly to my exhortation to be broad in our ideals, charitable to each other's views, and merciless to those who lower our standards of conduct.

"Mr. Nicholson is a fine clairvoyant and claims that among other spirits who assist him is that of William Terriss, whom I had met in the flesh before his lamented murder. Such a statement cannot be checked, but what can be checked, and will bear checking, is that he pours out a stream of messages to his congregation, containing names and knowledge which he can get by no normal means. It is, of course, only the old 'discerning of spirits' named by Paul as one of the signs of a true gospel teacher, but the Churches have wandered so far away from early Christian ideas that it stands out now as a wonderful novelty. No one could be present and have the least doubt of the honesty of the gift, though I suppose that, like all spiritual powers, it ebbs and flows.

"Even more wonderful was Mr. Wiggin. His audience had sent him up innumerable notes with questions for their dead. The pastor sat with the papers heaped before him. He wore a pair of opaque spectacles. Sitting beside him and watching him closely, I could see that there was no trick of any kind, though I had no assurance that the paper he was holding was always the one that he was answering. He dealt with about thirty, and the appearance of the people who admitted the correctness of the answers made collusion quite impossible. The exactness of the detail was wonderful.

"Sometimes there were comic touches at both sittings. 'Your wife is here. She tells me you got rid of the furniture after her death.

You gave it away, did you not?' 'Well, practically,' said the widower in a gloomy voice, and everyone laughed. So they did also when Mr. Wiggin called some name, and received in reply an explosive 'Yep!' which told how eagerly the inquirer was waiting for his answer.

"It was all an example of what St. Paul meant when he said that he taught the Gospel not merely by words but also by power. So long as a clergyman and medium can be united in one person, all is simple. Mr. Wiggin has a claim for another phase of mediumship, which is both more interesting and more questionable. It is that at times the greatest of all world figures, Jesus of Nazareth, descends to the earthly plane and uses him as a means of communication. I am quite convinced of Mr. Wiggin's psychic power and of his honesty in the matter, but it is very possible that he is being duped by Spirit on the other side, impersonating something higher than himself in order to give force to his utterance.

"Someone must have alerted the Press to my presence, for when I departed Wiggin's Unitary Spiritualist Church, I was accosted by a pack of the hounds, though thankfully, none of the ruffians I had earlier encountered at the train station. It is amusing to watch the genesis of some wild statement in the newspapers. I hope that the public does not take seriously all that I am reported to have said. It works like this. Enter a very young and frivolous female reporter. 'Well now, Mr. Doyle, say! Do they have golf in the next world?' She has come to make you say they have, as it has occurred to the sub-editor that it would make a good headline. Fight as you may, you will most certainly have to say it, 'No,' you answer, 'I have no reason to say they do.' 'You never heard them speak of golf?' she asks. 'No, I never have.' 'Well, you said they had amusements,' she says. 'Yes, they say they have more than we,' you answer. 'Well, maybe golf is among them,' she says. 'I never heard them say so,' you reply. Next morning, you open the paper. 'Doyle says they play golf in Heaven.'

"Tomorrow, is the main event at Symphony Hall. Mr. Burns cautioned me about this. Mr. Widdecombe has picked up whispers today of anti-Spiritualist demonstrations that might be afoot. I am grateful that Burns is on the pitch with me."

Monday evening was fine, so Doyle and his party elected to walk from the hotel to Symphony Hall, a magnificent red brick and limestone edifice done in the Italian Renaissance revival style. Approaching the Massachusetts Avenue entrance, they caught sight of a milling crowd. At first, taking them for attendees, Doyle commented that it augured well for attendance. That was before they saw the placards and heard the anti-Spiritualist chants.

"We are not wading through those waters," Burns declared. "Guide us to the stage entrance, Widdecombe."

The director of Symphony Hall and the stage manager greeted Doyle and apologized for the unruly protesters. Burns sought assurances that they would not be allowed to attend the lecture, but the best they could offer was that no one carrying placards or openly spouting invectives would be granted entry.

"We cannot interrogate all ticketholders as to their views on the Spiritualist question," the director said. "However, I can assure you that our ushers will escort out anyone brandishing ripe cabbages."

Doyle looked amused. "I was a boxer in my youth. I am quite capable of dodging vegetables."

In the wings of the theater, Widdecombe was seen to be conferring with a gentleman who passed him something. In time, he approached Doyle and Burns, waving a folded newspaper.

"Here's the explanation," Widdecombe said. "A Catholic paper, *The Pilot*, is closely tracking your Boston engagements, Sir Arthur. It's whipping up their readers with hard-line anti-Spiritualism."

"*The Pilot*? Never heard of it," Doyle said.

"It's influential in these parts," Widdecombe said.

"Who is the author?" Doyle demanded. "I want to challenge him to a public debate. Best way to deal with a scoundrel, short of fisticuffs."

"The article about you is signed, An anonymous clergyman."

"Typical," Doyle spat. "Typical and spineless."

"Who was that fellow you were speaking to?" Burns asked.

"A compatriot of mine with an ear to the ground," Widdecombe said. "I asked him what we can expect the next few days."

"What *can* we expect?" Burns asked.

"More of the same, it seems. Cardinal O'Connell spoke against

Sir Arthur at his Sunday Mass. A number of Protestant congregations were riled up, too."

"Let me read the damned article," Burns said, patting his pockets for the one with spectacles. "If I had known, I would have signed on more men from my bureau."

"Fear not, gentlemen," Doyle said. "The worst that can happen is also the best—a journey across the River Styx to the glorious world that lies beyond. Now, then, it is time to enlighten and inform the populace."

Doyle strode onto the stage of the auditorium, a narrow and high shoebox hall with a coffered ceiling in cream-and-gold, its walls broken by pilasters and statue niches. He took to the lectern on the proscenium under a central Beethoven cartouche and surveyed the politely clapping audience. Unlike his Carnegie Hall appearance, it was not a packed house. Undeterred, he cleared his throat and began.

"Ladies and gentlemen. It warms my heart to return to your fine city, the cultural center of the American continent, to speak to you tonight about the singularly most important truth that awaits us all."

~

Doyle took afternoon tea in his suite, nestled in a comfortable armchair with copies spread before him of that day's Boston newspapers, organized by morning and evening editions. When Widdecombe delivered them to his rooms, Doyle had been astonished that a city of this size had no fewer than nine dailies.

"This impresses me greatly," Doyle had said. "We have not many more in London, a city four times the size!"

"You may be less impressed after you've read them," Widdecombe said.

After the tumult of the previous night, Doyle had spent a congenial day in quiet contemplation, friendly meetings, and sightseeing. It began with an hour in the Mount Auburn Cemetery, where he browsed the gravestones of the great American thinkers, and left flowers upon his favorite essayist, Oliver Wendell Holmes. Whenever he was asked whether he had named his famous detective after the writer, Doyle would smile, Sphinxlike, and say, "I couldn't possibly comment."

From there, he went to Harvard to meet with Mr. Charles Damon, an assistant professor with an interest in alchemy. The young fellow took him to the Widener Library to show him several ancient alchemical texts which seemed to allude directly to ectoplasm, showing that, according to Damon, medieval philosophers were really a good deal ahead of their time in some phases of psychic knowledge.

Finally, he concluded the daylight hours with a visit to Bunker Hill, scene of the famous Revolutionary War battle, which he was surprised to learn was closer to town than imagined, and not a hill at all, but a mere mound.

The tea was quite acceptable by American standards and put him in the mood to suffer the slings and arrows of the Boston press corps. He perused the offerings and plucked the *Boston Daily Globe* from the pile for a review of his lecture. For the most part, the article was a faithful summary of the night's proceedings, describing the somber audience, many dressed in mourning clothes, including mothers of sons lost in the war, listening attentively to the arguments and claims of the great British novelist. It contrasted the respectful tone within Symphony Hall with the riotous events that later unfolded outside, when the Boston Police were called in to clear a path for Conan Doyle and his party to reach an awaiting taxi. A fractious and vocal mob of placard-waving anti-Spiritualist demonstrators, including a contingent of clergymen and women, surrounded the stage door, effectively trapping the novelist until the police arrived. As he exited, bottles were thrown, one sailing perilously close to the great man's head. Arrests were made.

Doyle shuffled the rest of the pile and went for a copy of the *Boston Evening Globe,* drawn to its irresistible headline:

Preachers Rap Spiritualism: Doyle Fails to Produce Evidence

Could be Done by Trickery, Mr Kingdon's View

The reporter had interviewed several religious leaders in the city, including a few who had actually attended the lecture and had rather scathing opinions as to what they had heard.

Doyle lit his pipe and was in the middle of a paragraph when someone came to his door.

The clergymen interviewed take the ground generally that his so-called evidence is insufficient or not of a character to warrant either his inferences or conclusions. And they are surprised that a man of such standing should go around preaching a doctrine of belief on the kind of evidence he presents.

"Come in," Doyle shouted. "It is unlocked."

Widdecombe and Burns sauntered in, both looking glum.

"You gentlemen look worse than me," Doyle said, "and I have been reading a skewering in the evening paper."

"It's about tonight," Burns said. "We think you should skip the sitting."

"Remind me, please, where are we to go?"

"It's in the Brighton area of the city," Widdecombe said, "at the house of a medium named Mrs. Slattery. I had her put on your schedule because the local Spiritualists, including Nicholson and Wiggin, touted her as one of the most talented mediums in town."

"Talented as in spectacular or talented as in genuine?"

"Both, so they say. She's meant to be the real deal."

"Then, what could possibly be the problem?"

Burns took to a sofa, lit a small cigar, and said, "Word on the street is that the scoundrels from last night know you're going to be there. We can expect more of the same, or worse. I'm told Slattery's house is on a narrow street where a mob can easily block access and egress. That means the police may have trouble getting in, and we may have trouble getting out."

"What, pray tell, is Mrs. Slattery's given name?"

Widdecombe checked his book and said, "Irene."

"Gentlemen!" Doyle said expansively. "Providence requires us to attend the sitting. Irene is the name of my favorite female protagonist, Irene Adler, whom I wrote about in *A Scandal in Bohemia.* She was one of the very few of my characters to outwit Sherlock Holmes. Onwards to Brighton!"

CHAPTER FIFTEEN

Cal strode through Saint Peter's Square, its colonnades sweeping pilgrims toward the Basilica, to the bronze doorway of the Apostolic Palace, the Portone di Bronzo, where Swiss Guards in Renaissance-style uniforms stood watch. How many times had he trodden these cobblestones to visit the last two popes? He'd lost count.

He showed his passport to the Guards who checked his name against the guest list, wanded him with a magnetometer, and asked him to wait in the Cortile di San Damaso, the palace's three-story Renaissance courtyard enclosed by arcaded loggias.

Vatican officials and clergy crisscrossed the courtyard, a cloistered space very much quieter than the tourist-choked Piazza. One of them, a Portuguese bishop, recognized Cal and peeled off from his companion to have a word.

"Ah, Professor! How good to see you."

"And you, Bishop Pereira. You're looking well."

"What brings you to the Vatican?"

"I was at a conference and asked to see the Holy Father."

Cal noticed an almost imperceptible headshake. "I still catch myself thinking it's our old friend Rodrigo upstairs," Pereira said.

The death of their beloved Pope John XXIV still hung heavy in the air. Cal reached for the bishop's shoulder and said, "I like to think he's still upstairs, just a little higher than the palace."

"Very well put," the bishop said.

The pope's private secretary, an American monsignor who had served as the then-Cardinal Macy's secretary in New York, came to fetch Cal, greeting him warmly.

"Professor Donovan. Right on time. Thank you."

"I wasn't going to be late, was I, Monsignor Lopez?"

"I can tell you that this is a meeting the Holy Father has been looking forward to."

"You mean he doesn't look forward to every meeting?" Cal asked wickedly.

"Hardly. Come. You know the way. I don't have to play tour guide."

As they headed up the Scala Regia, the palace's grand ceremonial stairway, Cal asked the monsignor how long it had been since he did a stint at the Vatican.

"Twelve years."

"What's changed?"

"My office is bigger."

They moved through the richly decorated corridors and reception rooms of the Second Loggia, through the anteroom and then the door of the Papal Library. Lopez knocked lightly and flung open the doors to a room that Cal knew well, a long, dignified hall with a coffered ceiling, patterned marble floor, and walls lined with bookcases and paintings. At one end of a carpeted area was the simple trestle table where popes received visitors.

Pope John XXV rose from his high-backed chair and came around to clasp Cal's hand, towering over him. As a young man, he had been a basketball player, an all-star at the University of Notre Dame. If not for knee injuries, he might have gone to the NBA rather than the priesthood. He used to display a framed copy of the front page of his hometown newspaper in his New York diocesan office with the headline: **Basketball God Decides To Become a Priest**. It wouldn't do to hang it in the

Papal Library, but he kept it in his private study in the Papal Apartment.

"Sight for sore eyes! My God, it's good to see you, Cal."

"Holy Father," Cal said, "greetings from Boston. I come bearing gifts."

Cal pulled a wrapped picture from his bag and watched him tear it open. It was a team photo of the Boston Celtics signed by the players and coaches.

"I'll give it pride of place," the pope said with a belly laugh, "until the Knicks come to visit." He handed it to his secretary and said, "Manny, you can take off. Note-taking not required. You want a coffee, Cal?"

"I'm good, thanks."

"So, give me all the news. What's going on Stateside?"

"Nothing you don't already know about, I'm sure."

The pope winked. "My intelligence operation isn't as sophisticated as you'd think. For instance, I don't have any idea how Eli's doing at Hah-vahd," he said, affecting a posh accent. "We miss her. Cardinal Santagati's a good man, but I wish she'd stayed. Methinks you made her a better offer."

"I don't know about me, but the university made a pretty good one. She's doing an amazing job. It's like she's been teaching her whole career. The students love her. They treat her like the rock star she is."

"No surprise there. What's she doing about her vows?"

"To be determined," Cal said. "She's thinking about it. She's ditched the habit for now—taking the temperature of secular life."

"She'll make the right decision," the pope said. "Her dues have been paid in full. Tell her to come and visit next time she's in town."

"I will."

"I hear you were at a conference at the Pontifical Gregorian University."

"It finished yesterday. They put on good events."

"I also hear you're going to roam the Archives today."

Cal chuckled. "Your intelligence operation is doing just fine. But, yes. What can I say? Got to get my Archives fix."

"There are worse addictions. Want to know something? The last time I was in there was—I can't even remember. But back then, it was called the Secret Archives. I kind of liked the old name. Think I should change it back?"

"That'll start conspiratorial tongues wagging," Cal said.

"Yeah, maybe I'll leave it be. I owe myself a tour one day. There's no time now—I've been drinking through the proverbial fire hose. Looking for anything in particular?"

Cal asked if he'd heard about the Wellspring House murders, and it came as no surprise that he'd been briefed on the matter, up to and including Father Malloy's suicide. The pope was fascinated by Cal's description of his and Eli's séance, and said he could understand her interest in the Vatican's historical positions on Spiritualism.

Monsignor Lopez showed his head, reminding the pontiff of his next meeting.

"You tell Eli to send me her article when she's written it," Pope John said, getting to his feet. "Tell me—you think Father Malloy definitely killed those nuns?"

"Probably? Yes. Definitely? No."

"Well, that's the kind of intelligent answer I'd expect from a Hah-vahd man."

~

Cal entered the Vatican Apostolic Archives at the Cortile del Belvedere and waited in the reception area for his friend, Maurizio Orlando, the Vice Prefect. Orlando emerged from his office in his signature sweater-vest, emanating the spicy aftershave vapors that Cal had come to associate with the quiet, bearded academic.

"Cal, my friend," he gushed. "I welcome you, once again."

"Maurizio, it's good to see you. You're looking well."

"It's kind of you to say so. Is there anything I can help you with today? What are you researching?"

"It's not me, actually. I'm carrying water for someone while I'm in Rome. You'll be pleased to hear it's Elisabetta Celestino."

"Ah! How is the Madam Secretary?"

"She's well—she's a born professor. She's gotten interested in—well, an interesting subject: the nineteenth and early twentieth-century Spiritualism movement and the Vatican's reactions to it."

"I've heard of it, Cal, but you've found a topic in which I'm largely ignorant."

Cal laughed. "There's a first time for everything."

"Tell me more about your ambitions."

"To put a pin in a calendar, she wants to look at communications between the Holy See and the major diocese in America and Britain in and around 1920 when the movement was at its peak."

The archivist paused, deep in thought, then demonstrated his command of Vatican history. "Then, you'll need to pay attention to two pontificates. Benedict XV was pope until January 1922. Pius XI became pope in February of that year. The Secretary of State, whose office was the likely way-station for the kind of diocesan communications you're looking for, was Cardinal Pietro Gasparri, who served both pontiffs. Now, let me think: in New York, we have archbishop Patrick Joseph Hayes. He wasn't made cardinal until 1924, I believe. In Boston, we have Cardinal William O'Connell. In London, we have Cardinal Francis Bourne."

"You're amazing, Maurizio."

"Why, thank you, Cal! I do try."

"Where do you think I should look—the ASRS?"

The ASRS—the Archivio Storico della Sezione per i Rapporti con gli Stati was the repository of records relating to the business of the Secretariat of State with foreign states and international organizations.

"I should think that almost everything you need will be there," Orlando said. "Have you rooted around that section before?"

"A bit modern for me."

"Then, you should know that these archives are voluminous, and I'm afraid there's no rational filing system. It's basically done by region and date, although this is not inviolate. I've found material decades out of place—American correspondence amidst African and Asian material—you name it."

Cal looked at his wristwatch and said, "I'm heading home tomorrow, so I'd better get moving."

"I think you know where to go. Please, see me before you leave. I'll be here until half-past five."

He did know his way around. The first time he used Pope Celestine's golden library card, he took a long walk through twelve centuries of history. He started at the top floor of the Archives, the brightly frescoed Tower of the Winds, built in the sixteenth century as a solar observatory by Pope Gregory XIII. Then he went to the musty second level, the Diplomatic Floor, commissioned in the seventeenth century by Pope Alexander VII as a central depository of the complete diplomatic correspondence of Holy See legates and nuncios.

His next stop was the thirteen kilometers of documents housed in the long gallery built in the early twentieth century to the west of the Cortile del Belvedere. Dubbed by insiders as the Gallery of Metal Shelves, the documents there included the archival material of the Curial offices and various Vatican commissions. Nearby was another archive, the so-called Soffittoni, built after the Second World War above the gallery of geographical maps in the Vatican Museum, containing the documentary history of the Congregation for Bishops and other Vatican congregations.

Lastly, he descended to the basement to explore the most recently added archival space, affectionately known to insiders as the Bunker. There, under the Cortile della Pigna of the Vatican Museums, were forty-three kilometers of shelving in a two-story climate-controlled concrete behemoth. The Bunker housed a huge array of documents, ancient and modern. To his delight, he was even allowed to enter the most secure storerooms adjacent to the bunker where the greatest treasures of the archives were kept—among others, the letter from English noblemen to the Pope Clement VII concerning the "Great Matter" of Henry VIII's divorce, the Edict of Worms with the signature of Emperor Charles, and the bull excommunicating Martin Luther. He remembered how he felt when he emerged, celebratory, from his inaugural visit, and how, those days being those days, he'd gone to the nearest bar to drink himself silly.

Cal went through the study room where academics from around the world sat at desks, waiting for the archival staff to bring them their requested documents, or reading and taking notes. There were a few curious stares and jealous looks as he glided toward the staff entrance of the storage areas.

Suddenly, an archivist in her early twenties called out in Italian, "Excuse me, Sir. You can't go in there."

Cal stopped, smiled at the pretty young woman, and thought about how to respond without coming off as pompous. Fortunately, he didn't need to. Another more senior archivist heard the raised voice and approached her.

"That's Professor Donovan. He has papal permission to go wherever he likes."

Cal heard the young woman whisper, "Really? Why?"

"I'll tell you about him later," the more senior woman said. She approached Cal. "It's okay, Professor. Sorry for that."

"Not a problem," he said cheerfully.

He entered the storage area and took the lift down to the two-story Bunker under the Cortile della Pigna, and listened to the thrum of the HVAC system and the echoes of his footsteps on the concrete floor as he walked past countless steel shelves and gray archival boxes.

He followed metal placards and shelf-end boards until he arrived at the ASRS section, and once there, he tried to scope out the magnitude of the search. It didn't take long to understand that this was going to make finding a needle in a haystack look easy. For just a single search criterion about communications between the Vatican and the United States, there were row upon row of boxes labeled *Affari Ecclesiastici Straordinari, Stati Uniti d'America, Benedict XV, 1915-1922.*

He decided to dive in, if only to take the water's temperature, and pulling an eye-level box at random, he took it to the ground. It wasn't his first rodeo—he knew the storage areas weren't like the stacks in a university or public library. There were no chairs or tables for researchers, so he sat on the hard floor, using shelves as a backrest, and began rifling through the box under the harsh overhead lights.

It was immediately apparent that there was at least a small silver lining to the monumental task. Most of the correspondence from the era was typewritten, so he didn't have to decipher a clerk's handwriting. Incoming letters were on paper; copies of outgoing ones were on flimsy sheets of carbon paper. From notations, it appeared the letters and directives had been transmitted by diplomatic pouches via ocean liner, with as long as a month's interval between a communication's date and its receipt log. Many letters had handwritten marginalia signed with a *Bened. P.P. XV*, for Pope Benedict and *P. Card. G.*, for Cardinal Gasparri.

Then and there, he narrowed his expectations. The best he could do today was make a start through boxes of correspondence between the Secretariat and Boston's Cardinal O'Connell. Anything more ambitious would have to wait.

CAL APPEARED at Maurizio Orlando's office as the archivist was packing his briefcase for the evening. Sunset was approaching, and from his windows overlooking the Cortile della Biblioteca, he could see that the lights of the fountain were on.

"How did you make out?" Orlando asked.

"I'm reminded of Hercules and the Augean stables."

Orlando laughed. "That much manure to wade through? Hercules, if I recall, had to divert rivers to flush them out. I hope you didn't flood my Archives. You found nothing of interest?"

"Only a single December 1921 letter from Cardinal O'Connell to Secretary Gasparri that was very much on point. I was hoping to make a copy."

Orlando took it from him, read it quickly, and placed it onto his office copier.

"Arthur Conan Doyle?" he said with surprise. "I didn't know he was a Spiritualist."

"I didn't either until recently. He was probably its most famous adherent. It looks like Cardinal O'Connell was worried about how to handle the Boston stop of his 1922 American tour. I'd like to see how the Vatican formally responded, but I ran out of time. I never even got to crack a single box of New York or London correspondence."

"How time sensitive is this, Cal?"

"Not especially. I'm sure that Elisabetta will be back in Rome before too long to visit with her family."

"Leave it with me. We're getting a couple of interns soon. It would be a nice project for them."

"You're a prince, Maurizio."

"More like a pauper, but a happy one. I work in the best library in the world."

Cal stopped in the now-empty reading room to take a picture of the letter for Eli. He texted it to her with the note:

> The plot thickens. Mrs. Slattery? Eva Nevins' grandmother?

Archdiocese of Boston
127 Lake Street
Brighton, Massachusetts

Dec. 6, 1921

All'Eminentissimo e Reverendissimo Signore
Il Signor Cardinale Pietro Gasparri
Segretario di Stato di Sua Santità
Palazzo Apostolico, Vaticano
Roma
Italia

Most Eminent and Most Reverend Lord Cardinal,

I write to seek guidance on a sensitive matter. The Spiritualist, Sir Arthur Conan Doyle, will be stopping in Boston this coming May to give a series of lectures on the controversial topic. I am led to believe that various congregants within my diocese, including members of the clergy hostile to his nefarious teachings, plan to conduct demonstrations at his lecture halls and "séances" with local mediums, including one with a Mrs. Slattery in Brighton, less than a mile from the archdiocese! Please urgently advise regarding our public stance and clergy attendance at demonstrations.

+ Wm. Card. O'Connell
Archbishop of Boston
Cardinal Priest of the Title of St. Clement

IN THE MARGIN, there was a scribbled note in a tight hand: *Caveant de falsis necromantibus—coord. con N.Y." P. Card. G.*

Beware of false necromancers—coordinate with New York. Cardinal Gasparri.

CHAPTER SIXTEEN

An officer at the front desk of One Schroeder Plaza called upstairs looking for Detective Santos. Someone found him microwaving soup on the floor's galley kitchen.

"Detective, I've got a walk-in downstairs who says she's got something for us about the priest who offed himself in Dorchester."

"What kind of something?"

"No clue."

"Is she a fruitcake?"

"Again, no clue."

Santos grumbled to himself about having to re-heat his soup and went down to the busy lobby, where a middle-aged woman was waiting with her young child.

"Hello, ma'am, I'm Sergeant Detective Santos. How can I help you?"

She gave her name, said she lived nearby in Roslindale, and launched into an apologia about hoping she wasn't wasting their time, and that her local police station told her she needed to talk to the homicide detectives. Santos could tell she wasn't a fruitcake and asked what was concerning her.

"I was over at my dad's house this morning and he told me something about Father Malloy—you know the priest—"

"I know who Father Malloy is."

"Yes, of course you do."

Her preschool son was restless as hell, bopping all over the lobby. Mom had to keep getting up to corral him in.

"Where does your father live?"

The address got Santos' attention, and he called out to the officer behind the counter, "Hey, do we have any of those plastic badges from the time we did the neighborhood thing?"

The officer found one, and Santos gave it to the kid, telling him he was being deputized to sit still. After his mother pinned it to his shirt, the boy obediently climbed onto a chair.

"Go on, ma'am," Santos said.

"I haven't seen my father since this happened. When I went there today to bring him some things, we got to talking about it. He told me he saw someone at Father Malloy's house the night before he was found dead. I knew from the TV there were a lot of police on the block, and I asked Dad if he told any of the officers what he saw. He said he didn't. I thought maybe he should have. That's why I came in."

"What time did your father see someone?"

"He just said nighttime."

"Does he know who it was?"

"He didn't, but it was a man."

"That's it? A man? Young? Old?"

"I didn't ask. But he did say it was a priest."

Mitchell Blum's McLellan Street residence was directly across from Father Malloy's ramshackle house. Unlike his neighbor's place, Blum's house was immaculate. The lawn was lush, neatly mowed, and raked clean of leaves. The pre-war house was in tip-top condition inside and out. Blum was a spry octogenarian in golfing slacks and a fleece pullover with a shock of white hair and a matching goatee. He had Detectives Santos and Trinh wait in his living room while he brought them the sodas he insisted they have.

"Perfect view of the house," Trinh said, looking through the picture window, "but why are we here? The case is closed, remember?"

"I remember, and it'll stay closed. But what are we supposed to do? We talk to the guy and we're done. No loose ends. I never want to get hauled downtown again."

Blum came in, balancing a tray and said, "Boy, oh boy, I hope someone buys that place and tears it down. I've watched it slowly going to hell for over fifty years."

"Did you know Father Malloy well?" Santos asked.

"Nooo. Probably haven't exchanged more than a hundred words in all the years we've been neighbors. He's almost—he *was* almost never outside. As you can see, he never did a lick of yard work. I'd say he was a recluse. Plus, I'm Jewish. What do I know from Catholics?"

"But you knew about his legal troubles, right?" Trinh said.

"You bet I did. All the neighbors knew. The rest of us—you know, five or six houses on both sides of the street—are pretty close. The Browns in the house next to him have been petitioning the town about getting him to do something with his yard to make the place less of an eyesore, but they weren't getting anywhere. We were talking about hiring a lawyer. That was before he was arrested."

Santos squirmed, anxious to move things along. "So, Mr. Blum, your daughter told us you saw someone at his house the night he died."

Blum dismissed his daughter with an air swat. "I told her not to bother you guys. You got more important things to do than come talk to me."

"It's no bother—it's our job. You want to walk us through what you remember?"

"Sure—here's the short and sweet. I was sitting right here that night watching TV. See there? I've got a straight-shot view of his house. I used to have a shrub that blocked it, but it got some sort of a blight—so out it went."

"We noticed the view," Trinh said. "Tell us what you saw."

"I saw a car pull up and park right in front of Emily's house."

"Emily?" Santos said.

"Oh, sorry, I still call it her house—Father Malloy's mother, Emily. She was a nice lady. We were all sorry when she died. Her son was living there, and he kept the place."

"Go on," Santos said.

"So, a car pulls up at—I'd say, a minute or two before eight."

"How are you that precise?" Trinh asked.

"Easy. I was waiting for my eight o'clock show to come on, and they were playing the commercials just before it. I thought it was kind of unusual. He never has visitors, and we neighbors have been on edge because of his arrest. That's why I paid attention. A guy got out and went to the front door. There's a porch light—if you can call that disaster a porch—and that's when I saw it was a priest."

Trinh stood at the window and said, "You must have pretty good vision to tell if someone across the street was a priest."

"Me? My vision is terrible."

Santos sighed and gave his partner a little wheels-up sign.

"That's why I use this," Blum said, grabbing a pair of binoculars.

"You watched him through binoculars?" Santos said.

"You bet. I saw him clearly. A youngish—definitely not an old guy—with a black shirt and a white priest collar."

"Had you ever seen him before?"

"I don't think so. I didn't get a good look at his face, anyway."

"How long did he stay?" Trinh asked.

"Almost an hour. He left before my nine o'clock show started. Not that I watched the one at eight. I was keeping an eye out."

"Why?"

"Because I read that Malloy was on house arrest, and he never has visitors, so it piqued my interest."

"How did this priest seem when he left? Did he walk to his car slowly? Did he run?"

"Nothing suspicious, if that's what you mean. It was raining, so he had his head down when he went back to his car. If I thought it was suspicious, I would have called you guys. I don't know why my daughter got so fired up."

"What kind of car did he drive? Any chance you remember that?" Trinh asked.

Blum grinned and said, "It was a brown, late-model Toyota Camry with Mass plates. I only caught the last digit as he drove off. It was a three."

The detectives looked at each other before Santos sputtered, "That's pretty specific, Mr. Blum. You seem pretty sure about the make and model. What makes you say it was a late-model Toyota?"

"The Camrys did a major redesign in 2018. The car I saw had a post-2018 body style. This was my business. I owned used car lots. I sold hundreds of them."

"Was it a sedan or a coupe?"

"Since 2008, they only made sedans."

"Sure about the color?"

"Toyota Brownstone—that's what they called it."

"And the license plate number? You sure about that, too?"

Blum held up his binoculars and smiled again.

BACK AT THE OFFICE, Santos told Trinh to run a CJIS/RMV query requisition for the make, model, and color with a plate ending with a 3.

Then he added, "I hope to hell we're not making a ton of work for ourselves. This is probably nothing, but—"

"I know—no loose ends," Trinh said.

"I mean, how many cars like that are going to be registered in the state?"

He thought it was a hypothetical question, but after lunch, his partner came to him with an answer.

"The RMV responded already?"

"Of course not. I ran some numbers myself. Want to hear?"

He grunted.

"There are about four million passenger cars registered in the state. Camrys are like the most popular make, representing about two percent of all cars. From what I can find, about half of the 2018 and later models are still on the road—so we're talking about a lot of Camrys. But the brown paint narrows it considerably. People hate brown. Only about half a percent of them are brown. Then we've got the last digit of the tag: a three. That cuts the number of tags by ninety percent. So, what do you think the expected numbers of brown, late-model Camrys with a last digit of three?"

"For fuck's sake, Maria. I wasn't doing the math in my head."

"About twenty. So, worst case, we won't be drowning in loose ends."

"Good, because unlike this solved case, we've got unsolved ones," Santos said, opening a different file.

Two days later, Detective Santos had a déjà-vu moment when he came in with his morning coffee and saw his partner sitting in his chair.

"How many times have I told you not to—"

Trinh didn't wait for him to complete his gripe. "I was off by a couple," she said. "Sixteen cars in the RMV database that match the description."

"Congratulations. Gold star. Now, run them down and get out of my chair."

She gave him a smug little head shake and said, "Don't need to. Want to know why?"

"For fuck's sake—why?"

"Because one of them is registered to a priest in Roslindale. Want to guess his name?"

Santos looked sick. "Come on, you're joking, right?"

They let the priest marinate in an interview room at the Homicide Unit a good long while to soften him up. The tactic didn't work as well as hoped because he had a lawyer with him providing reassurance. Both men stood when the detectives entered.

"Father Bouchard," Santos said. "Thanks for coming in today, and sorry for keeping you waiting."

Bouchard acknowledged the detectives wordlessly.

"I'm Phil Ragland, an attorney for the diocese," the lawyer said. "Here's my card. For the record, Father Bouchard is attending this interview voluntarily, but if I think he shouldn't answer a question, I'll advise him. Can I confirm that he is free to leave at any time and is not the target of a criminal investigation?"

"He's free to leave, whenever he likes," Santos said. "We just have a few questions about Father Malloy."

"Ask away," the lawyer said, sitting next to his client.

Santos faced them with Trinh and said, "Father Bouchard, when we were in your office a while back, you told us you'd only been to Father Malloy's house once in three years."

The priest nodded. "I recall."

"Since that interview, did you have occasion to go over to his house again?"

"I'm sorry, but what does this have to do with the Wellspring House case?" the lawyer asked.

"Who said anything about that?" Santos said. "We're conducting an inquiry into Father Malloy's death."

"His death has been reported as a suicide," Ragland said.

"I'm aware," Santos said. "What about it, Father? Did you go to his house again?"

Bouchard looked to his lawyer, who told him it was all right to answer.

"I did, actually, yes."

"The night before he was found dead," Trinh said.

"Yes. How did you know that?"

"A neighbor saw you," Santos said. "I guess we were a little surprised you were in contact with him. He was the prime suspect in a murder investigation, he was confined to his home, and it was your tip that led us to him. You were probably going to be called to give testimony at his trial. Did your superiors tell you it was okay to see him?"

He waited for his lawyer's nod and said, "Actually, I was told not to talk to him."

"Then, why did you?" Trinh asked.

"I took pity on the poor soul. He was cut off from all human contact, and it ate me up thinking about the spiritual crisis he was undoubtedly facing."

"That night—was he? In crisis?" Santos asked.

"He was down—he looked defeated, a shell of himself. I was shocked at how he'd deteriorated."

"How do you mean?"

"He looked gaunt. I doubt he'd been eating properly. His hygiene was poor. He offered me a drink, and when I declined, he poured himself a glass of vodka. He lifted his pants and showed me an alcohol detector, and told me he expected to get a call."

When Trinh checked into it, she found that the SCRAM detector pinged at 20:22, but the modem failed to push the alert that night. It was only picked up after his body was discovered.

"What did the two of you talk about?"

"I tried to bring him a semblance of normality. We mostly talked about parish affairs. We prayed together. I heard his confession."

Trinh asked aggressively. "Did you talk about his case?"

After a whispered exchange with his lawyer, he said, "Essentially nothing during our non-confessional conversations."

"What are you saying?" Trinh demanded. "That he confessed to the murders during his confession?"

Ragland held up his hand and said, "I'll take that one. You know that Father Bouchard cannot comment in any way about what might or might not have been said under the seal of confession."

Santos eyeballed his partner to stand down and said, "We understand. Let's talk about the stuff that was said before and after you heard his confession. You said *essentially* nothing. What does that mean?"

"When we initially sat down in his kitchen, he told me he was innocent. That was the extent of it."

"Did he tell you he was suicidal?"

"If he had, or I thought he was, I would have done something—notified someone—the police, the diocese—I've invoked Section 12 commitments before."

"Even if that meant letting the diocese know you violated their no-contact directive?"

"Of course."

"But you never told your superiors you went to his house, did you?"

The priest looked at the table, not the questioner. "I didn't, no."

"How much did he drink while you were there?"

"Two small tumblers—maybe three. It was concerning. He said he was tired. I assumed he'd go to bed."

"That's where we found him," Trinh said bitingly.

"Is there anything else you can tell us that would help our investigation?" Santos said.

"I don't think so."

"What do you think, Father? Do you think he killed those nuns?"

The lawyer interjected, saying they were skating too close to the confessional seal.

"One more thing," Santos said. "Have you ever been in trouble with the law?"

"Trouble? No. I mean, when I was a young priest in Montreal, I had a car accident and was charged with reckless driving. My license was suspended for a few months. That was my only brush with the authorities."

"Okay, good to know. What did you decide about letting us have a look at your phone?"

"I'm sorry—what were you hoping to learn?" the lawyer asked.

"Father Bouchard told us he's got several social media accounts. We wanted to see if he and any of the nuns, particularly Sister Kristin, exchanged messages."

"Yeah, that's not going to happen," the lawyer said with a forced smile.

"Okay, I hear you," Santos said, getting up. "Maybe we'll get a search warrant. We'll see."

"No judge is going to sign off on that based on the totality of facts and circumstances," Ragland said. "I'm sorry your prime suspect never made it to trial, Detective, but Father Bouchard is done here."

A WEEK LATER, Santos's commanding officer angrily summoned him to his office. On the way, he let Trinh know that he was getting firing-squad vibes.

"Want me to go with you?" she asked.

"Nope. You're young. You got your whole life in front of you. I'll take the bullet."

"Oh, fuck off," she said sympathetically.

The lieutenant started in on him before he had a chance to close the door.

"What the hell are you doing bothering Cardinal Archer, Zé?"

"We just had a couple of questions for him. Can I sit?"

"Yeah, sit. I just got reamed from the sixth floor. The Commissioner got a call from a fancy lawyer for the diocese named—"

"Ragland?"

"Yeah, that's the one. The Commissioner wants to know why you're still making inquiries on a closed case."

"Hell, without a confession or conviction, the case is only closed on paper, not in my head. Something didn't sit right about Father Bouchard—I told you about him, remember? He turns in his assistant pastor, he visits with the guy the night before he's found dead, he says he's on social media, but he doesn't remember if he and the young nun who was shot ever messaged each other. Trinh and I thought that Bouchard deserved more scrutiny. So, we've made some inquiries."

"Like what?"

"We asked him if he'd ever been in trouble, and he said he had a reckless driving charge in Canada years ago. We checked with the Montreal police, and it was more than simple. He rolled his car late at night, driving fast in a residential area. His passenger, who wasn't wearing a seatbelt, was killed. And listen to this: she was a twenty-four-year-old nun. His BAC was barely legal. There was a whiff of scandal, but it didn't kill his career. We were told that the Cardinal of Montreal asked his pal, Cardinal Archer, to do him a favor and find him a job down here. He's been in Roslindale ever since. We called Cardinal Archer to ask about him. We caught him cold. Before he decided he didn't want to talk to us, he said he was aware of Bouchard's car crash before he approved of his transfer to Boston, and that he's done well in his parish. I guess his next call was to his lawyer."

The lieutenant ran his hands through his bristly hair. "Unless you've got more than a vague suspicion about Bouchard, you've got to drop this. That's not just from me. It's from the Commissioner."

"I'll do whatever you want, boss," Santos said, "but I'd hate to think that someone was getting away with murder."

"You and me both, but I'm a hundred-percent sure the priest killed himself with pills and liquor like the ME said." When Santos threw up a hand in a maybe gesture, the lieutenant said, "Where do you peg the odds?"

"I'm at ninety percent," Santos said. "Trinh, who's good, although a royal pain in my butt, is at fifty-fifty."

"Fine. I'll go with you, Zé. Ninety percent says stop. Ten percent says do what you want to do—quietly. I don't want any more calls from the sixth floor."

CHAPTER SEVENTEEN

A MONTH PASSED, AND THE COLD NOVEMBER MORNINGS BORE witness to the coming winter. Eli had resisted dressing like an American, but she broke down and bought herself a loose, functional down jacket to replace her Italian piumini, which was slimmer, belted, and more stylish, but not as practical for cycling.

If she had to choose one word to summarize her feelings about her first months at Harvard, it would have been contentment. Her lectures were going well, her first academic paper was taking shape, her father, by all accounts, was copacetic, and her relationship with Cal was where she wanted it to be—although she knew it was a good distance from where he wanted it.

She was developing a network of friends and participating in social events that were a far cry from the stylized banquets with Curial officials and diplomats she had to slog through during her years as Secretary of State. Ruth Steinberg and Grace Olufemi Gregory included her in a group of Divinity School women who periodically met for meals and book discussions, and Cal invited her to all the soirées with his Cambridge and Boston pals. Her calendar was pleasantly full.

In the darkness of the elongating evenings, her favorite haunt was Cal's library, where she liked to work in front of a good fire with a glass of wine while he racked up points for teetotaling. On a night when they were tapping away in silence on their laptops—Cal writing his Cathars book and Eli, the speech she was scheduled to give to the upcoming LCWR convention—his phone dinged lightly. He glanced at it and went sour.

"Look."

It was a *Globe* news alert: *Boston Archdiocese Announces the Death of Two Nuns in Jamaica Plain: Developing Story.*

They couldn't find anything more online, so Cal suggested they watch the eleven o'clock news. They decamped to the living room when the hour ticked over.

"It can't have anything to do with Wellspring, can it?" she asked.

"Ray Malloy is dead and buried," he said. "So, no, I think not."

The broadcast led with the story, with a reporter positioned in front of a mostly dark, low-slung building set on a grassy rise.

"This is Kelly Murphy at Jamaica Plain's Holy Name Nursing Home, where late this afternoon, two nuns were found unresponsive in their beds. Medical staff attempted unsuccessfully to resuscitate them, and they were both declared dead at the scene. According to the director of the home, Sister Leslie Coyne, although both women were chronically ill, their deaths had not been expected. As you can imagine, following the murders of three nuns two months ago in Brighton, residents in this neighborhood are on edge. The priest charged with those murders, Father Ray Malloy, took his life while on house arrest. So far, the Boston Police and the Archdiocese of Boston have not issued statements. Earlier, I talked to some of the neighbors of the nursing home to get their reactions."

Cal turned the volume down and said, "I know what you're thinking, but this is going to be a coincidence."

"That's what I said about the 1944 killings," she said. "Don't you think there are too many coincidences?"

"Absent more information, no. I'll stick with association bias."

"Fancy term for coincidence," she laughed.

"I heard a psychology professor use it once, and I've been waiting for the opportunity to casually toss it out."

SANTOS AND TRINH weren't on call for new cases, but they caught these anyway.

"Congratulations. We're the dead nun detectives," he told her on the way to Jamaica Plain.

The Holy Name Nursing Home, a drab yellow-brick facility built in the 1970s, was owned by the Boston Archdiocese and provided care for sick and retired clergymen and women, as well as Catholic laity. They were met by the home's director, a thin-lipped, no-nonsense nun who reminded Santos, unpleasantly, of one of his elementary school teachers. On the elevator, he asked for information on the deceased.

"Sisters Melissa and Carmen were both in their seventies. They've been roommates for two weeks now and—"

Trinh cut her off. "Roommates?"

With a withering look, Sister Leslie snapped, "That's what I said. Roommates."

As the elevator door slid open, Trinh swore under her breath.

"I heard that," the nun said.

"Sorry," Trinh said. "It's just nobody told us they were in the same room."

There was a gaggle of people at the far end of the hallway.

"That's a significant piece of information," Santos said. "Tell us more about them."

"This is our wing for women who require skilled nursing care. We moved Sister Melissa here when she returned from the hospital, where she was treated for a bad case of cellulitis. On discharge, she required continuation of intravenous antibiotics. Sister Carmen had several operations for intestinal blockages. She's been on this floor for several months, receiving nutritional support. The two of them were getting along well, I'm told."

Outside the room, Santos asked for details of what happened that afternoon.

"The nurses were changing shifts at three, when they heard a clatter down the hall—it was Sister Melissa's lunch tray that hadn't been picked up yet, hitting the floor. When the nurses checked, both women were convulsing."

"Both of them?" Trinh asked.

"Detective, do you have a hearing problem?"

"It's just that what you're telling us is kind of remarkable, don't you think?"

"It's only what I know. The staff called 911, and the two registered nurses on duty began CPR. When the paramedics arrived, they continued to work on them, but nothing could be done. They were pronounced dead sometime after four."

"Give us an idea about their health before this incident," Santos said. "Were they talking? Were they with it?"

"Mentally, they were in fine shape. They watched TV, prayed the rosary every day, went to Mass in our chapel—by wheelchair, of course. Sister Carmen read a lot. She'd been a teacher."

They'd brought their own gloves and booties and began to put them on outside their room.

"Did they have any visitors today?" Trinh asked.

"They didn't. The visiting hours for the facility are in the evening."

"Did they get special meals?"

"Sister Melissa got the same meals as all the residents on solid food. Sister Carmen received an intravenous feeding formula."

"Could other residents visit their rooms?"

"Nothing is stopping them, but there isn't a lot of mobility in this wing."

"What about cameras?" Santos asked, looking around the hallway.

"We don't have interior cameras."

"Thank you, Sister. If we need you—"

"Yes, yes. I'll be in my office."

The CSI techs hadn't arrived yet, and the room was still. Two elderly ladies in hospital gowns lay prone in bed, their glassy eyes eerily fixed on the ceiling. The paramedics had left the detritus of their trade scattered on the floor along with the remains of Sister

Melissa's lunch. Without touching the bodies, they did a cursory inspection for signs of trauma, bullet, or knife wounds.

"This doesn't look like anything like Wellspring," Santos said.

They had a rummage through the personal possessions the women kept in their bedside tables, closets, and bathroom, and finding nothing of interest, they left the room and peeled off their protective gear.

"What do you think?" Santos asked.

"I think I want to know where Father Bouchard was earlier today."

"If your theory is that he had something going with Sister Kristin and he killed her to keep it quiet, then how do two old women fit into the picture?" Santos asked.

"Dunno, but I still think he's a creep."

"You got his picture on your phone?" Santos said. "We can show it around—see if anyone recognizes him. We need to pull staff rosters and question the nurses and aides who work on this floor. Also, the people responsible for facility security."

Halfway down the hall, Trinh said, "Didn't Sister Leslie say that the two nuns prayed the rosary?"

"Yeah."

"I didn't see any rosary beads in there, did you?"

Santos stopped to look at her. "Fuck me, I didn't either."

~

THE OCCASION for the dinner at Harvest in Harvard Square was to welcome Charles and Grace Olufemi Gregory back to dry land after their three-week Caribbean. Recounting their days at sea, Grace, who wasn't teaching this semester, said she caught up on pleasure reading, and Charles cranked out an amusing column contrasting the personality of American versus European passengers. After recapping as much of their adventure as they thought Cal and Eli could handle, Grace asked what they'd missed while away.

"Two more nuns have died in Boston," Eli said.

"We saw that," Charles said, spouting out factoids. Cal seemed surprised at his level of knowledge, to which Charles replied, "They have this new invention on ships these days. It's called the Internet."

"I get it, but I thought you were the type to tune out and power down during a vacation."

"No, no, no," Grace said. "You're mistaking my husband for normal. Every bloody second, he's asking me, 'What do you think of this idea for a column or that idea for a book?'"

"It's true," Charles said with a grin. "Maybe I'll wander over to the nursing home and see if I can talk to some folks. I haven't seen anything from the police yet. Personally, this reads like a malpractice case—that's what my new best friend, the ship's doctor, told me, and it makes sense. Some buffoon gave them the wrong meds."

"It's a tragedy, but I hope that's the explanation, Charles," Eli said. "I'd hate to think that someone's continuing to kill nuns."

"Yes, but the priest who committed the Wellspring murders is dead," Grace said. "So, that's not possible."

"He wasn't convicted at trial," Eli said.

"Speaking of coincidence," Charles said, "I was finally able to do some online sleuthing on the 1944 murders you tipped me on."

"In Jamaica, he stayed on board doing that while I took a trip to a waterfall with real people," Grace said.

"Seen one waterfall, seen them all," Charles said. "Eli, to answer your question, I'm pretty certain the police never found the person who killed those women. In case I missed anything—"

"He never misses anything," Grace said.

"Thank you, dear, but in case I did, I lobbed in a query to a cold-case homicide detective I know."

"What coincidence do you speak of?" Eli asked.

"Well, a couple of months after the St. Joseph murders, there was another suspicious case in Brighton involving nuns in a different convent, Our Lady of the Presentation on Lake Street—neither of these convents exists today, by the way."

"What happened?" Cal asked.

"Two nuns, and, if I might add, one cat, died after falling acutely ill. The women were fairly young, under forty, I think. The coroner suspected food poisoning, even though no one else at the convent was ill. But circa 1944, during the war—who knows how thorough the investigation was? That's what I meant by coincidence. Five dead nuns in two months then, five dead nuns in two months now."

Eli shot Cal a look of defiance and said tartly, "It's not a coincidence. It's an association bias."

"I think we're on the outside looking in on something, Charles," Grace said.

~

Santos and Trinh arrived late to a meeting at the Office of the Chief Medical Examiner on Albany Street, and the Deputy Chief ME was irritated and unforgiving.

"I've got a hard stop at half past," she said. "So, make it quick."

"Yeah, sorry," Santos said. "We're trying to keep a lot of people happy on this one. Let's get to it. What do you have?"

The ME flipped open a folder and said, "I'm calling the manner of deaths homicides. I just can't say if they were intentional or unintentional."

"What do you mean?" Trinh asked.

"I'll explain, but first, here's what I didn't find. Both women had underlying health issues, but they weren't the proximate causes of their deaths. We sent samples of the residual food and drink from Sister Melissa's lunch tray for analysis. Other than being unappetizing, they were not contaminated with toxins or pathogenic bacteria. That leads us to the significant finding. Although neither woman was diabetic, we found post-mortem lab values from blood and vitreous humor consistent with the administration of insulin: extremely low blood and vitreal sugars, sky-high insulin levels, and low C-peptide levels. We sent the sealed IV tubing for residue testing, and the results came back positive for insulin precipitants by LC/MS—don't worry, it'll all be in my report. The witnessed convulsions were caused by hypoglycemia, i.e., low blood sugar. Bottom line: someone intentionally or accidentally gave these ladies fatal doses of insulin. I'd say it's more likely intentional, because it's rare to give insulin intravenously, but I can't exclude sheer incompetence. That's for you nice people to figure out. Where are you with your investigation? I thought your nun killer was dead. What's his name again?"

"Father Malloy didn't do it," Trinh said.

"Thank you, Detective. "You're a credit to the department."

"We'll go back and question the people at the home about insulin, but none of the caregivers gave us any cause for suspicion," Santos said. "There's another priest in Roslindale who we've been looking at. He says he was sick at home the day of the murders, and he has no connection to these new victims. Plus, no one at the nursing home recognizes him. Security cameras outside the nursing home only showed the normal comings and goings of staff that day."

"You've got yourself a real head-scratcher," the doctor said.

Trinh said, "Besides the victims being nuns, the only thing that links both cases is that all their rosary beads are missing."

The ME got up and made for the door. "Well, that's not nothing, as my mother used to say."

CHAPTER EIGHTEEN

Cal had no idea how to connect with the right person within the Boston Police Department, so he turned to a friend who taught criminal law at Harvard Law School. That professor, something of a legend within HLS and the Boston legal community, simply called his acquaintance, the BPD Commissioner, and asked. Problem solved, and Cal had the phone number of Detective Sergeant Jose Santos.

Following the unusual call, Santos wavered on whether he should follow up by interviewing Cal in person. A call from the Commissioner's office to Santos's lieutenant inquiring what a Harvard professor had to say about the recent murders was all he needed to get off the fence and into his car.

Santos and Trinh looked uncomfortable in the unfamiliar environs of the Divinity School and sat stiffly in Cal's office while he finished up an overseas call in Italian. When he hung up, he apologized for keeping them hanging then asked for their further indulgence to wait for Professor Celestino, who was running late.

Eli glided in, stylishly dressed and subtlety perfumed, and she, too, apologized. On the car ride back to the office, Trinh would later tell her partner she was blindsided by the glamour in the room and felt like they were interviewing a couple of movie stars, not professors. Santos admitted that he, too, was wrongfooted, thinking that people in a divinity school would look like monks.

Santos began the interview tentatively. "Yeah, so we're here to follow up on the phone call you made the other day, Professor Donovan. You said that you and Professor Celestino uncovered some old cases that you think have a bearing on the recent ones?"

"That's correct," Cal said. "Professor Celestino's the one who found the earlier cases. Eli, did you have the printouts?"

Eli passed them copies of the newspaper articles and said she could make one for each of them.

"We'll share," Santos said. He quickly read the first article on the 1944 shooting of the three nuns—too quickly for Cal's liking—and passed it to Trinh. He did the same with the subsequent articles on the fatal illnesses of the other women, then awkwardly waited while his young partner perused them more diligently.

"All set?" Santos asked Trinh to egg her on.

"Yeah, almost. Give me a sec."

She nodded when she was done and sat quietly, looking puzzled.

"Professors," Santos said, "To be honest with you, we're here because the Wellspring murders attracted a lot of attention, from the public and within the police department. And because both of you are prominent members of the community. At this time, we have a high level of confidence that we'd have obtained a conviction if Father Malloy had gone to trial. With his death, the case has been closed. The deaths at the Holy Name Nursing Home are under investigation. I can understand how these old cases caught your interest, but I don't see how they're helpful."

"As a nun, I have been deeply affected by the murders of the Sisters of the Living Well," Eli said. "Cardinal Archer has encouraged our outreach to the order. There are some strange elements to the case, don't you think, like the prediction about a priest and an old gun? We talked to the medium, Mrs. Nevins, and we have no explanations for what she foresaw."

Trinh suddenly got interested. "You went to see Eva Nevins?"

"Yes, as I said. Now we have two more unexplained deaths,

bringing the toll to five, all within a month or so. In 1944, the city of Boston saw five nuns die within the same short period. The similarities are striking, don't you think?"

Santos held his breath, then let it out in a huff. "Well, five then, five now, sure, but 1944 was a long time ago. I mean, if the killer were a baby, then, they'd be in their eighties now, so—"

"I don't think we were suggesting the murders were done by the same person," Cal said.

"Okay, then what were you suggesting?" Santos said, getting to his feet.

"We're not suggesting anything. We thought you should have the information," Cal said. "If it's useful, we'll be pleased we could be of help. If it's not, then we apologize for wasting your time."

"No, problem. Happy to take a ride and see how people in Cambridge live," Santos said, signaling his partner, who was still seated. "Don't worry. We'll log your tip and see where it goes."

"Can I keep these?" Trinh asked.

"Of course," Eli said, and the detective folded the pages.

"Just so you know," Cal said, "an acquaintance, a columnist for *The Globe,* is writing a story on the 1944 murders. We're told it will be in the Sunday paper."

"Outstanding," Santos said, clearly not meaning it.

On the way to their car, Trinh listened to Santos complain about once again about being forced by know-nothing higher-ups to waste their time on dumb inquiries.

"What if it's not dumb?" she said when he had finished his rant.

"C'mon, Maria."

"I mean it. It'll come out in a day or two that the new cases are also homicides. What are the odds of look-alike cases separated by eighty years—?"

He interrupted her. "Don't know. Don't care. It's called a fucking coincidence."

"Yeah, maybe. Probably," she said. "I'm going to do some digging into the old cases, if it's okay with you?"

He grunted and said, "Do it on your day off, all right? We've got lots of real work to do."

~

Boston is a small, big city. Within a few hours of Charles Gregory's new column speculating on the eerie similarities between the present-day and the 1944 murders, the talk shows took up the conversation, and social media began filling with all manner of sane and insane conversations. It was against this backdrop that Cal and Eli, following morning Mass and lunch in the Square, headed to Brighton for another appointment with Eva Nevins.

When they arrived and no one answered the door, they retreated to the warmth of the car, rang Eva's phone, which also went unanswered, and discussed leaving. As Cal scribbled a note to slip under her door, a medical van pulled up. A short young woman with an odd haircut, black lipstick, and facial piercings jumped out and waited for the driver to open the sliding door and activate the wheelchair lift. Eva Nevins, bundled against the cold, was lowered to the ground where the woman began pushing her toward the house ramp.

"Let me check on this," Cal said.

He called out to Eva, who turned and weakly said, "Oh, Professor Donovan. How rude of me to keep you waiting. I should have contacted you to tell you I was at the hospital."

"It's not a problem, Mrs. Nevins. We can reschedule."

"Nonsense. Come inside. I'll just change."

"Eva—" the young woman said, forcefully.

"I'll be fine, dear. I'm right as rain. Professor, this is my friend and trainee, Felicia King."

Felicia coldly stared at him in lieu of a greeting.

"I insist you come in," Eva said. "I won't be long."

~

Santos was with his family at Cosco, inspecting a pork loin, when his phone rang.

"Who's calling on a Sunday?" his wife asked.

"Spam, I'm sure," he said, his finger hovering.

"Then, why are you answering?"

"I like to fuck with them."

"Oh, grow up, Zé," she said, walking off.

He answered and exuberantly said, "I ain't buying whatever the hell it is you're selling."

The rejoinder from the caller was, "Detective Sergeant, you'd damn well better buy what I'm selling. This is Commissioner Stevens."

"Oh, sorry, sir. The number didn't register."

"It's my personal cell phone, and it just lit up with a call from the mayor about this pot-stirrer, Charles Gregory's new column. She wanted to be briefed on these 1944 cases, which I've never heard of. Do *you* know about them?"

"Only that they exist."

"I know that your lieutenant doesn't know about them either, because I just called him. When were you going to tell him?"

Santos looked to the slab of glistening meat for inspiration.

"As you can see, sir, the connection to our cases is speculative at best. Before sending it up the chain, we wanted to pull the records on the old cases. We didn't know that Gregory was going to do another article, or we would have put what we knew on the table."

"Well? What have you dug up?"

"My partner's all over it. I'll send you a report the second we have something."

"I've got a meeting with the mayor on Tuesday morning. I'll expect a report before that meeting."

~

Felicia slowly descended the staircase as the chairlift whirred Eva to the ground floor. She had been transformed from a pale hospital patient in a bathrobe into a properly dressed, coiffed, and perfumed medium, ready for business. As the four of them settled around her parlor table, Eva refused Cal's envelope, saying that she couldn't possibly accept payment given the delay.

"I haven't been well lately," she volunteered, "but I've been receiving marvelous care at the Massachusetts General Hospital. I know the hospital has a new name, but I'm hide-bound. I don't like change."

"I do hope it's not serious," Eli said.

"I'm still on the sunny side of the grass," she said. "Are you ready to begin? Felicia is a talented medium in her own right, but I'm teaching her some of the finer points. She'll join us, if that's all right with you."

"Of course," Cal said, looking at the imperious Edwardian man staring down from over the mantel. "Before we begin, I ran across an old letter from the Vatican to the Archdiocese of Boston about Arthur Conan Doyle's lecture tour in Boston. It mentions that he was going to have a séance in Brighton at a Mrs. Slattery's house. I presume that's this house?"

It was the first time they'd seen her smile. Years seemed to fall from her lined face.

"Yes, indeed. I believe I told you that the great man graced this very room with his presence. Mrs. Irene Slattery was my grandmother. According to my mother, it was the zenith of her life. Now, let us hold hands."

The four of them sat close and formed a tight circle. Cal took Eli's hand; they knew the drill. In time, Eva said she had made contact with her spirit guide, Kay, who, as usual, professed to being "well enough."

"Who do you wish to contact?" Eva asked them.

"We don't know," Eli said. "We're looking for answers."

Felicia's scowl annoyed Cal, but he let it pass.

"To what?" Eva asked.

"In 1944, three nuns were shot in Boston, and shortly afterwards, two more died from an unexplained illness," Eli said. "We want to know if these deaths have any connection to the five nuns who recently lost their lives in Boston."

"That's not how this works," Felicia said. "It's not like Kay can Google shit. She can only put you in touch with dead people."

"Well," Cal said evenly, "Let's ask Kay to find someone who knows about the dead nuns."

"Very well," Eva said. She repeated Eli's prompt to Kay and asked whether anyone in her sphere could help. After an uncomfortably long pause, Eva said, "Kay says that she can find no one with knowledge of the events you've described. Is there a specific person who has passed who might have the knowledge you seek?"

"Perhaps one of the murdered nuns," Eli said. "Would you like their names?"

"Very well," Eva said. "Tell me."

Cal was not surprised that Eli had the names committed to memory. Very little about this remarkable woman surprised him.

Eva repeated the names to Kay, and they waited once again.

"Kay says that she cannot locate them."

"Please ask her to try again," Eli said.

"Very well."

During an even longer wait, Cal observed Eva's chin falling to her chest and Felicia leaning over to whisper. He couldn't tell if she was in a trance or asleep. Then, Eva opened her eyes and said, "Kay has located one of the women, Sister Angelica Catherine. What would you like to ask her?"

Cal and Eli looked at each other, nonplussed. Cal didn't know if she had questions prepared, but she immediately asked, "Sister Angelica, tell us about your life."

Eva was soon channeling Kay. "She says she was born in Boston before the Great War. Her father enlisted and was sent to France, where he died. She was a heartbroken girl who, upon hearing the news, decided to become a nun. When she reached her majority, she entered the order of the Sisters of the Immaculate Shepherd and lived with her fellow nuns at St. Joseph's Convent, where she was content."

"Please ask her what happened the night she died," Eli asked.

"I was in bed at the convent. My cell was on the third floor. The hinges of my door always creaked, and when I heard the squeal, I awoke. A dark figure approached me, and before I could ask who it was, I felt a sharp pain below my right eye, and then, I was here. It was so fast."

"Before this happened, were you aware of any threats made against you or your fellow sisters?"

"I was not."

"Have you met your fellow sisters where you now dwell?"

"Alas, no. There are so many souls here."

"One last question. Are you happy?"

"I am nearer to God than during life, so yes, I am happy."

"Perhaps we could try to contact one of the nuns who recently died," Eli said.

Eva sighed, and Felicia abruptly released Eli's hand. "I think we'll have to end it here," she said. "Eva is tired. I need to get her to bed."

"Of course," Eli said.

"I'll see you out, then take her up," Felicia said.

Cal and Eli thanked Eva and followed the young woman to the front door, where she told them that Eva wanted her clients to know that she was sick with cancer. When she tires, it's not that she has lost interest in a sitting.

"The doctors don't give her much time," she added.

"Very sorry to hear that," Cal said. "She didn't have to see us today."

"She's old school," Felicia said. "She's agreed to be my spirit guide when she dies, you know."

Eli looked at Cal and said, "That's very generous of her."

In the car, Cal was first to speak. "Well, that was weird."

"On many levels," Eli agreed.

"You didn't actually think you were speaking to one of the murdered nuns?" he asked.

"At this point, I don't know what I believe."

CHAPTER NINETEEN

Detective Trinh started her search at the BPD cold case archives located in the basement of her office building at One Schroeder Plaza, but came up empty—1944 cases weren't cold—they were frozen. The chief archivist told her there was a chance, and not a good one, that if the case had been important enough in its day, its files could have been transferred to the City of Boston Archives on Rivermoor Street.

The City of Boston Archives was housed in a modern industrial warehouse on Cow Island Pond, a wide bend of the Charles River in West Roxbury. Trinh showed up on a day when flu had thinned the ranks of the staff, and the only archivist on duty didn't have the bandwidth to drop everything to search for her. The detective pushed back on the suggestion of returning in a week and pressed her case, saying that her mission was important. The archivist allowed to perform the search herself with a caveat. When the archive was opened in the 1980s, boxes arrived in bulk, and some were sent straight to the stacks without sorting.

Trinh found herself in soulless corridors lined with pull-out file drawers that seemed to go on forever. She'd been told that old police files were one of the smaller components of the archives, which existed primarily to preserve historical records of the Boston city government such as city council and mayoral records and correspondence, tax records, and photographs. Her only strategy was to find boxes from 1944 and start rummaging.

Trinh's mother never wanted her to be a police officer—it was dirty and dangerous work, not the clean, safe, prestigious kind of job Vietnamese immigrants wanted for their kids. Her brother and two of her cousins were hot-shot lawyers. But after several hours in the sterile, climate-controlled environment of the Archives, Trinh knew she would have withered on the vine in an office job. When she was working a case, there was never enough time. Down here, time stood still.

She opened another box, and her eyes glazed over with folder after folder of exciting proceedings of the budget committee of the city council for fiscal year 1944. She realized she was nodding off when her phone delivered a jolt.

"Hey, Zé."

"Find anything?"

"Papercuts."

"Funny. Nothing?"

"Folks back then were even more boring than folks today. It's all city government crap—mountains of it. I haven't found a single BPD file. They told me that high-profile cases could have been preserved, but I haven't seen any yet."

"Keep at it."

"They close at five."

"See if they'll let you stay later."

She grunted at that. "Funny how when I first mentioned it, you were like—do it on your own time—and now, it's keep at it all night."

"What can I say? The Commissioner's involved now. I told him I'd get him a report before he meets the mayor tomorrow."

"And what are you doing at five o'clock?"

"Going home. Rank has its privileges. Some day, you'll treat a rookie like shit. Call me if you have something."

Trinh jawboned permission to stay after hours; the night security guard was alerted to her presence and would let her out when she was done. There was a vending machine upstairs that took credit cards, and for the next couple of hours, she alternated between sweet and salty munchies until she was positively green.

"I'm done—last damn box," she muttered to herself, as she dragged one out and lugged it to the reading table. Among the old city council hanging files was a thick manila envelope which she recognized as an oddity. Plucking it, her eyes widened at the stamped lettering: ***Boston Police Department, Station 14—Brighton/Allston***, and when she opened it and turned it upside down to pull out the papers, something clunked onto the floor.

She got on all fours to look for whatever it was and spotted it a few feet away.

"Holy shit!"

~

Sister Gabriela had been dreading the job, but the time had come. Reverend Mother Pauline, the leader of the Sisters of the Living Well, had notified her that three new nuns were being assigned to the Boston order and that their accommodations needed to be arranged.

She finished boxing up Sister Dora's belongings and moved to Sister Kristin's room, where she began with the clothes in her closet. The sight of each familiar garment worn by the vivacious young woman tugged at Gabriela's heart. When they were packed, she gathered up her toiletries and clucked, disapprovingly at the bottles of makeup and tubes of lipstick. Then, she started on her books. Kristin was an avid reader, and she had stacks of paperbacks on her dresser, which filled two cartons. With a heavy heart, the old nun reached for Kristin's Bible, and was about to add it to the box, when she noticed the edge of a card sticking out. She didn't give it much thought, but she sat on the bed and opened it out of curiosity.

"Dear God!" she exclaimed, as the Bible slipped from her lap.

TRINH DROVE BACK to her desk at the Homicide Unit and called Santos.

"I'm having my dinner," he said. "Is it important?"

"What are you having?"

"Chicken."

"It's more important than chicken. You need to come in."

"What did you find?"

"Trust me. Come."

He appeared a half-hour later with a this better be good expression.

"Okay," she said, "I found the file of the investigation into the June 14, 1944, shooting at St. Joseph's Convent."

"I assumed. What's more interesting about it than my wife's chicken?"

"It's like reading the Wellspring file. The similarities are crazy. The killer breaks into a convent house in the middle of the night, goes to the top floor, and shoots three nuns in their beds."

"Which we knew from the newspaper articles," Santos said.

"According to the investigators, they were shot with .22 LR rounds, just like Wellspring."

"So what? It was probably the most popular ammo back then."

"I looked it up. You're wrong for the millionth time in your life," she said with enough of a smile to defuse him. "It was a distant second to .38 specials."

"So, number two most popular. I miss my chicken."

Suddenly, he was looking at the object she found on the archive floor, pinched between her thumb and forefinger.

"Look familiar?" she said.

"They kept the bullets?"

"One of them. Tell me what you see."

"It's a spent slug. Deformed."

"Color?"

"Dull gray."

"Here's a picture of the rounds recovered from our Wellspring victims. Dull gray. They look identical."

"Not impressed. There's bound to be similarity between 1920s and 1940s ammo."

"Maybe, but look at the markings. Here's a magnified picture I took of the 1944 round. Here's a picture from the FBI report on Wellspring. See these curved grooves? They look the same, don't you think?"

"What am I—a ballistics specialist? And you aren't either. If you're telling me that you think the same gun fired these bullets, I'd say you're loonier than that medium in Brighton."

"Okay, go back to your chicken, Zé. I'm going to send this to the FBI for comparison. And I'm going to look for anything I can find on the deaths of the other two nuns in 1944."

Santos got up and put his coat back on. "Shit," he said.

"What?"

"I've got to send the Commissioner a report tonight. What the hell am I supposed to say?"

"Like you always tell me—stick to the facts."

"Fine. You write it and shoot it to me."

~

Two days later, Santos and Trinh were at their office in Roxbury Crossing when Santos received a call from his lieutenant, who asked him to come to his office.

"What did I do now?" he muttered to his partner.

"Want me to answer?"

"No."

The former Marine looked up from his desk and told him to sit down.

"Problem?" Santos said.

"Potentially. I got a call from one of the monsignors on Cardinal Archer's staff. He says that they were made aware of a piece of evidence from Wellspring House. He had it sent over by courier. It was found in one of the victim's Bibles—Sister Kristin, the young one. Have a look."

When Santos saw it was a card, he asked about gloves, but the lieutenant said that everyone and their cousins had already handled it. He slid it from an envelope addressed to Sister Kristin LaMattina with no return address. It was a birthday card with a watercolor cake and candles. Inside, the note read: *The very best birthday wishes to a special person. I know we decided to stop seeing each other. But in the eyes of God, how can something that feels so right be wrong? Tim*

"Tim?" Santos said, followed by, "Fuck me. Father Timothy Bouchard?"

"Yep," the lieutenant said.

"We're going to have to reopen the case," Santos said.

"Jesus, not publicly. But you've got to run this down and do it fast."

~

Father Bouchard shifted nervously on an uncomfortable chair in one of the spare interview rooms of the Homicide Unit. Santos and Trinh had been double-teaming him with questions, and he looked pale and frayed. The diocese's lawyer, Phil Ragland, sat at his side, taking notes and advising him not to answer some of them.

"When we spoke with you a while back at your rectory, you told us you didn't recall if you followed Sister Kristin on TikTok."

"I recall that I didn't recall."

"Cute," Santos said. "Did you check to see if you did?"

"I don't think I ever did."

"Do you have your phone with you?" Trinh asked.

"I do."

"Good. Because we have a search warrant for your phone and all your electronic devices. Please let us have it."

"What, now?"

The lawyer asked to see a copy of the warrant, read it, and told his client he had to comply.

"And your passcode," Trinh said.

Bouchard slid it across the table and said, "Do I have to give them my code?"

Santos answered before Ragland could. "We also have a decryption order."

The priest sighed heavily and coughed it up.

"I cannot understand this line of questioning about my whereabouts on the night of the murders. You caught the killer, and he is dead."

Santos gave his partner the sign to play the trump card—in this case, the birthday card.

Bouchard knew it was coming, but the sight of it had a visceral effect, and he looked like he might be ill.

"It was in Kristin's Bible," Trinh said.

"I was told," he said. "Look, I—" He stopped mid-sentence, struggling for words. "I know this doesn't look good, but I had nothing to do with her death or the death of the other women."

"Doesn't look good?" Santos said, his voice rising. "What are you smoking, Father? How can it look any worse? Let's start with your relationship with Kristin LaMattina. Tell us about it."

"There's not much to tell," he said, looking to his lawyer for moral support. "We were friends. We had a lot in common. I met her for coffee a few times at her workplace. She visited me at my rectory on two occasions. Regrettably, we were intimate both times, but we thought the better of it and made the mutual decision to end it."

"This card says otherwise, doesn't it?" Santos said. "You wanted your relationship to start up again."

"The card was a mistake. She never acknowledged it, and I never brought it up again."

"But maybe it ate at you," Santos said. "Maybe it made you mad as hell she wasn't reciprocating. Maybe you tried that night to get her to change her mind, and it didn't go so well. You shot her, and it woke up the other women."

Bouchard swung his head in slow arcs. "No, no, no. It never happened. I wasn't there that night."

"Where'd you get the gun?" Trinh said quickly. "Family heirloom? We checked. They were sold in Canada at the turn of the last century."

"I don't know anything about a gun. I've never owned one, shot one, even held one in my hand."

"Come on, Detectives," Ragland said. "You're grasping at smoke."

"You know what I say? I say it's smoky as hell," Santos said. "First, your client comes to us to implicate Father Malloy. Then, he violates a no-contact policy put in place by your diocese and visits Malloy the night he conveniently kills himself. He's got no alibi—just his word that he was alone in his apartment that night. And now, this birthday card's been discovered, which provides a motive for the shootings."

"Was there a question in there?" the lawyer asked.

"A bunch of them," Santos said. "Did you frame Father Malloy?"

"No, I did not."

"Did you encourage Father Malloy to kill himself?"

"Absolutely not."

"Did you kill those women?"

"No, I did not."

Ragland patted Bouchard on the shoulder and told him that it was time to call it quits.

"Stay in touch with your whereabouts," Santos said. "And don't head home right away. We've got some officers executing a search warrant on your apartment. It should take them a couple of hours."

"You won't find anything of interest."

"We'll see."

"When can I get my phone back?"

"Hard to know. If we decide not to bring charges, you'll get it then."

"It's very inconvenient."

"I'll bet it is."

Just before the session ended, Ragland said, "For your information, Detectives, Father Bouchard has tendered his resignation as

Pastor of the Sacred Heart Church. He plans to return to Montreal to stay with his parents."

"We can't stop you from going," Santos said, "but give your lawyer your contact info. And counsel, I want a forty-eight-hour notice of travel. Nice thing about Canada is, we've got a great extradition treaty with them."

CHAPTER TWENTY

Cal was on his early morning jog along the Charles, sucking in chilly air and fantasizing about keeping going until he got to Eli's apartment, when he felt his phone buzzing with an email notification. He'd set an insistent vibration for high-priority emails, and his butt alerted him to a VIP message.

He peeled off to a grassy verge to get out of the way of other runners and had a look at his phone. What he read gave him a legitimate excuse to satisfy his fantasy, and he set off at a fast pace.

He called outside Eli's apartment building and caught her fresh from the shower.

"Good morning," he said. "What's your coffee situation?"

"Is that a hypothetical question?"

"It is not. I'm outside your building."

"I see," she said lightly. "Then, you'd better come up."

He could tell she'd dressed quickly because her blouse was untucked from her skirt, and she was barefoot. He noticed her glance at his skimpy running shorts and cold-reddened thighs, and was amused when her neck turned a similar color.

"Espresso?"

"Of course."

Over the sound of the grinder, she asked, "Long run, no?"

"Longer than planned. I just got an email I wanted to share with you."

She tamped the grind and said with a laugh, "Has the forward button on your email stopped working?"

He sat at her dinette, hiding his legs under the table. "Let's just say, I was in the neighborhood."

He waited for her to pull two shots and join him, complimented her on the quality of the coffee, and entertained a fleeting thought of how terrific it would be if morning coffee with her were a daily occurrence.

"My mother taught me at a young age," she said. "Your email?"

"It's from Maurizio Orlando. One of his interns found a letter from 1922 in the Archives from Boston Cardinal O'Connell to Cardinal Gasparri. It's a follow-up to the letter I found where O'Connell asked for guidance on how to handle Conan Doyle's lecture tour."

"Gasparri was a predecessor of mine at the Secretariat," she said. "Quite a good one, apparently."

"I prefer women secretaries of state."

"I'm sure you do. Okay, show me."

He clicked on the attachment and passed his phone.

~

Archdiocese of Boston
127 Lake Street
Brighton, Massachusetts

May 5, 1922

All'Eminentissimo e Reverendissimo Signore
Il Signor Cardinale Pietro Gasparri
Segretario di Stato di Sua Santità
Palazzo Apostolico, Vaticano
Roma

Italia

Most Eminent and Most Reverend Lord Cardinal,

I am uncertain whether the Roman newspapers will report upon a distressing incident connected with the lecture visit of Sir Arthur Conan Doyle, and so I take the liberty of informing Your Eminence directly.

Until now, demonstrations surrounding the Spiritualist's appearances have been largely restrained. Both laymen and clergy have gathered with placards and prayers, offering a peaceful witness against doctrines that lead souls astray. Regrettably, matters took a grave and wholly unexpected turn last night.

A crowd assembled outside a private residence in Brighton where Sir Arthur was said to be participating in a so-called "séance." Some clergy of this Archdiocese were present among the onlookers. It has been reported to me that certain members of the public, apparently under the influence of intoxicants, became disorderly. Stones were thrown, breaking windows. More seriously, an unidentified ruffian cast a flaming bottle—evidently containing spirits—through an upper window, igniting a fire.

From my rectory, I could hear the engines of the fire brigade. Details remain incomplete, but I have received sober word that there were casualties, possibly among children.

We shall condemn this criminal act in the strongest public terms and take all prudent measures to distance the Holy Church from the misconduct of individuals who acted without sanction and contrary to Christian charity.

I remain,

Your Eminence's obedient servant in Christ,
+ Wm. Card. O'Connell
Archbishop of Boston

Cardinal Priest of the Title of St. Clement

"How awful," Eli said, laying down the phone. "Children! He doesn't write where this happened."

"He says he could hear the sirens from his rectory. It could have happened at Eva Nevins' house. She told us that Conan Doyle was at the house with her grandmother. We should ask her what she knows about it."

"The woman is sick. We shouldn't bother her."

"Tell you what," Cal said, "I'll ask Charles Gregory to search the *Globe* archives for stories on the fire. He's on a roll. He'll thank us if he can spin out another column."

"I'm not sure I'm happy with that," she said. "I don't want to cause Mrs. Nevins any distress."

"I'll tell him she's sick. If he writes something, he'll be respectful. What's your morning looking like?"

"I've got an early meeting. Want to ride on the back of my bicycle?"

He was hoping against hope she'd invite him to stay, but he didn't whine.

"My run's only half done," he said, rising—suddenly self-conscious about his running shorts. "See you later at the office. I'll let you know if Charles digs up anything."

With the sale of their historic property to Boston College in 2008, the Archdiocese of Boston moved from Brighton to a decidedly non-historic former office building in Braintree. Father Bouchard was summoned there for an exit meeting with the Vicar General, the Most Reverend Richard Dickens, a recently appointed bishop with the personality of an administrator, not a pastor.

"Father Bouchard, come in, please," Dickens said.

It was a corner office with an uninspiring view of traffic on Route 1.

"You've met with HR, right?"

"I have, Your Excellency."

"Good, good. Well, I wanted to speak with you briefly before you left the area for Montreal, I was told."

"I'm from there."

"Yes, yes. I take it that up until recently, your tenure in Roslindale would have been considered a success."

"I like to think that's the case. I cherished my parishioners. I hope they thought fondly of me. I would have liked to have said a formal goodbye beyond an email, but I was instructed otherwise."

The bishop cleared his throat. "Well—under the circumstances."

"Yes, of course."

"I wanted to see what your plans were going forward."

"I haven't been thinking much beyond returning to Canada."

"And what are your feelings about continuing as a priest?"

The question landed like a gut punch, and Bouchard responded forcefully. "I have no intention to submit to voluntary laicization. I plan to meet with the diocese of Montreal, explain my situation, and request a pastoral assignment, after an appropriate leave of absence. I know I crossed a serious line, but I am mindful and penitent. I believe I can still serve the Lord in the capacity of a pastor."

"That line you crossed was wide and flashing red!" Dickens exclaimed.

"I understand that. I will use my temporary weakness to make the rest of my life stronger."

"Did your last temporary weakness make you stronger?"

"I'm sorry?"

"I'm referring to the incident in Canada before your posting to Boston, where your passenger, a young nun, was killed when you crashed your car."

"I was absolved of any crime, Your Excellency. Otherwise, Cardinal Archer would not have offered me a position in Boston. It was a snowy night, and unfortunately, the sister was not wearing a seat belt."

The Vicar General leaned back in his chair and searched the acoustic ceiling tiles. "Yes, His Eminence is benevolent. There is a concern, Father Bouchard, that your transgressions might be greater than motor vehicle accidents and sexual affairs. The diocese is aware that the police consider you a person of interest in the Wellspring atrocity."

Bouchard was breathing fast now, on the verge of hyperventilation. "The police are only doing their job, I know this. However, they are misguided. As God is my witness, I had nothing to do with these murders! It's an absurd notion. We all know that Father Malloy was the prime suspect. He had the murder weapon! It was likely his guilty conscience that led to suicide. However, in the event that he was innocent, there is another person the police should be investigating."

"Who?"

"The information I have is subject to the seal of confession."

A look of horror clouded Dickens's face, and he held up his hands as if fending off a physical assault. "The seal of confession is absolute and unbreakable. A priest may never reveal anything he hears in confession to anyone, not to his confessor, not to another priest, not to a superior, not even to save his own life or to prevent a crime. So, stop right there, Father! Say nothing more."

"I understand, Your Excellency. I only raise the subject to make you aware that someone else committed this crime. I am innocent."

Cal was correct that Charles Gregory would be happy to dig for information on the house fire in Cardinal O'Connell's 1922 letter. They spoke on the day the police announced that they were now investigating the deaths of the two nuns at the Holy Name Nursing Home as murders. Charles mentioned that his two articles on the Wellspring murders had generated more online shares and comments than all his other articles combined over the past year.

"Of course, I'm interested," he said. "I feel like a prospector following a seam of gold that keeps getting wider and wider."

That evening, Eli came over to Cal's for dinner. They ate slowly, chitchatting about work, but mostly about the tragedy that befell the Slattery family. Cal had just stacked the dishes when his phone chimed. It was Charles with uncanny timing.

"I've got something," he said, his voice oozing with triumph. "You're going to want to see this."

Twenty minutes later, Charles and his wife, Grace, were at the door. Charles held a folded printout like a dispatch from the front.

"Come in," Cal said, kissing Grace on the cheek.

In the kitchen, Grace sniffed at the lingering fragrant smells and asked who had cooked.

"Cal did," Eli said. "Lamb tagine. It was delicious."

"Charles—hear that? Cal cooks. All you can do is eat."

Her husband grinned. "I suck around the kitchen, but I'm a wizard at finding stuff online."

"What do you have?" Cal asked.

"Behold. *The Boston Globe*—May 4, 1922."

Fire Follows Disturbance At Brighton Seance;: Three Children Perish In Night-Time Blaze

Mob Gathers Outside Home of Medium After Visit of Sir Arthur Conan Doyle —Molotov Bomb Hurled Through Window — Mother and One Child Escape — Investigators Seek Identities of Assailants

Boston, May 4, 1922 — Brighton was the scene of uncommon disorder last evening when a crowd of several dozen persons assembled outside the residence of Mrs. Irene (Nell) Slattery, a well-known local Spiritualist, following a private séance attended by Sir Arthur Conan Doyle, the celebrated British author and advocate of psychical research. Before the night was through, the Slattery home, a Queen Anne–style dwelling on a quiet suburban street, was in flames, and three of Mrs. Slattery's young children lay dead.

According to neighbors, the gathering began shortly after dusk as word spread that Sir Arthur was calling upon Mrs. Slattery during his stay in the city. Several nuns, accompanied by two priests and carrying placards condemning Spiritualism, were observed praying aloud on the sidewalk. They were joined by curious onlookers and a handful of rough-mannered men who, residents report, appeared to have been drinking.

Witnesses state that Sir Arthur exited the home shortly after nine o'clock and was met with jeers from the more excitable elements of the assembly. As he departed in an awaiting motorcar, two men began throwing stones toward the house, shattering at least three windows on the upper floors. Efforts by several bystanders and by the clergy present to quiet the agitators appear to have been unavailing.

Moments later, in what authorities now describe as a deliberate act of incendiarism, unidentified men produced bottles filled with a flammable liquid, lit a rag affixed to its mouth, and hurled it toward the dwelling. Two projectiles entered a second-story window, and within seconds flames were visible from the street. The crowd dispersed in confusion as smoke poured from the upper chambers.

Fire apparatus from the Brighton station responded promptly, but the blaze had already gained a firm hold in one of the children's bedrooms. Firemen, battling smoke and heat, discovered three of the Slattery youngsters—two girls and a boy—lifeless. Two additional children were removed and conveyed to St. Elizabeth's Hospital, where their condition at press time was described as "grave." Mrs. Slattery and her eldest surviving daughter, Winifred, escaped without injury. Thanks to the fast action of the firemen, the house was saved from destruction.

Mrs. Slattery, a widow who supports her family through her Spiritualist practice, was said to be overcome with grief, yet able to answer a few brief questions. "My children were asleep," she said. "They never did harm to a soul." She declined further comment.

Police questioned several of the nuns who had been present earlier in the evening. One sister expressed sorrow for the loss of life but added, "We stand firmly against the false practices that lead people away from the true faith." When asked whether any among their number had witnessed the assailants, the nuns deferred, saying only that they had come to pray against "the dangers of superstition."

Lieutenant John F. Fitzgerald of the District 14 station stated that investi-

gators are seeking information regarding the men who threw stones and the individual who cast the incendiary device. "This was a lawless and cowardly act," he said. "We will pursue every lead."

The tragedy has cast a pall over the neighborhood, where residents today spoke in hushed tones of the children's deaths and expressed dismay that such violence could erupt on their ordinarily peaceful street. Whether the disturbance was spontaneous or instigated remains under inquiry. The authorities urge any citizen with knowledge of the perpetrators to come forward.

"My God," Eli said. It's even worse than what's in O'Connell's letter."

"The poor family," Cal said.

"What happened to other children, I wonder?" Eli said.

"Here's your answer," Charles said, happily producing another printout. "*The Boston Evening Globe*—July 15, 1922. It was a damn good newspaper then, it's a damn good newspaper now."

Fifth Child of Brighton Medium Succumbs to Injuries; Mother Vows to Remain in Damaged Home

By Staff Correspondent

Boston, July 15, 1922 — The tragic story of the Slattery family of Chestnut Hill Avenue gained two more sorrowful chapters yesterday with the deaths of Kay, aged 16, and Bronwyn, aged 12, who had been under continuous treatment at St. Elizabeth's Hospital since the Spiritualist disturbance and fire which swept their home late on the night of May 3.

The two youngsters, gravely injured by burns and smoke inhalation, survived for nearly two months under the attentive care of physicians and nurses, but neither child rallied sufficiently to overcome the damage done. Their passing brings the number of victims of the blaze to five. Three chil-

dren—Vern, 10; Sarah, 9; and Darlene, 13—were lost on the night of the fire.

Recalls Night of Alarm

The fire followed a well-attended séance conducted by their mother, Mrs. Irene (Nell) Slattery, a widowed Spiritualist medium known in local circles. Sir Arthur Conan Doyle, the noted British author and advocate of Spiritualism, had attended the event earlier that evening while on his Boston lecture tour.

During the gathering, a crowd estimated at over one hundred persons assembled on the ordinarily quiet street. Several members of nearby religious communities, including nuns and a small number of priests, stood among the demonstrators, praying aloud and carrying placards denouncing Spiritualist practices. Some lay members of the crowd, thought to have been under the influence of liquor, grew unruly. When Sir Arthur departed the premises, stones were thrown, shattering windows. A short time later, an unidentified man was seen hurling a flaming bottle, later believed to be a "bomb," through a second-floor window.

Flames spread rapidly through the upper rooms where the children were abed. Firemen from the Brighton station responded quickly, but three were beyond rescue by the time the blaze was brought under control.

Perpetrators Still Unfound

Despite police investigation, no arrests have been made, and authorities say they have been unable to identify the man who threw the incendiary device. Witnesses have given conflicting descriptions. The presence of nuns and clergy, widely discussed in the days following the tragedy, has been acknowledged, though no evidence has ever placed any religious personnel among the violent actors.

Cardinal O'Connell Offers Condolences

His Eminence William Cardinal O'Connell yesterday issued a statement from the Chancery on Lake Street extending "the prayerful sympathies of the Archdiocese to Mrs. Slattery in this renewed season of loss." The Cardinal added that "certain members of religious communities were present that evening in peaceful witness against practices the Church holds to be harmful," but stressed that "no priest or nun took part in unlawful acts nor bore responsibility for the violent outbursts of others." He urged "charity in all judgments" as the authorities continue their inquiry.

Mother's Vow to Remain

At the Slattery home—a Queen Anne residence, still scarred though partially repaired—Mrs. Slattery spoke softly but with resolve.

"My children were innocent, every one of them," she said, standing near the boarded windows of the second floor. "This house is all we have left of our life together. I will rebuild it, room by room, and I will not be driven out."

She added that she intends to continue her Spiritualist work, saying, "If God permits it, I shall speak with my children again. I shall reach for them in the next world as surely as I held them in this one."

Funeral arrangements for Kay and Bronwyn will be announced later this week.

"She lost five of her six children," Eli said sadly.

"It's awful," Grace said. "Did they ever catch the man who threw the firebomb, Charles?"

"I didn't find anything, so maybe not. I'm sure the diocese wanted the story to go away, so maybe the police weren't all that diligent. Who knows?"

"Do we think that Winifred was Eva Nevins' mother?" Cal asked.

"We should find out," Eli said.

Cal saw the way that Charles was grinning, and he suspected he was holding out on them.

"What? Do you already know?"

"What kind of newspaperman do you think you're dealing with, friends?" Charles said. "I spent a couple of hours today at the Massachusetts Registry of Vital Records and Statistics in Dorchester."

His wife punched him in the arm. "And—?"

He produced a cheat sheet. "I made a pretty little family tree. Winifred Slattery, the only child to survive the fire, was born in 1914 to Irene Slattery and Dennis Slattery, who passed away in 1918. Winifred, aka Winnie, married Edwin Nevins in 1932. On their marriage certificate, he's listed as an electrician; she's listed as a cleaner. They had only one child, Eva, born in 1949, so it looks like they'd been trying to have a kid for years. Winnie was thirty-five when Eva was born. Winnie passed in 1978 from a stroke, Edwin in 1963 from a car accident."

"That's when Eva was paralyzed," Cal said.

"Eva never married and didn't have children," Charles said. "The family tree ends with her."

"So you think Winnie was a medium, too?" Grace asked.

"You know what? I'm going to interview Eva," Charles said. "I'm going to ask about her mother, and I'm going to ask what she knows about the house fire. If I write the story I think I can write, my editor is going to toss rose petals down the newsroom whenever I come in."

"Tell him, Cal," Eli said.

"Tell me what?"

"We found out that Eva's got terminal cancer," Cal said. "She's not long for this world."

"Then, I'd better hurry," Charles said.

"You're such a dope," Grace said. "Eli wants you to leave the poor woman alone. Write your story if you must, but leave Eva Nevins out of it—and be respectful, for Christ's sake."

FATHER BOUCHARD ARRIVED UNEXPECTEDLY at Wellspring House after the sisters had finished dinner. Sister Gabriela was more than surprised to see him, and showed her discomfort. The nuns were aware he'd been relieved of his post, and they talked among themselves in the living room, while Gabriela took the priest into the kitchen.

"How can I help you, Father?" she said stiffly.

"It was important that I speak with you," he said.

"I received your email," she said. "It was self-explanatory. A monsignor from the diocese told us we wouldn't see you again, yet, here you are."

His voice was higher-pitched than usual, and his words tumbled out. "I know I sinned. I know I was weak. I should never have gotten as close as I did with Sister Kristin. I have paid the price, and I will continue to pay the price. This is a matter between God and me. But, the Lord knows I never killed Kristin, Lidia, or Dora. Someone else did. Was it Father Malloy?" He pointed a finger. "Or was it someone else?"

"What are you saying?" the nun said.

"We cannot have this discussion unless we enter into confession. Will you have confession with me?"

"What, now?"

"Yes, please, Sister Gabriela. This will probably be the last time we see each other. I've been a faithful servant to the Sacred Heart community and to your order. Do me this courtesy."

"Here?"

He closed the kitchen door and sat at the table. "Here."

Gabriela went stiff, as if frozen inside. She sat slowly opposite him, staring in anger and distrust.

When they heard the door close, Sisters Fabienne and Claudine, the Haitian cousins, hovered outside the kitchen, listening for trouble.

The priest began, "In the name of the Father, and of the Son, and of the Holy Spirit. Amen."

The nun hesitated a few seconds before saying automatically, "Bless me, Father, for I have sinned. It has been three weeks since my last confession."

"May the Lord be in your heart and help you make a good confession. You may begin."

"I think they're having a confession," Claudine whispered.

"Don't listen!" Fabienne said, stepping back.

Gabriela's discomfort and anger were clear as glass. She forced out,

"I don't have any grave sins to confess, but I have struggled with small things. I've grown impatient a few times with the younger sisters, especially when I'm tired. I've allowed myself moments of discouragement, doubting whether I'm still useful in the community. And I've failed in charity once or twice by speaking too sharply when I should have been gentler. For these and all the sins of my life, I am truly sorry."

He didn't offer the characteristic comfort or suggest a gentle penance. Instead, he said, "During a confession a month after the sisters were killed, you confessed to me that you were enraged by Sister Kristin's behavior—her incessant social media use, her excessive use of cosmetics, her flirtations. Do you recall that?"

"I do."

"And do you recall that you confessed that you thought she was an unhealthy influence on other sisters?"

"Yes."

"And do you recall that you confessed that you got so angry at times, you had murderous thoughts?"

Gabriela placed both palms on the table and said, "This is ridiculous. Are you suggesting I killed her?"

"What I want to suggest to you under confessional seal is that you go to the police if you had anything to do with this crime. Unburden yourself. I cannot compel you, and I cannot go to the police to tell them about the murderous thoughts you expressed during confession."

Gabriela stood up so abruptly that her chair almost toppled. "We are done, Father. Leave this house."

Bouchard trembled at the outburst. "I'm sorry if I upset you," he said, his voice cracking. "I will go. Know that God is with you. Do the right thing, Sister."

~

Cal was having a fitful sleep, tossing and turning. Fragmented dreams were flitting through his mind, when he awoke suddenly. His mouth was dry as a desert, and he gulped some water. That's when it came to him. He didn't care whether it was a spontaneous thought or the remembrance of a dream.

"Fuck me," he said out loud.

He scribbled it down before it slipped away.

(3+2) x 3

CAL CALLED Eli the first thing in the morning to tell her about his revelation.

He allowed her a long silence before she said, "Cal Donovan, you clever man. You must be right. How can it be a coincidence?"

"What should we do about it?" he asked.

"I know she's ill, but I'm going to call Eva. I'm going to ask about her mother."

EVA WAS IN THE KITCHEN, having a coughing fit, when she heard the phone. She was too hoarse to answer, so she let her answering machine, an old piece of tech, screen the call and record the message. She listened to the machine playing Eli's message in real time and stared at the flashing light when it was done. Her cough returned, more violently than before, and when the spasm abated, her wad of tissues was wet with blood.

CHAPTER TWENTY-ONE

1965, Brighton, Massachusetts

By eight o'clock at night, the house would grow quiet.

The last of the sitters were gone, their envelopes placed into the blue China bowl on the hall table. The front door was locked, footsteps faded down Chestnut Hill Avenue, and the voices that had filled the parlor left an echo behind them, something that wasn't quite sound.

Eva waited where she always waited, in the front hall, just outside the parlor door. Her wheelchair faced the coat rack and the framed black and white photograph of a young family from a generation long gone. If she craned her neck, she could see a sliver of the parlor rug and the imposing portrait hanging over the mantel.

Her job was to collect the envelopes when people arrived, smile, say thank you, and place them in the bowl. Her mother said it made the guests comfortable, seeing her daughter downstairs and not tucked away. It reminded them that the money was put to good use.

The lamp bulb hummed faintly. Somewhere in the back of the house, the boiler kicked on with a metallic clank.

The parlor door opened. Her mother stepped out, closing it halfway behind her.

"Be a dear and wait here. I simply must get out of this dress."

Winnie Slattery returned from her bedroom, having replaced her long dark dress with a skirt, blouse, and cardigan. She'd let her white hair down from a tight bun into a ponytail. Faint red marks persisted on the bridge of her nose where her glasses had rested.

"Well," she said, exhaling. "That's done."

"How did it go?" Eva asked.

"As it usually goes," Winnie said. "A husband adrift without his wife. A sister who died young. A boy lost in Vietnam. They all want reassurance." She rubbed her forehead with the heel of her hand. "Kay was tired. I told them the spirits were weak tonight. They were a little disappointed, but they'll come back." She looked down at Eva. "You did well at the door. Mrs. Hanley told me you have a very kind smile."

Eva shrugged. "She's lonely. She likes to talk."

"That's half my work," Winnie said. "Lonely people." She paused, studying her daughter. "How's your pain?"

"Fine," Eva said automatically. Her legs felt like nothing at all. Her shoulders cramped from wheeling in and out of the narrow hall all evening, but she was used to that.

Her mother glanced at the clock over the stairs. "We have a little time before I have to clear up."

"Time for what?" Eva asked.

"For you," Winnie said. "If you still want it."

Eva's fingers tightened on the rims of her wheels. "You mean—"

"Yes," Winnie said. "Tonight you can come in."

There had been other nights when she almost said it and didn't. Eva knew the signs: her mother would stand in the doorway, thoughtful, then decide she was too tired or Eva wasn't ready. Tonight, something had tipped.

"You're not just being kind—?" Eva said, nodding down at the chair.

"Don't be ridiculous," Winnie said. "You were probably ready before the accident. You're sixteen. You're more ready now. You see things differently." She opened the parlor door fully. "Come. When you're older, you'll need a way to make a living."

"What about—?"

"Don't worry about her. She's busy."

Eva swallowed. The line she'd never been allowed to cross lay right there, a strip of worn threshold wood. She unlocked the wheels, pushed forward, and rolled into the room.

It felt like stepping inside an old photograph.

The parlor was a time capsule. Her grandmother's time. The air had that dense, polished smell: furniture wax, lamp oil, dust that was always being wiped but never gone. Dark wallpaper patterned with climbing vines, faded at the seams. Heavy curtains drawn over the street-facing windows, letting in a narrow strip of sodium-orange light from the lamp outside. The same oval rug with a floral border, threadbare where countless chairs had stood.

And above the mantel, the portrait.

She'd glimpsed it from the hall since childhood but never straight on. Now she saw the man fully. Thick moustache. Receding hair swept back from a broad forehead. Dark suit, high collar, a watch chain across a solid chest. His gaze was direct, a little sad, and seemed to take in the whole room.

"Who is he?" Eva asked, without looking away.

"Sir Arthur Conan Doyle," her mother said. "The writer. Sherlock Holmes."

"I've seen the books at the library," Eva said.

"He came here," Winnie said simply. "Long before you were born. I was only eight. I got a glimpse of him from the stairs. The aroma of tobacco reached my nostrils. He sat right at that table with your grandmother. He admired her very much." She started toward the center of the room. "We'll talk about that another time. Come along."

The round table stood under the gas fixture that had been converted to electricity. The shade cast a warm, limited circle of light. Six high-backed chairs surrounded it.

"Which side?" Eva asked.

"Here, beside me. Let's see if Kay is up to meeting you."

"Kay," Eva repeated. The name had floated through conversations all her life, usually lowered on the last syllable, as if it should be spoken softly. "She's the one you talk to the most."

"She's the one who talks to me," Winnie said. "Do you know who she is?"

"Your sister," Eva said. "She died in the fire. In my bedroom."

"She and Vern, Sarah, Darlene, and Bronwyn. The others seem to have drifted away. Kay lingered."

"I've felt her," Eva said. "Sometimes at night. In my room."

"I know you have. That's how I know you have the gift."

Eva wheeled up, angling her chair under the table. The edge pressed gently against her ribs. She locked the wheels and put her hands in her lap.

"What was she like?" she asked. "Before."

"She was a lovely girl, bright as a penny, on the cusp of womanhood," Winnie said. "Mischievous. She liked to climb trees. You'd have liked her."

"How is she now?"

"She still is lovely, but she's not playful anymore. She's serious."

"I thought you always said children moved on quickly," Eva said. Why didn't she?"

"Most do," Winnie said. "Kay stayed. Some ties are stronger. She and I were close. I was the youngest, she was the eldest. Mama was busy, and she took care of me like I was her baby. Your grandmother's grief was strong. She had a powerful gift, and she called for all the children. Kay was the only one who answered."

The story of the fire had come to Eva in fragments. Her grandmother, Irene, a medium. A sitting. Angry people in the street. Bottles of burning alcohol thrown through a window on the second floor. Flames in the children's room. Firemen pulling out three small bodies and two more, barely alive. Vern, Sarah, Darlene. Then Kay and Bronwyn, weeks later, at St. Elizabeth's. The old folks in the neighborhood still lowered their voices when they mentioned it.

Spiritualists had come forward with money and carpenters. The charred upper floor had been rebuilt. The furniture was replaced.

The house looked whole again. But people said that if you listened late at night, you could still hear screaming children.

"What if she doesn't come?" Eva asked.

"I believe she will," Winnie said. "She told me she likes you. She's been near you for a long time."

Eva thought about the times she had felt watched in this house. Little shivers at the top of the stairs. Soft drafts where the windows were shut. She had always assumed it was her imagination or the lingering trauma of the crash.

Her mother turned off the overhead light. The room shrank to the lamp on the table.

"Take my hands," Winnie said. "Relax your fingers. We're not doing any tricks. We're just making a circuit."

Eva did as she was told. She felt her mother clamping her knuckles.

"Breathe normally," Winnie said. "Don't force it. Just listen."

"To what?"

"To whatever you hear."

The house settled around them. There was a faint car sound from the street—tires on damp asphalt, and the tick of the hallway clock. Somewhere upstairs, a pipe clanged, then went quiet.

Her mother began to speak, not loudly, not in a made-up tone, just as if she were talking to someone in the next room.

"Friends and loved ones in spirit," she said. "We gather with respect. We ask only for the presence of those who come in light and truth." She paused. "Kay, if you're about, we would be glad of you."

Eva stared at the table. At first, she felt nothing. Then, very gradually, there was a sense of pressure in her ears. Her skin prickled along her forearms.

It's just the draft, she told herself.

Her mother's voice dropped a little. "There now," she said, as if to a child who had just entered the room. "Come on, then."

A breath touched Eva's right cheek. Not air, exactly, but the idea of a breath—a soft, cool awareness stopping just short of her skin. She flinched.

"Do you feel that?" Winnie asked quietly.

"Yes."

"That's Kay."

Something brushed the back of Eva's right hand, lighter than a moth's wing. Her fingers curled.

"It's all right," Winnie murmured. "She won't hurt you."

Another brush, this time circling her wrist. Then a definite impression: a hand on her wrist. It was neither warm nor cold. It was just there.

Eva's eyes stung. She stared straight ahead, afraid that if she looked, she would see nothing and that the feeling would dissipate.

"Kay," Winnie said, "this is your niece, Eva. You've watched her enough. You know her. She would like to know you."

A faint pressure squeezed Eva's wrist, a quick, nervous squeeze.

"Can she hear me?" Eva asked.

"Start by thinking at her," Winnie said. "Words get in the way sometimes. When I'm with clients, I use words to keep them involved, but you can just put the thought clearly in your mind."

Eva closed her eyes. *Hello,* she thought, as plainly as she could. *I'm Eva.*

Behind her eyelids, she saw a blur of green—not the wallpaper, a different green, bright, like summer grass. It shifted quickly. A tree trunk. A girl's bare foot on a branch. Then nothing.

"Did you see that?" Winnie asked.

Eva said, "Yes," in a breathy exhalation.

"She's showing off," Winnie said quietly. "She's fond of that tree. Your grandmother hated it. Said she'd break her neck one day climbing. You saw it quickly. That's good."

The small hand slid further up Eva's arm, to her forearm, stopping halfway. The touch was firmer now, as if the child had gained confidence. A thin, clear sensation followed, not quite words, more like an emotion poured down the line of contact. It felt like curiosity, mixed with something like relief.

"She's glad you're here," Winnie murmured. "She says you're stubborn."

I'm not, Eva thought, and then realized the absurdity of arguing with a dead girl.

A sense of amusement came down the line, bright and quick. Eva found herself giving a little huff of laughter.

"It's like she's inside my head," she said.

"That's how it works sometimes," Winnie said. "Especially with guides."

"Is she my guide?" Eva asked.

"She can be," Winnie said simply. "If you'll have her."

The question rose before Eva could stop it. *If you're a guide, why didn't you save your sisters? You were the oldest. Why didn't you save yourself?*

The instant the thought formed, Eva regretted it. But it had already gone.

The hand on her arm tightened once, then loosened. She felt something like a dull ache, an old, old sorrow, worn down by time but still present. Then a different feeling overlaid it, gentle and firm, like someone placing a blanket over something left in the cold. It was a sense of acceptance, of having moved past the question long ago.

"I'm sorry," Eva whispered aloud.

Her mother watched her closely. "What did you ask?"

"Nothing important," Eva said.

The hand traced a slow circle on her forearm, forgiving.

"She's not angry," Winnie said, as if she had, in fact, heard the exchange. "She knows what happened. She's had a long time to think about it. She sees more than we do."

Eva let out a breath she hadn't realized she was holding.

"Ask her something useful," Winnie said. "You get maybe one good question the first time. Don't waste it. You can think it. "

There were too many things to ask. Why had her father driven so fast that rainy night on the highway? Was he all right now? Did he blame her for the accident because she was being difficult in the back seat? Would she ever walk again? Was this life—chair, envelopes—going to be the whole of it?

Her mind skittered over all of that and landed somewhere simpler.

Will you help me? she thought.

The answer came back without pause. Not as voice, but as a complete feeling, dropped into her like a stone into water: *Yes.*

It rippled outward—steady, uncomplicated. It was not a promise that things would be easy; it was just a statement.

"She said yes," Eva murmured.

"I know," Winnie said. Her expression softened, the worry lines at the corners of her mouth easing. "All right, then. That's settled."

"How do you know?" Eva asked.

"Because she helped me," Winnie said. "And she'll help you. But you must listen. You can't use her like a performing monkey. Guides don't like that."

The pressure on Eva's arm began to fade, as if a hand were slowly being withdrawn. A faint coolness moved away from her shoulder toward the far side of the room.

"Kay," Winnie said, "thank you. You may go now. Rest."

The room lightened. The ringing in Eva's ears eased. She became aware again of the clock in the hall, the faint traffic, the weight of her own body in the chair.

Her mother reached for the lamp and turned it up a notch. "How do you feel?"

"Tired," Eva said. "And, sort of full."

Winnie smiled briefly. "That's normal. First contact is like that. You'll sleep well tonight." She stood and began to blow out the candles. "Just listen to Kay. See what dreams you have. Keep a notebook."

"I don't keep a diary," Eva said.

"It's not a diary," Winnie replied. "It's work. You'll see."

Eva unlocked her wheels and backed away from the table. At the doorway, she stopped and looked back.

The portrait of Conan Doyle watched her go, as he had watched for forty-three years. She wondered what he would think of a sixteen-year-old girl in a wheelchair talking to a dead aunt in a Boston parlor in 1965.

Probably, he would approve.

Her mother came to the door. "Do you want help onto the lift? I can call her."

"I can manage," Eva said.

She pushed herself out into the hall. The house felt different—not safer, not more dangerous, just less empty.

At the foot of the stairs, where the light from the parlor fell into the gloom, she paused at the electric chair lift that one of her mother's wealthy clients had purchased for them after the accident. The air brushed her cheek again, playful this time.

"Hi," she said softly, under her breath.

There was no reply she could name, but something like a small, satisfied presence settled just above her right shoulder, as if a girl had perched there, legs swinging, ready to whisper whenever she was needed.

Eva rode the lift to her bedroom, already composing the questions she would write down before she slept.

CHAPTER TWENTY-TWO

Eli spread her note cards across Cal's library table, grouping them into clusters—historical context here, theological framing there, personal remarks she wasn't sure she wanted to use there. Her address to the National Conference of Women Religious at the Hynes Center was only a week away, and she was only now starting to work in earnest on the keynote speech. The theme had been hers to choose, and she was going with *Witness to a Changing Church.* It was broad enough that she could steer it where she wanted, but sharp enough that she risked stepping on land mines with candid personal disclosures. Her mouth was stuck in a frown.

Cal sat across from her, elbows on the table, pretending he wasn't staring.

"It looks like you're thinking too hard," he said.

"I know they want me to spill the tea—isn't that what kids say?—but I need to be cautious. Pope John doesn't need more headaches than he already has."

"You'll find the right balance."

"I should have started earlier. Lectures, student papers, committee assignments—my God, they all take so much time. How do you manage to write your books? You've got a heavier teaching load than I do."

"It gets easier. You'll recycle old lectures. You'll write new ones faster. You'll say no to committee invitations and outside speaking engagements. You'll see."

He lifted one of the cards and read the line she'd scribbled: *Faith without courage is merely consent.*

He raised an eyebrow. "Planning on starting a schism?"

"No," she said, playfully snatching the card back. "Anyway, I'll be careful. A little red meat for these reform-minded women, but not too much."

He leaned back and folded his arms. "You'll be great."

She didn't answer right away. She was working on two problems at once: the speech and Cal's equation.

(3 + 2) × 3

Cal had called early that morning, excited, convinced he'd cracked something, only to realize, after both of them stared at it from every angle, that there was no there, there. It was nothing but a thin, tantalizing reed.

Eli sipped her wine and brought it up again.

"I'm embarrassed," he said, rubbing his forehead. "My brain woke me up like it had solved your dad's Goldbach Conjecture."

"Your brain is enthusiastic," she said gently. "It's speculative, but it feels right."

He had one of his periodic cravings for a cold vodka. "We should tell the detectives anyway."

"What are we going to say? That you dreamt the numbers?"

"It wasn't a dream. At least, I don't think it was."

"Whatever it was," she said. "There's no substance. The police won't take it seriously. They'll dismiss it as coincidence."

He let out a long breath and pushed away from the table. "You're right," he said. "We'll hold it. For now."

Eli slid her cards into a stack, squared the edges with her palms, and sighed. "I need to concentrate on one thing only. It's like trying to sew a dress during an earthquake."

"You want to switch to coffee?" he asked.

She nodded. "Please."

"I don't have to give a speech next week to a ballroom filled with fawning nuns," he said. "I'll keep thinking how we can persuade the police we're onto something."

He stepped behind her chair and squeezed her shoulder—not too long, just enough for her to feel it.

She looked at the empty doorway after he was gone.

~

EVA NEVINS SAT at the table in her darkened parlor, staring at the candle she'd lit. The flame flickered in the faint draft from the sash windows—that old wood, always shifting. The room smelled faintly of the same brand of lavender polish her mother had used.

The parlor hadn't changed in a hundred years. There were the same heavy drapes, the oval table with its carved knuckles of walnut, the portrait of Conan Doyle on the wall—his eyes following you, no matter where you sat. It was as if the 1920s had never ended here.

Eva's wheelchair sat close enough to the table for her to rest her forearms on its edge. She wheezed faintly from the effort of transferring into position. Even small movements taxed her now.

She took in a breath and let it leak out. *Kay*, she thought. *I'm ready.* When she was alone, she didn't need to speak to Kay. Thoughts worked just as well.

The room answered with stillness. Eva knew better than to rush.

She closed her eyes.

When Kay came, she never arrived with theatrics. There were never gusts of cold air or rattling of objects. There was only a shift, like someone quietly entering a church pew beside her.

Eva's eyes fluttered open.

The candlelight quivered. A pressure touched the air, a presence small and weightless, old as the house itself.

Eva.

The voice was a breath, high and young but threaded with

something that wasn't childlike at all, but possessed a steadiness and intelligence of someone who had watched far too long.

I'm here.

Kay's shape was never more than suggestion. It was a faint luminescence near the wall, like the outline of a girl glimpsed through glass fogged with winter. But her tone carried perfectly.

Kay came to her as a voice within her head. *You're not well*, she said.

I'm having trouble with my lungs.

I sense the shortening of your days.

Eva swallowed hard. *It's getting worse.*

How long? Kay asked.

Weeks, the doctor said. Or days.

Kay was silent for several seconds. *When you die, I'll die a second time.*

The words slapped Eva like a cold wave. She blinked rapidly, tears forming against her will.

We don't know that.

Kay said. *I'm afraid. You're the last of us who remembers. When your mind slips away, will there will be no doorway left for me? No path back? Will I fall into whatever awaits forgotten children?*

Eva coughed and covered her mouth. *Kay—please—*

It's only the truth.

Eva bowed her head.

Kay waited in patient silence. She had always been patient—more patient than any sixteen-year-old girl could have been in life. Eva wondered sometimes whether Kay had aged, not in body, but in the strange dimension where memory lived. Whether a century of being half-alive had made her into something wiser and lonelier than any child should ever be.

You're thinking about her, Kay said at last. *The nun.*

Elisabetta Celestino, Eva acknowledged.

She worries you.

Eva lifted her head. *She's strong. Stronger than she knows. I almost like her. In another life, perhaps I would have.*

And you fear her.

Yes.

Kay's glow dimmed slightly, as though thinking. *She is close to knowing,* she said.

Eva adjusted her grip on the table's edge. *I've been thinking about what we must do. Before I'm gone.*

Kay's presence tightened, sharpening like a breeze turning suddenly cold.

A final blow, Kay whispered. *A last clearing of shadows.*

Eva's throat bobbed with a painful swallow. *Yes.*

A blow against those who did us harm, Kay said. *Against those who wear the mask of holiness. Against those who forget girls like me.*

Eva let out a trembling breath.

Are you frightened? Kay asked

Yes.

You won't be alone. I'll be waiting for you.

Eva lifted her eyes toward the portrait of Conan Doyle. His gaze seemed to meet hers, grave and stern. She'd grown up under that stare, hearing her mother speak of him as though he'd been an old family friend. It comforted her now, in an odd way.

She rolled her chair away from the table and into the harsh light of the kitchen, where her laptop sat charging.

The screen lit her pale face.

She typed slowly: **Elisabetta Celestino, Harvard Divinity School**.

The results popped up instantly—so many of them. She was famous and celebrated. Eva scrolled until she saw something that made her stare into the glow.

Annual National Conference of Women Religious – Keynote Speaker: Elisabetta Celestino, Professor at the Harvard Divinity School and former Vatican Secretary of State. Hynes Convention Center, Boston.

Eva clicked the link and read the program description: A thousand American nuns. Sessions on renewal, healing, and institutional accountability. Plenary sessions. Lectures. Breakout panels.

Eva closed the computer with shaking hands and realized that Kay was still with her.

How? Kay asked.

I'll think it through.

Kay's voice softened. *I trust you, as I trusted our mother.*

Eva closed her eyes and let the silence stretch. Her lungs rasped, struggling for rhythm. When she opened her eyes again, Kay was there, wavering like a reflection in disturbed water.

You should rest, Kay said.

I will.

And then Kay was gone, pulled back into whatever thin place she lived in, leaving behind a hollow coldness.

CHAPTER TWENTY-THREE

1922, Brighton, Massachusetts

THE EVENING OF THE THIRD OF MAY SETTLED OVER ACADEMY HILL Road, the last of the spring light thinning behind a veil of low cloud. The Slattery house, large for the neighborhood but worn at the edges, glowed behind its lace curtains. The lamps were lit in the front rooms, throwing a soft brightness that made the street outside seem darker than usual. The smell of damp earth from the afternoon rain mixed with a trace of coal smoke from nearby chimneys. It had never been the kind of street where history happened, but the people who were gathering outside the Slattery house that evening sensed something unusual.

Inside the house, the children had been shepherded upstairs with strict instructions to remain in the bedroom. Their mother wanted no giggling on the landing, no questions shouted down the stairs, and no small heads peering around doorframes. She wanted the house orderly for her guests, and she wanted the children safe. The youngest, Winnie, was already in her nightdress and robe, perched cross-legged on the edge of the bed she shared with Sarah.

Her hair was braided in two tight rows and she kept tugging at her satin bows.

Darlene, thirteen, stood near the window, trying to see down the street through a gap in the curtains. She was tall for her age and already carried herself as if she belonged somewhere other than the crowded bedroom. Vern, ten, knelt beside the radiator and pushed a tin soldier back and forth as if forcing the toy to march through combat. Sarah, nine, sat close to Winnie, her hands folded in her lap and her eyes wide. Bronwyn, twelve, moved restlessly around the room, keeping an ear trained on the muffled sounds below. Kay, sixteen, the oldest and the one who acted as second mother whenever Irene Slattery was occupied with the demands of her practice, sat on the straight-backed wooden chair near the door. She tapped one foot lightly, watching the younger siblings without taking her eyes completely off the hallway.

The children were no strangers to late-night gatherings in the parlor. Their mother's Spiritualist sittings had grown more frequent in recent months as word of her skill spread. People came to Brighton from Back Bay, Cambridge, Dorchester, Newton—even from Rhode Island and New Hampshire. Some came alone, some with friends and family, sometimes bringing photographs, locks of hair, or written questions prepared with trembling hands. Most left lighter and more unburdened than they had arrived.

Irene never promised certainty, but she gave comfort, and comfort was scarce in households recovering from wartime losses. Tonight, however, the throng outside the house and the children inside knew that tonight's visitor was different from the usual bereaved husband or grieving mother. The children had been warned to behave, to stay in their room, and to make no sounds. Their mother had polished the mantel, the walnut table, and the candlesticks. She had donned her Sunday-best black dress and pinned her hair so tightly it lifted her forehead.

The celebrity arrived precisely on time in a chauffeured limousine that braked cautiously on the curb as the multitude gave way for it. A murmur ran through the crowd. At dusk, there had been only a few nuns gathered, Sisters of Saint Joseph of Boston, who had arrived in twos and threes with rosaries wound tightly in their hands. As the evening wore on, they were joined by Sisters of Charity of Saint Vincent de Paul and Sisters of Mercy, all of them notified by leaflets of a celebrated Spiritualist sitting in the heart of the diocese. Several parish priests joined them, carrying placards that read, **Truth Is Found Only in the Gospels and Spiritualism Leads Souls Astray**. Word had spread throughout Brighton, and in the local taverns along Washington Street, Catholic men, fired up by drink, poured out the doors and stumbled along gas-lamp-lit Chestnut Hill Avenue toward the Slattery house. The neighborhood had grown accustomed to small pockets of protestors, but this was something else altogether.

When the motorcar's headlights illuminated the wet road, more people emerged from the shadows. Men who smelled of cheap whiskey and cigarette ash stood shoulder to shoulder, their coats unbuttoned on a warm May evening. A few laughed too loudly with boozy bravado. Others muttered to one another, glancing at the automobile, as if expecting the devil himself to step out.

As the car came to a stop, the crowd pressed forward. The nuns began their hymn, and the familiar rise of *Salve Regina* floated over the street with a sweetness that contrasted with their hard expressions. Behind the nuns, one of the priests raised his placard higher, his jaw set in indignation.

The motorcar door opened and Sir Arthur Conan Doyle stepped out with a deliberate composure. He was dressed in a dark overcoat, buttoned high, with a matching hat. His moustache was neatly trimmed, and he carried an air of purpose.

One man's shout turned into a din of opposition. Despite the furor, Doyle maintained a calm bearing, although he paused briefly as if gauging the tension in the air.

"Oh, good Lord," he muttered to Captain Widdecombe, the ex-soldier and Boston aide, and the detective, William Burns. "I expected opposition, but this is rather spirited."

"Come, let's proceed inside apace," Burns said.

A second car pulled up and the Spiritualist minister, Mr. Wiggin and his wife got out, blinking at the demonstrators.

. . .

Doyle made for the house, where the porch light cast a halo on the freshly swept steps. Irene Slattery stood in the doorway, her hands clasped at her waist, glancing briefly at the disapproving crowd, then shifting her gaze to the great man.

"Mrs. Slattery," Doyle said when he reached the porch. "Thank you for receiving us."

"Welcome, Sir Arthur," she said. "Please come in quickly. The evening has grown unsettled."

"A familiar condition, I fear," he replied with a rueful smile. "Nevertheless, I have never been turned away by a friend of the spirit world."

As the rest of the entourage disappeared into the house, the men in the crowd started jeering. Irene firmly shut the door and greeted the others in the safety of the hall.

Upstairs, the children listened as the front door's lock clicked into place. A murmur drifted up, then the sound of coats being removed and hung, and the familiar creak of the parlor door. Kay leaned toward the hallway and motioned for the younger ones to stay where they were. Winnie begged to be allowed to sit on the stairs to see the visitors, then broke away for a moment and from the top of the stairs, snuck a peak of the famous visitor before Kay pulled her back to the bedroom, shushed her, and told her to behave. Winnie made a face and pressed the heel of her hand against her mouth. Bronwyn moved to the bed and sat, her hands clasped between her knees. Vern went to the window again, unable to resist the pull of the commotion outside.

He parted the curtains another inch. "More people are coming," he whispered. "They are walking down the street with lanterns."

"Do not frighten Winnie," Kay said. "Move aside."

He stepped away so she could look. She saw the bobbing lights and the shifting shapes in the fog. The nun's hymns rose and fell like the tide. The priests stood stiffly, and the men in the crowd pressed forward. One of them spotted her and began shaking his fist. She'd never seen anything like this, and she was afraid.

"We will stay in the room," she said. "That is what Mama told us to do. Everything will be fine. Nothing will happen."

Winnie stared at her older sister. "Will there be trouble?"

Kay hesitated. "No one will trouble us inside the house."

"The shouting scares me."

"Stick your fingers in your ears."

Irene guided her guests into the parlor. The curtains were drawn completely. The walnut table had been polished to a mirror finish. She gestured toward the chairs, and Doyle lowered himself slowly onto his seat, surveying the room with interest. He complimented the spareness of the space and its aura.

"Mrs. Slattery," he said, "I have long heard about the quality of your work and wished to witness it firsthand. Mr. Wiggin here speaks highly of you. What is it you said, Wiggin?"

"I told you that she possesses an unusually steady sensitivity."

"Thank you, Mr. Wiggin. It is a pleasure hosting you again."

"Please—all of you—understand that I cannot guarantee what will happen tonight. Spirits do not always respond when called."

"Of course," Doyle said. "I would be suspicious if you promised certainty."

Captain Widdecombe nodded in agreement. Although he was not a dyed-in-the-wool Spiritualist, he had been impressed by what he had seen these last days and he possessed an open mind. He placed a notebook on the table in case he wished to record anything of importance.

Outside, the nuns' hymn shifted to another familiar piece, their voices straining to rise above the louder men. A few ruffians were shouting at one another, their arguments melding with the song. One of them threw a beer bottle that skittered across the pavement and shattered on the curb. A fistfight ensued that extinguished as fast as it had begun.

"Pay the baying mob no mind," Doyle said. "Outside is darkness, inside is light."

Irene closed her eyes for a moment, gathered her breath, and began the ritual with a calm, even voice. She invited only those who came in goodwill to hold each other's hands.

"Ah, you are of the hand-holding school," Doyle said. "Very well."

He bowed his head slightly and took Irene's and Mrs. Wiggin's hands.

"May I inquire as to your spirit guide, Mrs. Slattery?" Doyle asked.

"Her name is Belinda. She passed in 1801 when the country was young. She came to me when I was but a girl, and she has been with me ever since, through thick and thin."

Widdecombe looked like he wanted to jot that down, but his hands were occupied.

Despite the noise outside, the room took on a sort of stillness. Doyle had described such moments as the heaviness before a door swings open. It was a sensation he had come to recognize during his years of exploration and debate. His hands lightly grasped those of his compatriots, and he kept his breathing slow, hoping for clarity despite the racket beyond the walls.

Irene's voice changed ever so slightly. "I seek my spirit guide, Belinda. Belinda, make your presence known. Everyone, grasp each other's hands tighter and concentrate all your mental energies on summoning her."

Earnest faces scrunched in concentration.

"Belinda, thank you for coming. How do you fare?"

Irene channeled the response. "I am well enough."

Doyle shook his large head in satisfaction.

"There is someone near," Irene said. "A young man."

Doyle's spine straightened. "Is it my son?"

Irene said, "There is hesitation."

"Hesitation?"

"He wants to speak, but the conditions here are agitated. He brings a word."

Doyle waited.

"Floreat."

The word landed with force. Doyle's son, Kingsley, had been

proud of his years at Eton. The school motto, *Floreat Etona*, May Eton Flourish, had always pleased him. It had carried through letters, inside jokes, and on the rare occasions when father and son had debated the worth of tradition.

Doyle swallowed with difficulty. "Do you see him?"

"I only heard him utter the word," Irene said. "Sometimes a word is all we can manage."

Doyle nodded. He dared not wipe the tear from his cheek, lest the chain be broken. "It is enough."

The others exchanged glances. The Wiggins smiled broadly. Widdecombe had the astonished look of a new believer. Burns was there, but not there. He seemed focused on the events outside the window.

Irene breathed deeply, her eyes clamped shut. Her shoulders shifted. Her facial muscles tightened in the way that often preceded a different presence.

"A man steps forward," Irene said. "He says his name is Myers."

Doyle inhaled deeply, struck by the possibility that this was a moment of import. Frederic W. H. Myers had died more than two decades earlier, leaving behind a body of psychical research and essays that had shaped the foundations of the movement.

"Myers wishes to address you, Sir Arthur," Irene said.

Irene began to speak, and her words came with a vocabulary and cadence that startled everyone at the table, for they were different to the woman's usual pattern of speech. She discussed the nature of belief, the narrowing of religious thought, and the way new revelations challenged old institutions.

At one point Doyle muttered, "This must be Myers. I recognize his arguments."

The dissertation continued until Doyle asked, "Do you attend my lectures in spirit?"

"I have stood beside you when the hall was full."

The claim was not unknown to him. A researcher in Philadelphia had once insisted he had seen Myers standing near the stage. Even a true believer like Doyle, who had experienced myriad contacts with the other realm, quivered at the twin communications with his son and Frederick Myers.

Outside, another bottle shattered against the sidewalk. The nuns faltered in their singing, only to regain their harmony moments later. Their voices rose higher and more defiant, as if some of them weren't so much singing, but shouting at the top of their lungs. The priests moved closer, trying to keep the drunkards at bay, but they lacked the numbers or, seemingly, the moral authority to tame the worst of them.

Upstairs, the children huddled together. Winnie clutched Sarah's hand. Bronwyn wrapped an arm around Vern's shoulders. Kay watched the door, listening to each new sound as if she could decode danger on the other side of the windowpanes.

Winnie cried out, "Why do the nuns sound so angry?"

"They are angry because they are frightened of Mama," Kay said. "Don't worry. They cannot hurt us."

Downstairs, Irene struggled to keep the sitting intact. She recognized the signs. As the outside noise grew more pronounced, Belinda withdrew. She always did so when confusion mounted and negativity seeped into the room.

Doyle recognized the shift as well. He turned toward the drawn curtains.

"Perhaps we should conclude," he said quietly.

"Yes, we should," Burns said emphatically.

Irene nodded. "Belinda and the others are fading away. It is no longer safe for them to speak."

The circle of hands broke and the table fell silent. Doyle and his companions prepared to leave, and Irene walked them to the front hall.

Before he reached the door, Doyle slipped something small and hard into her hand and whispered in her ear. She looked down without revealing it to the guests or the children overhead. His eyes said everything and she accepted it with gratitude.

"Thank you."

"Take this too," he said, reaching into an overcoat pocket.

She looked at it and nodded.

"You show courage tonight," Doyle replied. "Hold fast to it. This movement needs people like you."

She managed a faint smile. "You have been very kind."

When she opened the front door, the full force of the mob greeted them. The hymns continued, deafening now. She didn't know that women could sing so loudly. The men hurled insults at Doyle, calling him a deceiver and a corrupter. The priests held their ground, though they had lost control of the most volatile elements. One man raised a bottle threateningly but lowered it when Burns shouted at him, pointed menacingly and thrust his other hand into his jacket, as if reaching for a weapon.

Doyle hurried toward his limousine, his companions following behind. He bade the Wiggins farewell as they ducked into their automobile. Doyle's driver, rattled by what he had seen and heard, pulled away from the curb before the door had fully shut behind them. As the car accelerated, another round of jeers erupted, mixed with the unwavering hymn of the nuns.

Inside the house, Irene locked the door. She pressed her palm against the weighed-down pocket holding Doyle's gifts, and remained still for a long moment before starting toward the stairs.

Kay was waiting in the doorway of the children's bedroom.

"Is he gone?" she asked.

"Yes," Irene said.

"Will the people go home now?"

"I believe they will. I hope they will go now."

Kay looked past her mother toward the hall window, where the lantern lights continued to dance through the lace curtains.

She put her hands over her ears and said, "Why won't those nuns stop their infernal singing?"

CHAPTER TWENTY-FOUR

ELI KEPT HER OFFICE DOOR CRACKED OPEN AS A SIGN TO HER colleagues that she was amenable to drop-ins. The late-autumn sun, thin and pale, flooded the window overlooking the Francis Street quad. The students had mostly cleared out for the day, and the quad was nearly empty. Papers lay stacked in neat piles across her desk, and her annotated note cards sat in a wooden tray along with the collection of feather quills that Cal had given her as a joke about her "monastic indexing system."

She was working through another revision of her keynote address. She wanted the speech to feel grounded in the reality she had lived, without sounding confessional or combative. She was aiming for a clear tone—honest, hopeful, unafraid. The recipe was not yet perfected.

She leaned back and looked at the line she kept returning to. *When institutions resist change, it is nearly always because change threatens the stories they tell themselves.* It felt true enough, though she was unsure whether it belonged at the beginning or the end.

Her phone rang, and she beamed as she answered. "Ciao, Mic."

"Ciao, sorella," Micaela said. "Drowning in work?"

"Up to the eyebrows."

"You sound tired."

"I'm fine," Eli said, though it was not quite true. She was overworked and homesick. "I was thinking about our Christmas plans."

She spoke in the Romanesco dialect they always fell into.

"That's why I'm calling. Papa wants to know your arrival date so he can book a table. He also wants to know whether you prefer your old room or the guest room. He thinks you'll sleep better away from the street."

"How is he?"

"Why don't you ask him? I brought the girls over tonight. We're leaving soon."

"Papa!" she said. "I can't wait to see you."

His voice tobacco-dry. "It won't be like usual, but at least you'll be here."

"I know, Papa, I know. Without Emilio, it will never be the same. How have you been?"

"What can I say?"

"The truth?"

"The truth is, I sit and smoke."

"It's not good for you."

"You think I care?"

"You're a Professore Emerito. You can go to seminars at Sapienza. You can get out of the house."

"I don't want to see those bums."

"They're not bums. Are you working at least? How's our friend, Goldbach?"

"Fuck Goldbach. I'm done with him."

"Don't say that. You'll find the proof one day, I know you will."

"Did you tell Micaela which room you want."

"My old room, please."

"All right, all right. Here's your sister. Give her your arrival date and I'll book a table."

They shifted to lighter matters, and Micaela delivered a story about a neighbor's cat that delivered a rabbit to their front door as a gift. The girls were hysterical, and Arturo, the emergency room doctor, did CPR on it, reviving the stunned bunny. Micaela told it with her usual theatrical flair until Eli snorted.

"I needed that laugh," she said.

"I know exactly what you need," Micaela replied.

"And what is that?"

"I don't want to be crude with a nun. How *is* Cal?"

"You're terrible."

"I'm serious. What are you waiting for? Rainbows and unicorns and a sign from God?"

"Two out of three," Eli said.

She finished the call, let the quiet return, and returned to her draft. But her attention drifted aimlessly to Eva Nevins, Emilio, the murdered nuns, and Cal Donovan, that restless soul who was down the hall, probably thinking about her.

~

Cal was slammed with late-semester chores, the unglamorous side of being a university professor. He pushed aside a half-read dissertation chapter, thought about wandering down the hall to Eli's office, but didn't want to be a pest. He was aware he'd become a bit of a joke around the office, particularly among the younger admins. When he headed in her direction, tongues wagged in the offices he passed. "It's like a salmon run, but with more tweed" or "there goes the tomcat with tenure."

Unsure how to spend the rest of the afternoon, he was saved by one of his teaching assistants who lightly rapped on the door and saw himself in, wielding a folder as thick as the New Testament.

"Done," he said, handing it over. "It's everything I could find. Now, will you tell me why you wanted it?"

"Stealth project," Cal grinned.

"Planning on writing a detective novel?"

"You know, Ken, that's not a bad idea. Thanks for doing this. Two gold stars and cheeseburgers for life."

"I'm a vegan."

"I know you are—hence, my offer."

THE EMAIL HIT every faculty member's inboxes simultaneously and commanded attention with the all-caps header: URGENT FACULTY MEETING – MANDATORY ATTENDANCE

Eli read it and began to fume.

Dear Colleagues,

I apologize for the short notice, but I must ask you to clear your calendars for an emergency faculty meeting on Dec 4, 12-1, in the Sperry Room, Schwartz Hall.

The Provost's Office informed me that the multi-school "Strategic Academic Reorganization" proposal will be brought before the Corporation at its January meeting, with specific implications for the Divinity School's budget, degree programs, and faculty lines. We have been given a narrow window to respond to a draft framework that, among other things, raises the possibility of folding our MTS program into a larger "Religion and Public Life" umbrella degree and imposing a hiring freeze for the next three years. I need your guidance before I respond on behalf of the School. I recognize that the date and time may not be ideal, and that some of you will have longstanding commitments. However, the stakes are significant enough that I must stress that attendance is expected unless you are away from the area.

With thanks,

Gil Daniels
Dean, Harvard Divinity School

It was Eli who migrated down the hall this time, appearing in Cal's office, with the printed email.

"Did you see this?"

"Just read it."

She spoke in animated Italian. "Gil and I were talking just this morning, and I mentioned I was giving a keynote address on Wednesday in Boston. Is it possible he picked the day and time to conflict with my schedule?"

"We're talking about Gil," Cal said. "It's not possible, it's probable. He's jealous of you."

"What should I do?"

He said it in English, "Do you know the expression, tell him to pound sand?"

"No, what does it mean?"

"It means, get lost."

"Ah. We say, "Vai a farti friggere."

"Go get yourself fried," he said, delighted. "I'll remember that. Just let him know on Tuesday that, regrettably, as he is aware, you have a major commitment."

"He'll be angry."

"It doesn't matter. You're untouchable. He's not. You'll have his job in a few years, if you want it. As for me, I wasn't going to crash your event, but now I've decided: I'm definitely coming. Thank you, Gil, for providing clarity."

She laughed and took one of the chairs in front of his desk. "I suppose that you're untouchable too."

"I'd make an exception for you."

She saw off his flirt with a sly smile and pointed at the stack of printouts. "What's that?"

"This is me avoiding work," he said. "I had one of my TAs find every contemporary newspaper story about Arthur Conan Doyle he could find online."

"Is that a legitimate use of a TAs time?"

"It most certainly is not," he said with a grin. "Nevertheless, it's done. If we're going to push the police to investigate Eva, we've got to find something that connects her to the murders. Here's what we know—he got up to his whiteboard, erased a bunch of stuff about the historicity of Jesus, and began jotting down bullet points.

(3 + 2) x 3. This has got to be the key, right?"

"I think so," she said.

He continued furiously writing out his points in sentence fragments: Conan Doyle was at a séance at Eva's grandmother's house the night of the fire. The fire killed three kids outright. Two more died two months later. Fast forward to 1944, when Eva's mother, Winnifred, the only surviving child, is thirty. Three nuns are shot dead. Two months later, two more nuns die of "food poisoning." Fast forward to the present. Three nuns are shot with what the police have said is an antique gun engraved with the word Piggy. Two months later, two more nuns are killed, this time, per the last police press conference, with insulin overdoses.

"But the gun was found in Father Malloy's house," she said.

"Yes, it was, and he was dead before the killings at Sacred Name," he said, so someone else did it.

"Maybe he killed the Wellspring sisters and someone else killed the other two."

"Okay, maybe—but it doesn't seem likely, does it?"

Then he wrote the last bullet point. **Eva Nevins**, and underlined it.

"She's a paralyzed, sick woman," Eli said.

"Yep," he agreed. "That's a problem. But here's what I'm thinking. What if Conan Doyle or someone in his group who attended the séance at Irene Slattery's house in May 1922 saw the mob outside and slipped her a gun for protection? What if that's the gun used in the shootings?"

"How are you going to prove that?"

"I don't know, but maybe there's something in these articles about Conan Doyle. He was garrulous as hell. He talked to any reporter with a notepad on both sides of the Atlantic. Feel like taking half the stack?"

"Hand it over," she said. "Anything to take me away from my speech."

OUTSIDE CAL'S OFFICE, the color drained from the sky and the streetlights glowed. At five o'clock, Cal got up, stretched a little, and asked Eli if she wanted a hot chocolate.

She sparked to the suggestion. "The one with the little marshmallows," she said.

When he returned, she was standing.

"What?"

She waved a single sheet of paper. "In 1933, a reporter in England interviewed a man named George Barber," she said. "Read the interview and give me my chocolate as a reward".

THE EVENING TELEGRAPH, AUGUST 16, 1933: I SPARRED WITH CONAN DOYLE

Some secrets are more well kept than others. For the first time we can now reveal a previously unknown nickname of Arthur Conan Doyle.

As a young medical student, only 20 years old, Conan Doyle spent eight months in Birmingham, working as an assistant to Dr. Reginald Hoare. It was a lucrative inner-city general practice, and Conan Doyle joined Dr. Hoare on his rounds and assisted in the surgery. Conan Doyle liked both Dr. Hoare and his wife Amy, and he felt more like a son than an assistant. In his spare time he started to write fiction, trying to get a story published for the first time.

Furthermore, Conan Doyle, who was quite athletic, spent some time boxing at the Lion Gymnasium. There he fell in with the 17 year-old George Barber, who worked at the Kynoch percussion cap factory in Witton. One day Barber, who also played football in the newly formed Aston Villa F.C., was sparring with Conan Doyle, when the latter landed a blow which considerably damaged Barber's nose.

Many years later, at the age of 71, Barber remembered the incident. "That," he said with some pride, "is my souvenir to-day of Sir Arthur Conan Doyle."

Barber also remembered one more thing – the nickname of his opponent. The hefty youth at the Lion Gymnasium was not Arthur Conan Doyle among the Birmingham boxers. He was instead – and here it comes – "Piggy" Doyle.

THE WAY CAL SAID, "FUCK ME," made her giggle. "Piggy Doyle. Do you think detectives go home at five?"

"This, I don't know."

He found Sergeant Detective Santos's card, called his mobile number on speaker, and gave Eli a thumbs-up when Santos answered. Cal told him they'd found a piece of evidence potentially linking a gun belonging to Arthur Conan Doyle to Eva Nevin's grandmother, and walked him through the items on his whiteboard.

He didn't get the reaction they expected.

"What do you expect me to do with this, Professor?"

Santos had him on speaker with his partner listening in.

"I don't know—you're the detective."

"You've got a piece of hearsay from an old newspaper that says the guy was called Piggy. Maybe he was, maybe he wasn't. Other people have been called Piggy. Ever seen Sesame Street? You can't tie him to the weapon used in the Wellspring murders based on a nickname."

"Isn't it enough to take a closer look at Eva Nevins on the theory that the gun has been in her family? Question her? Search her house?"

"That's a hard no. This isn't actionable. There isn't a judge on the Massachusetts bench who'd grant a search warrant based on this. And, believe me, we have questioned this old lady who—if you haven't noticed—is confined to a wheelchair!"

"What would you need?" Cal asked.

"It would have to be something that ties her directly to the weapon."

"How am I supposed to do that?"

"You're not. You're a college professor. I'm a police detective. That's my job."

Santos hit the mute button long enough to say to Trinh, "Fucking eggheads."

Cal signed off, rolled his eyes, and said to Eli, "That went well. Want to get some dinner?"

"Give me an hour," she said. "I need to do more real work."

WHEN SHE CAME BACK with her puffy jacket and shoulder bag, Cal was collecting his papers for the night.

"Don't tell the great detective Jose Santos, who, by the way, could never be confused with Sherlock Holmes, that I did more sleuthing."

"Oh yes?"

"It turns out that most of Conan Doyle's personal papers wound up in an archive managed by the city of Portsmouth, where he practiced medicine for several years. They've got over sixty thousand items. It's not digitized and searchable, but they allow researchers to study the material. I just sent them an email telling them I was looking for anything linking him to a particular pistol and to Mrs. Irene Slattery, a medium he encountered in Boston on his 1922 American tour."

"Do they say how long it would take to get an answer?"

"Nope. I'll call them in the morning."

"I've got a better idea," she said. "Maybe my good friend, the Cardinal of Westminster, would lend us a retired priest from the Portsmouth area to go there in person. You make your call, I'll make mine."

CHAPTER TWENTY-FIVE

Cal rolled into Francis Street after his morning seminar and deliberately took a route through the building that passed her office. He heard laughter from a few doors down and recognized Ruth Goldberg's distinctive New York accent.

Putting his head in, Ruth exulted, "Now! My two favorite people in one place. My day can't get any better."

"And it's good to see you, too, Ruth," he said, kissing both cheeks.

"Eli was just telling me she told Gil that she wasn't coming to his ridiculous meeting tomorrow. He doesn't need a faculty meeting to tell the Provost to jump in a lake. I happen to agree with you that he chose the day and time to complicate Eli's speech."

"What did he say?" Cal asked.

"He tried to make me feel guilty. He told me that an adverse decision by the Provost wouldn't affect a professor of practice such as myself, but all the poor junior faculty would suffer without the support of those with tenure or tenure track."

"Oh my God," Cal said. "Give the man an Academy Award nomination. What a load of crap."

"Tell Cal what you told him," Ruth said. "She is so clever."

"I told him that I couldn't possibly renege on my speaking commitment, but that I'd be happy to meet with the Provost in person to argue the case for HDS."

"Brilliant," Cal declared. "You threatened to upstage him. He probably soiled himself."

"I don't know about that," Eli laughed, "but he didn't look pleased."

"I've got to hop on a call," Cal said. "Did you hear anything from Portsmouth?"

"Nothing yet."

~

MARIA TRINH HAD a new vision of Hell: The City of Boston Archives.

She had spent a week of her life sifting through musty paperwork in this sterile warehouse, and the very thought of returning made her sick to her stomach. At this point, she was seriously doubting she'd ever find anything about the two nuns who died in 1944 at Our Lady of the Presentation Convent, but at least she had company. The Police Commissioner, who'd been feeling the heat ever since the public learned that the nuns at Sacred Name were also murder victims, sent her two patrolmen languishing on desk duty following officer-involved shootings, to help look through boxes.

The two officers were not best pleased to be sitting on the hard floor, sifting through ancient City Council records, but they were warm bodies and misery loves company.

She was telling them, by way of motivation, that there were only a dozen shelves of material to go through until they hit the end of the 1944 records, when she got a call from a number she didn't recognize.

"Probably spam," she grumbled, answering anyway.

When she realized it was important, she sprinted for the stairs and ran outside to get a better signal. Against the backdrop of the cold, black waters of Cow Island Pond, she had a brief, animated conversation with the caller, working hard to sound like a professional, not an excited rookie. She rang her partner the second she hung up.

"Zé," she said. "Big fucking news. The FBI just called."

"Yeah?"

"The bullet from the 1944 case? It's a match. It's the exact same composition as the Wellspring slugs, and they're ninety-eight percent sure the same gun fired it."

"Ninety-eight's not the same as a hundred."

"Will you listen to yourself? It's the same murder weapon used eighty years apart. They're sending their report."

"So, Malloy got the gun from a murderer."

"Then, who killed the Sacred Name nuns? Look, I think we've got to take the eggheads seriously. We need to go back to Eva Nevins."

"Nothing's changed on that score," Santos said. "There's not enough to get a search warrant. You let me know if that changes. And send me the ballistics report when you get it, so I can torture the Commissioner with it. I'm trying to reverse the flow of shit by sending it upstream. When are you wrapping things up down there?"

"We're running out of real estate—by the end of the day—ninety-eight percent sure."

~

Cal persuaded Eli to come over for dinner the night before her speech. She wanted to get an early night, so he arranged for delivery and went home early to tidy up—he'd been in full bachelor mode the past week and had left dishes in the sink and clothes everywhere.

She arrived at six, and he microwaved the tubs of Indian food, which arrived a little cold. They were just about to tuck into their meal when her phone chimed with a text.

"You going to look at it?" he asked.

"Not now."

Five minutes later, her phone rang from a UK number.

"Oh, hello. Have I reached Professor Celestino?"

"You have."

"Oh, good. This is Father Jeremy Coates from Portsmouth. I've been looking through the Conan Doyle Archives for you. I wonder if you received the text I just sent."

"Oh, yes, let me check," she said. "I heard it coming in, but I haven't looked yet."

"I believe it may be helpful for your query."

She thanked him profusely, ended the call, and went to her messages. The priest had sent her two photos of a two-page handwritten letter.

"Cal!"

Academy Hill Road
Brighton, Massachusetts
July 29, 1922

Windlesham Manor
Crowborough, Sussex
England

My dear Sir Arthur,

I have received your most compassionate letter of condolence, and I cannot adequately express what comfort your words have brought to me in these desolate weeks. It is a rare blessing, in a time of such affliction, to feel that one's sorrow is met with sincere understanding, and your kindness has been a balm to my wounded spirit. I thank you with all my heart.

You asked for some further account of the tragic night, and though it pains me to revisit it, I feel I owe you the truth of what befell us. The crowd outside my home had grown hostile as the evening wore on. A cadre of nuns—members of various local orders—stood in the roadway chanting their hymns with an obstinate fervor that seemed directed as much at us as at Heaven. A few priests remained with them, holding placards denouncing my work. I cannot say they took any active hand in what followed, but neither did they lift a voice to restrain the drunken men who had been lingering amongst them. Whether out of fear, indifference, or misguided righteousness, they allowed matters to escalate unchecked.

Those men, in their stupor or malice, hurled two flaming bottles through the second-floor windows. In moments, the upper hall was ablaze, and my dear children were trapped. I attempted to reach them, but the flames were too strong and drove me back. By the time the fire brigade arrived, the upper floor of the house was near consumed. My Bronwyn and my brave Kay were carried out alive, though terribly injured. My three other dear souls had perished. I remained with Bronwyn and Kay during their long struggle at St. Elizabeth's Hospital, praying for their deliverance. For a time, the physicians held out some hope, but the burns and the smoke were too grievous to overcome. Bronwyn slipped away at dawn on the fifteenth day. Kay endured a little longer, though she never regained her voice. She passed on the twenty-third, with her hand in mine.

It consoles me to believe that they died in innocence and courage, and I trust that God, in His infinite mercy, received them gently. I am left now with only my youngest, little Winnie, who clings to me with a tenderness that breaks and sustains me in equal measure.

Before you departed, you placed a small silver pistol in my hands, urging me to keep it for protection. I confess I had never touched such a thing before, nor did I have occasion to use it. Yet I am grateful to possess it still. It shall remain in my keeping as a token of your friendship and of the faith you placed in my work. More than that, I regard it now as a safeguard for my dear Winnie, whose safety is my only earthly purpose.

Please accept my profound gratitude for your solicitude, and know that your goodness has not been forgotten in this sorrowing home.

With deepest respect,
Irene Slattery

~

Trinh walked into the Homicide Unit at Roxbury Crossing, looking a bit too smug for Santos's liking.

"Good, you're still here," she said.

"I'm in no rush," he said. "My mother-in-law's still at the house. What's with you? You win the lottery?"

"Better. One of the patrol guys found something. And I never have to go back to that fucking warehouse ever again."

He had his feet up on the desk, glasses on top of his head, and didn't look like he wanted to tax himself by reading something with small print.

"Just tell me."

"It's the final coroner's report from 1944 on the two nuns and one cat found dead at the Our Lady of the Preservation Convent. Bottom line: blood, urine, and organ levels had astronomical levels of arsenic. They were poisoned."

"Damn. Five murdered nuns," he said.

"Are you going to listen to the eggheads now?" she said.

"It's weird as fuck, but it doesn't change anything. It's still not enough to get a search warrant."

~

Trinh was writing up a report on the arsenic cases while Santos was getting his coat on. He'd gotten the all-clear that his mother-in-law had gone home.

When his phone rang, he said, "You're not going to believe it. It's Donovan again."

"Put it on speaker," she said.

"Professor, how can I help you?" Santos said with an attitude.

"Remember, you said we needed something that tied Eva Nevins directly to the murder weapon?"

"I do remember."

"Well, I'm calling to tell you we can't do that."

"Well, thanks anyway for the call," Santos said, looking bemused.

"But we can tie the murder weapon directly to her grandmother. Can I text you what we found? It's photos of the original letter from a Conan Doyle archive in England."

Santos waited for it to come through, read it with his partner over his shoulder like a parrot, and said, "Now we've got enough for a warrant. You write it up, and I'll try and find a judge."

CHAPTER TWENTY-SIX

1922, Brighton, Massachusetts

As the taillights of Sir Arthur Conan Doyle's hired motorcar faded into the darkness, the crowd surged. Some men, a couple of shots short of being paralytically drunk, staggered down the road after it. A clamor rose up—cheers, mostly. Some demonstrators started to leave; others persisted, aiming their ire at those who remained inside the darkening house.

Irene stood at her sitting-room window, her eyes fixed on the dark shapes lingering on the street. Some of the nuns must have departed because the singing was less insistent. She was caught in a moment between pride and irritation—pride in Sir Arthur's admiration for her work, irritation that the mob had truncated his stay.

She turned at her youngest child's whimpering. Kay had let little Winnie come down the stairs.

Winnie stood in her nightdress, small and sorrowful, rubbing her eyes with the back of her hand. She had been crying. The older children wanted to stay up for a while to talk and play. Winnie wanted sleep, or perhaps comfort from the scary voices and shadows. Irene sank heavily onto the sofa and let the girl climb onto her lap, where she stroked her hair and whispered reassurances.

Winnie pressed herself against Irene's bosom, looking up with damp eyes.

"I still hear them," she said.

"They will leave soon. There is nothing more to see."

Crowds sometimes take on a life of their own. This one didn't seem to know whether it was living or dying. Although it had thinned by half, the remaining elements grew bolder. The most fervent nuns stayed on, belting out new hymns in defiance of one of the neighbors who leaned out a window, threatening to call the police if they didn't shut up. A couple of priests kept their placards waving in solidarity. Drunken men got drunker and louder, so much so that Irene left Winnie on the sofa and returned to the window. An electric street light atop a pole across the street cast shadows over the wall of women, their black-and-white habits pressed against one another. Her stomach churned with bitterness at these closed-minded, pious ladies.

Go away, she thought. *You've done enough tonight.*

She was tempted to open the window and demand to know what gave them the right to stand in judgment of her. She wanted to ask whether they imagined themselves exempt from human decency. Instead, she returned to Winnie and smoothed her hair.

"You need your bed."

"Can't I stay with you?"

"All right, my sweet. Let me put more coal on the fire."

She stoked the cast-iron stove, laid Winnie's head on a pillow, and placed a blanket over her shoulders and up around her ears to dampen the foolishness outside.

Irene returned to the parlor to straighten the remnants of the séance. A faint odor of candle smoke clung to the curtains. She blew the candles out and returned them to their proper place. It was then that she noticed a shawl under Mrs. Wiggin's chair.

"Oh dear. What a shame," she said, gathering it up and folding it carefully.

When she moved toward the hall, her arm brushed against her

bulging hip pocket. She reached inside and felt the small silver revolver and box of bullets that Sir Arthur had pressed into her hands as he whispered, "For your protection."

She had never touched a gun, and couldn't imagine ever firing one, but it felt like a protective talisman bequeathed by a great man.

She quickly climbed the stairs, put an ear to the bedroom door, and heard that the children were still awake.

"Go to your rooms, boys and girls," she called through the door. "I'll be back up in five minutes. Kay, get them brushing and washing, please."

She relied on her oldest daughter. When Irene's husband fell in the Meuse-Argonne offensive in the waning days of the Great War, Kay's childhood ended, and she became the household's second mother. Irene was so very proud of her, and tonight, she resolved to praise her more and not take her for granted.

Irene retreated down the stairs and returned to Winnie. The child was already asleep, and she lowered her head to plant a gentle kiss on a peach-fuzz cheek.

A sudden noise made her raise her head.

It was a man whooping like a savage.

She crossed to the window and parted the curtain. A row of nuns stood firm in song, but the men around them had grown dangerously animated. Several waved bottles. One man lurched against another, laughing. She saw a flicker of fire rise briefly in the air, perhaps a match struck fiercely. The moment passed, and the two men stumbled away from the streetlight.

Irene's pulse quickened. She closed the drape and went to the front and rear doors, making sure she'd locked them properly. She was halfway across the kitchen when she heard the faint sound of glass breaking upstairs.

Her first thought was that the children—Vern especially—had been roughhousing and broken a lamp. But then, only a moment or two later, there was a second crash, louder, sharper, followed by a thump and a whoosh.

She heard a high-pitched scream—she knew each of her children's voices and cries. This was Bronwyn. Then Darlene screamed. Then, Vern.

She smelled smoke.

Her body reacted before her mind could form coherent thoughts. She raced up the stairs, shouting the children's names, and on the landing she saw fire blooming like a field of infernal flowers. The flames licked at the curling wallpaper and crawled across the ceiling. She tried to reach the children's bedroom, but the heat forced her back. She covered her face with her arm and attempted again, only to retreat as embers floated down, burning holes in her dress.

Inside the children's room, Kay looked in horror as flames, fanned by the wind blowing through the broken windowpane, consumed the curtains and a dresser. As her sisters and brother wailed, she tried to push open the door, but a wall of heat and fire made her slam it shut. Vern and Darlene were crying hysterically. Bronwyn had her hands pressed to her ears in panic. Sarah crawled toward the flaming window when Kay dragged her back and screamed as loudly as she had ever screamed.

"Mother! Help!"

The air was thickening by the second, as acrid smoke spread from burning wallpaper to the wood lath of the walls. Kay urged the younger children onto the floor, ripped the blanket off the bed, and beat it against the window to no avail.

There was nothing Irene could do. The hallway had become a tunnel of flame. Heat forced her halfway down the stairs, where she screamed out to Kay.

"Stay there! Wait for the firemen!"

The fire roared in answer.

She felt the revolver in her pocket, and although it was senseless, she raised her arm, pointing the weapon as if she could threaten the inferno.

"Mama!" Kay screamed. "We're trapped!"

Irene sobbed and tried again to climb toward the heat. She heard a beam cracking, and staggered backward, gasping, and that's when she heard Winnie crying out from the sitting room.

Kay gathered the children around. Her voice stayed remarkably steady, even as the room filled with smoke.

"Come here," she said, spreading the blanket on the floor. "Pretend it's a tent. We're all going to crawl under it until the firemen come and get us."

Irene heard another groan overhead as the floorboards began to fail. She ran to the sitting room, scooped up Winnie, and carried her toward the front door. She hesitated at the threshold, torn between staying and fleeing, and shouted into the night for help.

The nuns were screaming and pointing at the second floor. The drunkards, including the men who had flung burning bottles through a bedroom and hall window, had already fled. One of the priests still on scene ran toward Irene, dragging her off the porch, pleading to know if there was anyone else inside.

"My children," she gasped. "Upstairs."

He ran a short way down the hall, had a look up the stairs at the burning landing, and retreated.

"I'm sorry—there's nothing—"

Another priest ran to the nearest neighbor and told them to call the fire department. The man of the house got on the party line, yelled at someone to get the hell off the line, and had the operator ring through to Engine Company 29 and Ladder Company 11 on nearby Chestnut Hill Avenue.

The first ladder and motorized pumper trucks arrived within five minutes. One of Irene's neighbors tried to get her to come inside with little Winnie, but she refused to leave the lawn, standing mutely as the firemen set their hoses and connected to the nearest hydrant.

Water arced toward the flames from a pair of hoses. What was left of the original crowd retreated to a safe distance where the nuns who remained knelt in prayer. Irene held Winnie to her chest, staring at them with black eyes, until she could bear it no longer.

"Go away! Leave us alone! My children are in there! You did this!"

The firemen entered the house from the ground level and the second story, beating back flames with their hoses.

Minutes passed in disjointed fragments of noise and motion. A fire chaplain appeared at Irene's side, and she collapsed to her knees.

"Ma'am, your neighbor here wants to take the child inside her house," the chaplain said.

"She stays with me."

At last, after an eternity of smoke and water and ash, two firemen emerged from the inferno carrying small shapes. They shouted for blankets. And an ambulance. Onlookers surged forward.

Irene rose unsteadily, watching as the firemen laid the children on the cool grass. She saw Bronwyn first. Her face was smeared with soot, but she was breathing. The fireman beside her was weeping.

The other figure lay motionless. Then Kay's chest rose in a shallow spasm.

Irene stumbled forward, taking Winnie with her. She sank beside Kay, touching her burned and brittle hair. Kay's eyes fluttered but didn't open.

"The others—" Irene asked the nearest fireman.

The big man dropped to his knees and shook his head.

They tried to move her back so they could work, but she refused to budge, and when the ambulance crew arrived with a stretcher and placed Bronwyn and Kay side by side on it, Irene climbed into the ambulance and rode with them to St. Elizabeth's Hospital.

She didn't leave their sides for two months until the first of their funerals.

CHAPTER TWENTY-SEVEN

The next morning at 8 o'clock sharp, Detective Santos, flanked by his partner and a posse of other detectives from the Homicide Unit, pounded on Eva Nevins' front door and shouted, "Boston Police with a search warrant! Eva Nevins, come to the door!"

When there was no reply, he repeated his command.

Just as he was debating forcing entry, the door slowly opened, and a young woman in pajamas looked out.

"Hello?" she said. "What's going on?"

Santos recognized the pierced face of Eva's young protegee.

"We've got a search warrant for the property. Where's Eva Nevins?"

"She's not here."

"Where is she?"

"None of your business."

"Wrong answer," Santos said, pressing forward. "We're coming in."

"This is private property!"

He brandished the warrant on a clipboard. "I'm giving you a lawful order. Step aside or we'll put you in cuffs for obstruction."

The detectives flooded the hall, moving Felicia back as if she were a piece of flotsam caught in the tide.

"I'm asking you again," Santos said. "Where is she?"

This time, she answered. "She's in the hospital. She felt sick yesterday, so I came over. She had bad stomach pains last night. I called an ambulance. They took her to Mass General."

"So, why are you here?" Trinh asked.

"It was late, so I stayed."

"Maria, call over to MGB and see if she's there," Santos said. Then, turning to the young woman, "It's Miss King, right? Miss King, you need to leave the property while we conduct our search."

Felicia got stroppy with him. "You can't kick me out. Eva said I could stay."

"This piece of paper says I can have you removed during our search. It's your decision—leave voluntarily, or you'll be detained and put in the back of a police car."

"Can I at least go upstairs to get my clothes?"

Santos told one of the female detectives to go with her.

Suddenly, Felicia said. "Is that a body cam?"

"Everything's being recorded," he said.

"Record this, asshole," she said, opening her shirt, exposing pierced nipples and a chest full of black tattoos—a riot of magical sigils. "See you on YouTube."

"Keeping it classy," Santos said. "Get dressed, Miss King, and hit the road."

Santos assigned three teams of two, one to cover the ground floor, another, the second floor, and the third, the attic, basement, and garage. The attic/basement/garage team started in on him, asking whether the department would pay for dry cleaning.

"Find something, and I'll sign the requisition," he deadpanned.

Trinh reappeared. "Eva was admitted at 2 a.m.," she said. "She's listed as critical."

Felicia came down the stairs fully clothed, grabbed her coat from the rack, and at the door, said, "The poor woman's in the hospital. She's probably dying. You have no idea what she's been through," she shouted, her voice cracking, before the bravado returned. "You should be ashamed of yourselves."

"All right," Santos told his people, "let's get moving. It's a big house. You find anything remotely of interest, give me or Maria a shout. Eyes on the prize. We need to figure out how an old woman in a wheelchair managed to kill five people."

Santos started in the séance parlor, opening the heavy curtains to let in the morning light. The room was sparsely decorated, and there weren't many places to search, so he wrapped it up quickly.

Before he exited, he had a staring contest with the old photo of Arthur Conan Doyle hanging over the mantel and said, "How's it going, Piggy? Should have held onto your fucking gun."

The living room was potentially more fertile ground, and he began opening drawers and cabinets and pulling books from their shelves. His mood usually dictated how a search went. If he was feeling mellow, he was neat and respectful. If he was angry, he wasn't. He was angry as hell at Eva Nevins, so he trashed the place.

When Santos got to the kitchen, another detective had already started removing pots and pans and placing them in neat piles on the counter.

"Christ, John, you're gonna take all day like this," Santos said, pulling out a drawer and dumping cutlery on the floor.

"Sure thing, Zé. You want it rough, I'll give you rough," he said, scattering a drawerful of utensils. "There was a piece of paper next to the toaster, if it's any interest.

Santos looked at the note scribbled on the back of a used heating oil company envelope.

Sister Elisabetta Celestino
12/4, Hynes Auditorium, 11-12

"It's for something today," Santos told the detective. "Bag it, and we'll figure it out later."

The morning dragged on, and Santos was getting frustrated. He did a whip around to the other floors, and no one was having any luck. He found Trinh in Eva's bedroom, with a pile of old-lady underwear on the bed.

"I need you downstairs," he said.

"Why?"

"I just started on the room across from the kitchen. It's an office. There's more filing cabinets and papers in there than I can stomach. You're the queen of files. Go for it."

"Seriously?"

"Do I look like I'm kidding?"

She tossed him an ample bra. "Then this is all yours."

He swatted it away like he'd been attacked by a rabid bat.

"By the way," she said. "Eva's a diabetic. There's insulin in her medicine chest."

"Interesting," Santos said, "but it doesn't prove shit. Half the world's got diabetes—at least half of my family. We'll need more than that to tie her to those murders."

~

TWO HOURS into the morning's search, Santos entered Eva's walk-in closet, a claustrophobic hanging garden of perfumed gowns, dresses, and handbags, and started pulling at fabric and tossing garments onto the bedroom rug. When he was done denuding the space, he glowered at the mountain of clothes and bags he'd made. He was tempted to move on, but a voice in his head told him he'd have reamed out a rookie cop for not checking the hand bags.

He went for the modern ones first, and found tissues, spare change, and the occasional tube of lipstick. The older bags looked like museum pieces; he guessed they were family heirlooms, like some of the vintage sequined evening gowns he'd ripped off their hangers. He snatched a beaded evening bag from the pile and had a look at the elaborate floral beadwork of silver, black, sapphire, emerald, and ruby-colored glass beads with a hanging fringe. When he pulled open the drawstring pouch and reached into it, he was confused by what he felt, because his hand filled with more beads, and he wondered if there was a smaller bag inside.

When he pulled his hand out, he dropped to his knees onto the clothes mountain and opened his throat to shout, "Maria! Get up here! Maria?"

Trinh came bounding up the stairs and looked at him quizzically until he opened his gloved hand to reveal a wad of rosaries.

"Oh, hell no!" she exclaimed. "How many?"

He untangled them and counted them out in front of her.

"One, two, three—" He laid them out on a dresser, one by one. "—four, five, six—"

Maria leaned over the dresser.

"—seven, eight, nine, ten!"

"Lemme see," she said, putting on a pair of gloves.

"How do we know these are from our vics?" he said. "Do they label rosaries? I left my glasses in the car."

"No idea," she said, inspecting one. "No markings on this one." She kept looking and exclaimed, "This one's got SIS engraved on the back of the crucifix. Hang on—this one, too. And this one!"

"What's SIS?" he asked.

"It's got to be Sisters of the Immaculate Shepherd. The three nuns shot in 1944. It's their order."

"Jackpot," Santos said.

She kept looking at the others. "Okay, this one's got a tiny brass tag on it. The writing's too small. Let me blow it up."

She laid it down, took a picture of the tag, and magnified it as far as it would go.

"To Kristin, From Mom," she said. "These are Kristin LaMattina's rosary beads."

"That sick fuck kept trophies of her kills," Santos said.

"So did her mother," Trinh said.

"But who pulled the trigger?" Santos said. "It wasn't Eva. We don't think it was Malloy. Or metal-face Felicia. Anything in the files?"

"Family and household paperwork. Deeds, repair records, insurance documents, tons of letters, bills—you name it."

"Keep at it. I'm going to take a victory lap and see how the others are doing."

Another hour passed. Santos was in one of the guest bedrooms when his phone rang. He glanced at it and muttered, "What the hell?" Answering it, he said, "Why are you calling me? I'm upstairs."

"Because I've been yelling my head off and you haven't answered. You're not the only one who can find shit."

He hurtled down the stairs to the office, where Trinh had a yellowed folder open on the desk.

"It's papers from a Boston adoption agency."

"Who's adopted?" Santos asked.

"In 1963, Winifred Nevins, Eva's mother, applied to this agency to adopt a child. She was rejected a few times because she was a single mother, but in 1964, they finally agreed to let her adopt a nine-year-old girl they couldn't place elsewhere. Her name was Mary Adamos, who'd been in an orphanage for years. In 1965, her name was legally changed to Mary Nevins.'

"Is she still alive?"

"I don't know, but look at this," Trinh said. "I've got a copy of her marriage certificate. In 1975, at the age of twenty, she married someone named George Carey. It gives his occupation as a truck driver and hers as a house cleaner."

"Why was she hard to adopt?" he asked. "Her age?"

"The report from the orphanage says she was, quote-unquote, slow. The kid wasn't all there, I guess."

"I don't get it," Santos said. "Winifred Nevins is a single mother with a daughter who's recently paralyzed, and she decides to adopt a kid who's not all there? What was she doing—adopting another daughter or a mother's little helper?"

"I don't know, Zé. I'll keep looking. If she's alive, she'd be seventy-one."

It was 11:30 now, and Santos was hoping to wrap things up before lunchtime. He made a pass through the house to see if the others were finishing and found the team that pulled the dirty work in a dank basement, packed solid with junk.

"Anything?" he called out.

The space was lit by a couple of low-wattage, naked bulbs, and the two detectives looked miserable.

"I've never seen so much crap in my life," the female detective said. "It's just old furniture, broken appliances, and rusty car parts. It's a waste of time."

"I hear you," Santos said, looking around at the mess. "Attic? Garage?"

"The attic's pretty clean, surprisingly," the male detective said. "The garage, not so much. It makes junkyards look good. There's cans of old paint everywhere, bug spray, pesticides."

"Oh yeah?"

"It looked like someone's been into them recently," he said.

"How do you know?" Santos asked.

"One of the cans is sitting on a brown puddle and something's running down the side."

"Where is it?"

"On a metal shelf. Near the fuse box."

A front had blown in during the morning, and it was raining hard now. Santos pulled his jacket to his neck, sprinted to the detached garage, and pulled the door open. He squeezed past an old Buick on deflated tires that had to be sixty years old and found the metal shelf.

The can sitting on a brown puddle was rusty and filthy, but he made out a skull and crossbones. He put on another pair of gloves and dangled it by its handle. There was a wet brown streak running down one side, but it didn't seem to be leaking. That's when he noticed a funnel on the floor, wet with the same brown liquid.

He couldn't make out the label through all the grime, so he put the can onto the hood of the Buick and found an old rag to wipe it down.

~

ORCHARD-GUARD
LEAD ARSENATE SPRAY

Patented 1931 – Reg. U.S. Dept. of Agriculture
For Control of Codling Moth, Apple Maggot, and Other Orchard Pests
Active Ingredients:
Lead Arsenate ($PbHAsO_4$) 98%
Inert Ingredients 2%
Net Weight 5 LBS.
Prepared by:
New England AgroChem Co.
Woburn, Massachusetts

~

TRINH ANSWERED HER PHONE, "Zé, WHAT?"

"Arsenic!" he shouted. "There's arsenic in the garage, freshly poured. There's going to be a poisoning!"

CHAPTER TWENTY-EIGHT

1964

THE GIRL WAS PLAIN IN EVERY WAY—PLAIN FACE, NEITHER attractive nor ugly, plain, mousy hair, plain body of average height for her age, doughy, but not fat.

Winnie Nevins paid the taxi driver and said, "This is your home now. What do you think?"

The girl was clutching the small bag that held all her earthly possessions. She raised her head to take in the sprawling Victorian house surrounded by majestic trees.

"It's good."

"Is that all you can say?"

"It's big."

"All right, then. Let's go meet your new sister."

Inside, Eva heard the taxi and was nervously waiting in the hall. Her mother had fussed with her hair and laid out her best dress before she left for the orphanage. Eva had seen a picture of the girl stapled to her orphanage records, but she had no idea what she was like or how her presence would change her world.

The door opened, and she was there.

Eva's animation and excitement were quenched at first sight.

The girl's expression was dull and unsmiling, and she made her way down the hall with the halting cadence of someone being led to the gallows.

If Eva could walk again, she knew she'd be running and skipping—making good use of God's gift—not plodding like this girl.

Winnie pried the bag from the girl's tight grasp and said, "Eva, this is your new sister, Mary. Mary, this is your new sister, Eva. Mary, go and kiss her."

Mary took a halting step forward and stared at the older girl.

"Why are you in the chair?" were her first words to her.

"My legs don't work anymore."

"Go on, kiss her," Winnie said.

The girl didn't budge. "No."

"Why not?"

"I don't want to."

"It's okay," Eva said. "You don't have to. Do you want to see your room?"

Mary nodded.

"Come on, then."

Kay rolled herself to the stairs, and Mary watched with a gaze devoid of curiosity as she transferred herself to the chair lift. When the loud motor began moving her, Mary climbed, too, keeping a step behind.

At the top of the stairs, Eva transferred to her upstairs wheelchair.

"I've got strong arms," she said, hoping to spark a conversation, but there was no spark, and Mary stayed mute.

She rolled into the third bedroom, and the girl followed.

"This is your room. That one's mine. The one at the end is Mama's. We share a bathroom, so you can't hog it. How old are you?"

She knew the answer, but she wanted to hear the girl say it.

"Nine." The girl was looking at the big bed with a cascade of fancy pillows.

"I'm fifteen. You can lie on it, if you like."

Winnie came in and admonished Mary for lying down.

"Why are you lounging? There's a lot to do." She counted the chores out. "You've got to put your things away, organize your little shelf in the bathroom, then help me with lunch. You'll be helping with all the meals. I'm a busy woman. I've got clients coming for sittings at all hours. Afterwards, we'll go to the supermarket. Then we'll teach you what you need to know to take care of your sister, Eva. She gets on pretty well, but she needs help with certain delicate things. In the evening, you can watch a television show with us. Then, and only then, young lady, you can lounge on your bed."

"What about school, Mama?" Eva asked.

"She'll go to Winship like you did. I'm going to register her."

Mary was standing now. "I don't want to go to school."

"Well, you have to. It's the law," Winnie said. "You've got to go till you're sixteen."

"How long is that?" Mary asked.

"You're nine," Kay said patiently. "Sixteen take away nine. How many years is that?"

The girl stared blankly.

"Do you know how to add and subtract?" Kay asked.

Mary shook her head.

"Well, they said she was simple," Winnie said, "and I guess she is."

~

1965

When Eva returned to her bedroom after her first séance with Kay, Mary wandered across the hall from her room.

"What were you doing down there?" the ten-year-old asked.

"I had my first sitting. Mama taught me how to talk to dead people. I have an aunt named Kay. She's nice."

"She's dead?"

"She died in this room."

"When?"

"A long time ago."

"Will Mama teach me how to talk to dead people?"

Winnie had come upstairs and was at the door, listening.

"Child, you will never do what Eva can do. You don't have the gift. It would be like trying to teach a chimpanzee how to recite the Gettysburg Address."

Mary teared up. "What's the Gettysburg Address?"

"You see?" Winnie said. "That's what I'm talking about. Where are you with supper? Did you peel the potatoes like I asked?"

"Not yet."

"Well, why are you still here? Go on, then. Your sister has homework to do. Eva, here's a fresh notebook to record your memories in case Kay comes to you at night."

"Can I have a notebook, too?" Mary asked.

"Notebooks are for special girls," Winnie said. "Now go do your chores!"

1978

WINNIE WAS AN OLD SIXTY-FOUR. High blood pressure and diabetes were rotting her body from within. She had suffered two strokes, one inconsequential, the other thickening her speech. Some of her clients were put off by her slurred diction and had stopped coming to her sittings, so she was pressing Eva into service.

Her daughter liked doing them and was popular with clients, but she only wanted to work on weekends. When she got home from typing all day at John Hancock Insurance, she was too tired and stiff for sittings. And she had read that you needed a license to be a medium in Boston, so she was worried about not having one. Winnie dismissed the concern out of hand, calling it ridiculous, like requiring a license to pray to God.

Mary was twenty-three with the battle-worn countenance of a young woman who'd been working full-time as a house cleaner since she left school at sixteen, and had to do most of the cooking and cleaning at home.

One night, over dinner, Mary said she had something to tell them.

"I'm getting married," she said.

It came completely out of the blue. They weren't even aware she'd been seeing someone.

Before Eva could start asking all the obvious questions, Winnie said, "That's absurd. You are not getting married. You don't even know any young men."

"I know George. He likes me and I like him."

"George who?" Winnie demanded.

"George Carey."

"Where did you meet this boy?"

"At the supermarket. He's a bagger. He always bags my groceries, and he smiles at me. George is going to be a truck driver. He got his license, so he asked me to marry him, and I said I would."

"Did you sleep with this boy?"

"No."

"You'd better tell me, young lady."

"I didn't sleep with George. He wants to. He's getting his own place. I'll live there with him."

"Well, I'm not having it. You can't get married."

Mary began to cry, and Eva reached over to console her.

"Why can't she get married, Mama? I'm sure George is nice."

"I'll tell both of you why," his mother said, spitting mad. "Eva is never getting out of that chair. She'll need help for life. No man is going to marry a woman in her situation. And I'm not getting any younger. I won't be around forever. I didn't rescue you from that horrible orphanage and give you my name and let you live in this wonderful house just to have you run off and shack up with a bagger in a supermarket."

"He's going to be a—" Mary protested.

"—or a truck driver," Winnie said. "I won't hear another word about it."

A week later, Mary got up early as usual and brought her mother her morning cup of tea in bed. Winnie was stone-cold dead. Mary invited George Carey to the funeral. Kay didn't much like him. He wasn't just rough around the edges—he was rough all over. On the day Mary moved out of the old house to go live with George, she promised Eva that she'd always be there for her.

"I hated Mama, but I love you," she said.

1982

"Big day," Eva said, looking up at the raw concrete of Boston City Hall from its broad, red-brick plaza.

"Ready?" Mary said.

Eva, dressed in pastel colors, looked demure and pretty. Mary always wore drab colors, and she spent little time on her appearance. She was a big-boned woman with a mottled complexion and perpetually red hands from cleaning products.

"I'm nervous, but I'm ready."

"You'll be smarter than everyone there," Mary said.

"Thank you for taking the day off to help me."

"George said I shouldn't have missed work."

"Well, thank George for me. Let's go in."

While they were attending the meeting of the Boston Licensing Board, where Eva presented her application for a license to tell fortunes for hire, the sun had come out and City Hall Plaza looked more inviting.

"We should celebrate!" Eva said. "Let's get lunch."

"Okay, but don't tell George," Mary said. "He'll say I should have gone back to work."

"I won't. And you don't tell him I gave you money for helping me today. That money's for you."

"I won't tell."

"Let's go to Quincy Market," Eva said. "They've got ramps."

Soon, they were sitting in the market's central rotunda eating Regina's pizza, and Eva couldn't stop smiling.

"Once I get my license, I'm going to start advertising for my sittings. Word of mouth is fine, but there's nothing like a good advertisement in the papers. And Yellow Pages! I'll put myself in the Yellow Pages, too. I truly believe that I can make a good enough living doing what I love, so I can ditch the secretarial work."

Mary was avoiding eye contact, and Eva asked what the matter was.

"I was scared to tell you."

"Tell me what?"

"I'm moving."

Kay put down her slice. "Moving where?"

"Indiana."

"What? Why?"

"George got a new job driving for a company in Indiana. He says he'll have more work because it's in the middle of the country. He says I can get a cleaning job anywhere."

"When would you move?"

"Two weeks."

Kay was shocked into speechlessness, and Mary began to cry.

"I knew you'd be mad."

"I'm not mad at you, silly. I'm just going to miss you, is all."

"Will you be all right?" Mary said, wiping her face with a napkin.

"I'm going to make good money now. If I need help around the house, I'll find someone. I know you don't like to write, but will you call?"

"Indiana is far. Those calls will be expensive. George won't like that."

"Then, I'll call you. I'm not going to lose contact with my only sister."

2023

Eva took a taxi to South Station and the elevator to the Greyhound terminal. Kind people treated her as the elderly, wheelchair-bound lady she was, offering to push her and helping her get to the right place, where she waited patiently for the bus from Indianapolis to arrive. She hardly recognized the heavy-haunched, slack-faced, gray-haired woman who approached her, wheeling a small suitcase. She hadn't seen Mary in forty years, although they had continued to talk at least once a month, and Mary wasn't one to send pictures or post on Facebook.

Mary spotted her first, because how many old women in wheelchairs were waiting for her bus?

"Hello, sister," Eva said, accepting a hand.

"Hello, sister," Mary said.

George had a heart attack while driving a big rig and drove it over a bridge into a river in Kentucky. It was in the news. Eva persuaded her to return to Boston, telling her she was getting old and needed her help.

"All these years, you didn't need my help. Why do you need my help now? Are you sick?"

"A little. They found a spot on my lung, but I'm okay at present."

"You still talk to Kay?"

"A day doesn't go by."

Eva sent her money for her ticket and expenses and rented her a studio apartment on Warren Street, less than a mile from the old house on Academy Hill Road. It would have been cheaper and easier if she had wanted to move in with her, but that was a nonstarter.

"I'll never live there again," Mary half-shouted into the telephone. "I want to live on my own."

Eva didn't press the matter. She heard the panic in her voice. She was a witness to Mary's traumatic childhood in that house and carried the guilt of not shielding her from the worst of Winnie's cruelty.

Eva showed her the ground-floor apartment and gave her the keys. It was handicapped-accessible, although she doubted she'd visit much. She stocked it with food and bought a few cheerful decorations to brighten the furniture's monochromatic colors, but Mary, as overwhelmed by the relocation as she had been the day she left the orphanage, could only sit on the bed and stare.

"Good news," Eva said. "I got you a job."

"Doing what?"

"Cleaning, of course."

"I'm good at that."

"I know you are. I made a resume for you and sent it to a good company. They hired you sight unseen."

"What will I clean?"

"It's a mixture—some residential properties and some facilities like nursing homes. The cleaning company has a contract with the Diocese of Boston."

"What's that?"

"You know—the Catholic Church. Nuns and priests."

"I don't like nuns and priests. Mother didn't like them."

"I know that. But I think it will be perfect, and Kay thinks so, too."

The Present

Kay invited Mary over for dinner, cooked her a nice meal, and served it in the formal dining room. She had never seen Mary looking so tired and worn out.

"Why are we eating in here?" she asked. "We never eat in here."

"I wanted it to be special."

"Why?"

"I'll tell you, but first, I'm worried about you. I think you're working too hard."

"My boss tells me where to go and I go. She says I'm her best worker."

"I'm sure you are. Have you thought about retiring?"

"No."

"You should. You've been working hard your whole life. You're what now—seventy-one?"

"You're older than I am. You're still working."

"But I enjoy my job."

"I like cleaning, too."

"All right. I'm just saying. It's an option to consider. This is what I want to tell you, Mary. My health hasn't been good."

"Your diabetes?"

"It's the cancer that's the problem."

"Are you going to die?"

"I'm afraid I am—at least that's what my doctors say. It won't be long now. I want to make you aware of certain arrangements."

"Okay—"

"I've got a will—you know what that is, right?"

"I know."

"Well, in that will, I'm leaving everything to you—this house and all the money I've saved."

"I don't want to live here."

"I hope you'll reconsider, Mary. It's been in the family for a very long time. I'd hate to think that someone other than family would be living here."

"I'm not from the family."

"Of course you are. Don't say that. Mother was difficult, I'll admit that, but she's been gone for a very long time. Will you think about it, Mary?"

"Could I have your room?"

"Yes, you can have my room. I want to tell you about a young lady I've been working with. Her name is Felicia. She has the gift."

"For dead people?"

"That's right. She's ready to be a medium. When I pass, I'd like her to be able to use the parlor and help my clients keep speaking to their loved ones. She would pay you part of what she earns—like rent. Would that be all right with you?"

"Yes."

"Now, one more thing. There's one last job I need you to do for me."

"Killing people, like Mama did?"

"Nuns. Only nuns."

Eva had test-fired Arthur Conan Doyle's old pistol in the basement and taught Mary how to use it. She was the cleaner at the Wellspring House and had the house key. After she shot the nuns, Eva had her hide the gun and bullets in Father Malloy's house during a cleaning visit. And she gave her a syringe filled with her insulin to inject into the IVs of the nuns at the Holy Name Nursing Home, where she was a cleaner.

"You said five nuns had to die," Mary said. "I killed five nuns."

"I know, but when I'm gone, there won't be anyone left with blood ties to avenge what the nuns did to our family. Kay wants more to die. One last job, Mary, and you won't have to kill again. When it's time for you to die, you'll have so many grateful people waiting for you on the other side."

"What do I have to do?"

"I got you a temporary job with the caterers for the big convention center in Boston. There's a convention of nuns next week. You'll be one of the food servers. I'll give you something to put in the food—a poison. When Mother was young, she killed five nuns—one for each child who died, just like you did. Mother is so proud of you. Maybe, one day she'll tell you herself when you're on the other side."

"I don't want to see her there," Mary said, getting upset. "I never want to see her again."

Kay wheeled herself over to Mary and tugged at her arm until her head was close enough to plant a kiss.

"Don't worry about that. I'll be there and I'll make sure that mother never bothers you again."

CHAPTER TWENTY-NINE

Cal steered his car into the parking complex under the Prudential Center. Eli hadn't said much during the drive, and he had left her to her silence. When he pulled into a space and turned the motor off, they both sat belted for a few moments.

"You okay?" he asked.

"Yes, fine."

"You sure? You're not coming down with something, are you?"

She shook her head, released her seatbelt, and adjusted her silk scarf.

He didn't think she'd be nervous giving a speech to a hall of nuns. This was someone who had brought the United Nations General Assembly to their feet.

"Do we have to stay underground, or can we get some fresh air?" she asked.

"We can go outside."

They walked the short stretch of Boylston Street through the morning cold. The sky had that pale, undecided color Boston carried in early December, neither silver nor white, and the air smelled faintly of salt and car exhaust.

"You're going to be magnificent," he said.

She let the compliment slide. "I want to get this right. This is the first time I'll be speaking from on the outside. The speech will be live-streamed. A dozen officials in the Curia will dissect it, and by dinner time, they'll have a report in Pope John's inbox. I want to make my points, but be respectful of the institution."

"You always did that well on the inside."

"This feels different. I'll go farther than I did when I was an insider."

She hadn't shared the text with him; he hadn't asked to see it.

"You know where to draw the line."

"I hope I drew it well," she replied. "This group is important. They actually believe change is possible."

"Your life has made them believe it."

She gave him a look. "You're overstating."

He laughed and play-punched her shoulder. "And you're underselling."

Inside the Hynes's broad lobby, directional signs and welcome banners lined the walls. The Leadership Conference of Women Religious had filled the place with color. Tables were set with pamphlets about renewal, reform, service, justice, and the future of the Church. Exhibitors drank coffee from paper cups as they set up their books and brochures for the day. The registration desks were busy, but the atmosphere felt buoyant, like a gathering of women who had decided they would not apologize for wanting a seat at the table.

Eli was immediately recognized, and several nuns clamored forward to say something or ask for her autograph. She obliged them like the gracious celebrity she was. Her business attire was in keeping with the gathering. Almost all the members of the group eschewed the traditional habit. Ever since the Second Vatican Council, most women in the LCWR had opted to discontinue traditional garb in favor of modern attire, although some of the older women chose modified habits.

Eli was greeted by a volunteer in a navy blazer with the conference logo stitched on her pocket and guided them through the cavernous Veterans' Memorial Auditorium, which was rapidly filling with conferees. In a backstage prep room, Eli was given a speaker's badge and a conference packet, and Cal received a visitor's badge. Sister Lisetta Houseman, the conference president, bounded in and made a straight shot for Eli, effusively thanking her for blessing their event with her presence. Cal was pretty sure he'd never seen a more excited person.

"This is the largest attendance at a national event we've ever had," Houseman said. "Twelve hundred women! We only had eight hundred last year. You are a rock star, Madame Secretary."

"Hardly," Eli said, embarrassed. "I'd like to introduce a colleague of mine at the Harvard Divinity School, Cal Donovan."

After a brief exchange where the president mentioned she'd heard of him, she turned her attention back to Eli. Cal couldn't have been happier playing second fiddle.

"If you have a thumb drive, we can load your speech onto the teleprompter," Houseman said.

"I don't like them so much," Eli said. "I have my text."

"Old school!" the president said. "I love it. All right, we'll give the ladies another few minutes to take their seats, then we'll start at eleven-fifteen. You're still willing to do a question and answer session from the stage?"

"Yes, of course."

"Afterwards, we'll have lunch in Ballroom B. Can you join us, Professor Donovan?"

"I've got to peel away after the speech to interview someone for a faculty position. I'll be back after lunch to ferry the rock star to Cambridge."

"Aren't you the best chauffeur!"

"I'll be front and center, Eli," he whispered to you. "Knock 'em dead."

~

In the main kitchen off the ballrooms, the caterers were getting ready for the luncheon service. Deliverymen brought carts of prepared food up the elevator to the storage room, where the catering manager, a hard-boiled woman checked them against the manifest.

"I see the chicken and fish mains. Where the hell's the beef?"

One of the delivery guys said, "I think it's coming with the salad and sides."

"It better be. Okay, ladies, I need you to get these heated. It's a cold day." She called her assistant manager over. "Debbie, make sure they put the trays in the right buffet warmers. They're labeled, but who knows if the new girls are gonna pay attention?"

One of the catering company's regulars was an open, friendly woman who tried to make small talk with one of the temps.

"Hi. I'm Theresa."

The big-boned woman with chafed hands and gray hair answered uncomfortably. "I'm Mary."

"I haven't seen you before."

"I've never been here before."

"We have three events on the same day, so they had to hire temps. How much are they paying you?"

"I don't know."

"How could you not know?"

"I don't know."

"You ever done catering before?"

She shook her head. "I'm a cleaner."

"Is that why your hands are like that?"

"Yes."

"We have to wear gloves anyway. I'll show you what to do."

"Okay, thanks."

"Do you like the aprons? They're new."

"I like them."

The woman pointed at the thermos in Mary's hand. "Whatcha got?"

"Coffee."

"You brought your own. That's smart. They give us coffee when we're finished, but it's not good coffee like from home. Okay, Debbie wants us to get the trays onto the warmers. Just do like I do."

CAL FOUND a seat in the middle aisle, five rows from the stage. The ballroom had the capacity for larger conventions, so they were using only the middle section which was full of murmuring, excited nuns. When Sister Houseman stepped to the podium, the chatter died down.

"Good morning, sisters," she said. "It is my privilege to introduce our keynote speaker, someone whose name you know. All of you have followed her work with admiration, some with astonishment, and all with a sense of possibility. She is a scholar, a leader, and a woman who has lived at the very heart, indeed, the pinnacle of the modern Church. Please welcome Sister Elisabetta Celestino, or I should say, Madame Secretary."

The applause crashed like a wave. Cal watched Eli stepping out, carrying herself with the same quiet confidence she displayed in the classroom. He felt his chest tighten with pride.

Eli thanked Houseman, then looked out at the sea of women.

"Welcome to Boston, my wonderful new home. We don't have the Coliseum and gladiators like my old home, but we have the Boston Garden and the Celtics," she began, earning a gentle laugh. "My theme today is witness. Specifically, what it means to be a witness to a changing Church, and how that work transforms us, whether we expect it or not."

She spoke slowly, without drama, with a manner of someone interested in clarity, not rhetoric. She talked about her early years in Rome, the joy of her formation, the beauty of communal prayer, and the call she had felt as a young woman, a graduate student in archaeology at the University of Rome. She spoke of her years as a teaching nun at a primary school before Pope Celestine called her to the Vatican to work as a pontifical archaeologist. She breezed through her progression of Vatican positions before Pope John XXIV shattered the glass ceiling by making her Secretary of State. And from that perch, she spoke of sitting at tables where she had once believed women would never be allowed.

She didn't gossip or indict. She told the truth simply.

"There were days when the work felt like sunlight in winter. A narrow warmth that reminded me of the goodness of my calling. And there were days when I felt the weight of the institution like a hand on my back, pushing me in a direction that was difficult to reconcile with the Gospel."

Women nodded and leaned forward.

"I learned," she said, "that institutions resist change not because they are wicked, but because they are afraid. They fear losing the stories they tell about themselves. They fear uncertainty. But the Gospels do not promise certainty. They promise truth."

~

SANTOS HUDDLED with his partner in Eva's small office.

"It's no good," Trinh said. "I can't log on with my personal phone. We've got to use the laptop in the car."

They ran to Santos's car and shivered until the heater kicked in.

Trinh swiveled the computer mount toward the passenger seat, logged onto the RMV database, and entered Mary's name and the social security number they found in Eva's file.

"Got her," she said. "Mary Carey, 122 Warren Street, Apartment 6. She doesn't have a driver's license, but she's got an ID card."

Mary's ID photo showed a dull-eyed, elderly lady with a sagging face, and Trinh snapped a picture of it.

"Where's Warren Street?" Santos said.

"Less than a mile from here."

Santos jumped out and called over to a couple of the detectives milling on Eva's porch.

"Get over to 122 Warren Street, Apartment 6. We're looking for a 71-year-old woman named Mary Carey. If she's there, bring her in for questioning. Maria's going to text you her photo."

He hurried back to the driver's seat and said. "Can you find out if she works anywhere?"

She logged onto the CLEAR Investigator Platform, navigated some menus, and soon had the answer.

"She's employed at a company called Archer Facility Services in Sommerville."

"What do they do?" Santos asked.

She Googled it and scrolled through the company's website. "They're a cleaning company that services residential and commercial customers. Blah, blah, blah—oh, shit!"

"What?"

"There's a customer list. One of them's the Diocese of Boston."

~

Eli was holding her audience in a spellbound silence. She talked about her difficult decision to leave the Vatican, described her move to Harvard, the joy of academic freedom, and the discovery of new forms of service. She spoke tenderly of her students, of their hunger to reconcile faith with the world as it actually existed, not as older generations imagined it.

And then she came to the part she had revised half a dozen times.

"I want to close with a reflection on the role of women in the Church," she said. "Not the role assigned to us, but the role already being lived by so many of you here. You lead hospitals, schools, parishes, and refugee centers. You carry out the works of mercy every day without fanfare. You do not need permission to do these things. You never have."

She let the words settle.

"My request of you," she said, "is simple. Do not apologize for your influence. Do not diminish the authority that comes from service. And do not allow yourselves to be convinced that a future with a greater voice for women is a threat to the Church. It is a gift to it."

A murmur moved through the room—part agreement, part emotion.

"I have lived inside the machinery of the Vatican. I have seen its strengths and its failures. And I believe, with all the faith I possess, that the Holy Spirit is moving us toward a Church in which women do not merely serve the mission. We shape it."

The applause rose instantly, a sound so loud it startled Cal. Women stood and wiped their eyes, and Cal felt something catch in his throat.

Houseman embraced Eli at the podium, a long, heartfelt hug, then turned to the microphone.

"Thank you, Madame Secretary! I have personally never been so moved! We have time for questions before lunch," she said. "Sister Elisabetta has generously agreed to take as many as we can manage."

Cal stood briefly, catching Eli's eye. He mouthed *brava*, then *magnificent*, but she squinted, not understanding. He shaped a heart with his hands, and at that, she smiled softly and nodded.

He slipped out of the row and hurried up the aisle. He'd have to hustle to make it on time for his lunch at the Harvard Club.

~

SANTOS TOOK a call and told his partner that no one was answering at Mary Carey's apartment.

She was on the phone, nodded, and said, "This is Detective Trinh from the Boston Police. I need to speak to the supervisor of one of your employees, Mary Carey. No, I can't hold. It's important." She told Santos, "They're transferring me."

Santos muttered, "We've got to—"

Trinh got through and introduced herself again, and put the call on speaker mode. "Who am I speaking to?"

"Carmen Lopez."

"You're Mary Carey's supervisor?"

"Her manager. What's wrong?"

"Nothing's wrong. We need to speak with her. Is she at work today?"

"She called in sick. She's not here."

"We checked her apartment. She's not there either."

"Well, I don't know where she is. If she's sick, maybe she's at the doctor."

"Your company has a contract with the Diocese of Boston. Does Mary work at any of the diocese properties?"

"That's all she does."

"Can you be more specific?"

"Let me get her roster. Hang on a sec. Okay, she cleans at Saint Columbkille Church in Brighton, Saint Anthony Parish in Allston, the Holy Name Nursing Home in Jamaica Plain—"

Santos drew a sharp breath.

"—a couple of private priest residences, and the Wellspring House in Roslindale, you know, the place where the nuns were shot."

Trinh's mouth opened.

"This is Sergeant Detective Santos. Let me ask you, ma'am. Did she ever work over at a Father Raymond Malloy's house in Dorchester?"

"Oh, yeah! She cleaned there. She's the one who found the poor man's body."

Trinh looked hard at Mary's photo and hit the mute button. "She's the fucking cleaner we interviewed, Zé!"

She unmuted and said, "Mrs. Lopez, you've been very helpful. It's important that we find Mary. Is there anyone at the company who might know where she is today? One of her co-workers?"

"I'll call one of the girls Mary's friendly with. Is she in trouble?"

"We just need to ask her a few questions."

"I'll call you back if I find anything out."

"Please. It's very important."

Santos and Trinh looked at each other, waiting to see who'd say something first.

It was Trinh. "Eva Nevins sat in her wheelchair and had her sister do the dirty work for her."

"Motive?" Santos asked.

"It's like the professors said—revenge for the fire that wiped out her family."

"It was a hundred years ago," Santos said.

Trinh shrugged. "I guess for her, it was like yesterday."

Her phone rang. "Trinh, here."

"This is Carmen Lopez. I just spoke to one of Mary's friends. Mary's not sick."

"She's not?"

"She called in sick, but she took another temp job today. She's not supposed to do that."

"Did her friend say where?"

"It's called Commonwealth Caterers."

Santos told Trinh to call Commonwealth Caterers while he tried to get an emergency warrant to break into Mary's apartment.

He was pacing on the sidewalk, waiting to connect to a judge's chambers, when Maria came running out of the car.

"Zé! I talked to the company. They're catering a lunch at the Hynes today. It's a convention of nuns. I looked it up. The main speaker is Elisabetta Celestino."

CHAPTER THIRTY

The Harvard Club of Boston's Georgian revival mansion on Commonwealth Avenue was only a third of a mile from the Convention Center, and Cal fast-walked it through the light rain in five minutes. He arrived at the Veritas Restaurant, greeted the maître d', and was shown to his table, where a man with a beard like a medieval scholar was waiting. The fellow was a star Associate Professor of Western Esotericism at the University of Michigan, and HDS was keen to poach him. He'd arrived the night before, stayed at the club, and had a day of on-campus interviews ahead of him.

"Brian, sorry, I'm late," Cal said. "I was watching one of our professors giving a speech at a national convention, and it ran a little late."

"No problem, Cal. I've had a luxuriously lazy morning. I'd forgotten how much I liked Boston."

"Music to my ears," Cal said. "Boston is a recruiter's ace in the hole." He glanced at the menu, and when they'd ordered, he said, "So, at Princeton you studied under my old pal, Milton Hartsfield."

"Oh! I didn't know that you and Milton knew each other."

"Let me tell you something about Milton you probably don't know and he probably doesn't want you to know—"

~

SANTOS AND TRINH were both trying to reach someone at the management or security offices at the Hynes, but it was lunchtime and all they got was voicemail.

"Get in the car," Santos said.

"It's going to take us a quarter of an hour to get there even with lights and siren," Trinh said.

"It'll take forever if we stay here," he said.

With siren blaring, he gunned his car down Chestnut Hill Avenue and made a screeching right onto Washington Street, heading toward town.

"Call the nun," he said.

"Celestino?"

"Who else?"

"I don't have her mobile."

"Call her office, for fuck's sake, and get it!"

"Okay, okay."

She reached the HDS main number, identified herself, and said she needed Professor Celestino's number due to an emergency. She was shuttled to an admin who was reluctant to hand out her private info over the phone.

Trinh lost it and screamed, "Listen to me! This is a life-or-death situation! I know she's at the Hynes Center. There's a credible threat to her life. If you don't fork it over, you're going to have to live with the consequences for the rest of your life."

"Christ! All right. Here it is," the admin said. "Do you want Professor Donovan's, too?"

"Why him?"

"Because he's with her."

~

Debbie, the assistant manager at Commonwealth Caterers, had her regular employee, Theresa, and the temp, Mary, wheel the food trays to the row of serving tables at the rear of Ballroom B.

"Theresa, you know how to stage them," she said. "Show her, then help me set up the coffee and dessert service."

Theresa patiently explained the order: salad and bread trays first, then the chicken, fish, and beef entrees, and finally rice, potatoes, and mixed vegetables.

"Got it?" she asked.

"I think so," Mary said.

Theresa noticed her thermos on the cart and asked her why it was there.

"I didn't want anyone to take it."

Theresa laughed. "It must be good coffee. Maybe you'll give me a cup later."

Mary vigorously shook her head. "You can't have any."

Theresa soured and walked off, saying, "All right. Be that way."

Alone in the ballroom, Mary played Eva's instructions in her head.

Pour a cup of liquid into each tray of food and give it a good stir.

Don't worry about getting caught out. It doesn't smell or have a taste.

It works pretty fast. Try to leave once they start getting sick.

She did what her sister wanted. The creamed chicken and beef stew were easy to mix. The baked fish confused her because the fillets were fragile, so she just splashed the pesticide over them.

When Theresa reappeared, she lifted each cover, checking the order of presentation. "Oh, dear, you've got the salad on the wrong end. They get their salad first. Help me shift every tray down one." When they were done, she adjusted the Sterno flames and, being an open person, said, "I've got to get this off my chest. I don't know why you were being unfriendly before. I thought I was being nice to you."

"I wasn't," Mary said, tearing up a little. "I just didn't want you to drink my coffee."

"It's all right, dear," she said, touching latex gloves. "I didn't want a coffee anyway. When they come in to get their food, stand behind the table, and when a tray is almost empty, go to the back for another one. Got it?"

"You're a nice person," Mary said. "Do you ever eat the food?"

"We're not allowed," Theresa said.

Mary smiled. "Good."

~

ELI WAS on stage in the middle of an animated Q&A session with her phone in her bag on mute.

Trinh called her number three times before saying. "It's going to voicemail, Zé. Should we get Dispatch to roll a patrol unit to Hynes?"

"We're ten minutes out. It'll take five for uniforms to get there. Try Donovan."

Cal had his suit jacket off, slung over his chair, and was munching bread and listening to the Michigan recruit talk about his book on Renaissance Kabbalah, when he heard his muted phone buzzing behind him. He apologized for checking, and when he didn't recognize the number, he put the phone down.

A few seconds later, the same number rang, and he hit the end button again, mumbling something about spam, but when it rang a third time, he said, "Sorry, Brian, I'd better check this."

The caller's urgency startled him.

"Professor Donovan! Thank God! It's Detective Trinh. Are you at the Hynes?"

"What? No!"

"Where are you?"

"At the Harvard Club on Comm Ave. Why?"

"Is Professor Celestino with you? We can't reach her."

"She's at the Hynes. What's going on?"

"Eva Nevins has a sister we didn't know about," she spouted. "She's working for the caterer at the nun's convention. We think she's poisoning the food. We're ten minutes away. Can you get there faster?"

"A lot faster," he said. "I'll keep the line open." He sprang up and said, "Brian—huge emergency. Have your lunch. I'll see you on campus tomorrow. Apologies."

Before his guest could respond, Cal was gone, leaving his jacket hanging on the chair.

~

TWO MIDDLE-AGED NUNS entered the ballroom and navigated the array of empty round tables, heading for the buffet.

One of them waved at Mary, who was standing, po-faced, against the wall, and said, "Oh, hello! We're from the organizing committee. We chose the entrees. Mind if we have a look?"

Mary shook her head. "I don't mind."

"Oh, good." She took a plate and said, "We'll just have a taste before the stampede. They're wrapping up in there."

"Quality control!" the other nun joked.

It was more than a taste. The women heaped generous portions of all three entrées onto their plates and went to sit at a peripheral table.

As Mary watched them eat, she heard Eva in her head.

They deserve what we're giving them. The nuns sang while Mama's brother and sisters burned. If I could walk, I'd do it, but I can't. Mama was hard on you, I know that, but she is so proud of you. Kay told her what you've done.

Is she really proud of me?

Oh, yes. She says you're a good daughter.

~

CAL GLANCED at his watch and burst out of the Harvard Club onto Commonwealth Avenue in his shirtsleeves, the cold hitting him like a pane of glass. He launched himself east through the drizzle, his loafers slapping the wet pavement hard enough to sting. Wind knifed through his white dress shirt, snapped his tie over his shoulder, and turned his breath into steam. A group exiting the Eliot Hotel pointed at him—a guy in half a suit and loafers running like he'd stolen something.

He swung right onto Mass Ave at full tilt, legs churning, lungs already burning. Traffic surged both ways, a chaos of buses and cars, but he darted through an opening of crawling traffic. A horn blared; a driver shouted; Cal didn't turn his head. He hit the opposite curb hard, almost stumbled, caught himself, and forced his legs to keep churning at the speed of a man half his age.

Left onto Boylston.

A straight shot.

He ran past the Berklee buildings, past the sandwich shops and the glassy storefronts lining the wide corridor of Boylston Street. His loafers slipped on a patch of grit near the fire station, but he corrected, pushing harder, accelerating toward the wide rise where the Prudential tower loomed over the street. His chest was on fire, a sharp, metallic burn deep behind the sternum, but he ignored it and barreled on.

The wind off the open boulevard sliced his face, but he kept cutting through it, skittering past the pedestrians flattening themselves against the building fronts to get out of his path, crossing Boylston at a gap in the traffic. He saw the glass awning of the Hynes entrance ahead, close now, within reach. His stride didn't break. He emptied everything he had into the last stretch, running with the form of a trained runner and the desperation of a man sprinting toward the woman he loved, praying he wasn't too late.

~

THE BALLROOM WENT from empty to full in a flash, as hungry conventioneers poured across the hall from the auditorium. A fast-moving line formed at the buffet table, and the tables began to fill.

President Houseman guided Eli by the arm through the crowd, raving about how wonderful the event had been.

At the sight of the buffet line, she called out, "Ladies, Sister Elisabetta can't stay much longer. We need to cut in front."

The Red Sea parted, and Eli was soon at the front of the line. She'd skipped breakfast and compensated by filling her plate with fish, chicken, and sides. Houseman took her to the head table where the leadership group began showering her with praise.

Debbie, the assistant manager, peeked into the ballroom and said, "Oh no! What's she doing?" and then marched over to Mary, who was a statue against the wall. "What's wrong with you?" she whispered. "The beef tray's empty!"

Mary mutely headed to the kitchen, taking her thermos with her.

~

CAL DARTED through the entrance of the Convention Center, catching a glimpse of his time.

Two minutes, door-to-door.

He retraced their morning route, and kept running toward the ballroom.

~

LEAD ARSENATE, the active agent in Eva's old cans of pesticide, dissolves in stomach acid, slowly releasing arsenic ions into the bloodstream. But most of the action happens in the small intestine, where, a few minutes after ingestion, the absorption of poisonous ions skyrockets.

Within five minutes, the two early-eaters on the organizing committee began feeling sick to their stomachs. After the first few mouthfuls, one of them mentioned her throat felt scratchy, and when the same thing happened to the other, the two Florida women grumbled about catching colds up north.

"I don't feel well," one said. "I think I need to go to the restroom."

The woman who stayed at the table suddenly felt a stab of abdominal pain, put her hand to her belly, and ran after her colleague.

At the head table, Houseman scolded her leadership team for

not letting their guest eat. Eli smiled at her and pierced a piece of chicken with her fork.

AT THE ENTRANCE to Ballroom B, a couple of security guards saw a man running toward them and exchanged worried looks.

"Who's this asshole?" one of them said.

They stepped in his way, and he ground to a halt, his chest working like a bellows.

"Do you have a badge, Sir?"

Cal looked down and realized it was in his suit jacket.

"It's an emergency," he panted. "Let me through."

"No badge, no entry," the bigger one said.

"I'm going in," Cal said.

"No, you're not."

The beefier guard made the mistake of putting a hand on Cal, unaware that the guy in a tie had been a champion boxer in his youth..

Cal caught him with a right hook, full on the side of his face, knocking him back a few feet, and creating enough space to charge through the nearest ballroom door.

He blinked once, getting his bearings. The room was packed with nuns—a dozen to a table, with a buffet line at the back. He didn't spot Eli right away, but as soon as he started yelling, she saw him and put her fork down.

"Don't eat the food!" he screamed, running toward the buffet table. "It's poisoned! Don't eat it!"

He covered the length of the room in a few seconds, pushed some women away from the table, and began upending each section, toppling the serving trays in a terrible clatter. A Sterno heater caught the edge of the tablecloth on fire, and he stamped on it.

Women screamed at the violent intrusion. Others, who were beginning to feel the effects of the arsenic, were clutching their abdomens and beginning to retch. In the women's room, the two early-eaters were lying on the tiles, vomiting uncontrollably and writhing in pain.

Eli ran up to Cal, spouting in Italian. "Have you gone mad?"

He was too out of breath for full sentences. "The police. Eva's got a sister. She's here. With poison."

That's when they noticed something was seriously wrong in the ballroom. At one table, a woman was crying. At another, a nun fell off her chair. The sound of vomiting was everywhere.

"Did you?"

"I didn't have anything."

"Thank God."

As he reached to touch her, he realized the phone in his left hand was still live.

"Hello? You still there?"

Trinh answered. "We're almost there. We've been listening."

"We need ambulances," Cal said. "Lots of them."

~

Santos and Trinh rushed in as the first EMTs were arriving, trying to decide whom to treat first.

One of the EMTs shouted to no one in particular, "Does anyone know what they took?"

Trinh yelled back. "Arsenic!"

The EMT got on his radio and said, "Let all the area ERs know we've got a mass arsenic poisoning at the Hynes. Tell them to get dimercaprol injections prepped."

They saw Cal and Eli kneeling beside one stricken woman and asked if they'd seen the poisoner.

"We've got no idea who she is," Cal said. "We need more medics."

"Every ambulance in Boston's on the way," Santos said. "Which way's the kitchen?"

Trinh pointed toward the back, and they ran off.

The kitchen and catering staff were huddled in shock. One

gray-haired woman stood apart by the refrigerators, holding something in her hand.

Santos recognized her from the day they responded to Father Malloy's suicide.

"She's got a knife," Trinh said, drawing her pistol.

"Mary Carey," Santos shouted, lining his pistol sights with the logo on the catering company's apron. "Put the knife down."

Mary appeared emotionless as she walked toward them, the raised kitchen knife in hand.

In her mind, she was asking her sister a question.

Eva, you promised me I wouldn't have to see Mama again. You'd better keep that promise. I hope you're there soon. If I'm lost, will you find me?

Mary slowly advanced into Santos's and Trinh's shouts and a hail of bullets.

~

IT WAS nighttime when the detectives arrived at Mass General Brigham to interview Eva. The Mayor and the Commissioner of Police had already given their first press conference outside the ER at Boston Medical Center, where they confirmed three fatalities and seventy-five nuns in area hospitals, all expected to recover. They praised the excellent police work of the city's detectives and the quick-thinking actions of a member of the public who prevented a much greater disaster.

On Eva's medical floor, Santos and Trinh asked to speak with her doctor, and a nurse called the senior resident.

Trinh's Vietnamese radar went off when she saw the young Vietnamese doctor coming down the hall.

"I'm Dr. Duong," she said.

"I'm Sergeant Detective Santos, and she's Detective Trinh. We need to speak with Eva Nevins. How is she?"

"She's dying."

"Then, we'd better hurry up and see her," he said.

"Yeah, that's not going to happen," the resident said. "She's not strong enough."

"Is she conscious?" Trinh asked.

"In and out."

"Do you know about the arsenic poisonings?" Trinh asked.

"Surely, you jest," the resident said, fingering her stethoscope. "I personally admitted six victims this afternoon."

"She's the one responsible for it," Trinh said. "We need to talk to her before it's too late."

"I don't care what she did or didn't do. She's my patient, and given her condition, it's inappropriate to question her."

"Listen—" Santos said.

The doctor didn't let him finish. "No, you listen. You need to turn around and get off my ward."

Walking off, Trinh said, "Jesus, Zé. She's me in medicine."

EVA LAY on her hospital bed, her arms folded, her eyes closed. She had been listening to each successive breath grow shallower. She didn't have the strength to curl her mouth, but inside, she felt herself smiling.

Oh, there you are, Kay. I've been waiting all my life for this. I hope you're as excited to meet me as I am to meet you.

CHAPTER THIRTY-ONE

Cal wasn't one to decorate his house for the holidays, but as a surprise for Eli, he wanted it to look very American and very Christmas-y. She arrived by Uber for dinner and squealed with delight at the fairy lights wrapped around the bushes, the wreaths, the decorations, and—the pièce de résistance—the tinsel-draped Christmas tree in the living room, topped with an angel.

She was leaving the next morning for Rome, but he promised to keep the decorations up through the new year so she could enjoy them on her return.

"I hope there will be snow," she said.

"There will be," he said. "We'll have a snowball fight."

"I was thinking more of a snowman. I've always wanted to make one. A big one."

Cal had left work early that afternoon to make a coq-au-vin, and he served it in the infrequently used dining room, which made the evening feel special. Over dinner, they talked about her trip, her family, the upcoming spring semester, Divinity School gossip and politics—everything but the elephant in the room—the questions that hung in the air about Eva Nevins. It had been two weeks since the luncheon at the Hynes, and neither of them seemed ready to talk about it.

"I'll miss you," he said.

"It's only two weeks. You'll be skiing with your friends. You won't even think of me."

"That's so not true," he said. "Can I give you an early Christmas present?"

She laughed. "If you insist."

It was a small box with a bow comically too large for it—the only one he had lying around, he admitted. Inside was a pendant on a chain, a solid-gold heart studded with small rubies and diamonds.

"It's too nice!" she said, briefly rising to kiss him. "I've never had something like this."

"As my Jewish mother used to say, wear it in good health."

"So," she said. "I have two presents for you. Here's your riddle. They are very light, they have no monetary value—unlike this beautiful necklace—but I hope they will please you."

She went to her handbag and returned to the table with two plain white envelopes.

"Let's see. I think this one is first."

With a look of perplexed amusement, he ripped the envelope open.

Sister Elisabetta Celestino
Augustinian Sisters Servants of Jesus and Mary
Harvard Divinity School
Cambridge, Massachusetts

Reverend Mother Sister Marthese Attard
Mother Superior
Augustinian Sisters Servants of Jesus and Mary

Dear Reverend Mother,

Peace in Christ.

I write to you after a long period of prayer and discernment. This letter is not easy to compose, nor is the decision behind it one I make lightly. With deep respect for you and for our community, I must state my intention to request a dispensation from my perpetual vows and to seek release from membership in the Augustinian Sisters Servants of Jesus and Mary.

My years in the Institute have been a profound grace. Everything I am—my formation as a theologian, my vocation to service, my fidelity to the Gospel—has its roots in the life we lived together. For all of this, I remain sincerely grateful.

In these past months, however, I have come to recognize that I am no longer able to live the vows of poverty, chastity, and obedience with the integrity required by our Constitutions. The discernment has been painful, but consistent: I believe the Lord is calling me to serve Him differently, outside the consecrated life, and in a context where I can fully respond to the responsibilities that have arisen in my new academic work.

This is not a rejection of the charism I have cherished, nor of the bonds of sisterhood that have shaped me. Rather, it is an acknowledgment—after sincere prayer—that I can no longer, in conscience, commit myself to the life demanded by the vow of obedience and to the communal availability that our apostolate requires. My recent appointment at Harvard has made this increasingly clear, and I fear that remaining in the Institute would be neither honest nor fair to the community.

For these reasons, and in fidelity to the truth as I have come to understand it through grace, I humbly petition you to initiate the process outlined in Canon Law for my dispensation from perpetual vows.

I assure you, Reverend Mother, that this request comes with no bitterness and no loss of affection for the Sisters. I remain deeply grateful for your guidance, for the love I have received, and for the witness of each member of our community. I will continue to hold the Sisters in prayer and to honor the charism of Saint Augustine in the way I live and teach.

Should you wish to speak with me further, either in person or by correspondence, I am entirely at your disposal.

With respect and gratitude in Christ,
Sister Elisabetta Celestino

~

Cal put the letter down and said, "Eli, are you sure you want to do this?"

"One-hundred-percent sure," she said, smiling. "Honestly, Cal, it's the longest I've thought about something since I decided to become a nun. I'm ready for the next chapter. Which brings me to the second letter."

He ripped this one open even faster.

~

Prof. Elisabetta Celestino
Harvard Divinity School
Cambridge, MA

Office of Residential Leasing
Harvard University Housing
1350 Massachusetts Avenue
Cambridge, MA 02138

Dear Sir or Madam:

I am writing to inform you that I do not intend to renew my lease for the upcoming spring semester. My current lease for my apartment ends at the end of the fall term, and I will vacate the residence no later than the required move-out date. Please let me know if there are any forms or procedures I should complete before my departure. I will ensure that the unit is left in good order. Thank you for your assistance during my tenancy.

Sincerely,
Professor Elisabetta Celestino

HE LOOKED at her in stunned silence.

"Well?" she said.

"Where will you live?"

"This is a nice house."

He grinned. "Where will you sleep?"

"You have so many bedrooms."

"Have you seen mine?"

"I've seen it, but I don't remember it very well."

"Care to have a look?"

"Why not?"

Climbing the stairs, she casually mentioned that she had left her suitcase for tomorrow's trip in his garage, in case she didn't return to her apartment tonight.

"You planned this out to perfection," he said.

At the threshold to his bedroom, she stopped and said, "I want to know what you think."

"About this? You know what I think."

"Not about this. About Eva. Her séances. Emilio. Was any of it real?"

He pulled her toward the bed and said, "Maybe we'll find out one day, but I hope like hell it won't be for a very long time."

EPILOGUE

Four inches of snow had already fallen, and more was coming. The conditions were pretty much a white-out on Academy Hill Road. A tall man dressed in heavy winter gear stood on Eva Nevins' porch looking expectantly toward Chestnut Hill Avenue. Finally, he spotted someone coming his way, leaning into the wind.

The woman plodded down the unplowed street and up the unshoveled walkway, taking the stairs rather than the wheelchair ramp.

"Is that Miss King?" he asked.

"That's me."

He extended a hand, and his gloves touched hers. "Steven Halperin, Mrs. Nevins' trust and estate attorney. You're late."

"The Green Line sucks during storms."

"Indeed. Shall we?"

He kicked the snow off his boots, opened the door, and shed his outer clothes. Felicia did the same.

"Chilly in here," he said.

"I'll turn up the thermostat," she said, collapsing Eva's wheelchair, which was blocking the way. "It's down the hall."

Felicia turned the lights on and asked where he wanted to do this.

"It doesn't matter," he said. "Somewhere with a table. The kitchen would be fine. That's where I did documents with Eva in the past."

The room was a shambles—the contents of the cupboards and pantry on the floor.

"The police made a mess of the place," he said. "It hasn't been touched since."

"I'll take care of it," she said, nonplussed.

He sat across from her, trying not to stare at her piercings and tattoos.

"May I see some form of identification?" he said.

She passed him her driver's license, which he photographed with his phone.

"Social security number?"

He took it down and pulled a folder from his briefcase.

"You're a fortunate young woman," he said.

"Am I?"

"Well, I'd say so. Eva's estate plan left everything to her sister, Mary, with a provision that if Mary died before she did, the estate pass to you. Mary died a few hours before Eva."

"I'm aware. So, what do I get?"

"The house, of course, and a trust account." He produced a summary page. "Here's the balance as of yesterday. It's not a fortune, I'm afraid."

"It's a lot more than I have right now."

"The house is something of a white elephant. Utilities, real estate taxes, insurance, repairs. Eva worked right up to the end to keep it going. What work do you do, if I could ask?"

"I was a masseuse."

"Was?"

"I quit last week."

"I see. Do you intend to sell the house?"

"Hell no. I love it. I'm going to live here."

"How will you manage?"

"With my new job."

"Which is?"

"I'm a medium. I've got Eva's client list. I'm going to charge more than she did. I think she left money on the table."

"You're a medium?"

"Yeah, don't look so surprised. Eva said I had the gift. I always thought I did, but she confirmed it. She taught me the fine points. I loved that lady. I've got my first sitting tomorrow night with a few of her regulars."

He gave her a lawyerly smile. "Well, then. We'd better take care of the paperwork."

WHEN SHE WAS ALONE, Felicia walked through the house, taking stock, figuring out where to begin her cleanup. She stripped the sheets and spread from Eva's bed, then laid out some fresh linen for later. When the kettle whistled, she slowly descended on the chairlift for a laugh.

When she'd had her tea, she went into the parlor with a dustcloth, gave the old walnut table a polish, drew the curtains until it was dark, and lit the candles.

She pulled a chair to Eva's usual spot and sat there, palms on the table, surveying the empty chairs.

Then, she closed her eyes and concentrated hard on the task at hand, until, after a few minutes, a smile creased her pierced face.

"Hello, Eva. There you are. How do you fare?"

"I am well enough."

"Well, here I am, at your table."

"It is your table now."

"Yeah, that's crazy, right?"

"It's not crazy at all. It was meant to be yours."

"Are you alone?"

"I am not alone."

"Who is with you?"

The voices chimed in, as if in a roll call.

First, a familiar one.

"Hello, Felicia. It's Kay."

Then, children's voices.

"I'm Bronwyn."

"I'm Vern."

"I'm Sarah."

"I'm Darlene."

Then, the voices of women.

"I'm Winnie Nevin, Eva's mother."

"I am Winnie's mother, Irene Slattery—Eva's grandmother."

Felicia was sobbing now. "Eva, you found them all. Your whole family."

"They were waiting for me," Eva said. "Kay's sisters and brother came from far away. It was quite the reception."

"I'm so happy for you."

"Thank you, my dear. There's one more I'd like to introduce to you."

"Okay—"

Felicia heard a deep, booming voice in her head. "Hello there, Miss King. Arthur Conan Doyle, at your service."

The End

ABOUT THE AUTHOR

Glenn Cooper is an internationally published thriller writer with over eight million copies sold in thirty translations. Many of his twenty novels have been top-ten bestsellers. Cooper has a degree in archaeology from Harvard College and a medical degree from Tufts University School of Medicine. He practiced internal medicine and infectious diseases before becoming a biomedical researcher and biotech CEO. He has also written numerous screenplays and produced three feature films. He draws on his experiences and studies to create fast-paced thrillers with historical, philosophical, religious, and scientific themes.

For more information visit his website:
glenncooperbooks.com

facebook.com/GlennCooperUSA
amazon.com/stores/author/B002L10BFU
bookbub.com/authors/glenn-cooper
goodreads.com/glenn_cooper

ALSO BY GLENN COOPER

THE WILL PIPER TRILOGY:

Library of the Dead

Book of Souls

The Keepers of the Library

THE DOWN TRILOGY:

Down: Pinhole

Down: Portal

Down: Floodgate

THE CAL DONOVAN SERIES:

The Sign of the Cross

Three Marys

The Debt

The Showstone

The Fourth Prophecy

The Lost Pope

The Last Conclave

OTHERS:

The Tenth Chamber

Near Death

The Resurrection Maker

The Devil Will Come

The Cure

The Taken Girls

The Cosmos Keys

The Silence of Flesh

The Physician of Nineveh

Printed in Dunstable, United Kingdom

80575011R00178